THE INNOCENCE OF TRUST

The third of the Sam Green novels

By

Roland Ladley

Copyright © Roland Ladley 2017
This book is sold subject to the condition that it shall not, by way of trade or otherwise, be lent, resold, hired out, or otherwise circulated without the publisher's prior consent in any form of binding or cover other than that in which it is published and without a similar condition including this condition being imposed on the subsequent publisher.
The moral right of Roland Ladley has been asserted.
ISBN-13: 978-1548227357
ISBN-10: 1548227358

To Ned, who started all of this…

CONTENTS

PROLOGUE 1

DECEPTION 11
    Chapter 1 .... *12*
    Chapter 2 .... *34*
    Chapter 3 .... *63*
    Chapter 4 .... *85*
    Chapter 5 .... *112*
    Chapter 6 .... *137*
    Chapter 7 .... *163*

DISINTEGRATION 193
    Chapter 8 .... *194*
    Chapter 9 .... *223*
    Chapter 10 .... *249*
    Chapter 11 .... *274*
    Chapter 12 .... *297*
    Chapter 13 .... *317*
    Chapter 14 .... *342*
    Chapter 15 .... *366*
    Chapter 16 .... *397*
    Chapter 17 .... *423*

DESTRUCTION 453
    Chapter 18 .... *454*
    Chapter 19 .... *478*
    Chapter 20 .... *507*

EPILOGUE 542

This is a work of fiction. Names, characters, businesses, organizations, places, events and incidents either are the product of the author's imagination or are used fictitiously. Any resemblance to actual persons, living or dead, events, or locales is entirely coincidental.

'Power corrupts, absolute power corrupts absolutely.'
- Lord Acton, 1887

Prologue

Inner German Border Crossing Point, 20 Kilometres East of Osterode, West Germany

18 November 1983

Major Peter Brown's warm breath met the forest air and immediately condensed into a fine cloud of water vapour. It was cold. Not yet proper, mid-European winter cold. The sort where snow lies six feet deep and hangs perilously from the tall, straight firs, falling with a *clump* on anything unsuspecting below when the branches give way. And not so cold that, whilst you'd never mention it, you wear your wife's tights under the trousers of your blue woollen uniform; and two vests to protect against the penetrating temperatures. But cold enough. Today it was accompanied by that horrible wetness lingering from previously heavy rain. Everything Peter touched was damp. The sleeves and shoulders of his blue naval jacket were covered in a sheen of dew that sparkled under the glare of an arc light that had been especially illuminated for the evening's exchange.

His issue black leather gloves were soaking. They had got wet as he unlocked the massive padlock that secured the single red and white-striped gate pole that lay suspended horizontally between two posts. An obstruction that barred access to a road that, until the Inner German Border was fortified, connected two villages previously part of the same district – families torn apart by the enforced segregation. His gloves had taken on more water as he had assisted his East German Grenztruppen counterpart open the tall, concertina-wire topped gate which straddled the road. The gate, along with the fence that ran hundreds of kilometres north to the Baltic and south to Czechoslovakia, was the last line of security preventing those in the East heading west to freedom.

He had counted six 'Grenzers' at the border point. They wore much more sensible khaki fatigues and warm berets. He had exchanged a few words in German with the man on the opposite side of the gate. There had been no smiles. No handshakes.

Once the crossing was open, Peter moved back from the road to the treeline. His other two colleagues, dressed similarly to him in their issued naval-styled uniform, including an incongruous white-banded peaked cap, were stood by a hard-topped, Series 3 Land Rover. One was taking a swig from a silver hip-flask.

Their job was done.

The border was open. And it was secure.

Peter squeezed his hands together. His black gloves dripped water into the puddle between his feet.

Superstitiously he reached behind his back and felt for his Belgian FN Self-Loading Rifle. He knew it was there, its weight pulling on the sling that gently dug into his shoulder. But he had to check. Fidgeting further, he looked at his watch: 10.21pm. The exchange was due in 19 minutes.

Other than his team of three members of the British Frontier Service (BFS), and a captain from the Household Cavalry (who was sat in the front seat of the Land Rover), there was no one else on their side of the crossing point. He knew the captain's troop of lightweight Scimitar tanks were in a holding area, half a mile back down the road. Every so often the officer's radio burst into life with a 'radio-check' call from, he guessed, a nervous NCO making sure he could still contact his boss. There was no radio silence for this exchange. The other side needed to know that they weren't alone.

The dark and dank sky to his left lit up as a distant searchlight patrolled the border zone. He knew if he moved back out of the treeline and glanced to his right, he would see the same effect from another concrete tower in the distance. There was no escaping the watchful eye of the Grenzers.

He reminded himself of the defences that had been put in place by the government of the GDR (G for German, R for Republic and D, inappropriately, for Democratic), to prevent its citizens from escaping to the West. The 400-yard, manmade gap in the forest was known as the 'Zone Area'. Would-be escapees had to cross three high metal fences – one of which was electrified. Interspersed among the fences was a minefield, an anti-tank ditch, two sets of barbed wire, a dog-run, and an illuminated vehicle path, which was patrolled regularly by armed members of the Grenztruppen. Every couple of hundred yards was a manned watchtower. Added to this, the Grenzers had authority to shoot first and ask questions later. It didn't surprise Peter that only a few East Germans had been brave enough to attempt to cross the border.

Today, if everything went well, some people would be crossing without being shot. As just a mere major in the BFS, he didn't know of details of the exchange; who the British were handing over to the East; and whom they were getting back in return. As far as he was aware prisoner swaps normally took place on Berlin's Gleinicke Bridge, over the river Havel. The *Bridge of Spies*, as it was known. That was where all high-profile exchanges took place: Berlin.

Normally.

But not today.

MI6 were the ones running the show. He'd spoken on the phone to a man in London named Derek, who insisted on calling his BFS team 'you chaps'. They were the ones who had chosen this little-used border crossing. And that crossing happened to be in his patch.

He and the Grenzer had had such difficulty opening the gate on his side of the 'Zone', he wouldn't have been surprised if it had never been used before. He assumed the powers-that-be knew what they were up to.

There was commotion on the far side of the Zone Area. Lit by arc lights, Peter picked out a couple of military trucks and a black car. He lifted his binoculars to his eyes, but dropped them quickly. He reached into his pocket for a handkerchief and wiped away condensation from the eye-pieces. Looking again, he saw two Zittau Robor LO 4x4 military trucks. The car was a Zil 4104, a prestigious limousine used by the great and the good from Moscow. His vehicle recognition was pretty sharp.

'Blimey,' Peter whispered under his breath.

What's the Zil doing here? Who exactly do they have on board?

'Sir!' It was a call from one of his team. 'Car coming, sir.'

Peter looked to his left, back down the road into the dark of the forest. The headlights of a car flashed and dimmed as the vehicle bounced down the potholed road in their direction. He walked out onto the tarmac, reaching for his military-issue, right-angled torch which was clipped to his belt. He stood in the middle of the road and turned the torch on, pointing it at the oncoming car. He swung the torch from side-to-side, the beam following.

Slow down!

The car came to halt in front of him. The passenger door opened. A mid-sized man in an untidy tweed overcoat got out.

'Hello, old chap. Are you Major Brown?'

Peter turned off his torch and stepped forward.

'Yes. I'm Major Brown.' He offered his gloved hand. The man, whose face was now illuminated by the lights of the Zone Area, took it limply and shook it. He looked pale and deskbound. But didn't seem unduly concerned to be out in the forest near midnight, opposite the not inconsiderable firepower and minefields of the Grenztruppen.

'I'm Derek. Good to meet you.' He looked around, picking out Peter's team and the Army captain, who waved at him nonchalantly from the driver's window. He then looked through Peter and across at the entourage on the far side of the Zone Area.

'Binos?' He pointed at Peter's binos whilst continuing to look across the 400-hundred-yard gap to the far side of the Zone. His eyes closed slightly as if picking out something in particular.

Peter, a little frustrated by the man's directness, took the binos from around his neck and thrust them into the other man's hands.

'Derek' spent some time looking at the other side, fiddling with the focus on one of the eyepieces.

'Mmm. Perfect. Two Robors and a 4104. Good. Just as expected.' He was having a conversation with himself. The man then lowered the binos and gave them back to Peter. 'We'll take it from here. You chaps just do what you do. I'm sure everything will be fine.'

And with that he turned around and got back in the car.

What the...?

Peter moved quickly to one side as the car's engine revved. It then took off in the direction of the open crossing. The car shot past the black, red, and yellow border post which supported the white-metalled sign displaying, 'Halt! Heir Grenze!' It was now in the Zone Area.

He had been surprised by the speed of it all. No paperwork. No detailed explanation. No nothing.

The border was open. MI6 were now heading on through. He was a bystander.

'Oh well…' He shrugged.

He watched the British car, a dark brown Ford Granada, make its way into the Zone Area. It slowed as it crossed the makeshift wooden bridge that the Grenztruppen had laid earlier in the afternoon, allowing vehicles to cross the anti-tank ditch. And then it stopped about halfway between both sides of the Zone. One of the street lights from the patrol road picked out the car's brown vinyl roof.

Peter raised his binos, adjusting the eyepiece. From the far side, the Zil had also taken off, leaving the two trucks behind. It moved forward slowly. After about a minute it stopped ten yards short of the Granada.

Then nothing happened. Both vehicles were stationary, all doors remaining firmly closed.

Still, nothing happened.

What if the shit hits the fan? What if somebody starts shooting?

In that instance, it occurred to him that they had nothing planned. There was no contingency. This was his first ever exchange. If this didn't go well, he had no idea what to do. Yes, he had a troop of the Army's best on call. But, if they were needed, wouldn't that be a precursor to World War Three? Could this evening turn out to be the equivalent of the assassination of Archduke Ferdinand? Was Osterode the present-day Sarajevo? As his mind whirled through all the possibilities, his back became drenched with sweat.

What have I got myself involved in?

After 25 years loyal service in the Army, Peter had only made it to the rank of major. Realising that he was going no further, and having married a local German girl, he'd applied for, and was accepted into, the BFS – an organisation where little of consequence happened. You patrolled the border, took photographs of installations, and accompanied senior people on visits. The latter was a sort of military tourism. And then you went home in time for crumpets and medals. It was a retired officer's dream.

I didn't expect this!

He shivered as the cold finally caught up with the sweat that clung to his back.

He had to concentrate.

Blinking, he focused back on the two cars.

Still nothing. No one had moved.

Then one of the Zil doors opened; a man got out. Immediately the passenger door of the Granada did the same. Derek got out. Both men walked forward, meeting in the gap between the cars. Peter had a good view. They appeared to be having a fairly relaxed exchange. But there was no shaking of hands. The talking finished, Peter saw Derek nod his head, and both men returned to their cars.

THE INNOCENCE OF TRUST

Derek opened the rear door of the Granada. A big man, who had to stoop to get out of the back seat, stood up and looked east. Peter guessed he was staring toward his homeland. He wore a long, dark coat. His hands were tied in front of him.

A second man got out of the Zil. He was smaller and dressed in a jacket, a light-coloured shirt and a tie. His hands weren't tied.

He must be cold.

All four men walked back to the centre. They stopped a few yards short of each other. Peter kept the binos firmly pressed against his eyes.

The tall prisoner (*or spy?*) with Derek stood impassively. He towered above the other three men, nonchalantly looking around, taking in the scene.

He slowly turned his head to his right, glancing back over his shoulder. He seemed to be looking directly at Peter.

'Shit!' Peter exclaimed under his breath.

He didn't recognise the tall man. But he would never forget him: a square face; a crew cut; and a thin mouth. Even at this distance, you couldn't miss the man's eyes; they were penetrating. And then Peter saw the scar on the right side of his face. A deep line from his forehead to his cheek. With the horizontal shadow of his brow, it created a cross on his face – like an aiming mark. Add that to his size, Peter knew that he was looking at a man who he wouldn't want to meet in a dark alley.

It was a fleeting exchange. The man wasn't really

looking at him – he was too far away to make a connection. But the experience unnerved him to his core.

Peter shivered.

And then it was over. The tall man and the cold man changed places; the latter shuffling – the former crossing the gap in a couple of strides. The cold man shook hands with Derek, and the tall man embraced the passenger from the Zil, almost smothering him.

Then they all got into their cars. The Zil started to reverse along the track and the Granada did a three-point turn using the vehicle patrol lane. As the Zil continued its slow reverse, the Granada gingerly crossed the makeshift bridge, and then picked up speed as it left the Zone Area. It didn't stop at his checkpoint, but drove unceremoniously through a muddy puddle a few feet from Peter. Dirty water splashed his trousers and covered his boots.

'You bastard.' Peter spat out the words as his eyes followed the Granada into the darkness of the forest.

He looked back to the Zone Area. The Zil's rear tail lights were flickering in the distance, soon to be extinguished by the brow of a hill. The two Robors were manoeuvring themselves so that could also drive away.

It was over. Mission accomplished.

That's that then?

DECEPTION

Chapter 1

Komsomolskiy Road, Moscow, Russia

Present Day

Sam spotted Alexei across the busy road, standing at the Frunzenskaya 3-ya bus stop. He was dressed casually: blue jeans, grey sneakers, a cream shirt and a light blue sweat top. He was carrying a black neoprene, laptop-sized case. He wasn't looking in her direction, instead he was staring intently at, what Sam guessed was, the bus timetable. There were four other people with him. They looked like strangers.

Good.

That was the first signal: him, unflustered at the bus stop, checking the timetable. Once he had caught sight of her, he would take the next bus heading northwest, and travel just two stops. He would alight at the 1-ya stop and go into a cafe, *The Karsotty*, just off the Komsomolskiy Road to the south. He'd find a booth in the corner where his back could be against the wall.

There would be at least one spare seat at the booth, and one of the seats would have a view of the main door. He'd order a drink, recce the toilets to see if there was a rear entrance/exit, and then he'd retake his seat. If he was uncomfortable with the meet he would abandon the cafe and make his way home. If that were the case, Sam would arrive, sit on her own, drink something – taking her time – and then go home. They'd arrange a new meet later.

The fact that he was at the bus stop, reading the timetable, was the first indication that all was well and their planned meet could go ahead.

Sam bent down to tie a shoelace. Not only were Doc Martens a very comfortable boot for field work, they had the advantage of having shoelaces that could be tightened when you wanted to pause without drawing unnecessary attention to yourself.

She glanced back across the road. A white single-storey LiAZ bus with green livery had pulled up. It obscured her view. A few seconds later it pulled away leaving an empty bus stop. Alexei was on the bus.

Sam stood up and nodded gently to herself.

So far so good.

If she dawdled it would take her 20 minutes to get to the cafe. By which time Alexei would hopefully be sitting comfortably, halfway down a latte and ready for their meet. It was standard Secret Intelligence Service (SIS) practice for low-level 'collaborations' – the 5 Cs: *Contact, Check, Carry, Connect, Communicate*. They'd done *Contact* and *Check*. They were now onto the *Carry*. She was surprised that couples having affairs didn't approach liaisons with the same level of furtiveness.

Sam checked her watch. It was 6.45pm and, after a warmish day in Moscow, it was starting to get dark. Crossing the Moskva River on the way here, she'd noticed a thick band of clouds heading in from the east. With it would come colder temperatures, heavy rain, and, after a few days of unbroken sunshine, probably some thunder. The kitchen window in her flat would leak all over the worktop. She was glad she had remembered to move the breadbasket this morning.

Sam was halfway to the cafe. Using the organisation's excellent IT system (colloquially named 'Cynthia'), she had recced the route using their souped-up version of Google Street View. It was indelibly etched onto her memory. She knew where all the building fronts started and finished. She picked out trees she recognised from the clip, signposts and pedestrian crossings. The only unfamiliar things were the vehicles and the people. And a hole in the pavement where some workers looked like they were digging in a new pipe. When she was training in Portsmouth, she would test herself. *And the colour of the main door into the second building is? Is it the next lamp post that has 'Residents Only' parking sign on it? Or the one after?* She had always answered her own questions correctly. She never missed a thing. It was a gift that had served her well, both as an analyst in the Army, and latterly with SIS. She didn't mean to be boastful, but she knew she had an extraordinary eye for detail, and a retentive memory that appeared to be boundless.

'A good number of pixels and a decent hard drive.' That was the call from her instructor at Fort Monkton as he tapped his head with a finger. As an analyst – and even as a 'case-officer' (the title was a surprise to Sam; she'd expected to be called an agent), you needed an eye for detail equivalent to a top-of-the-range camera. And a memory the size of a supercomputer. Training had helped hone these skills. But mostly, she thought, this was something you were born with.

So, today's route wasn't a surprise. She'd be turning right in 250 metres. Immediately after a red-brick four-storey building with five lower-floor windows. And a bottom-floor entrance that had white pillars, and a blue double-door. It was the offices of a law firm: *Mayokoskaya*. It was 17A; the number was on the left-hand door below a semi-circular window. In brass.

First – *here it comes* – she had to cross a small cul-de-sac where the houses were set back slightly from the pavement, and their very short front yards defined by black railings. With arrowheads on top.

Gotcha!

She was always looking out for the unexpected. Not necessarily things that shouldn't be there. Instead, things that should be there, but weren't. It was the key to unlocking images, data and real-time intel: photos, videos, routes, scenes, websites, computer programmes. And people. An empty street on a busy day. A woman wearing a jumper when it's hot. A man with no shades – when it's brilliantly sunny.

No tears at a funeral.

People are animate. Calculating. They did most things for a reason. And when they didn't, Sam had an ability to spot the gap. No matter how inconsequential, or casual. She could read people as well as she could read an air photograph. She didn't have to try very hard. It was innate.

So, whatever she was doing – she was looking for the gaps. It didn't always make for the most interesting of lives, and it often bored her. And she knew she was dull company to go for a drink with. But she had a knack. And so far, it had served her well.

Sam got to the end of the red-brick building and hovered for a split second. She looked right, down the side road and spotted *The Karsotty*. It was 50 metres down the road, on the left-hand side. Cars were parked on both sides. The lowering sun caught a second-floor window of the house to the right of the cafe, glinting as it did. She was momentarily distracted.

She was about to take off when she spotted a man in a blue suit on the opposite side of the road; he was walking quickly toward the junction. He looked like any normal businessman heading home after a hard day at the office. He wore a pink shirt and a blue spotted tie. *Very Savile Row*. But there was one thing that made Sam's mind pause. He wasn't carrying anything. There was no briefcase or laptop bag. No man bag, not even an umbrella. He was rushing home for a bus or a train, but had left the office without any accoutrements. It was going to pour down soon and he would get very wet (maybe that's why he was moving quickly?).

Make sense?

She dismissed the thought and carried on walking toward *The Karsotty*.

Then somebody messed with her day.

All explosions follow the same pattern. Combustible material is instantaneously converted into hot gases. This conversion creates light and heat. It's the light you see first – blinding light, just like looking into the sun. Next, travelling supersonically, is the blast wave of highly compressed air. The molecules at the front of the wave are so tightly squeezed together, they're like a solid object travelling through space. Depending on the size of the explosion and where you're standing, this will take the wind out of your lungs, or knock you off your feet. Or kill you. Next is the fireball, burning at up to 3,000 degrees. Caught up in all of this, and more often than not unwitting passengers in the process, is shrapnel: the debris of terror. The fire loses its energy quickly, transferring it to nearby objects, burning savagely. The shrapnel, travelling close to the speed of sound, falls where it lands. Or where it's stopped.

A piece of shrapnel, later identified as glass, caught Sam just below her right eye. She was lucky. Even though her brain had registered the blinding light and had started the reflex process of closing her eyelids, the object hit her well before the body's emergency procedure had finished its job. A centimetre higher and she would have lost the sight in one eye.

In fact, she was lucky in many ways. When the bomb tore through *The Karsotty* and everyone in it, she was still 40 metres from the centre of the explosion. And there was a red Lada Samara between her and the seat of the blast. The car had rocked, its wheels closest to the cafe lifting. At this distance it survived being blown over, unlike many of the cars closer to the cafe. Luckily for Sam it had also taken the brunt of the heat – the paintwork on the front left wing peeling. Most of the shrapnel heading in Sam's direction slammed into the car, piercing panels and smashing glass.

Sam was still blown off her feet. And she was still peppered with debris – and she had a chunk of glass in her face that would forever leave a scar. Her face would take a couple of days to recover from the burn inflicted by the heat. Her ears, overpressured from the shockwave, rang like an annoying car alarm. And the wind had been taken out of her lungs.

She lay on the floor, struggling to find her breath.

But none of this stopped her mind from working. From spinning. She knew that Alexei was dead. He couldn't have survived the blast if he were in the cafe. And their liaison meant that the blast was almost certainly designed for him. *Wasn't it?*

And for me? Shit!

What should she do now?

Come on!

As the shower of explosive flotsam continued to fall to the ground in a percussion of noise, and the roar of the fire became intermingled with human screams, Sam lifted her head from the pavement and glanced over her left shoulder through a gap in the cars. She could make out the spot where, momentarily before, strode the man in the blue suit. With the spotted tie. And no bags.

Moving quickly away from the scene?

She had caught sight of his face. OK, so it was only side-on. But she had seen him. And, as a result, she would remember him. Perfectly. That's what she did. She could get Cynthia's excellent photofit programme to make an exact likeness. If he were part of all this, they would know what he looked like.

Yes, that's what I should do now...

Arbat Village, Eastern Urals, Russia

Sabine Roux was desperately tired. It had been another 12-hour day. She had just closed the clinic and now needed to make sense of her notes. At the same time, she'd use the incredibly slow internet connection, which had been provided by the local administration, to upload her notes to the *Médecins Sans Frontières* (MSF) account in the Cloud. She needed to do this before her head hit the pillow. And at some point, she really should eat.

She sat in front of her dusty laptop, pressed the start button, and imagined all the little people inside working the steam engines to boot it into life. It had seen better days. But money was always tight in any charity and she was at the end of a very long supply chain. She'd probably get hers updated when everyone else had moved onto a brand-new form of the technology. That didn't bother her at the moment. She was more concerned about falling asleep where she sat.

Her fingers hovered above the keyboard, waiting

for the machine to stop whirring. She looked at her fingernails. Even though they were reasonably short, half were broken or chipped. As a doctor, she didn't keep them long – plastic gloves *et al*. But at the rate she was working and with little useful help (that wasn't fair – Dimitri was a *chéri*, and was honing his nursing skills nicely; he was also a decent interpreter), she didn't have time to keep them pristine. *I must give them a trim.*

That reminded her. She must also take some of her own blood and get it into the centrifuge and under the microscope. The day before yesterday, as she was lancing a lesion on a sweet three-year-old girl's arm, mixed fluid had somehow or other bypassed her protective glasses and splashed into her eye. There were all sorts of diseases she'd need to look out for.

Her screen settled down. Using a temperamental mouse, she double-clicked on the MSF icon. Her laptop, the ancient router, the telephone system, and some magical contraption in the Cloud, all began their merry dance. If the last three days were anything to go by, making the connection would take a while. Thankfully, when she eventually got the document open, it hardly ever crashed.

Sabine had a number of cases to update, and three new ones to generate. The latest three were all from the village. In fact, *all* her cases were from the village. That was what was so extraordinary. Her current patient list was 64. Sixty-four 'unexplained' illnesses and infections, from a population of just 350. She had heard that the next-door village (next door being over 50 kilometres away) also had a good number of unusual ailments; she had already cleared with her boss in Moscow that she would move there as soon as she could.

Her three new patients were typical. There was a 68-year-old man who had severe abdominal pain and internal bleeding – his stools were jet black. She'd taken blood and, during her short lunch break, found he had aplastic anaemia – a big drop in blood cells; white ones in particular. As a result, his body was wide open to infection. She couldn't do anything about the internal bleeding without an ultrasound (which she didn't have), and so she had referred him to the hospital in Kushva. The second and third patients were young children. Both had patches of red skin on their arms and torsos, and they were listless and vomiting. She prescribed and administered an anti-inflammatory cream for the skin, and had taken blood and stool samples to establish what was causing the nausea. The stools would go to the hospital and she would do what she could with the blood using the limited equipment she had. In the meantime, the children's mothers had been instructed to restrict their diet. They had left with a few days' worth of small-dose Hyoscine for the nausea.

So far there was no pattern. There were plenty of symptoms, many were similar, but a chunk were irregular. Very few patients came to the clinic with exactly the same set of ailments.

And that's why she had been sent here.

Find the pattern.

The village had a visiting doctor and the local hospital was 80 kilometres away, along some of the worst roads in Russia. The spate of undiagnosed illnesses in this very confined area had been brought to the attention of the chairman of the local Chelyabinsk district. As he was a cousin of a senior politician in Moscow, MSF had been asked to send someone to see if they could establish what was going on.

It's not 'what you know' ...

Sabine had arrived four days ago; it was just her, her trusty Toyota Hilux and a boot full of medical equipment. The journey from Moscow had taken two days. The first day was a slog across the Steppes. It had been a combination of a straight road, fields of wheat and corn, a distant horizon, and a huge, blue sky decorated with fluffy white clouds. The second was more spectacular: all ravines and peaks. The roads up and over the Ural Mountains; at one point the map said they were as high as 1,500 metres. She could best describe their condition as 'passable'. As such, the drive was entertaining. After five years of MSF field work in Asia and Africa, difficult driving conditions rarely fazed her. The trip over the Urals had been a breeze.

Sabine had been surprised at how well organised things had been at Chelyabinsk. Arriving late afternoon, she'd been met by the chairman at the town hall and he'd led her straight to the village. She'd followed his tatty Lada Riva, which dealt with the rough pebble and sand roads equally as well as her Toyota – at times she had struggled to keep up. After about an hour, and then in darkness, they pulled into the village. It was not much more than a hamlet at the base of a rocky escarpment (from what she could make out in the dark). Sabine thought she picked out a Russian Orthodox church beyond the square where they stopped, its gold-painted, onion-shaped dome glinting in the moonlight. The chairman led her to what looked like an old-school house – it was an off-white, single-storey building with large windows and a rusty bike rack by the front door. In a small front garden there was an old climbing frame, which needed several coats of paint.

Inside there were four rooms. One was classroom-sized, furnished with 20 infant chairs and no desks. She immediately designated this 'the waiting room'. She used a second, smaller room as her surgery. There was a bed in the third, and she put all her medical equipment in the fourth. There was a bath and a loo, the former supplied with rusty warm water from a heating system that clanked loudly when it was operating. But no heating. That was fine. She didn't need that. Yet.

That was then. It seemed like an age ago. Now, 64 patients later, she was no further forward in establishing a link between the symptoms. MSF had given her two weeks and then she'd have to return to Moscow. The charity had only a handful of doctors in the country. Sabine thought they had 12 in Chechnya providing clinics in the conflict area, and five in Moscow, supporting the burgeoning homeless population. She was needed elsewhere. Time was always of the essence.

The spreadsheet opened on the screen.

Viola! Allons-y!

Her English was very good, but she wasn't yet fluent enough to think and dream in the language.

Sabine looked across at her notes and started to type. She pressed 'Ctrl-S' regularly to ensure that the spreadsheet saved what she had inputted.

She was halfway through the update when her concentration was broken. There was commotion outside. Sabine pressed 'Ctrl-S', took a deep breath and breathed out through her nose.

Dimitri burst into the surgery looking like he had run a marathon. In between breaths, he said something which resembled '*Rapidement médecin!*' His French was poor and his Russian accent didn't aid communication.

'English, Dimitri! *Pas Français.*' Whilst French was the dominant language in MSF, English was often first choice. 'Slow down. Tell me what's happening?' Sabine was already on her feet and reaching for her coat.

'The child. From this morning. Peter. His mother thinks he is dying! You must come at once.'

Sabine grabbed her medical bag and picked up a high-powered torch. Very few of the houses had guaranteed electricity.

'OK Dimitri.' She motioned with her hand. '*Apres-vous.*'

Flat 17, 3125, Prechistenskiy Road, Moscow

Tears ran down Sam's face as her right hand worked in a circular motion, wiping up the rainwater that had made it through the gaps between her apartment's kitchen window and its frame. The wind was still howling outside and the tissue she had just stuck in the biggest hole was already soaked. It was an endless task. She was glad she had her PADI open water scuba qualification; she might have need of it soon. Humour in the face of despair. It was an old army trick.

She stopped wiping. Another tear fell and landed on her hand. She stared at it, watching the small drop follow the contours of her skin, before slipping between a gap in her fingers and joining the puddle that she was meant to be mopping up. The small dressing covering the gash in her face was acting as a dam against the reservoir of tears seeping from her right eye. It wouldn't hold out much longer. Later she'd have to re-dress the wound herself. She had some plasters in the bathroom.

What a shit day.

It had been, without doubt, her worst day in Moscow so far. And that was saying some.

She hadn't enjoyed the move to Russia. At first, being selected by her outgoing bosses' boss, David, for case-officer training, had been such a boost. Especially after the trials of the German affair. At that point she had been down, possibly as low as she had ever been. The loss of her last living relative, Uncle Pete, and the mayhem that followed as she chased around Europe clutching at conspiratorial straws, had all taken its toll. Things didn't get any better when she realised, soon afterward, that some of the people responsible for the terror were still at large. She wasn't a coward, but knowing that Ralph Bell, the ex-CIA operative and all-round monster, was not behind bars, played on her mind. She couldn't look at a can of Diet Coke, his consistent tipple, without shivering inwardly. On the plus side, since the crash of the Air France plane there had been no more air disasters. That was a positive.

Field training had gone well and she'd really enjoyed it. She hadn't come out top of the class; her final report said something along the lines of, 'Sam Green will make a sound case-officer. At times slightly maverick, she will need the usual level of supervision.' But she had passed. She guessed a posting to Moscow was a sensible choice – she wouldn't be operating on her own much, and with a large team around her, there'd be plenty of people to 'keep an eye'.

Before the move, SIS had planned two years of Russian language training: an initial at year at Warwick University; and then a second year with a Russian-speaking family in Vilnius, Lithuania. Sam had really fretted about that bit of the jigsaw – she spoke French (badly) and had picked up some phrases of German as she was gallivanting around the country with Wolfgang. She wasn't a natural linguist. *Am I?* But she needn't have worried. Her tutor at Warwick gave her the green light after just six months. And five months of Lithuanian submersion later, she was fluent – the Embassy's language expert in Vilnius had said that she couldn't tell Sam apart from a local.

And then onto fourth floor of the British Embassy in Moscow where it had all gone downhill.

She had taken an immediate dislike to the head of section in Moscow, 'M'. She didn't know what it was about him, but there was something in the way he looked at her and the way he spoke to her. He got right up her nose. She had taken over from M34 (Moscow, the 34th member of the team) and had assumed his nomenclature. The boss, M's, real name was Simon Page. But he clung to the superior, old-world title of 'M' – when everyone else in the business was on first-name terms. For Sam's portfolio, he'd stripped away some of the previous M34's responsibilities, and she was left with one objective: co-operating with FSB, the Federal Security Service for Russia – MI5's equivalent, responsible for internal affairs. The work was low-level intelligence cooperation: looking at the movement of drugs into Russia; organised crime; and some illegal arms exports. It didn't fill her day and, not unexpectedly, the Russian FSB team she dealt with treated her like a woman – she wasn't afforded much respect, and she was often ignored altogether.

Typical.

During training it had surprised her to learn that SIS staff would openly assist other nations, especially former sworn enemies such as Russia. It quickly became clear that none of them on the fourth floor were undercover spies *per se*. The Russians knew every member of the SIS team. She might hold the Embassy title 'Projects Officer', and have a fancy ID card with that title on it her, but the FSB *knew* that she was SIS. To make the point, when she moved into her apartment (the flat came with the post), there was a small box of Russian chocolates and a litre of very expensive vodka on the kitchen table. Next to it was a card with her name on it. Her predecessor, who was showing her around before flying home to a welcome retirement, had said, 'It's from the FSB. They'll keep an eye on you from here on in. Just accept it and plan accordingly.'

So, the work was dull – and her boss was an idiot. In six months she had made few friends that she could count on, and the only release she felt was when she worked out in the Embassy's basement gym.

That was until she met Alexei Orlov.

He had caught her at an Embassy party four months ago – both were on the right side of 40, unlike most of the guests. They'd chatted about this and that. He was a journalist for the fledgling e-magazine, *Moscow Talks*. It was a live website which gave information on the local nightlife, usable emerging technologies – such as the latest mobile phones, and other fashion ideas. For Sam, the highlight was the excellent weekly editorial called '*Abroad*'. It was written by Alexei and gave a Russian slant on world news. Alexei was smart and funny. But Sam knew all the rules when having a conversation with someone like him; she'd given nothing away, whilst really enjoying his company.

A couple of weeks later she received an email from him asking that they meet. She cleared the liaison with M, who was dismissive, and they had met openly at a cafe just around the corner from the Embassy. They didn't discuss much, but as he left he slipped her a bit of paper with a Hotmail address on it.

That had been the start of her first, home-grown agent. From then on they had exchanged emails using the reasonably opaque Hotmail, sending them to each other via third-party servers. And they had met on five occasions. As their meetings progressed, so had the level of information and intelligence they shared. Alexei didn't want anything in particular from Sam, but was keen to share snippets of anti-government intel that he was collecting. By not answering some of his questions directly, she confirmed a couple of his lines of enquiry. Soon, a second weekly editorial entitled simply, '*Freedom*', blossomed on *Moscow Talks*. Sam was impressed with the edge to the journalism – it was honest and hard-hitting. Most of it focused on government corruption and cronyism.

As if catching up with its younger sibling, *Abroad* also became more pointed, and started commenting on Russian involvement in world affairs, such as their military's presence in Syria and, much closer to home, the conflict in Ukraine.

Not surprisingly Alexei had had a couple of visitations without coffee from the Ministry of Internal Affairs (MVD). But *Moscow Talks* had stuck to its guns. Last week's edition covered both the Russian involvement in hacking the US presidential candidates' email accounts, as well as major military manoeuvres on the Baltic States' borders. Sam had given nothing to Alexei on either of these two issues, so he was obvious getting his information from a variety of sources.

They met every three weeks; each time a different day of the week and a different final location. They always made initial contact at a bus stop a short distance from the final RV. Locations and dates were agreed face-to-face at the previous meeting, and no changes could be made by email, so there was little chance of intercept.

Except for this afternoon. The meeting at *The Karsotty* had been impromptu, arranged two days ago after Sam had received an opaque email from Alexei:

It would be good to meet as soon as we can, please. We need to talk about SH and his work down south. I hope you're having a fun time. Pass my regards to Martin.

The flowery language was a simple aid to camouflage – but Sam recognised the immediacy of the need to meet. *To talk about SH?* She had no idea who or what that was.

Sam almost sought advice from one of her SIS colleagues as to how to proceed, but as most of them regarded her as wet behind the ears, she didn't bother.

Sod them.

She arranged the meeting.

A meeting destined to end in death and disaster.

And now here she was, sobbing uncontrollably in her kitchen. A tough six months had just dissolved into abject misery. Someone had turned the lights off without asking her.

Sam knew that most of the tears were from shock – a delayed reaction to having almost been murdered for the fourth time in her life. She knew it was shock, as she couldn't get rid of the accompanying cold strip that ran down her spine. Cold, shivering and uncontrolled emotion. The body's reaction to things it couldn't comprehend.

She also knew the shock was exacerbated by losing Alexei. Almost a friend. Someone who treated her like an adult. Her very first agent. A prize.

And her miscalculation had cost him his life.

She knew he was dead. One of the organisation's analysts had checked as soon as she'd got back to the Embassy. And it was her fault? She had arranged the meeting – he had died. He had something to tell her about *SH* and that had cost him his life. Surely that was the case?

Sam had visited the Embassy's medical centre to get her cheek seen to as soon as she got into the building. She'd pulled out the glass as she jogged away from the scene and had stopped the bleeding by pressing her hanky to the wound. The Embassy's medical staff had stitched her up on the spot and given her some cream for the light burns to her face. Once on the fourth floor, a few of her colleagues had gathered round and listened to her story and offered condolences. One of the team, with responsibility for internal affairs, had questioned her on the location of the explosion and what she thought the type of explosive might have been. By then, tiredness and anger had congealed. She had given monosyllabic answers.

M had come in just as she was heading home. Normally he would have walked straight through to his office, but for some reason he sauntered up to her desk.

'What's wrong with you, Green?'

Sam asked him if he had heard the news about the bombing. He had. She then explained about her meet with Alexei.

'Don't give yourself too much credit, Green. It's almost certainly: wrong place, wrong time. The Chechens are responsible. Trust me.'

She didn't, of course. Not as far as she could launch him from one of the fourth-floor windows – if they opened. Which they didn't. That was a good thing, as, as he stood beside her with his hands thrust into his trouser pockets fiddling with something unmentionable, she was sorely tempted to give it a go.

He walked off whistling 'I'm singing in the rain.' Sam looked to the closest window. It had just started to pour.

Now, back in her apartment, she was feeling incredibly sorry for herself. She was still staring vacantly at her hands, the blue, chequered dishcloth soggy and motionless on the worktop. Sam sensed the tension in the dressing on her cheek loosen and felt it drop from the top downwards, pivoting on the bottom tape which held firm. She couldn't see her face, but she had good imagination: curly, out-of-control auburn hair, pink eyes, red cheeks, an inflamed scar with three black stitches, and a wet dressing dangling from her face as if it was about to abseil to the floor.

Not a good look.

Sam sniffled and held back the tears. She looked out through the kitchen window, which now rattled against the ferocity of the wind. She was on her own. Completely. Yes, she could phone her old London boss, Jane, tomorrow and have a gas with her. But Jane had wider responsibility (which sadly didn't include Russia); she wouldn't be able to afford Sam much time.

So, and she didn't mean to repeat herself, she was on her own.

I am on my own.

With the initials *HS*.

And a dead journalist.

She had two choices.

She didn't need to rehearse them; she knew which one she was going to take.

And damn the consequences.

Chapter 2

No 7 ExtraOil Rig, Yamal Field, Northern Russia

Jim Dutton was not a happy man. It wasn't because, even in mid-autumn, the temperatures were already struggling to make it above freezing. He could cope with whatever the weather threw at him. Ten years on the North Sea rigs was enough to prepare any man for weather extremes. At least here on the Yamal Peninsula, looking out across the Kamal Sea, it was dry. On the exposed sea rigs, wind, rain and salt water were ever present. A single-degree drop in temperature was amplified five times. And the salt in the wind piled on the misery, irritating exposed flesh and penetrating cuts and sores. No, he could cope with the Arctic weather.

Neither was it the general dour atmosphere in which he worked, although he did miss the camaraderie of his previous rigs. Fun wasn't a word in the northern Russian's dictionary – unless it was accompanied by a vodka bath. So, he didn't expect much by way of teamwork. Everybody was working flat out and the conditions hardly encouraged merriment. He currently worked for *ExtraOil*, a part-state owned Russian start-up oil and gas company, hurried along by the need to produce more oil. Western sanctions against Russia, after their annexation of Crimea and partial invasion of Ukraine, were hitting hard. Very low crude oil prices had exacerbated the situation and, as a result, the Russian government were pushing ahead with new fields at a rate hitherto unseen anywhere in the world. *If you can't sell it high, make a lot of it.*

It was true to say that he didn't have many pals on the rig. Most of the crew were Russian. Out of the five English speakers he was the only Scotsman. There were a couple of Canadians, big men (in every way), who he shared a whiskey with every so often. There was a Kiwi, with whom he played the odd game of chess. And a Norwegian, Jürgen, who spoke very good English; he guessed he was as close to a friend as you could get in conditions where, what little time off you had, was spent either eating or sleeping. All of them worked 12-hour shifts, the benefit of which was six weeks on, two weeks off. For him, as getting home involved a 48-hour journey by way of a truck, a helicopter, a train and two planes, he worked a double-shift: 12 weeks and four. Taking off journey time, that gave him a luxurious three weeks at home.

As the QA (quality assurance) for the whole site, he didn't naturally make many friends. His job was to check all the industrial work and ensure that it was up to the required standard. On the Russian fields, the post also subsumed Health and Safety. Although, the owners seemed less worried about accidents involving their workers than they were insistent on the efficiency of the processes – keeping the oil and gas flowing. As a result, his job was tough. It was a full day, often in very inhospitable conditions. And when things weren't right, he had to give the bad news to the relevant senior engineer. They often disagreed with his assessment; they knew their business better than he did? Six times out of ten their dispute had to be run past the chief engineer for arbitration. Five times out of ten the chief sided with him – and the fault had to be rectified.

As the QA, making pals on a rig was always going to be difficult.

He didn't care. He was an outstanding oilfield operator with 32 years' experience; and QAs were notoriously unlikeable – it went with the territory. As a Scot, he was born with skin thicker than a rhino, and he had friends aplenty back in Aberdeen. Work was work. It was tough, but he could cope. He knew the oil business better than anyone on the field and he was meticulous with what he did – he made few, if any, mistakes. And he was proud of that.

And they paid him $125,000 a year. Tax free.

He could do without friends. And he could cope with the weather.

No, it was something else that was gnawing at him; something he had discovered three weeks ago.

It had been a chance find. He was in the chief's office waiting for him to get in from Salekhard, a small town 100 klicks to the south of the rig where *ExtraOil* had their local HQ. Getting to and from the town was quickest using the firm's helicopter, or their twin-engine *ChelAvia* P2006 light aircraft. Alternatively, the field's purpose-built railway ran a twice-daily freighter which had space for several passengers. The drive by 4x4, along the dirt road, was always problematic. In the short summer, it was often flooded as the ice melt took its own course, often taking bits of the road with it. In the winter, it was frozen solid, and whilst there was very little new snow (technically much of northern Russia was classified as desert), the ice fractured the road, and, between the cracks, it provided skid pans for unsuspecting drivers. The *ExtraOil* infrastructure maintenance team did what they could. But few travelled by road unless they had no other choice.

The chief's secretary said the boss was coming in by helicopter; it was delayed by 30 minutes for some technical reason. Touchdown was at 16.35pm.

Jim had walked round the chief's desk to the window to look out across the site at the Arctic Sea. When the weather was benign and the light just so, it was mesmerisingly beautiful. Everything was a shade of blue. The dark blue water, the piercingly bright blue sky, darker towards the heavens than at the horizon, and the floating ice – white with a hint of blue. He was pretty sure *Dulux* made a paint that colour – one of the 'almost whites' from their 1980s range.

He turned around and, with nothing else to entertain him, looked down at the chief's desk. And there it was. Among a pile of paper, just sticking out from what Jim thought might be the chief's overflowing pending tray.

He could see the top third of a paper. Other than a US company, *Drillmec's*, sales catalogue, it was the only document clearly in English. It was a three-page, loose memo. What caught Jim's eye was the header: COMMERCIAL SENSITIVE – CONFIDENTIAL. He checked his watch: 16.20pm. The chief would be back in about ten minutes. It was a windless day; he'd hear the helicopter well before it landed.

His Scottish inquisitiveness got the better of him.

Jim pulled the paper from the pile and read it. Cover to cover. And then he read it again.

What he read shocked him to the core.

He was a QA in the oil industry. He knew everything there was to know about getting the stuff out of the ground. Gas, fracked gas, crude oil. You name it; he knew about it. He'd seen it done well. And he'd seen it done badly. He knew what happened underground. And he knew what happened on the surface.

What he had just read wasn't right. It wasn't ethical. In fact, it was downright dangerous. He knew that. What was *ExtraOil* up to?

He heard the melodic *wocker-wocker* of the helicopter blades grow louder as the aircraft came into land. He carefully put the paper back where he had found it. And took a deep breath.

He couldn't recall the details of his subsequent meeting with the chief. It had been short and sharp. During the meeting his mind had been on other things, but the boss didn't seem to notice. Five minutes later he was back out on the rig checking the mud hydro-pneumatic units.

Since then, Jim had spent all his spare time researching what he had uncovered. He had access to the firm's databases and a good number of their e-files. He looked over the mud and slurry reports from the post-drilling records, and he checked the freight export log, both by rail and the few by road. He also got to know the company better. Where *ExtraOil's* rigs were. What and where they drilled. Who owned the company and what its subsidiaries were. And he checked their public accounts.

It had taken him about a week, but by then he knew a good deal about *ExtraOil*, its founder, its sister companies and their worldwide operations.

But what to do?

Ten days ago, he had emailed a pal of his in Moscow. He was an ex-North Sea engineer who had left the business and gone into lecturing at Moscow State University. He was now a professor, or something similar, with a PhD in oil exploration. They had become great friends about 15 years ago when they both worked on the *British Petroleum* Kittiwake oil platform. Which was a surprise, because his pal Grigori was Russian – 'White Russian' – Grigori had always corrected. Jim guessed the 'White' bit, from the mid-west of Russia, is what made him more Western – more likely to become a friend. They'd kept in touch over the years and Jim trusted him implicitly. Grigori was neither new nor old Russian. He was a realist and avoided politics as best he could. That's why Jim felt he could share his disturbing news with him without risk of bias.

Grigori had pinged back a holding email

immediately. And had replied in more detail a couple of days later. He response was one of incredulity. He asked whether or not he could share the detail with a trusted friend; the answer from Jim was, 'yes'. There'd had further short exchange a couple of days ago – but nothing since. Jim continued to trawl the internet looking for more clues, whilst keeping a close eye on the by-products of the *ExtraOil* field.

To ensure some degree of protection for himself, he deleted all his internet search records, as well as his email exchanges with Grigori. But he was also old-school; he couldn't stop himself from keeping a notebook full of his findings. He hid it in the last place anyone would look: in his protective clothing locker in his room, strapped to the underneath of a low shelf. It was hardly *Secret Squirrel*, but it gave him some comfort.

So, he wasn't happy. Certainly, he wasn't comfortable. And he was on the horns of a dilemma. He needed his job and the hefty final-salary pension that came with it. But he wasn't sure how much longer he could keep his little secret, secret.

The Lubyanka Building, HQ of the Border Guard Service of Russia, Moscow, Russia

Sam couldn't stop herself from pausing as she crossed the main square in front of the Lubyanka. It was an extraordinary building. A big, orange, late-19th century neo-Baroque monolith – out on its own, every other building giving it space. That was no surprise.

Previously it had been the HQ of the erstwhile KGB. Today it housed a political prison and some elements of the FSB – as well as the HQ of the Border Guard Service. It stank of fear. Nobody wanted anything to do with the place – other than those who worked there.

Sam worked there. Well, every so often. It was here that SIS met their Russian counterparts. She was involved with the planning of the FSB's latest joint operation: Op Michael. The operation was designed to blow a hole in the main opium conduit from Afghanistan; a route which took in Turkmenistan and a sea journey across the Caspian Sea, before entering into the Russian heartland.

The meeting was due to start at 11am, on the third floor. Room 313B. The building was an organised rabbit warren; one which benefited from beautiful parquet flooring and copious amounts of wood panelling. The meeting rooms were all cramped, and the Russians' technical facilities were at least a decade behind where SIS were. But, the staff were very earnest and uber-organised. It was just a shame that, as the only female on a team of five (she and four FSB agents), they rarely gave her ideas any credence. One small part of her thought that 'M' had assigned her to this role as he knew what their reaction would be to having a younger female on the team.

She was building up a long list of disgruntlements against the man.

It can't last.

Sam had walked the three klicks from the Embassy to Lubyanka. She could have got the metro or the bus, but she needed time out of the office to think. To try and put together a plan – who to talk to, and how best to make that happen. She couldn't think last night; the shock had taken what little energy she had left. Any room for spare thought was subsumed by trying to come to terms with Alexei's death. *Who would kill him?* The nagging pain in her cheek was an ever-present reminder that she could so easily have joined him. She had been exhausted.

After a quick fridge raid, she had had a bath and just about made it to her bed before her mind had shut down, her body rapidly following suit.

She had felt much better first thing – somebody had turned the lights back on. She was energised by the need for answers. And it had been a reasonably productive morning. Using Cynthia's photofit programme, she now had a close-to-exact likeness of 'Blue Suit'. The computer's face-recognition programme worked on finding a match among the millions of mugshots that were stored on all SIS databases. Sam had drummed her fingers while Cynthia went through every face they had. No luck. Rubbing her chin, she had forwarded Blue Suit's mugshot to an old pal of hers, Frank, in SIS's London HQ in Vauxhall (colloquially known as *Babylon*). He was the senior analyst for the Middle East and southern Europe. He also had connections in the UK with the Met's CID – who would access Interpol's database, as well as the National Counter Terrorism Security Office (NaCTSO) and the British military. Frank, with his usual efficiency, had pinged her back as soon as he had got into work – Moscow was two hours ahead of London. He was now on the case.

By way of a plan, en route to Lubyanka she had made the decision that she would visit the offices of *Moscow Talks* as soon as she could. It would be a highly irregular move by an SIS case-officer, but needs must. She had checked their website on her mobile as she walked and, as a result, knew the names of a couple of the other journalists. An email exchange, or phone call, might scare the horses; so, an impromptu face-to-face meeting was the way ahead – Sam got so much more from an exchange when you could see the person's pupils.

Sam reckoned she could tell if someone were lying by looking into their eyes. For inexperienced liars there were other, obvious giveaways: shaking uncontrollably and profuse sweating. But, even when she had dealt with experts, very few could prevent their eyes from telling the real story. To her, at least.

Sam had clocked *Moscow Talks'* address and would pop over after her Op Michael meeting. She also had Alexei's last email which she remembered word-for-word: *It would be good to meet as soon as we can, please. We need to talk about SH and his work down south. I hope you're having a fun time. Pass my regards to Martin.*

The 'Martin' bit was his teasing; that he knew SIS's head of mission was called 'M'. Anyone who watched James Bond, or did a cursory search of the internet, knew who 'M' was – but she allowed Alexei his little victory, without pointing out the obvious.

'*SH and his work down south*'? Now, that was a different thing altogether. Crimea was down south. So was Ukraine. So was Syria. And Iraq and Sudan. There were so many possibilities. On the other hand, the whole thing could have been a bouquet of flowers to pad out the need to meet. Maybe SH meant nothing?

Her only hope was that someone at *Moscow Talks* knew what he was onto. And/or, Frank came up with an identity for Blue Suit.

First, though, she had to get through the Op Michael meeting. Without fidgeting. *Or thumping a Russian.*

She was met at the main entrance by Vladislav Mikhailov, a 40-something FSB officer and her 'oppo' at the Lubyanka. He was wearing an open-necked shirt and dark, heavy cotton trousers. Balding, with a pale complexion, he displayed all the hallmarks of a middle-aged, middle-class Russian man: a vodka paunch, a reddening nose and eyes that needed a good night's sleep.

Stop being so judgemental!

Notwithstanding appearances, Sam liked Vlad. He was the only Russian in the building who seemed to take what she said remotely seriously. And he had a warm smile, which he used expertly. Sam reminded herself that he was a trained spy, which meant – in the case of the FSB, he was almost certainly a competent shot and useful in a tight spot. As he led her up the stairs to the third floor, she checked out his silhouette for a concealed weapon. *You never know.* But there was nothing.

Op Michael was a straightforward op. Julie, a contact of hers in the Embassy in Kabul, had recruited a local Afghan who'd agreed to be placed on a drugs convoy that was due to cross the Afghan border on Friday night. (She and Julie had been on the same training course – she'd come out top female, and hence a posting to Afghanistan.) Julie had issued the Afghan with a doctored mobile. As well as receiving locational information from GPS satellites – as all smartphones could, the planted SIS mobile also constantly pinged its position to a couple of European military satellites. This guaranteed that people with the right equipment could follow the phone, no matter the terrain. Even if it were turned off. With mobile towers few and far between outside of the major cities in Afghanistan, having a phone which provided guaranteed location information was an essential link in the Op Michael plan.

In an emergency, the Afghan could phone Julie and, with UK Special Forces (SF) on call, she'd made a half-promise to the man that it might be possible to extract him. When Sam was talking to Julie by phone a couple of days ago, Julie couldn't hide from Sam that SF would almost certainly *not* deploy for a lone Afghan informant. The man was on his own.

Sam couldn't find any particularly deep emotion for the informant. She'd hate for him to be lost. But this operation was as much about stopping drugs getting into Western Europe, as it was about preventing them from finding their way onto the streets of Russian cities. And the Op had the added advantage of forging closer links between the FSB and SIS. Risking a lone Afghan informant was probably worth it. *Probably*.

Once they were all sat down, one of Vlad's colleagues and the lead for the operation, updated everyone on the plan for the Turkmenistan side of the border. The projector threw up a series of slides as he spoke. On the table in front of them was a 1:25,000 paper map of the operational area. A Spetsnaz (Russian special forces) team would be prepositioned on the Turkmenistan side of the Afghan border and would intercept the convoy once it was through the crossing. A rep from the Border Guard Service confirmed that his men, who would be working alongside the Turkmenistanis on the ground, would let the convoy through without any hassle. Spetsnaz would then do the business a couple of klicks further down the road.

Sam, who had spoken to Julie briefly this morning, told everyone that the agent was already in place. The phone would boot up at 15.00 on Friday. Its battery should last for at least eighteen hours – well beyond the planned intercept. They had tested the phone with the designated Russian computer in the building, and it had all worked well. On Friday night, they would all be glued to the screen.

The Russian lead finished the briefing and asked for any questions.

There were a couple from his team which he dealt with expertly.

Sam was nervous about a fork in the road, a couple of klicks short of the border crossing. It had the potential to split the convoy, if that's what the smugglers wanted.

'Sorry. Ehh...' Sam, speaking Russian, leant forward so she could point at the junction on the paper map.

'Have we got any idea if the track leading north here can take vehicles? I'm just concerned that, if spooked, the convoy might take the fork and cross here.' Sam used her finger to follow the route from the fork to what looked like a second border crossing point.

She had mentioned this before during the pre-planning, but the team had patronised her with their apparent local knowledge. Sam had done the maths. None of them looked old enough to have served in the country during the Soviet occupation in the 80s. So, she wasn't sure how they'd know. To back up her concerns, this morning she had used Cynthia's enhanced 3-D satellite mapping to study the junction and the path that led to a second crossing point. She reckoned you could easily get a 4x4 over the border using the secondary route.

She pressed again now.

The lead Russian bristled.

'Our view is that the only viable vehicle route from Herat to the Caspian Sea is via Dugy, Narzi and across the border here,' the Russian used a wooden pointer, placing its tip firmly where the team were planning that the drugs would cross into Turkmenistan, 'and then onto Serhetabat. This other route you point out is a distraction.' His pointer described the alternative route.

Grrr.

Sam wasn't going to take no for an answer.

'Thanks. Got that. The thing is, I've e-recced the route using SIS mapping and I'm pretty sure you can get a 4x4 up the second track and across the border. The route also gives the added advantage of avoiding Serhetabat in Turkmenistan, a choke point for the convoy. Would it not be sensible to split the Spetsnaz team – or at least have eyes on the second crossing? Maybe something remote? Our Afghan agent's phone should give us some prior warning if the plan changes, but there isn't an easy route for your team to get from one crossing to another should that happen. We could lose the drugs and the carriers.' Throughout she looked the Russian lead directly in the eye.

Vlad glanced across the conference table and caught Sam's eye. He gave a hint of a smile. *Does he agree with me?*

'Out of the question, Miss Green. We need all of the Spetsnaz collocated for maximum impact, should that be necessary. We will not be splitting the team.' He paused for a second, purposefully not looking in Sam's direction.

'Any other questions?'

The room filled with shaking heads. Except Sam's – she screwed her face up as if she'd sucked on a lemon.

So, that's that then?

Arbat Village, Eastern Urals, Russia

'Yes, I've done that. Three times. The tests are all negative.' Sabine was talking in French to her MSF colleague in Moscow. She was sheltering from the biting easterly wind behind a shed on the old school playground. Mobile reception was better there.

Her conversation was about water quality — the most obvious answer to the spate of, now deadly, illnesses that were affecting her village. She'd only been there five days and it was already *her* village. Last night's death of the poor young lad, Peter, had ripped out a small piece of her heart. At the same time, it had lashed down a part of her which she knew would make leaving the village without a solution very difficult.

Sabine raised her free hand to her mouth and bit on a finger. She closed her eyes and fought back a tear. She was a doctor. She had seen death more times than she could remember. But there was something about the isolation here, in this forlorn, forgotten place, that made everything much more personal.

'Sorry Michele, it's been tough here.' She forced her mind to clear. 'Look, to repeat myself, I've used the water sanitation equipment to check for the full gamut of nasties. I've taken samples from five different taps across the village, and two wells. I've looked at all the samples under the microscope. Nothing... well, not quite nothing.' She paused. 'As per yesterday's report, chlorine levels are high, but that's a good thing in this semi-wilderness. And chlorine's not going to cause the infections, rashes, nausea, listlessness, dizziness — sorry, you know I could go on.'

'I understand, Sabine. Have you had the stool samples back from the hospital?'

'One set. All clear. No sign of salmonella,

campylobacter, typhoid – I've checked the whole lot. And the combination of the stomach upsets *and* rashes? It's bizarre…'

Michele started to speak, but Sabine carried on. 'And this morning, I've had a new case. A 70-year-old woman bleeding from her uterus. It's madness! The only common thread is that those affected are nearly all old and/or vulnerable.' The wind blew a particularly strong gust; Sabine's long dark hair whipped across her face. She used her spare hand to push it behind her ear. 'Most of the working-age men seem to be fine. They all slave away at the local cement factory. I've had one come in with severe headaches, with no prior history. I sent him away with some codeine. But apart from that they seem fit enough.'

Sabine spotted Dimitri walking briskly from the school building toward the shed. He was carrying a blanket which he gently placed around Sabine's shoulders. She forced a smile. *Ce chouchou.* She would struggle without Dimitri, that's for sure.

'Doctor. You must come. A lady is here. She very sick.' His tone was forceful, but reverent.

'Got to go, Michele. I'll call you later.' Sabine didn't wait for a reply. She thrust her mobile into her pocket and hurried into the surgery.

Where she discovered chaos.

Outside, buffeted by the wind that howled all the way from Siberia, she had been protected from the noise that greeted her in the waiting room. In the centre, sat uncomfortably on an infant-sized chair, was a middle-aged woman. Sabine guessed she was mid-

30s, but these people age so quickly – she could have been in her 20s. She wore standard village attire: a dark-coloured skirt, a white blouse, a heavy woollen cardigan and leather ankle boots. The colours were bland; the skirt may once have had vibrancy, but now, after countless washes, it was the colour of the local vegetation.

Except it wasn't. The hem and much of the front of the skirt was dark crimson. Sabine couldn't see the extent of the staining, as the woman had lifted her skirt up around her thighs, her legs wide apart. Her rounded, heavily-laden belly, which strained the buttons on her blouse, drooped over her pelvis. And the red continued to tell a story as it pooled between her feet. Blood splattered down her inner thighs, onto her calves and all over her off-white ankle socks.

She must have lost at least a litre of blood? And more on the way here?

Sabine was shaken from her momentary pause by the accompanying noise.

The woman was screaming at the top of her voice, only to stop and pant four or five times, before screaming again. Next to her, holding her hand, was a man – she guessed her husband. He was shouting all manner of Russian that Sabine didn't understand. Between them they made Sabine's ears hurt. As her mind translated her assessment into action, she quickly took in the other people sat around the waiting room. There were five. Only one looked able-bodied enough to be of help.

Now!

At the top of her voice Sabine cut through the noise. She was only 1.55m tall, but she had a big set of lungs.

'*TAIS-TOI!*' She took another breath. 'SHUT... UP!'

The man stopped yelling immediately, stunned by the petit French doctor. The woman, whose screaming was beginning to fade of its own accord, broke into a series of delirious pants. Her head was lolling on her neck, as though the muscles had been severed. The man used his spare hand to help her keep it upright.

She turned to Dimitri. Quieter now, but still forceful.

'This woman is having her baby. She has haemorrhaged and has lost a lot of blood. Carry her into the surgery. I will prep. Once she's on the table, get that woman,' Sabine pointed at the 20-something girl, sat like a rabbit staring down the barrel of a shotgun, 'to boil plenty of water. As much as she can. And keep it coming. We might be doing some surgery.'

The husband had started shouting again.

'And keep him out of my way!'

Those were the right instructions. But they weren't right enough.

The next 40 minutes were the worst of Sabine Roux's professional life. She was a moderately competent emergency surgeon, having spent 18 months working in Accident and Emergency at a hospital in Abidjan, Cote D'Ivoire. She'd dealt with some horrific gunshot injuries, vehicle accidents and knife wounds. But there, she had the benefit of an anaesthetist, a few nurses and some half-decent medical equipment.

Here, in a tiny village in the Eastern Urals, it was her, Dimitri, three scalpels, two forceps, a drip and some morphine. And a young woman working beyond herself to keep them all sterilised. And she couldn't use the morphine before the child was out, as she needed the woman to push.

But the woman didn't push. Because she didn't last more than two minutes on the table. She had lost too much blood. Sabine had put a drip in as soon as she could, but it was too little, too late.

She lost the child too. But that also wasn't due to Sabine's ineptitude.

That was because the child was dead on delivery.

Once the drip was up, Sabine checked the woman's vagina. The baby's head was showing. Where the blood had smeared clear of the scalp, she could see a tinge of blue. She had no time. The woman was close to death, or dying. Or dead. She was incapable of helping Sabine with the delivery. Her body had given up.

The baby was in the same state.

Sabine had no choice. She had to cut.

She cut so much she could, just about, get leverage on the baby's head with her bare hands. After a few seconds of monumental effort, the baby was out. It was so slippery, she almost dropped it. She immediately brought her ear to the poor thing's chest to listen for a heartbeat. But there was nothing. She listened some more.

Still nothing.

Sabine knew the baby was gone.

She lifted her head, the red slime of afterbirth and blood dripping from her ear. She looked at the blue and red bundle in her hands and followed the umbilical cord to the child's mother, who lay motionless on the table, her pelvic region a mess of blood and flesh.

And then she noticed it.

The baby.

The blue and red lifeless baby.

The blue and red lifeless baby that had stumps for arms.

Tsandera Street, Moscow

As Sam approached the offices of *Moscow Talks* she noticed a young woman locking a metal and glass door. The medium-height woman wore a knee-length, lemon-coloured wool coat. One of her hands was turning the key in the lock, the other held several files and a handbag.

Sam stopped short of the entrance and took in the scene. A two-storey, narrow office front. A single door, which probably led straight into a stairwell. And an adjoining, metal-framed window which started close to the pavement, finished at the ceiling and ran the length of the frontage.

But it wasn't a window. It was an ex-window, now boarded up inexpertly with cheap plywood. The wood looked new. The break was recent.

Sam glanced at the upper floor. Both windows were intact, off-white net curtains preventing onlookers across the road from gawping in. If Sam didn't know it was the home of *Moscow Talks*, she would have guessed at a private investigator's office. Or those of a street lawyer.

The woman finished locking up. As she turned away from the door, she registered Sam. She gave a half-jump, as if Sam was someone who had come back with a large piece of concrete intent on smashing the remaining windows.

Or to break something more vulnerable.

She shook her head, clearing her fright. And took off in the direction of the Ostankino TV tower, which rose in the middle-distance above northern Moscow, like a giant upturned golf tee.

Sam kept pace with her.

'Hi. My name is Elena. I'm a friend of Alexei.' Sam's accent was perfect.

Sam had four Russian aliases. All of them supported by the necessary paperwork. She always carried Elena's with her. She liked Elena. She was an office-worker from St Petersburg. She was in Moscow visiting her sick mother. Her mother, who was 84, lived in a grubby apartment in Bibirevo District, north of where they were now. She was dying of lung cancer.

Actually, the apartment was an SIS safe house. Her

mother would be pleased.

The pursued woman picked up the pace.

'Leave me alone! Leave me alone!' She spat out the words. 'I have a lot to do. If you continue to follow me, I shall call the police!'

Sam avoided a grey bin that was blocking her route and re-joined the woman after her detour.

'I know Alexei is dead. I was due to meet him when the explosion happened. I want to find out why.' *No harm in the truth.*

The woman stopped abruptly. Sam was caught off guard and skidded to a halt. She turned to face the woman, who had tears in her eyes.

'You're no friend of Alexei's.' Venom was ever present. 'I have known him all my adult life. He never mentioned an Elena. In any case. You saw the front window of the offices. And you say you saw the explosion. It's over!' She was breathing shallowly, as if they'd sprinted to where they were now. 'Leave – me – alone!' She was half-shouting now.

Even though the light was fading, Sam could see the woman's eyes clearly. Her pupils had dilated. She was scared. Glancing down, Sam could see the woman's hands shaking.

She wasn't scared. She was terrified.

Sam raised her hands in submission.

'I'm sorry. I am. But I must find out more. I work for *Russian Liberation.*' Sam was making it up as she went along. 'We think Alexei was onto something important.

My meeting with him...' Sam's sentence trailed off as the woman turned sharply and started walking again, quickening her pace. Introducing the infamous, anti-government, underground movement had been a poor choice. The wrong lie at the wrong time.

Oh well.

Sam quickly caught up with her.

'Go away!'

But Sam wasn't giving up. She spoke at the woman as they both trotted along the pavement.

'Help me. Please. Give me something. Something or somebody...' Sam avoided a lamp post, 'that Alexei has seen or spoken to recently. Please. This could be so important.'

They both had to stop at a junction, the pedestrian traffic light was showing a stationary red man and, on a separate screen, red numbers were counting down from 45. In front of them was a major road. Back-to-back cars plied their way up and down the main thoroughfare. The woman looked straight ahead. Stationary, Sam had a chance to study her face in more detail. Behind the austere pout, she was beautiful – there was no other word for it. Short dark hair in a bob, high cheekbones, pale complexion, just enough red lipstick and a pointy nose. A modern-day, Russian, Audrey Hepburn.

The woman turned her head toward Sam, who was momentarily embarrassed for staring.

Almost in a whisper. 'If I give you one name. Will you leave me alone? And...' she raised an index finger and pointed it at Sam accusingly, 'you find the bastards who did this to Alexei!'

Sam blew out, her cheeks expanding and her shoulders dropping as she did.

'Yes, I'll do my best.'

I really will.

The woman faced the front again. The lights had changed, the walking green man now illuminated. She strode off, Sam matching her pace-for-pace. They followed the minor road in the direction of the TV tower. The frontages of the buildings had changed – businesses giving way to accommodation. Both sides of the road were packed with parked cars.

The woman's pace didn't slow. She stared straight ahead. As Sam caught a glance, she noticed the woman's lips moving imperceptibly, as if rehearsing something. Sam was watching her so intently she caught her left hip on the wing mirror of a rather smart black Mercedes.

Bugger! That hurt.

'Professor Grigori Vasiliev. He lectures at Moscow University. Oil, I think.'

The woman stopped. Her red lips tight, her expression a frown.

'Now, will you leave me alone?'

Sam studied her face one more time. She was beautiful, that was true. But Sam now saw something more than the fear she'd picked up earlier. It was grief. A real depth of feeling at having lost someone very close.

Were she and Alexei…?

Sam had been there with her first love, Chris. She'd experienced the same terror in Afghanistan – a terror that had taken his life and destroyed hers; physically and emotionally. As she looked into the film-star eyes of the woman in a yellow woollen coat, she could see it now. This beauty and Alexei were an item. Yesterday's explosion had damaged Sam; she had a scar on her cheek for life to prove it. The same explosion had destroyed the woman in front of her. Sam knew that she would never fully recover from the experience. Sam knew. And that hurt like hell.

'Yes. I promise you, I will do everything in my power to find the people who killed Alexei.'

Prechistenskiy Road, Moscow

Sam hadn't bothered to go back to the office. It was well past 7pm by the time she came out of her local metro station. She'd checked her secure emails remotely, using SIS's encrypted smartphone. Frank had come back with nothing on 'Blue Suit'. But he wasn't giving up. There was a short acknowledgement from Julie that their agent was nicely holed up in the compound in Herat, where the drugs were currently piled high. And the op was still on for Friday, the day after tomorrow.

And she had Googled Professor Grigori Vasiliev. Sure enough, he lectured on oil exploration at Moscow

State University. She would do some more remote research on him at her desk tomorrow before, she thought, paying him a visit.

She also ran through all the possibilities to why and who had killed Alexei. Until this evening there was lingering doubt in Sam's mind that he (and she?) were the bomber's main target(s). Sure, Russian politicians had immediately blamed Chechen rebels for the attack and, as a result, scores of hapless immigrants had been rounded up, accompanied by a circus of media. 'Another vicious attack on Muscovite freedom', was this morning's headline in the broadsheet, *Izvestiya*.

But seeing the boarded-up front window of *Moscow Talks*, and the fearful state of one its reporters, Sam was clear that the bomb was designed to kill Alexei. He was onto something that someone else didn't want exploited.

Could the State be behind this? Were her colleagues in the Lubyanka building capable of murder? There was no hard SIS evidence (that she was aware of) that the FSB murdered political opponents. They had no need to. The Russian premier had such power that anyone who wilfully opposed him was arrested. Trials took forever, by which time the issue had gone away.

Organised crime, hidden superficially by big business – that was a different thing altogether. Oligarchs with more power and money than they could afford to lose, were capable of anything. Most were above reproach, but a few – a number of whom were under the watchful eye of some of her colleagues at the Embassy – operated lawlessly; bribing a Moscow political elite who enjoyed the privileges that the money could buy.

But, what was the connection between Alexei and the professor? A connection so damning that the former was dead. He, and now she, were onto something. She knew it.

Sam was 50 metres from her apartment, a five-room, reasonably decent pad on the fifth floor of the next-but-one block of flats. She could hear the glass of Malbec calling her.

As she turned half-right to cross the street between two parked cars (a battered Toyota Previa and a very old Lada Riva – always alert; she couldn't stop herself), she sensed something wasn't quite right. It was a peripheral thing. A combination of movement out of the corner of her eye, a non-mechanical sound, and an almost imperceptible increase in pressure. She almost managed to stop herself from crossing the road, but the momentum of her original pace kept her moving.

That's when the car hit her. It must have been traveling at around 30 miles an hour; easily enough to kill. She was just out from between the parked cars, but her sense of something not being quite right gave her a fraction of a second to react. A fraction of a second to propel her body upward, so that she went over the top of the car, rather than underneath it. She started to leap like a Fosbury-Flop high jumper: back arched, bum high, legs bent. And she had done some gymnastics at school. So, she remembered how to land – fingers, then palms, then the back of the head, bent forward to allow the shoulders to take most of the impact. And finally, a roll to enable the body's inertia to run its course.

A half-jump and a landing; the combination of both had turned what could have been a bad accident, into an opportunity.

As Sam came out of the roll she instinctively looked for the tailgate of the car speeding off into the distance. *It must be a hybrid. Driving on electric only?* It if had been burning fuel she would have heard it long before she had started to cross the road.

But it wasn't a hybrid. It was a Tesla Model S.

All electric.

No noise. *Ahh – that makes sense!*

And it was maroon (or blue; the light wasn't great).

And she had the number plate – indelibly etched onto her brain.

Now they weren't expecting that.

Chapter 3

Fourth floor, British Embassy, Moscow, Russia

'What's wrong with you, Green?'

Simon Page knew he was an unreasonable man. Until recently he'd managed to keep his disdain for his fellow human beings well and truly hidden. But, with his wife back in the UK on a temporary 'separation', and neither of his grown-up children really talking to him, he was struggling to keep his frustration with life unchecked. And his newbie, Sam Green, was an easy target.

He didn't like her. There were a couple of things. First, she was ex-Army. That really got his goat. SIS didn't generally target ex-Services people, because most of the good ones stayed in and got promoted to at least one rank above their competence. The ones they did employ had a misplaced self-assuredness that comes from a large dose of operational experience. Iraq and Afghanistan had a lot to answer for in his book. He loathed their self-confident air. And they all dressed the same, like something out of a Barbour catalogue. All wax-jackets, gilets and cords. No imagination. None of them.

Green was worse. She wasn't even a commissioned officer. An 'other-rank', and just an ex-sergeant at that. What was Vauxhall playing at? Yes, she was bright and sparky enough. He'd read her training course report. It was unremarkable, but solid. No obvious weaknesses. But, and it was a big 'but' in his book, she was a state school 'laddess'. Not Oxbridge. Not even from a Red-Brick university, or a tertiary qualification to her name. Down the pub she probably joked of having 'a degree from the University of Life'. Pathetic.

And she was a lesbian. It was obvious. She dressed more like a man than a woman. Doc Marten boots (*huh?*), jeans and a heavy jumper; no make-up and unkempt auburn hair. She was pretty, in her own way, and fit – she was always down the gym; another sign that she 'batted for the wrong side'. But Page knew who wore the trousers in Green's relationships. She was definitely the dominant one.

Actually, it was the whole of SIS that had gone down the pan. Over the last ten years much of the old order had been stripped away. It was now all 'open-plan spaces' and 'hot-desking'. He, thankfully, had his own office – and his own desk. And he kept his door well and truly shut. First-name terms? What was wrong with being called 'sir'? And, for Christ's sake, what was 'multi-agency teams' all about? In the halcyon days of the Iron Curtain, MI6/SIS were top-dog. You looked down on your MI5 colleagues. There's no way you'd countenance sharing intelligence with the Metropolitan

Police, let alone brushing shoulders with the SAS. Now, it was all tiger-teams: identify a problem, find a space in the office, call in your 'pals' from CID, MI5, the SAS and GCHQ, and then pull together a plan. 'Sharing' was the new 'secret'. It wasn't his game.

Nowadays, it was about data – overwhelmingly so. Phone and email intercept, breaking into the dark-web, pixel resolution on images shot from space, video-cams and CCTV. Whatever happened to dead-letter boxes and running agents? Gathering HUMINT was a skill beyond the comprehension of many of these puppies. And Green was the greenest of them all (*I like that*). But, he didn't like her. Her and her kind.

She had asked to see him first thing.

Green walked awkwardly into the office, limping slightly, as if carrying an injury. Her face was redder than normal, and she had stitches in her cheek. She'd looked a mess the night before last. She didn't look any better this morning. It was probably that time of the month.

'Someone tried to run me over last night. I clocked the number. "Cynthia's" running the details now. I should know in ten minutes if we have a match.'

Page snorted. What was this girl playing at?

'What do you mean, "someone tried to run you over"?'

Green seemed to look through him and out of his window. She didn't seem fazed by his aggressive approach. She was nonchalant. That made him dislike her more.

She sighed.

'I was heading back to my flat at about 7.30 last night. I stepped out onto the road between two parked cars and a Tesla crept up on me. I went over the bonnet and landed on the other side of its boot. It was a clear attempt to take me out. It's as though they hadn't finished the job from the day before yesterday.' She paused as if expecting a comment. He let her continue. 'I'm happy to pursue this on my own, but I thought I should let you know.' Her matter-of-fact tone further irritated Page.

What do you say? The girl's been here 15 minutes and she thinks she's a female Jane Bond. Page found himself caught between chastising her and dismissing her. Or both.

He closed his eyes in thought.

All of a sudden, he felt very tired. And very old. He was 58. Two years to retirement and a full, very fat, pension. And he had his nest egg – he couldn't forget that. He'd seen numerous Greens come and go. Straight out of training, into the field. A spook around every corner. Overcome by the glamour of it all. God's answer to protecting the nation. Their ambition and energy wore him out.

He didn't like her, that's for sure. But he couldn't afford a discrimination case against him. Not at this stage. He needed to rein back; a bit.

As the cogs turned and with Green continuing to stare through him, the devil on his shoulder almost got him to blurt out 'show us your bruise, Green'.

Thankfully order and sanity prevailed.

'Okay. Put a report together, along with any notes and findings from the cafe job and pass it to me. I'll look at it.'

Green checked herself.

'Thank you, sir. I'll get that to you by close of play.'

'Good. How's Op Michael looking?'

She seemed surprised by his question.

'On for tomorrow night. I'm not altogether happy that FSB have their bases covered, but I've done what I can.'

Page bit his tongue and stopped himself from smirking. *Who the hell do you think you are?*

'Well, I'm sure they know what they're doing. Anything else?'

'No, sir. Thanks.'

She turned and left the office, pulling the door to.

Page blew out and stretched in his chair. He closed his eyes and concentrated.

Of course, there was the other issue that always dogged him. He had it under control. He was confident of that. But, he'd have to continue to play his cards carefully to make sure that things remained 'just so'.

Sam was back at her desk in no time. She wrote on her pad: brief for M by COP.

What an idiot. Simon Page was a complex and difficult character. She knew that he was from a different age, and hadn't been able to keep up with change and progress. He was old-school; brought up in the Cold War. Blue versus red. Good versus evil. He couldn't cope with omnidirectional threats, multi-faceted intelligence, and cross-agency cooperation and planning. It was the speed of everything nowadays. It was, to an extent, a young person's game. Sometimes, even she struggled to keep up.

Straight out of training, Sam had kept herself to herself. But she had got to know the Moscow team very quickly, mostly by research rather than face-to-face. She'd discovered that five of the case-officers were Oxbridge grads. M, whose degree was from Bristol, treated them like royalty. Other than herself and one other, the remainder of the team had degrees from a half-decent university and were treated fairly. However, she and an ex-copper, Rich – who she was beginning to like, were graduates of nowhere. As a result, M barely gave them time of day.

The most frustrating thing was the way he treated women. His PA was a bit of a battle-axe and their relationship seemed fine. But the seven other women on the staff all got their fair share of being leered at. Except Sam. She never felt subject to his wandering eyes; she always felt fully-dressed when she was in his company. Perhaps he thought she was gay? *What a laugh.*

Stop!

Come on girl, work to do.

Cynthia was still looking, a little circular icon whirring away in the top-right corner of the screen.

But there was an email from Frank. She opened it:

Hi Sam,

Nothing on Blue Suit, I'm afraid. I guess your next step is the FSB? I'll keep looking. I've also had a dig around Moscow Talks. Again, nothing that I guess you don't know about. We were beginning to take the website seriously here, so that may have been a good enough reason for someone to close it down. And no connection to anyone with the initials SH either.

Sorry I can't help. Let me know if there's anything else I can do.

Keep safe.

Frank x (Jane sends her love…)

The last line hurt. She missed her old boss, Jane, and the team back at *Babylon*. It reminded her of how vulnerable she felt. It was unpleasant enough working for an idiot and having no friends to speak of. The fact that she was now on someone's hit list, having lost her only hand-picked agent, compounded the misery. Her side ached, work was dull, her Russian compadres treated her as if she were only there to make the coffee, and winter was coming. She'd caught the end of it when she'd arrived six months ago. The cold penetrated everything, and the dark evenings added to the gloom. What was she doing here?

What am I doing here?

'Hi, Sam, everything OK?' It was Rich, the ex-copper.

'Ehh, sure. Thanks.'

'I saw you hobbling about. Have you hurt yourself?' He had a concerned look on his face. The fact that someone in the building was taking an interest in her made her momentarily well up. She coughed, to hide any embarrassment.

'It's a long story. I got hit by a car yesterday. I got away with bruises, thankfully.'

'Shit. No way? Have you seen the doc?' He was gently shaking his head.

'No, Rich, thanks. It's just bruising. I'll be alright. Really.' She smiled at him.

'What sort of car was it?'

What? That's an odd question?

'Oh.' Sam laughed. 'A Tesla. You know, all electric. Crept up on me like a Marine. Didn't hear it coming.' She was about to continue with the whole story, but something stopped her. *Protect your sources.* 'It's my own fault. I'm an idiot. Should've paid more attention to the big green giant at school.'

'It's the Green Cross Code, Sam. You're thinking of the huge smiley bloke with the sweetcorn.'

Sam laughed. 'Yes, of course. You'd know. Ex-bobby 'n all.'

It was Rich's turn to laugh.

'Well, let me know if there's anything else I can do. I'm just over there.' He needlessly threw a glance across the office. She knew where he sat.

'Thanks Rich. Means a lot.'

Rich left for his desk just as Cynthia came up with an answer:

C 199 JK 67 – Tesla Model S – Maroon – Registered keeper: Bogdan Kuznetsov

Sam pushed back on her chair. She breathed in through pursed lips, making a whistling sound, and then exhaled, the pitch of the whistle lower as the air escaped. Deep down she hoped the keeper would be a Sacha Hagaev, or similar. *SH*. But, it was something; she was now considerably further ahead than she was five minutes ago.

Two leads: Professor Grigori Vasiliev; and now Bogdan Kuznetsov.

That's enough to be getting on with. She looked at her watch. It was 10am. An hour of further research on both men, ten kilometres on the treadmill, and then off to see Professor V. Before that she'd reply to Frank's email. Sam typed away:

Dear Frank,

Thanks. Could you be a darling and have a dig around a Bogdan Kuznetsov. It's linked to this whole thing.

Sam xx

She didn't want to share any more of the detail. She was already using Frank to access national and international security records, when doubtless he had plenty of work to do. But the desire to share everything she had with someone, nipped at her heels.

Farm Compound, On the Outskirts of Herat, Northwest Afghanistan

Haseeb Ahmadi wasn't coping well. He kept feeling in the pocket of his thawb for the mobile the British had given him; just to make sure it was still there. He was fidgety and, even though the temperatures were dropping after another blistering summer, he was constantly having to wipe his brow as the sweat dripped down from underneath his soft, brown pakol. He was feeling so self-conscious that he was sure one of the other men would notice.

Was he stupid to do this? To risk everything for a colonial favour?

No, there was no other choice. The British had made him an offer he couldn't refuse: he and his son would be out of Afghanistan by the end of winter. To set up a new life in the West. Away from the madness that was his beloved country.

It had to be worth it; *had to be.*

For what seemed like an eternity his life had been a sea of misery, punctuated by troughs of despair.

First, in the late 70s, were the Russians, bringing with them their tanks, their ill-discipline and their disrespectful ways. He'd lost his sister to a Russian soldier. She had been taken in the evening, dragged from their house by her hair. They hadn't seen her again. She was just 13.

Then the civil war, north versus south, Islam versus Islam. The Taliban were the stronger – protected by the Americans! Colour had been washed from his country over that decade. No music, no laughter, no culture. No kites. *No kites!* It was the darkest of times – religious fervour stronger than any state police; intra-family fear now a new building block of their fractured history. That's when Mohammed, his brother, was lost. Fighting for al-Qaeda against the 'infidels' in some far-off country.

The Americans were next. Cruise missiles, laser-guided bombs and more instant death than the country had ever experienced. The soldiers were kinder, but the devastation seemed more indiscriminate. At least the Russians had let the countryside run itself, focusing on the cities and major towns. The Americans and their allies meant well, but all they did was spread the horror. Yes, at first there was a semblance of peace, but nobody can run this lawless country. It was like pressing on a cow's bladder. Push too hard and someone gets wet. And smelly.

And that's when, heartbreak of heartbreaks, he'd lost his wife and daughter. It was an American or a British airstrike. They were shopping at the local market. He heard afterwards that a senior Taliban official had been killed.

They didn't report the collateral cost. One wife and one daughter – among ten others.

It was then, three years ago, that he'd made a vow to Allah: to find a better life for his only son.

Haseeb was a qualified engineer. He'd trained at Islamabad in Pakistan. Three years of hard graft. He'd worked as a surveyor, initially in Masar-i-Sharif; he'd followed the work to the north of his country, leaving his family in Kabul. But once the Russians had invaded, work dried up and he returned to Kabul to help tend his dead brother's land. Times were tough, but they were moderately happy. To keep his mind alive, he learnt English and Russian. He was colloquial in the former, having picked up a good deal at university; he was poor at the latter. What he didn't know was how useful being an English speaker would be later in his life.

After the civil war, and once the Americans were ensconced in Kabul's Green Zone, he'd applied for a job as an interpreter. What remained of his family bristled at the notion of him working for the Americans. For them it wasn't a religious thing. They were all honest Muslims; not extremists. They had coexisted with other religions all their lives. Allah was central to their existence, but so was compassion and neighbourliness. Everyone was welcome into their house. Colour and creed were irrelevant.

What his wider family feared were the repercussions because one of theirs was working for the 'infidels'. But they needed the money. And Haseeb had to use his brain.

In the last couple of years, whilst there remained an uneasy peace in Kabul, the Americans were drawing down and the Taliban was resurgent. The Afghan tricolour was replacing the Stars and Stripes. And with it came opportunity for the extremists.

It was about trust. Whilst you couldn't avoid their bombs, face-to-face you could trust the Americans. And the British. But who else could you trust? The Afghan soldiers may have been American trained, but what was in their hearts? The police were the same. Money was the only thing that glued everything together.

But fear was even stronger than money. Much stronger.

And Haseeb had made a vow to Allah – he was determined to keep it.

So, here he now was. Working for the British, after being approached in the Green Zone four weeks ago.

He was in a part of the country he didn't know. Close to the Iranian and Turkmenistan borders. And about to help deliver a group of hard-men into the hands of – he had no idea. The British didn't tell him. All he was told was to stay with the drugs and keep the mobile with him. He knew the route to the border and he knew when they were going to set off. He didn't know the final destination. And he didn't know when the convoy would be intercepted.

But, should everything go well, the British had promised to help him and his son leave the country to a better life. That, surely, was worth every risk?

And he trusted the British.

His right hand fell to his pocket as he checked again that he still had the mobile phone. His left, accompanied by a handkerchief, patted the sweat from his brow.

Moscow State University. Sparrow Hills, Southwest Moscow

Sam took in the 36-storey central tower of Moscow State University. She was in the park that stretched out in front of the huge, neoclassical sandstone building. She'd never been to the university before, so had read up on it this morning. It was big. In every way. The main tower was one of seven ordered to be built by Stalin throughout Moscow at turn of the last century. Labour was cheap – it was bussed in from the Gulags. But there was no denying the outcome: quantity having a quality all of its own. The place was massive. And attractive, in a 'bigger-than-you' sort of way.

Sam was just about to cross the main road that ran in front of the university when police sirens held her back.

Two blue and white Chevrolet Cruzes and a Mark 4 Ford Transit with barred windows.

She couldn't stop herself.

Then she was over the road. She sort of knew where the Geology department was and headed in its general direction. This morning she had looked for Professor Vasiliev on the staff list of the Gubkin University, which specialised in oil and gas. But hadn't found him. She eventually uncovered him on the staff at the main State campus, under 'Geology'.

Inside the building, directions were as limited and confusing as in a British hospital. Eventually, after 20 minutes of semi-aimless wandering, she found a big wooden sign above a doorway on a main corridor: Geology Faculty. Just inside, on a metallicised board with heavy plastic nametags, was a list of all the senior academics – accompanied by their room numbers. Halfway down she found: Prof Grigory Vasiliev PhD MSc BEng – Room 6157A.

Sam had another five minutes of fun down several minor corridors until she came across 6157A. Stood outside the door was a policeman. He looked about twelve; an oversized grey-topped, red-banded peaked cap plonked on the back of his head.

If he sneezes, it will fall off.

A couple of women were milling about, looking like they were busy but more probably were being nosey.

Sam walked up to the closest one and asked in Russian, 'Is Professor Vasiliev around?'

The woman was short and matronly. She wore a black and grey tweed skirt, a white blouse (which was only just managing contain her ample bosom) and a thick, black knitted cardigan. Sam assumed she had just fallen out of a bag of Liquorice Allsorts.

The woman blew out through her nose contemptibly and waved her arms at the policeman by the door.

'These pigs,' she dismissively shook her hand in the direction of the policemen, 'have taken Professor Vasiliev. And now they are ransacking his room.'

Sam thought she spotted dampness in the woman's eyes.

Like a caring daughter, Sam took the woman's elbow and drew her away from the professor's door. The woman waddled as she walked and, now with momentum, led Sam to another office. It was small and looked secretarial.

Sam spotted a kettle in the corner by the window.

'Can I make you some coffee?'

The woman plumped herself down in an office chair with a sigh, next to an ageing VDU computer screen. She replied, 'Yes please.'

Sam wasted no time.

'Why have they taken the professor away?'

The woman paused for a second. 'Who knows? Who ever knows? They took away the vice-chancellor last month without a by-your-leave. The State has gone mad. It's going backwards, into the dark ages.'

The woman's view surprised Sam. She was probably mid-40s. In Sam's experience, middle-aged Russians seemed to long for the stability and order of the communist era – a time where Russia was an international power, everyone had a job, and a blind eye was turned to a heavy-handed State that dealt swiftly with dissent.

Either this woman was unusual, or the arrest of the Professor had flicked a switch.

'Have you no idea? Was he working on something?' Sam checked herself. 'Sorry, are you his secretary?'

The woman took out a handkerchief and blew her nose. The noise filled the room.

'Yes, I am.' She dabbed her eyes. 'He was lovely. Kind, intelligent, normal. And very generous.'

Sam placed a black coffee in front of the woman, and sat on the only other chair in the room. She looked around for clues. What she got was an overriding sense of order and cleanliness, with files and books lined up smartly, like a company of soldiers. And, to the right of the woman, was a small area of personal effects placed on a couple of shelves. Photographs, neatly arranged postcards and set of babushka dolls – Sam counted ten, small to large, left to right. There was a small vase of wild flowers, and some pink ribbon hanging loosely from the top shelf. And then the veil lifted. The area was a shrine. The photos were all of the professor, or the woman with the professor. In the centre, pride-of-place, was an elaborate gold-framed photo. It was of the pair of them stood side-by-side, outside of the main university entrance.

Sam pointed to it.

'That's a nice photo.' She let the comment hang.

The woman looked at it wistfully.

'Yes, it was our 10th anniversary.'

That set too many cogs whirring for Sam.

'Of what?' Her enquiry was soft.

'Of me becoming his secretary.'

Sam could sense that the professor's secretary was

on the edge of tears. She glanced at her watch. She had to get back to the office tonight. Tomorrow was Op Michael, she had a brief to write for M, and she had several other things on her list. She placed her hand on the woman's shoulder. With the professor locked away, she needed an ally in the building.

'I'm so sorry. The State can be very heavy-handed.'

The woman turned to Sam, a fire burning behind the damp eyes.

'They're all bastards. From the top down. We had a chance when Mikhail was in charge, but the money has spoilt everything. Get rich quick and blow the consequences! And now, with that thug on the throne. What chance do we have?'

Sam assumed the Mikhail she was referring to was Mikhail Gorbachev. The president who allowed the Iron Curtain to fall.

'I know. I know. It's all very sad.' Sam now purposefully looked at her watch. 'Look, Miss…?'

'Mrs Popov.' The woman smiled, her mascara now beginning to show signs of moving south.

'I'm from *Moscow Talks*, the web-magazine. Did the professor ever mention it?'

The woman thought for a second. 'No, not that I remember.'

'One of my colleagues was in communication with the professor. His name was Alexei Sokolov. Unfortunately, he was killed in the cafe explosion the other day.' Sam let the woman think for a second and then continued. 'I wonder if you have any recollection of my colleague; any emails, anything that might help me piece together what the pair of them had been discussing. I think it's quite important.'

The woman bristled and pulled away from Sam.

'I couldn't possibly. I don't even know who you are.' She looked over her shoulder as if searching for one of the policemen. 'You could be one of them!'

Calm down.

'I'm not. Trust me. Please. The professor and my friend were discussing something which I think may have led to his arrest. If I can get to the bottom of it, I may be able to help him. And get revenge for my friend.' Sam thought she saw some cogs turning.

'Please.'

The woman turned to face her computer screen and with a deftness that belied her size, she expertly started working the keyboard and mouse.

'Let's beat these bastards!'

Sam left the university only slightly better informed than when she had arrived. The secretary had scoured the professor's calendar, his recent files and his work emails. Sam had helped her unearth double-deleted mail, a simple enough trick she'd been taught in training, but there wasn't a great deal to go on.

There was nothing in his diary that had Alexei's name on it. Nothing for *Moscow Talks*. And there was nothing unusual in his mail except a single exchange from an *ExtraOil* email address; a chap called Dutton,

ExtraOil's QA. What was interesting was that the email was in English. It read:

Hi Dimitri! It's been a while…

All's well here. Same old shit, different uniform.

I have something interesting to talk to you about that I don't want to share on company time. Do you have a personal email that we can use?

Thanks.

Next time I'm in Moscow we'll share a bottle. My shout.

Jim

The professor had replied and had copied into the reply his personal Gmail address, which Sam clocked. The secretary didn't have access to this new account. There may have been a trail on the professor's own machine, but with the Russian police currently all over it like a rash, there was little Sam could do at the moment.

Thinking ahead, the problem Sam had was that she'd need M's authority to hack the Gmail account – that was SIS protocol. Currently she had no authority at all. She'd add it to her brief. And if nothing was forthcoming, she could always rely on Frank. *Bless him.*

As she strode purposefully for the metro she checked her secure mail. There was something from Frank.

THE INNOCENCE OF TRUST

Sam,

Checked out Bogdan Kuznetsov. He's in the oligarch, Nikolay Sokolov's, inner circle. You may know him: owns a rugby Super-League club in the UK; made his money in Russian commodities; multiple businesses all over the world; has a huge superyacht. Important: he has the ear of the Russian premier. They served as KGB agents together in the early days.

We have a huge file on him in the cloud - but you have access to that. Cursory check is clean, but only just. Interestingly there is an orange marker on the file.

Seems to me that you have crossed a line. I obviously don't have the whole story, but you need to be careful.

Nothing else on Blue Suit. Sorry.

Be safe.

Frank x

Sam looked up from her phone and came to an abrupt halt.

Shit!

What was going on? She looked around. The entrance to the metro was a few hundred metres away across the park. There were a handful of people in the same space. A woman pushing a pram. A man sat on a bench. A jogger. Some others. Which one was keeping an eye on her? Whose sights was she in? She instinctively set off again, turning randomly left and right across the grass – like a rabbit with myxomatosis.

Stop! Stop it!

She checked herself again.

Come on! Get a grip!

She walked normally. Direction: the metro.

No one was going to take out an SIS case-officer in broad daylight? It was a question, not a statement.

She ran through what she knew: Alexei; *Moscow Talks* getting braver; a surprise call to meet Alexei to discuss 'SH' and his activities 'down south'; the explosion; Blue Suit; the beautiful and very scared reporter; Professor Grigory Vasiliev, who has been arrested for...?; the Tesla attack, *C 199 JK 67*, which was registered to Bogdan Kuznetsov – who works for Nikolay Sokolov, oligarch and ex-KGB agent – ear of the premier; and Jim Dutton – a QA for *ExtraOil* – probably of no relevance whatsoever.

And Nikolay Sokolov's SIS file has an orange marker on it. A very clear edict from someone at the top: *Special Care – Authorisation Required*.

She had two questions. Who knew about her relationship with Alexei? And what were Alexei and the professor discussing? And a third one just came to her: does Nikolay Sokolov, the oligarch, own *ExtraOil*?

Bugger.

She'd put all of this in her report to M this evening. And then focus on Op Michael – which, just now, definitely required her best attention.

Chapter 4

34°08'15.1"N 29°33'14.9"E, Somewhere in the Eastern Mediterranean

She was sore. The brute had hurt her last night. He always hurt her, but last night her body hadn't automatically responded to him. He had come at her regardless. He didn't seem to notice. He clearly didn't care. As a result, this morning she hurt. And, she knew if she checked, her inner thighs would be red and raw. She was probably bruised as well.

It was over quickly. That was a small relief. He smothered her. Not with a pillow. He just smothered her. He was big, over 1.90m tall and at least 230/240 pounds. Possibly more. Ugly. Something wasn't right with his face. And she was petite: 1.55m and now about 110 pounds. Her target weight was 130 – otherwise she knew she looked anorexic. But she'd lost 20 pounds since…

She couldn't complete the sentence in her head. Her thoughts were random. Skittish. It was too horrific to think about.

She hated herself. She hated the fact that her body responded to his assault. Even last night. Eventually. Even though she was crying throughout the ordeal.

Sobbing.

As she was now. Lying on the huge bed, wrapped in light grey, silk sheets. Surrounded by opulence, the water slapping up against the side of the boat. Gently rocking. Rocking and sobbing. There was no end to her tears.

She missed her mom. God, how she missed her mom. And she missed her brother. She struggled with the time difference, especially as she had no idea where she was. But she guessed she was still in Europe, and that he was six or seven hours behind. She opened her eyes and turned her head. The cool dampness of the tear-stained pillow on her cheek was a reminder of how she felt. Ragged. Spent.

Abused.

The gold-coloured clock on the bedside table read 6.45am. It would be close to midnight in Detroit. Would he be asleep? Would he be awake thinking about her? Where was she? Why hadn't she been in touch? It had been at least two weeks.

Two weeks.

Although, through the horror, she had to think hard about how long she'd been in this place.

She normally spoke to her brother every other day; WhatsApp or Skype. Checking in. Just passing time of day. Making sure she was OK.

She used to. Two weeks ago.

She let out a sob. A pathetic, frightened sob. More tears ran off her cheeks and dropped onto the pillow.

Surely someone would be looking for her? The US was a big country. An important country. It had embassies all over the world. It had the CIA. The FBI. The Army. Special soldiers that came in the night to rescue people. Men with guns that would land on the boat and kill the brute. And *that* woman. And everyone else on board. All of them.

She could feel herself smiling. Inwardly.

She had changed. She never used to think that way. About murder. And killing.

But now, between sleeping, overwhelming self-pity and uncontrollable crying, emerged revenge. *Kill them all.* All of them. One by one. Someone like Bruce Willis. Or even Arnold Schwarzenegger. Armed to the teeth. Guns and rockets. Death and destruction. No mercy.

Her brother liked the older films. She thought Bruce Willis was his fave. Or was it Tom Cruise? Cruise was more furtive with his killing. More discreet. Willis was up front. Shoot first, ask questions later. *Mission Impossible* versus *Die Hard*. Her brother had made his little sister watch the films. She'd have rather been watching *The Princess Diaries*. But now she understood the reality of the world, the *real* world, she knew it had been a good lesson. A lesson in life.

She heard the door to the vast cabin being unlocked and in came *that* woman.

She hated her. Did she hate her more than the brute? It wasn't possible. But *that* woman would be dead in her new world. The new world order. A world subsumed by the worst emotions possible. Fear, loathing, wretchedness, hate. *That* woman would be second in line. Back against the wall. After the brute. No mercy.

Just death.

Death? *Now there's a thought.*

Last night she had scoured the white-faced, gold-edged cupboards and drawers in the cabin for a sharp object. She'd turned the en-suite bathroom, with its immaculate white porcelain tub and basin, upside down for a razor. Nothing.

She may have wanted everyone on board dead, but last night she needed to hurt herself. She wanted to feel her own pain, generated by her own hand. She'd had plenty of someone else's enforced pain. That came regularly. Most evenings; sometimes twice. For the last two weeks.

Last night she'd wanted to inflict some of her own.

To have control.

To take out her feelings on herself. Feelings so acute, so deep that, if she could lay them on the dressing table they, themselves, would be sharp enough to cut. She wanted to slice. To see her blood. To feel the relief. To translate some of her grief into something else. Into a physical reality.

But she didn't want to die. Did she?

And she didn't want to smash one of the many

mirrors to find a weapon; the two on the dressing table, the one in the bathroom. The large set on the ceiling above the bed. She could have smashed them easily with one the three ornate chairs that were placed about the cabin. With the glass splinters she could cut herself so deep she wouldn't wake up. She'd seen it in the films. Fill the bath with warm water. Get in. Cut. Sleep. Die.

She didn't want to do that. Couldn't do that. She didn't want to break the place. Not yet, anyway. She wasn't quite there yet.

That woman was carrying breakfast as usual. A huge tray of the finest food. Buttered croissants, rich jam in silver bowls, grilled bacon, cured meats, toast, butter, fresh orange juice. All served on bone china. She wasn't an expert, but she thought the cutlery was heavy enough to be solid silver. The napkins were thick cotton, and the pepper and salt was served in an ornate, silver condiment set. It was like no other hotel she'd ever stayed in before. But it wasn't an hotel. It was a cell. On water.

That woman placed the tray down on a small table at the end of the bed. She went over to an electronic box on the wall by the entrance to the bathroom and fiddled with dial. The A/C kicked in.

She then came over to the side of the bed and, as per her daily ritual, spoke.

'Please move.' The accent was strong, but she had no idea where it came from. This was her first time abroad anywhere, away from the States – she wouldn't recognise a German accent over a Romanian one. She would probably guess correctly if it were French/Italian. She thought she'd be able to pick out the lightness; the lyricism. But this was a heavier accent. Guttural. Strong. Horrid.

Eastern European? No idea.

She moved gingerly off the bed, taking the top sheet with her. She was naked. She'd been naked since she'd first been put in the cabin. The only way to cover her modesty was with a bed sheet, or a towel. She staggered over in the direction of the bathroom, holding onto the doorframe to steady herself. She was weak.

She sat on the loo and peed. With the door open she could see *that* woman making the bed with, as usual, freshly clean sheets. Smelling of lavender; or roses. No expense spared. And then, as she always did, she seemed to check the bottom sheet for marks. It was an intense check. Looking for something that really mattered. Searching.

She knew there'd be some staining. Some of the brute's semen would have leaked from her during the night. She couldn't prevent that from happening. There would be a mark.

She cried again. Fitfully, her whole body shaking. The rise and fall of her shoulders sending tears in all directions. The crying an immediate reaction to the reminders.

Precautions hadn't been taken. Couldn't be taken. *That* woman, whose English was adequate, had spoken to her on her arrival. It was the first sign of the horror to come.

'You on the pill?'

What? OMG! No! She had cried at that point.

Until then, she had fought back. Two men had taken her and stuck a gag in her mouth. Eventually her arms and legs had been tied together as they threw her in the small rubber boat on the harbour side in Athens. Throughout she had thrashed about, trying to make contact. Protesting. She hadn't cried.

But she had cried then. In the cabin. When *that* woman had asked her about contraception. Cried at the enormity of what she was likely to face.

'No.' She'd blurted it out between sobs.

'Any contraception?'

'No.'

'Good.' At that point *that* woman had undressed her. Her protestations had been mild. Resigned. She was made to get in the warm bath – *that* woman had then disappeared. She had quickly got out, dripping on the lush cream carpet as she made her way to check the door. She gave it a good shake – it was locked. The single porthole was just above the waterline, but it was dark. She hadn't been able to see anything at all.

Then *that* woman had come back in with a tray of food. She left a short while later.

To be followed by the horror.

Two hours later, naked, sore, bereft and dumbstruck, she tried to take in the enormity of where she found herself.

But only tears came. Tears accompanied by a longing to be home. To be safe.

Now, sat on the loo looking at *that* woman, the monster who prepared her for her daily ordeal, tears continued to fall. Torrents of them.

As she sobbed, *that* woman came to the bathroom door. She was holding a sheet and pillowcases. She bent down and picked up the sheet that was on the bathroom floor.

'Eat.' It was accompanied by a point in the direction of the breakfast tray.

And with that order *that* woman left, the noise of the door bolting only just registering above the light drone of the A/C.

The Lubyanka Building, HQ of the Border Guard Service of Russia, Moscow

'Anyone like a coffee?' Sam stood up, moving away from the 32-inch screen they were all looking at. She headed toward the door.

There was a general murmuring of 'no thanks' from the Russian team, except Vlad who replied, 'I'd like one. I'll come with you.'

They both made their way down the corridor into the small kitchen. Sam filled the kettle while Vlad sorted out a couple of mugs.

'Do you still think the second border crossing is a problem?' Vlad was leaning against the worktop, his arms crossed.

Sam absently held the handle of the kettle and stared out of the window. It was just after 5pm and starting to get dark. It would be pitch black in Afghanistan now. She thought about their informant. She wondered what he might be doing. How he felt to be working for the British, now undercover with a bunch of militant drug smugglers. Whether he was frightened. *Or shit scared.* How he was coping. She was amazed at what some locals would do for a safe trip out of their country.

'I'm not sure. It looks like an oversight if you ask me. If I were them, I would tell my close team one thing – knowing that every group will leak the information if the price is right, and then do something else at the last minute. I don't know how the FSB train, but we work exclusively from the enemy's perspective. Get in their mind...'

Vlad interrupted her, 'Put yourselves in their shoes and wargame the operation. React as they would react. It's FSB teaching too, but it's not always followed. Tonight it will probably not matter. The Taliban are arrogant enough to think they know everything. But I can see that it's an opportunity for them. If they do take the drugs up the second route, we will have lost them.'

The kettle was boiling. Sam poured and Vlad offered some milk.

'Yes please.' She nodded. 'It's probably nothing, but this operation has been three months in the planning and, between us, it's costing in the order of 20 million roubles. That seems like a lot of money to be associated with a plan that's not bomb-proof.'

'You're right.' Vlad let Sam go through the door first. She led them back to the operations room. Just before they entered, Vlad stopped Sam by holding onto her elbow. She turned to face him, absently slopping coffee on the floor.

'Be careful, Sam.'

Sam had that really unattractive look of consternation on her face, all scrunched up.

'What do you mean?'

'Nothing. Just be careful.' He let her elbow go, and motioned to go into the operations room. The conversation was over.

What was that about?

The three other Russian officers were still sat staring at the small screen. Sam had offered to bring over an SIS Beemer to throw the image onto one of the walls. It would have been better for everyone's eyes. But, as per most of her suggestions, it was declined.

She and Vlad sat back in their chairs. Sam sipped her coffee while focusing on the screen. It displayed a map of about 500 square kilometres. At the bottom was Herat, Afghanistan. At the top was the southern tip of Turkmenistan, showing the border town of Serhetabat. There was a single road joining the two; north-south. Or in the case of the smugglers, south-north. The display gave little indication of the terrain, although they could switch on the satellite overlay if they wanted. On the FSB system, this slowed the updates to a frequency that was not helpful – so they kept it clean.

What was important was the flashing blue dot. That was the SIS mobile, pinging a satellite fix every three or four seconds. Assuming it was working, the team knew exactly where the phone was. Which was hopefully where the agent was. Which was hopefully where the drugs were.

Hopefully.

Sam had spoken with Julia earlier. The agent had been in touch with Kabul that afternoon. All was well. There were no changes to plan.

It was now 5.45pm; 8.15pm in Afghanistan. The flashing blue dot was three quarters of the way to the border following the main route, which on the map looked like an A-road; in reality it was an untarmacked, sand and rock track, just wide enough for two trucks to pass – if they did so carefully. The dot was moving at about ten kilometres per hour, the average speed for a jingly truck on the back roads of Afghanistan.

Sam had come across jingly trucks on her tour in Helmand five years ago. In Afghanistan they were as notorious as yellow cabs were in New York. Old Mercedes, GMs and other trucks, vans and buses, painted in outrageous colours and then highly decorated with flowers, icons, ribbons and metal streamers. The streamers were made from painted chains that hung from the bumpers. It was the chains that 'jingled', hence the name. The problem with the ornate decoration was that it made old, slow trucks even slower and unstable to the extra weight. And, with most of the windows also painted, drivers had more blind spots than a blinkered horse. They were fun to look at. But were to be avoided at all costs. Julia had told Sam that the convoy consisted of two jingly trucks: a Merc and a Datsun.

At this rate the convoy would be at the border in 40 minutes. And, Sam reckoned, at the earlier junction in 30. She sincerely hoped the flashing blue dot blinked its way past the junction without pausing.

They'd know soon enough.

35° 3' 55" N 62° 15' 25" E, On the A77 Heading North to the Turkmenistan Border, Afghanistan

Haseeb was woken from his fitful sleep by the sudden stopping of the truck. He checked his watch. It was 8.45pm. They should be at the border shortly. He stuck his head out of the back, pushing aside a tarpaulin which hung down to prevent dust from settling in the load bay.

It was pitch black, except for where the headlights of the lorries lit up some of the potholed road, the ditches either side and the rising banks which faded into darkness after a few yards. Both engines were still running, but above that sound he heard men talking. He recognised a couple: the leader and the driver of front truck; but there was a new voice which was unfamiliar to him. High pitched and agitated. He tried to listen for some words, but at this distance it was a blur.

He sat back in the truck, his backside on a sack of nuts which was part of the dummy cargo: around 150 hides and pelts, 10 bags of walnuts and 50 Afghan carpets and rugs.

And 250 bricks of congealed opium sap.

He knew how to make exportable opium. His brother's farm had a single field hidden in among other rudimentary crops, such as wheat. He'd helped slit the poppy seed pods, burnt black by the sun, and collected the browny gum in crude pottery bowls. And he'd seen his brother meld the thickening gum into a brick and cover it with leaves, further wrapping it in paper, and then tying the bundle with string. One brick weighed about a kilogramme.

And one brick was worth $100 under the counter on a good day at the Kabul bazaar – a tenth of its worth outside of the country. Haseeb could do the maths. In the back of his truck they had $250,000's worth of pure opium gum. The very best Afghan rug would sell in Islamabad for 10,000 rupees to a willing tourist; that's about $600. If you ignored trader mark-up, they'd need to be carrying ten times as many rugs as they currently were to get the equivalent value of their opium stash. And he knew the rugs they had were not good quality and worth a fraction of a decent one. Opium was considerably better value than carpets.

He'd read somewhere that Afghanistan produces around 2,500 fine rugs a year. Against that, the US illegally imports half a million kilograms of Afghan heroin.

Do the maths.

How anyone thought that eradicating poppy fields from his country without replacing the income with something sustainable was out of their minds.

He stared through the gap between the tarp and side of the truck. As he did, he checked the phone again, pressing a button – watching to see if the screen lit up to show that it was working. It was.

Relief.

His was in the rear of the two trucks; all he could see through the gap was a cloak of black, except for the shards of stars which lay like broken glass on the sky's dark coat. Twinkling. There was no one else on the road, not at this time of night. It was all blackness.

It was in that one moment of calm, the one time in the last couple of days when he actually felt some peace, that his world began to unravel.

'Haseeb! Out, now! We must move the cargo. Quickly.' The leader was unhooking the chain that held the large tailgate in place. It pivoted and fell with a loud, uncomfortable *clunk*, metal against metal, onto the bottom steel of the truck.

'Come, quickly – I will show you.'

Haseeb's mind was spinning. *What is happening? Where is the cargo moving to?*

He scrambled after the leader as the man strode to the front of the lead jingly truck. Where all became clear.

The headlights of the lead truck illuminated a branch in the road. The main road bore left slightly. To the right, a lesser track headed off into the blackness. There was no signpost; no indication of where it was heading. On the new track, with its back to them, was a dark coloured pick-up truck. And a man – someone Haseeb had not seen before.

'Here – you and Mohammed,' the leader gesticulated to another man who was travelling with the convoy and was now at Haseeb's side, 'put all of the cargo in the back of the Toyota. Understand?'

Haseeb nodded. He understood exactly. The drugs and the convoy were parting company; here at this junction. That was not good news for the British – nor him. Not good news at all.

Twenty minutes later he and Mohammed were close to finishing the transfer of the opium to the pick-up. The work had made him hot and sweaty, but what he was now about to do would raise his temperature further. He needed to use the phone. He needed to let the lady in Kabul know what was happening. And he needed to do that now.

As he finished putting the last three bricks into the back of the pick-up, he turned to the leader. 'I must go for pee.' Haseeb nodded his head in the direction of the back of the trucks, indicating where he would relieve himself.

And find somewhere to send an SMS. Somewhere safe.

'Go quickly. The convoy must move on. We are expected.' The leader unnecessarily tapped his wrist.

As Haseeb walked between the two trucks he raised his hand to acknowledge the driver of his truck. The man ignored him, as he had done throughout the journey. The side window was open. Haseeb was sure he smelt burning opium.

He walked a few metres past the truck and stopped by the edge of a ditch.

With his hands shaking, he lifted the hem of his thawb and went through the motions of going for a pee. At the same time, he used his spare hand to retrieve the mobile from his pocket. He tried to text with his free hand, but poor dexterity beat him. He couldn't even get his address book to open.

He looked over his shoulder. Nothing. Just two trucks with their headlights on and their engines running.

He used both hands. Within 15 seconds he had written:

At junction short of border. Drugs transferred to another truck. Looks likely to go in another direction.

He pressed 'Send'.

'What are you doing?'

Haseeb almost dropped the phone. He turned quickly and saw the driver of his vehicle stood menacingly behind him.

'Give that to me!' The man, who stank of opiate, grabbed Haseeb's hand.

'No, it's mine!' They wrestled for a few seconds.

Their short squabble was interrupted by another man's voice. The voice of someone who Haseeb knew would be the end of it all.

'Haseeb. What are you doing? What have you got there? Show it to me!'

It was the leader.

He wasn't high. He wasn't drunk.

He was a single-minded, ruthless smuggler. And most likely Taliban. He would get what he wanted. By whatever means. And Haseeb knew that, when asked, he would answer all his questions. What courage he had was gone. There would be no escape. There would be no future in the West for him and his son.

It was over.

Flat 17, 3125, Prechistenskiy Road, Moscow

It was 2.15am. Sam was feeling light headed. She was halfway down a bottle of the Embassy's reasonably quaffable Malbec. It had been a helluva day and now, drowning her sorrows with a bottle of red, she was finishing off her letter of resignation. The cursor on her secure Chromebook blinked at the end of the sentence, 'I understand that SIS expect all of their new case-officers to serve for at least three years; I am happy to pay back any monies owed to allow for my departure as soon as practical.'

She had £45,000 in savings, the product of a life devoted to work and not much else. She wasn't sure if that would be enough, but she didn't care. She would find the money somehow. She certainly couldn't go on like this.

Sam was surprised at how sanguine she was about it all. How calculating; unemotional. She wasn't tearful. She wasn't about to break down, to reach for a bottle of pills, or, as was normally the case when she felt this low, hit out at something. Last time she'd been this down – really down – was when she'd discovered that her only surviving relative, Uncle Pete, was dead. Then, she punched in a toilet door at SIS headquarters in London, breaking a finger in the process. Her frustration normally spat itself out as rage.

Now, after the loss of the Afghan agent (that was Julie's supposition when the phone stopped blinking), the failure of the Op, and the humiliating SMS she'd received just after midnight from M:

You'd better have a good reason as to why Op Michael has catastrophically failed. I expect a full report on my desk on Monday morning. We have some explaining to do to London.

…She felt detached. As if all of this was happening to someone else.

Add this to Alexei's death, and maybe M was right? Maybe she wasn't cut out to be a case-officer? Maybe her approach with Alexei had been naive. She'd been too keen, too quick. Cut too many corners? And Op Michael. Why hadn't she been persuasive enough to get the second crossing covered?

I am rubbish at this.

The Russians had been very quiet after she'd read

out the text from Julie.

Just got an SMS from our agent. Drugs have been cross-loaded to another vehicle and are heading in a different direction. The Op is compromised. I don't hold out much hope for our man on the ground.

The Russians hadn't acknowledged her previous protestations; that she'd made the point twice before to cover the second crossing. Instead, they had needlessly seen the operation through, even after the blue dot had paused for 20 minutes at the junction, and then headed off in a different direction. Spetsnaz had stopped the convoy an hour later; finding nothing – just carpets, hides and nuts. Then, the Lubyanka team had passed around a bottle of vodka. Ten minutes later, just as Sam was leaving, they had opened a second. Vlad, who hadn't been drinking, had followed Sam out. He'd said something along the lines of, 'You were right. All along. I'm sorry we didn't listen to you.' He'd then touched her shoulder and repeated the previous warning. 'Be careful Sam. Be careful.' She'd tried to get him to explain what he meant, but he'd shuffled her out of the front door of the Lubyanka building into the darkness.

What had he meant, 'be careful'?

Sam, unnerved a little by his concern and still edgy after the attempt on her life by Kuznetsov in the Tesla, took every precaution heading back to her flat. She hailed the second taxi – *never* the first (it might have been waiting for her) – straight home. And, on the way back, with so many conflicting thoughts in her mind, she decided that she would get out of Moscow. And out of SIS. Altogether. She knew she'd promised the beautiful reporter that she would find Alexei's killer. And she reminded herself that she'd said 'damn the consequences' only a couple of days ago to following that route.

But… it was hopeless. She was hopeless.

I am hopeless.

Sorry, but I am. Read the stats.

Her Chromebook pinged. *A message?* At this time of night, it was probably an advert. Earlier in the week, when she still assumed that she had a future in Russia, she'd been looking at downhill skis – winter was on its way and Sochi was a half-decent resort. Doubtless this was Amazon reminding her that she'd yet to order some poles, boots, salopettes, jacket. And Colin Firth.

Sam was a good skier, but she always skied at the very edge of her ability. As a result, she was only ever one misjudged turn away from skiing through the resort and into the pharmacy. She was a *Bridget Jones* fan, so could recall the imagery.

Colin Firth. Mmmm.

Sam topped up her glass. She was going to have a headache in the morning.

Except the email wasn't from Amazon. It was from Frank. Secure. She checked her watch. 2.30am. Half-past midnight in the UK.

What the hell was he doing in work at this time on a Friday night?

The fog cleared; sobriety returned, just.

The title of the email was: *Blue Suit*. It read:

Hi Sam,

CIA have eventually come back to me. They have an 85% prob on Blue Suit. His name is Iosif Ergorov. An ex-East German, and Stasi member. He's on the US's most wanted list. He's a pro, with several confirmed hits. Works to the highest bidder. They think it's unlikely he's linked to Russian state, but can't rule it out.

I've asked around the office here (I've yet to speak to Jane, but will do on Monday when we're both back in Babylon - she's currently in Tel Aviv), and the view is, if you mix Ergorov and Sokolov together, you get a highly explosive, ruthless and very thorough team. Everyone thinks you are poking at a wasps' nest with a very short stick.

Have you shared the case? If not, do so. This is bigger than you are, even if you do have the German Order of Merit!

Get real and be safe.

And you know where I am.

Finally, sorry about Op Michael. Julie has been in touch. Bad news all round. Poor man.

Frank

Sam's fingers hovered over the keys piecing together a reply. She thought better of it – *for now*. She reduced the email tab and stared at her letter of resignation. She read it. And then read it again. A tear formed in the corner of her left eye. It trickled down her cheek and fell onto her nightie, leaving a grey stain on the white cotton cloth. She reached for a tissue from the pack on the kitchen table.

Not tears again?

She sat there drying her eyes. For some reason, her mother came to mind. 'Now, pet. There, there, cheer up. It's not as bad as all that? You must do the right thing. Forget yourself. Help others. And they will help you. It all comes around.'

She leant back on her stool and stared at the ceiling. Tears welling up in her eyes with nowhere to go. Two small reservoirs on her face. *Pathetic.*

She was facing the same two choices. Fight or flight. What had she to lose? She had no friends in Moscow. She had few friends back home. And she'd made a promise to a beautiful stranger.

I made a promise.

It was Friday… *Doh! Wrong! Saturday morning.* She had a free weekend.

She looked back down at the kitchen table, drying her eyes as she did. She reached for a pen and pad and scribbled down a daisy-chain of connections: Her to Alexei. Alexei to Professor Vasiliev with some unknown communication which likely caused Alexei's death. The arrest of the prof. Alexei murdered by *Blue Suit*, aka Iosif Ergorov – an ex-Stasi pro. Me knocked down by Bogdan Kuznetsov. Bogdan Kuznetsov linked to oligarch Nikolay Sokolov, who had a case file that she had only had a chance to flick through. A case file with an orange marker: *Special Care – Authorisation Required.*

She stared at the paper. She drew a line through Alexei's name – *God, that hurt*. She then drew prison bars around the prof. She tapped her pen on the table. A repetitive sound. *Tap, tap, tap, tap*. Something was gnawing at her. *Think, girl, think!* She vowed never to drink again. *Yeah, like that's going to happen.*

At the bottom of the page she wrote down Alexei's message: 'We need to talk about SH and his work down south.'

Nothing.

Tap, tap, tap, tap.

Still nothing.

Tears again now. Not of sadness, but of frustration. She scrunched her fists up in a ball and gritted her teeth; tense as an overwound spring. She closed her eyes, a single tear rolling off her right cheek.

Come on!

Nothing. Then…

Shit, that's it! The final link. Squaring the circle! From yesterday afternoon at the university with Mrs Liquorice Allsorts – Professor Vasiliev's likely stalker (*Get a grip, girl, this is no time to be flippant*).

Professor Vasiliev's work email had a single exchange between himself and… (she scrunched her eyes together again, trying to remember the name – the wine still playing with her synapses). Jim Dutton, a QA at *ExtraOil*.

Jim Dutton.

She'd checked this morning on the *ExtraOil*

website: Dutton worked on the Yamal Field, just south of the Arctic Circle. And, *wait for it*, have a guess who owned *ExtraOil*?

Nikolay Sokolov. Oligarch-in-chief.

That was the circle. From her, through Alexei, to the professor, to Dutton. Back to Alexei. With Sokolov and his acolytes in the centre.

But it was better than that.

It had just come to her. She had it all now.

Alexei's message was a code; OK so it was rubbish code designed by a four-year old, but now it made sense. Below Nikolay Sokolov, Sam wrote down his name in Russian Cyrillic: *Николай Sokolov*.

Nikolay Sokolov, NS in English. But HS in Russian.

Or SH, if you write the Russian version backwards.

Alexei's message's read: 'We need to talk about *SH* and his work down *south*'. If you're a four-year old wannabe spy and you write things back to front, the original translates to: 'We need to talk about *HS* and his work up *north*'!

Up north. The Yamal oilfields. He'd composed the email the wrong way round to hide its meaning. And he used Sokolov's Russian initials.

Genius?

Hardly…

The chain was now unbroken. Throw in two cold-blooded killers, Kuznetsov and Ergorov, and you have all the ingredients of something very knotty indeed.

And it was still early Saturday morning. Work was 48 hours away. Could she extend that to 72, or 120 if she threw a sickie? Could she get to the Yamal oilfield and back within four days?

'Brrrrrr!'

'Shit! What the...' It was her doorbell. Her mind raced; her heartbeat easily keeping up. *Who the blazes is this?*

Trouble?

She used the tissue to dry her eyes and quickly made her way to the kitchen window. She looked down on the street below. Nothing. Well, there was a cat helping itself to an upturned bin, but nothing else.

'Brrrrrr!'

Her heart still racing, she dashed across the room to her front door — beside the reinforced door, secured with triple locks, was a video entrance system. She took a deep breath and turned on the screen.

It was Rich, the ex-copper. Sam's shoulders dropped in relief. She pressed the intercom.

'Rich! What the bloomin' hell are you doing here? It's almost three in the morning.'

'I'm a night owl. I saw that you were live on the organisation's system and I knew that Op Michael hadn't gone well. I thought you might like company?' He put on a sheepish smile and raised a bottle of red wine to the camera.

Sam dithered. What bizarre question had Rich asked in the office the night before last? *What was the make of car that had knocked her down?* It was out of place. Almost searching for something he didn't need to know. Or, he was just naturally inquisitive? *Maybe a car freak?*

She pressed the 'Open' button. A buzz and a click let him in.

Rich left just over an hour later. Sam hadn't helped him finish the bottle, she was too buzzed up, and she was making plans for the weekend as they chatted. He seemed genuine and, after half an hour, she really warmed to his laconic style and self-deprecating humour. He showed a lot of interest in her past; kind questions, nothing searching, just gentle enquiries. Fifteen minutes later Sam realised that his visit was as much about his own loneliness as it was about checking on her morale. His story was that he'd lost his wife to cancer ten years ago, left the police and became a spy. Two tours later he'd not made many friends in Moscow and saw Sam as a kindred spirit. He didn't flirt with her (he was definitely not her type – too much hair; probably all over his body if his neckline was anything to go by), but was friendly, relaxed and emanated trust.

Why wouldn't you trust an ex-copper-cum-spy?

Sam told Rich every detail of the last four days. She wanted to share her excitement with somebody, and she really did need to brief someone just in case things went tits up (she didn't want to keep bothering Frank). She finished off by telling him that as soon as he left, she would be packing a small bag and heading a long way north.

His response was odd.

'Have you thought that Alexei's death, the professor's arrest, the attempt on your life *and* the failure of Op Michael may be connected?'

Sam thought for a second, but couldn't make a connection.

'Sorry Rich, I don't see how.'

'Well maybe someone's ahead of you. Someone who's keeping track of what you're up to – undermining it all.'

'What, like a mole?'

'It's just a thought. Seems to me you've followed every procedure to the letter and yet you've been tripped at every turn. Coincidence?'

Sam didn't believe in coincidences.

Could this be all about me?

Chapter 5

40km north of Arbat Village, Eastern Urals, Russia

Sabine cradled her coffee in both hands. Steam rose from the mug as if it were a cooling tower of a power station. It was cold; temperatures had dropped dramatically in the past three days. The surgery in Arbat's sister village was a two-room affair. A small, cramped waiting room, and a treatment room which was just about large enough to fit Sabine, Dimitri and a patient. Originally there was a desk and two chairs, but she asked the local mayor to replace the desk with a bed – she would treat her patients, sat beside them. The mayor had done his best: an old, stained mattress on top of a smithy's workbench. Thankfully they had clean sheets, which the mayor's wife replaced daily. Everyone was doing their bit, but it seemed that the mayor and his wife were at the centre of getting things done.

Qu'ils soient bénis. Bless them.

In the corner of the small room was a sink, but the water that eventually emerged after much pipe clanking, smelt foul. And looked just as revolting. While Sabine was seeing patients yesterday morning, Dimitri had been to the local town and bought a hundred litres of bottled water. When they needed boiled water, they used a primus stove.

For the lavatory, Sabine used a one metre square, wooden privy in the back garden of the house next door. Pulling a chain consisted of throwing in a scoop-full of lime, which sat in a grey bucket next to the wooden seat. She washed her hands back in the surgery with carbolic soap and recently boiled water.

There was no heating. That wasn't strictly true. There was a fireplace in the waiting room, but it was boarded up. She survived by wearing plenty of clothes and drinking countless cups of instant coffee. This morning, a woman she had seen yesterday complaining of a rash all over her back, had brought in a pair of woollen fingerless gloves. The wool was black and oily, but they did the trick. At least now she could hold a pen even if the ink would probably congeal before it touched the paper. The locals all appeared much hardier and got away without layering up. But Sabine was clear that, even with thermals and a softie, she couldn't do this indefinitely – not without the mayor jacking up some electricity and plugging in a bar heater.

It was her second day. To get here, she and Dimitri left Arbat just as the sun lifted its head above the Siberian Plain. It took them an hour and a half to travel the 40 kilometres to the village, the road twisting and bending, dropping east off the lower Urals, then turning north, before heading back into the hills. The direct route would have been quicker – on a mule.

Yesterday they'd finished at 7pm and had eventually got back to Arbat just before 9pm. It had taken Sabine two hours to type up her notes onto the Cloud. She had seen 30 patients, all with a similar mix of ailments to the 82 who were registered in her village. Thankfully, after the death of the young Peter, and the pregnant woman and her deformed son, she'd not lost another patient. And, of the group she had treated here so far, none of them seemed particularly poorly. Still, most of them had a combination of ailments that were unusual for the area and time of year: rashes, lethargy, stomach upsets, dizziness and, most surprising of all for one old woman – hair loss.

She'd now had all of Arbat's blood, stool and water results back from the hospital, including a more detailed analysis of the water supply. There was nothing that she could point to that would disproportionately affect such a small population. The water, which came from local springs, was safe to drink. The PH was average, metallic elements and salts were consistent with the local chalk and clay, and sulphates, nitrates and fluorides all seemed normal. Only chlorine levels were higher than you'd get out of a Western tap, but that was because the local administrators put chlorine in the village's storage tanks.

In short, she was no further forward and didn't know what to do next to try and rationalise symptoms against causes. And she was tired. Dog tired. The sort of tired that makes your hospital colleagues insist you go home for fear of making a mistake. But Sabine didn't have 'colleagues' as such, she only had the lovely, hard-working Dimitri. She looked across at him over the brim of her mug. He was sat uncomfortably on a small wooden chair, squashed between the door and the makeshift bed. He was clearly as tired as she was. The back of his head was resting against the peeling plasterwork, his mouth open and his eyes closed. Since lunch, the rhythm of his manly snore had been the soundtrack to any gaps between patients.

Through the window Sabine caught a glimpse of someone heading for the surgery.

'Dimitri.' Sabine spoke gently.

She sipped some more of her coffee.

'Dimitri!' Louder this time.

But clearly not loud enough.

Sabine stood and stretched, her hands to the ceiling, her back arched. She'd go and meet the patient herself.

She took the three short steps necessary to reach the door. She gently nudged Dimitri's shoulder. He came to quickly; his eyes damp with sleep. Still dazed, he cleaned his teeth with his tongue and moved his fingers as if her were playing the piano. It was a real effort to break from his sleep.

'Sorry. I must have fallen asleep.'

'Don't worry, Dimitri. There's a new patient, I think. I'll go and usher them in.'

'No, no!' Dimitri sounded affronted. 'It's my job.' He made an effort to stand; Sabine put her hand back on his shoulder, keeping him still.

'I'll go. Make me another coffee, please. I've just finished the last one.' She smiled at him, missing his return smile as she slipped into the waiting room.

It was the mayor. He was mid-height and size, probably in his 50s. He wore a heavy green woollen jacket, a black roll neck, jeans and cowboy boots; sensible, utilitarian semi-official clothes. He walked over to Sabine and shook her hand. She noticed for the first time that he dragged his left leg.

'Hello doctor!'

Sabine knew that was the extent of the mayor's English.

'Hello Mr Mayor. Business or consultation?' Sabine knew that he wouldn't have understood what she had said. She raised both hands, holding the conversation.

'Dimitri. Here please.'

The door to the consultation room was still ajar. Dimitri stuck his head around and saw straight away that his interpreting skills were needed. He was at Sabine's side in a flash.

The mayor started the conversation in Russian.

'I have found a generator. My wife's brother is working on it now. It should be ready for tomorrow morning. Also, my cousin is bringing an electric heater this evening from his cowshed. I'm hoping we can have heating in your room tomorrow.' He spoke quickly, drawing images with his hands and smiling as he did.

Dimitri translated. Sabine's smile was as big as a crescent moon. *These people are so generous and efficient.*

She reached for the mayor's hand and shook it vigorously.

'Thank you, Mr Mayor, thank you.'

There was no need for translation. Still smiling, he nodded in return.

'It's the least we can do.'

Dimitri translated. A short embarrassing moment followed when no one had anything to say.

The mayor broke the silence. 'Well, I will return tomorrow!'

And with that, he backed off a few steps and turned for the door. As he did, he wavered a bit, almost a stagger; he had to catch himself by placing a hand on a wall.

'Are you okay, Mr Mayor?' Sabine knew straight away that something wasn't quite right. Dimitri translated immediately, his own voice carrying an air of concern.

The mayor looked over his shoulder toward Sabine, pain etched deep in the laughter lines emanating from the corner of his eyes.

'I'm fine. It's nothing.' He shook his head, but his stance and grimace told a different story.

Sabine didn't need a translation.

'Come into my room, Mr Mayor.' It was an uncompromising order from Sabine. Dimitri's interpretation was much longer than her statement. He'd obviously elaborated to make sure the mayor knew that Sabine wasn't taking prisoners.

She held the mayor's elbow and escorted him into the treatment room.

'Without Dimitri. Please.' The mayor gently waved at Dimitri, figuratively pushing him away.

Sabine understood what he had said.

'I can't examine you without having a conversation.'

Dimitri translated.

'No Dimitri. Please.'

Sabine took a deep breath and forced it out through pursed lips.

'Please leave us Dimitri. Take a seat on the bed, Mr Mayor.' She gestured with her hands. The mayor did as he was told.

'So, tell me what you can.'

The mayor, speaking at a pace which made any understanding impossible, backed up the jumble of Russian sounds by using his hands.

He had pain, 'down below'.

Sabine didn't reply; she didn't want to waste effort on potentially misunderstood, or misinterpreted words. She reached for his leather belt and started to remove his trousers. He helped her drop them, and his pants, down to his ankles. She then grabbed his legs, lifting and turning them so that lay on the bed.

She examined him.

It took her twenty minutes.

Nothing was said between them.

As she took off her disposable rubber gloves, placing them in the bin, Sabine sighed quietly. It was not good news. It was also perplexing.

She motioned for the mayor to get dressed and then called Dimitri back in. The mayor didn't protest. He could probably tell from Sabine's face that there was difficult news coming.

Dimitri stood reverently by the door.

'Mr Mayor. You have two lumps in your scrotum.' Sabine let Dimitri translate.

'And your prostate is enlarged. How do you find going for a wee?'

There was a further pause as Dimitri translated.

'It's difficult. I need to go all the time and when I do it's uncomfortable.'

'And sex?'

Dimitri obliged. He coughed an embarrassing cough as he finished.

The mayor wiggled on the bed; his legs, which didn't reach the ground, flapping about. He looked sheepishly at Dimitri and shook his head.

Sabine gave them all a few seconds.

'I need to take some bloods. And you must get to the hospital as soon as you can.' Dimitri translated. 'They will take a biopsy of the lumps in your testes and they will need to take an ultrasound or an x-ray of your prostate. They'll probably want to do some other tests.' Again, Dimitri translated, but Sabine let the pause hang before giving her provisional verdict.

'I think it's possible that you have cancer. To have symptoms of both testicular and prostate cancer is very unusual. But we will need to see what the hospital discovers. Do you have any other pain?'

After Dimitri's translation the mayor said, 'I have back pain, here.' He pointed to the area of his kidneys. 'It comes and goes.'

Sabine sighed inwardly.

'How long have you had a lump in your testes?'

'Not long. I know to check – my uncle was a doctor. The lumps have only been there for a few weeks. And much of the pain is very recent.'

'Is there any history of cancer in your family?'

'No, mostly heart trouble.'

Sabine knew where this was all heading. It was unusual for symptoms to raise themselves this quickly; possibly in three separate locations. But she wouldn't know anything for sure until the hospital had done their work. But the prognosis was not good. And, whatever the mayor had, it was moving very quickly.

There was another pause after Dimitri had translated. Sabine met the mayor's eyes. She saw dampness. She couldn't stop herself from responding. She swallowed deeply and held back tears. This was a man who was clearly the centre of the village. Who made things happen. It was possible that his symptoms meant nothing; but that was very unlikely. It was also possible that his cells had a propensity to turn cancerous, but with no family history, that what was also unlikely.

Or, and this really worried Sabine, the environmental factors that were causing the spate of illnesses in these two villages had the ability to destroy a man's life in this way. And, likely, leave a huge hole in the village hierarchy and administration.

C'est de la merde.

It was shit. It was all shit.

Departure Desks, Miami International Airport, Florida, USA

'I'm going to be fine, Daddy, I really am.'

Holly Mickelson understood her father's concern. She really did. She was heading to the US Consulate in Istanbul, the most western of all of Turkey's cities, for a six-month internship before taking her place at Princeton to study political sciences. In preparation, over the past three months she'd read an awful lot about Turkey. Since the failed coup, the country was a basket case. The current president was using the recent assault on the government to crack down on all his enemies and expand his powerbase. It was an only partially-concealed plan to cement his authority on the country, reduce the military's influence and reinforce Islamic law.

So, even though her father was a Florida congressman and a very well-read Democrat, she almost certainly knew more about the political and environmental situation in Turkey than he did.

And she'd be fine.

The Department of State's latest advice on travel to

Turkey was: *The U.S. Department of State continues to warn U.S. citizens of increased threats from terrorist groups throughout Turkey. U.S. citizens should still carefully consider the need to travel to Turkey at this time.* She knew that. After all her research, she didn't need to check the DoS's travel advice on Turkey. She could have written it herself.

That's why she *so* wanted to go. She hadn't told her family, but her ambition was to be a war correspondent. *New York Times? CNN?* All her family thought she was hoping to become a government administrator. And maybe later, a politician – like her daddy. That had been an early ambition of hers. But the latest Presidential election had shown politicians for what they really were: child-like narcissists; or elitist, self-serving bureaucrats. No, she wanted out. Out of the politics that had surrounded her life for as long as she could remember, and out of a country that was being torn apart by bigotry and in-fighting. And where better than the front line? OK, so Turkey wasn't Afghanistan, Syria, or Iraq. But it was the only half-dangerous country that was taking interns where her father had some reach.

And Istanbul looked such a fabulous place. East meets west. Christianity meets Islam. Asia meets Europe. The Blue Mosque, the Grand Bazaar – Topkapi Palace! She could smell the spices from 6,000 miles away. Holly really couldn't wait.

Her father was holding her hands in his. He had that 'deep concerned' look, the one that worked so well on the TV when Florida had been battered by storms. Or after there had been a mass shooting. And that was also part of the problem. Did she really know her daddy? He was perfect. Kind, loving, attentive... Just what any daughter wanted. But, how much of that was for show, even for her? Was it an act? Did he really love her? How could he love her that much, when he showed the same affection for everyone he met? Where did Daddy stop and Congressman Chad Mickelson start? Were they one of the same?

Holly smiled her biggest smile. She'd learnt a lot from him. She could act as well as he could. If he expected joy and laughter – she could deliver; homeliness – she could do that too; frightened? – that was easy. He was a master and she had been a very adept learner.

'I'll be fine, Daddy, I really will.' She held the smile. 'The staff are meeting me at Atatürk airport and I promise to follow every rule. I will hardly ever go outside of the Embassy grounds. My job is to listen and learn. Prepare for Princeton.' She paused. The smile still planted on her face. 'I promise.'

Her father titled his head to one side and then bent forward to kiss her on the cheek.

'OK, sweetie. You are your mother's daughter! Determined and persuasive.' He took a handkerchief out of his pocket and ceremoniously wiped an eye. 'Go now, and call *every day*. You have endless credit on your cell.'

She reached up and gave him one last kiss on the cheek.

Stay in the Embassy grounds? You've got to be kidding.

'I'll miss you, Daddy. But I'll come back a woman –

you'll see.'

And with that final farewell, Holly Mickelson picked up her carry-on luggage and made her way into the security zone prior to departure.

Salekhard Airport, Northern Russia

Sam was waiting for the 'fasten seat belts' sign to be extinguished. The Aeroflot badged Boeing 737 had taxied to its tie-down on the small concrete apron; the engines were whirring down. Looking out of the window she picked out a single set of travelling steps (she was sure they had an official name – she would Google it) moving into place beside the aircraft's front door. They would be getting off soon.

The weather looked workable. She'd checked the outside temperature on her in-flight screen as soon as they'd touched down: +2°C. There was snow on the ground, but just a smattering, like a thinly iced Christmas cake. The windsock on the coning tower fluttered; there was little wind. And no sun. A blanket of high cloud prevented that.

The airport looked small-to-medium sized. Sam had counted five commercial aircraft on the pan, an assortment of smaller prop planes and a handful of brightly coloured helicopters – mostly Russian Mi-8s. The Mi-8 was the workhorse of most air forces and businesses when they wanted a cheap and effective minibus with rotor blades. Sam had travelled in one a couple of times in Afghanistan, when the British had been collaborating with the Afghan air force. They were remarkably agricultural in comparison to the RAF's Merlin troop carriers. But, with over 12,000 in service across the world, they clearly were well thought of. She looked again at the four on the pan. One was painted in *ExtraOil* livery. *Tick!*

The journey had been remarkably easy so far. Last night, once Rich had left, she'd quickly pieced together an outbound route that worked. She booked a return Aeroflot flight from Moscow to Salekhard, leaving today at 12.25pm; returning Monday, leaving Salekhard at 17.15. Getting to the *ExtraOil* fields was more complicated, but it seemed that there were two options. She'd come across an angler's blog called *Fishin' Freezing*. It featured a sturdy Dutchman who went out of his way to fish in extremely cold climates. Nordkapp, the most northerly point of Europe, was his favourite place – although it was often 'full of tourists', which seemed to get right up the blogger's nose. Second on his list was the Yamal Peninsula, where she was now. The blog (which had too many photos of dead fish with their eyes popping out for Sam's taste) offered two options to get to the Arctic Ocean from Salekhard. First, hire a 4x4 – although the route was often dangerous; broken by ice melt during the short summer and fractured by the deep freeze for the rest of the year. Second, was the 'oil train', which ran twice daily between Salekhard and the sea; it took a few paying passengers.

Sam had checked the *ExtraOil* website and, after 20 minutes of interrogation, had found a map of the rigs they operated on the Yamal Peninsula. There were two, side-by-side: No 6 and No 7. And it seemed that the train served both rigs. *Perfect.*

By the time she'd booked her flight, worked out how to get to the oil field, and packed her things, it was 6am. She had six hours before her flight: an hour to check in; an hour to get to the airport; four hours spare.

Breakfast. Ibuprofen (the wine had set like cement in her head; it was making the gap between her ears throb). *Write report.*

As the coffee bubbled away on her hob and her *Shredded Wheat* (with dried cranberries) soaked up the milk, she tapped away at her Chromebook. She may be a maverick, and what she was about to do blew all SIS protocol out of the window and propelled it into space, but more often than not she did as she was told. M wanted a brief by Monday morning; M would get a brief by Monday morning. In fact, he would get one in 30 minutes' time.

Sam drafted reports quickly and accurately. Yes, she needed to check them, and there were always things she wanted to amend. But her first draft was always just about good enough. As she typed up her thoughts on why Op Michael had failed, she reminded herself of what Rich had said before he left: 'all these things may be connected; someone's ahead of you.' Who might be ahead of her? M? Frank? *Rich?* Someone else in the organisation?

No, can't be. She dismissed the notion.

Rubbish.

Her report was standard SIS style: conclusions and

recommendations to start; supporting documentation following on. She reread the front page:

Op Michael - Post-Op Report

Conclusions

1. Michael failed because the FSB disregarded SIS advice to cover a second, minor border crossing point into Turkmenistan. FSB procedures allow for reviewing enemy options, but resources were limited and only one crossing was covered.

2. There is currently no int that allows us to unpick why the smugglers chose to reroute their consignment. Options include: standard operating procedures that we were unaware of; a leak/informant within the Taliban/smugglers' operation.

3. Liaison between SIS in Kabul/Moscow worked well.

4. Kabul's agent and planted mobile worked extremely well. The agent gave timely information at the crux of the operation - an action which almost certainly cost him his life.

Recommendations

5. SIS/FSB joint operations should continue. However, the competence, seniority and gender of the assigned SIS case-officer requires further consideration

(Yeah, like I was clueless...)

6. Further investigation is required to establish Taliban/smugglers MOs; in the meantime, always assume secondary routes and methods.

She made a couple of changes and then pressed 'Send'. She blind-copied Julie in; Sam didn't want her outflanked by anything she'd written in the report. She'd send a further email to M tomorrow, making excuses for not being in the office on Monday. He'd probably get off on 'period pain', so she thought that it was safer to say something along the lines of 'a heavy cold'. Doubtless he would cast aspersion as to her flakiness – 'hasn't the backbone to face a good bollocking'.

The idiot could go and... She didn't finish the sentence in her head.

Her most knotty decision had been: 'who to travel as?' If someone was ahead of her, they would get a 'ping' if she booked a flight in her own name. If that someone was SIS, then it wouldn't matter which alias she used – she would be monitored. An added factor was that she had decided to take her work phone and tablet with her; she needed the intelligence horsepower. The phone was trackable from any SIS desk. That unnerved her a little. It would certainly give M all the ammunition he needed to sack her when she got back, if he bothered to check that she was above the Arctic circle, rather than under her duvet. But, at least it meant that should she get into trouble, Rich would know where she was.

Then there was the tricksome question of getting

onto the oil field to see Jim Dutton. She didn't think any of her foreign aliases would get her past the security guards. However, as an English-speaking cousin of Jim Dutton's, with family news that was best delivered face-to-face – that might just work.

Stuff it. Sam Green it was – Jim Dutton's English cousin. Coming all the way to Salekhard to tell him the good news – that he's been left a sizeable chunk of money in his aunt's will. *That will have to do.*

The seats in front of her were emptying. She stood, retrieved her only bag – a 45-litre grass-green Osprey rucksack (which she loved), and followed the queue to the aircraft's exit. Before she got there, a cold front of air from the outside hit her; the exposed tips of her ears, her tangled hair tucked away behind them, feeling the drop in temperature.

Damn. I forgot to bring a hat. Idiot.

The next 20 minutes passed quickly enough. Inside the not-unpleasing, curvy, metal and glass terminal, she followed the signs for security control. All flights to Salekhard were internal, but the Russians took their own brand of Islamic and Chechen terrorism seriously. After a five-minute wait she made it to the head of the queue.

Behind the glass front of a security pill box was a walrus of a woman; she was only short of a pair of tusks.

'Papers.'

Sam hadn't thought through whether to speak in Russian or English; would Jim's cousin be fluent? *Probably not.* She went for 'colloquial'. She handed over her UK passport.

The walrus was wearing a light brown, short-sleeved shirt which was struggling to contain the blubber she hoarded to keep her warm during the long winters. She looked at Sam's passport and work visa from every conceivable angle.

'British?' She spat it out. Since the numerous EU embargoes enforced on Russia after their annexation of Crimea, many Westerners were given a hard time from your average Russian. Sam was sympathetic to their predicament.

'Yes.' *It says so, on the front of the passport and in several places on the pretty pages in between.*

Flippancy was an ammunition of Sam's. It was an army thing. You weren't trained in it; well not exactly – you were smothered in it as soon as you joined up. It was hugely powerful in helping you to deal calmly with stressful situations. Humour was a glue among the ranks. It was as central to the British Army as corned beef hash. The Americans didn't get it. *They had the Humvee instead.* Thousands of them.

The walrus needed more information.

'Reasons for travel.'

Here goes...

What fascinated Sam about her new job as a 'spy' was that she wasn't a very good liar. She was, even if she said so herself, good at many other things: photo and image analysis; document review and dissection; as a HUMINT controller (natural empathy helped here – she and Alexei had hit it off immediately; she exuded trust).

But a good liar, she wasn't.

She gulped, trying to look unflustered. Her freckles hid a small rush of blood to her head.

'I'm visiting a cousin of mine. He's Scottish...' she was remembering to mispronounce some words, 'and works for *ExtraOil*, on the oilfields north of here.' Sam kept her response short, but accurate. Her interrogation training was unforgettable: be factual, but minimal; give them something to chew on, but don't overdo it; if they want more, they *will* come back to you.

That was OK?

The walrus looked at her as though she was manky seaweed caught in her flippers. She hesitated for a second. And then threw Sam's papers back at her, motioning with a flick of her head for Sam to move on.

You have a nice day too...

She was through.

Once in the main auditorium she got her bearings. She clearly recalled her route from a photographic replica of the Google Map overhead she'd seen last night: airport terminal to taxi rank; taxi to the train station.

Taxi rank: forward left.

But she didn't shift. The fleeting movement of a recognisable face transited through her left peripheral view? She turned her head sharply. Nothing. No one. If it were someone, and she couldn't place the blur, then that someone was gone. Or was her mind running away with itself?

Bugger.

Her mouth dried. Her heart rate quickened.

Slow down – calm.

Flippancy was banished. Adrenaline kicked in. Focus took over.

With her feet rooted to the spot, she dropped her rucksack from her shoulder and bent down to tie up her Doc Martens. A very quick panorama at knee height spotted a couple of further suspects. A middle-aged woman sat at a cafe, legs crossed and seemingly reading a paper, or completing a Sudoku, pencil in hand. She caught Sam's gaze and dropped her eyes back to the paper. She scribbled something. *Click*. Sam had her face and stature, even though she was sitting.

A man pulling a black cabin bag behind him. Tall, 6' 2", slim. Rugged attire, all beiges and browns, trousers with more pockets than you could possibly need, keys hanging from his belt; likely to be an oil worker. He was stationary when Sam had clocked him looking across at her. He was moving now. Right then left, toward the sign that pointed to the loos. *Click: two out of two.*

Any more?

She finished tying her second shoelace. She had ignored everyone in uniform, and there were plenty of those – all colours: blues, greys and greens. Uniformed military and police were incapable of blending in in a public space. They couldn't follow the yellow brick road. Tailing was an undercover job. It wasn't for them.

Nothing. No one. She steadied her breathing.

Move now.

Sam stood and quickly made her way right, away from the taxi rank, but toward the small bus station. She exited the terminal through a single glass door, and was immediately reminded by the tops of her ears that she'd forgotten her hat. She turned hard left and, as close to running as was comfortable, walked quickly along the front of the terminal to the taxi rank. There were five taxis, yellow Datsuns with a red '*taxi-nn.ru*' etched on their doors. Against the protestations of the first two, she took the third.

With no ceremony whatsoever, she got in passenger seat and ordered the driver to drive. In perfect Russian. No destination.

'Of course.' If the driver was confused, he didn't show it. He was dressed casually and looked very much a local – round face, thick, tough skin, black hair. And he didn't smell of vodka. *Result*.

Sam knew the route from the airport to the train station. She had used SIS's e-planner to visualise it; it was the last thing she had done before she left the apartment. She knew the local road network, where the traffic lights were, and where the road underpassed the main, southbound dual carriageway.

She kept an eye on the traffic behind her using the passenger wing mirror. She reached into her gilet pocket and pulled out her leather card holder. She opened it at her Embassy ID and flashed it at the driver. It was too quick for him to have seen any detail.

'FSB. Turn left here.' Sharp. Decisive. She pointed late, but the taxi driver, sensing he was dealing with someone not to be messed with, swung the car left just in time, its tyres protesting at the turn.

Sam checked behind. Nothing.

Then a black Mercedes 190 screeched round the corner 50 metres behind them. *Shit*. The taxi driver sensed what was happening; he was now alert. He looked across at Sam, fear in his eyes. *Dilated pupils*. Hold it together fella.

Sam's mind was racing. *What am I involved with?* These people, whoever they are, don't know where I'm going. They can't, can they? Could they have squared the circle as she had done last night?

Maybe. Possibly.

How did they know I was here?

She had to get to the train station without them realising that that was where she was heading.

'Left, here. Step on it.' Finger pointing, as well as verbal directions. The driver followed her instructions. 'Right here.' The taxi driver, sweat now dripping from his forehead, did exactly as he was told. They were now in traffic, the Merc five cars behind. 'Right again, next junction.' Sam kept giving orders as a plan coalesced in her mind. She reached into her wallet and took out a $100 bill. She waved it in front of the taxi driver and then forced it down between his legs; he involuntarily brought his knees together.

'You drive like this for 30 minutes? Then go back to the airport. Don't stop. Remember I'm FSB.' Sam tapped the side of her gilet, the one closest to the passenger door, hoping to signify that she was carrying a handgun.

The taxi driver nodded vigorously.

They stopped behind an orange Opel Corsa which was waiting for the lights to change. Sam looked – the Merc was still five cars back.

She referenced the map in her mind. They were two blocks from the railway station. Up until now the buildings on the side of the road had been a bit ramshackle; single story affairs. Industrial. Now, in the centre of town, the blocks were taller. Red-brick. More sturdy. Business-like. There were lot of pedestrians. It was busier.

The cars in front moved off slowly. The taxi driver followed suit. She unclipped her seat belt. The dashboard immediately started to bleep. She waited for exactly the right moment.

Now!

The road bent to the left. The pavement was at its busiest. Shop fronts; a cafe; a pedestrian crossing; a metre-high roadside box, probably containing electrical signalling and switching. Five or six people milling about.

In a flash, Sam flung open the passenger door and threw herself onto the pavement, her bag following in a splurge of green with grey piping, the door bouncing back closed. *Fuck!* Her right thigh hurt like hell as it took a second beating in under a week – but her gym teacher would have been proud of her shoulder roll and recovery. She was on her feet, a little unsteady, but striding into the *Maksim Cafe* before the taxi driver had registered her leaving.

Sure, there was commotion on the pavement. At least three people's gaze had followed her transit. One man had protested, his hands raised in horror. And a dog had yelped as she flew past its nose. But, as she glanced behind to check the progress of the Merc, she saw no recognition in the face of its passenger that something was untoward. She got a reasonably clear view of the man, but not the driver. It was fleeting; too much movement. But enough to recognise him again – *probably*. He seemed intent on keeping an eye on the taxi, rather than any commotion on the pavement.

She'd bought herself some time.

Sam took a deep breath and looked around the cafe. Almost everyone was staring at her. An elegant woman, wearing a Burberry check jacket, daintily suspended a coffee cup between the table and her mouth; her lips pursed ready to sip.

Sam took out her card case again, waving it around briefly.

'FSB. Nothing to see here.'

She'd always wanted to say that.

Chapter 6

40°44'37.9"N 28°07'54.9"E, in the Sea of Marmara, South of Istanbul

The brute had hit her yesterday. The back of his hand against her face. She'd never been hit by anyone before. Sure, her mom used to tap her thigh when she was a kid if she misbehaved. But no one had ever struck her before – not with the intent to hurt. He was on top of her. When, out of nowhere, she had screamed at the top of her voice – 'Get fucking off me, you fucking brute!' They were words she'd never used before. The 'f-word' wasn't in her vocabulary. The involuntary splurge of expletives had shocked her.

His ears couldn't have been more than a few inches from her mouth when she screamed, and she guessed it took him as much by surprise as it did her. And it probably made his ears ring.

It did the trick, though – well partially. He stopped.

Briefly.

His torso was raised above her, resting on his elbow. His eyes, which were normally closed, were wide open. She could see nothing behind them. No feeling. No emotion. Just blank.

Just his ugly, deformed face.

And then he smiled. It was a crooked sort of smile, more like a crack in his hard, disgusting face. A horrible smile. The smile of a deranged man. A man who systematically raped women.

A dribble of spit formed in the corner of his mouth. She watched it, mesmerised as it began its journey directly toward her own. It didn't drip, not to begin with. It just slowly dropped, hanging onto the brute's mouth by an extending piece of spittle. She knew the lifeline would break soon, that the globule would fall. And she knew whatever she tried to do the spit would fall on her face – somewhere. She could have turned her head to one side; at least then it would have landed on her cheek. But she didn't. She couldn't. She just watched as gravity took its course.

Splat. Her mouth was closed, and the brute's spit landed on her lips. His spit on her mouth. *Gross. Fucking gross.*

She focused back on his eyes. All she saw was that empty space. But he was still smiling, that crooked half-smile of an unhinged monster. Which is what he was. She knew nothing of him, so couldn't put him in a box. He didn't speak; he didn't show any kind of emotion. He just held her down. Did what he wanted to do. And then he left. Not a word.

Slap! The back of his hand smacked into her face

with the full force of a 200-pound lump.

Shit, that hurt!

Her head had been flung to one side by the force. She immediately sensed her cheek reddening as warm blood flooded the area to deal with the injury. She kept her head turned, tears of pain already welling up in her eyes. She didn't want to look at the brute again. She didn't want to do anything. In fact, just then, at that moment, she didn't want to be alive. She wanted to be dead. She longed for it. Something peaceful, to take away the pain; to remove the ignominy of it all. To find rest. Silence. Relief.

Her longing was broken; he had started again. It didn't matter. Nothing mattered any more.

That was last night. She felt a little better this morning, although her cheek still throbbed. She was still sore and still devoid of emotion, but she didn't think she could kill herself. Not this morning. Not with the sun streaming through the porthole; a glimpse that there was life outside of this hell. That every day she survived was a day closer to her rescuers breaking down the door and taking her home. Every day she got through, was a day closer to the end of this. She knew that.

The door unlocked and in came *that* woman carrying breakfast. She didn't wait to be asked, but swung her legs onto the floor, took up the top sheet and made her way to the bathroom.

As she peed she watched *that* woman examine the bottom sheet. Even from here she could see a different coloured discharge from normal. It wasn't usual grey/white left by the brute. There was red in it. Blood. Her blood. She knew she was having her period. She'd felt groggy for the last two days; it's probably why she screamed out last night. At least she wasn't carrying his child. Not this month.

'Come here.' *That* woman; an order to be obeyed.

She wiped herself and walked over to the bed, holding the silk sheet in front of her for imaginary protection.

'Lie down.'

She did as she was told. She thought she knew what was coming. She had no idea why, but she knew *that* woman was interested in whether she was menstruating.

She was right.

That woman prised open her legs; she didn't resist – two weeks of brutal rape and a heavy slap from a man who could probably snap her back over his knee, and compliance was easy. *That* woman peered down and then, using a corner of the top sheet, wiped between her legs, staring at the result, shaking her head.

She was confused. Scared. More scared than usual. She was having her period. That's all. These things happen – once a month. Maybe the brute didn't relish the idea of rape when it was accompanied by the lining of her uterus? Maybe she'd get some relief? Just a couple of days? That would be special. Fear headed to the door marked 'relief'. Maybe he'd be finished with her – for now?

Her thoughts were interrupted by *that* woman

leaving. A departure which was different from normal. Three things initially struck her as odd, that broke the routine. Three things that very quickly so unnerved her, she started to shake uncontrollably.

That woman left without the daily accompanying order: 'eat'.

She only took the bottom sheet, leaving the rest of the bed unmade.

And, as she left, she took the untouched breakfast tray with her.

On the Oil Train just short or the ExtraOil *Rigs, Yamal Field, Northern Russia*

The clanking of the carriage over a set of points woke Sam from a fitful sleep. She looked at her watch. It was 6.43am. She wiped sleep from her eye and stared out through the dirty window, out across hundreds of kilometres of very little. The sun was making itself known from behind the horizon, illuminating the eastern skyline with a vast palette of blues, reds and yellows – a skyline which included the curvature of the earth, such was the flatness of the terrain. It was the biggest sky Sam had ever seen. And it was one of the most beautiful. Dark blues, from above her, behind the train, merged with turquoises, scarlets and oranges, drawing naturally toward a focus on the horizon: that of a brightening yellow smudge where, very soon, the sun would announce the arrival of the day.

The landscape was equally as bewitching. It lacked the colour of the sky, just greys, dark greens and browns – and a patchwork of white. But it provided the perfect bottom frame for a vibrant sky; a combination of snow-covered tundra, a few trees and, close to the track, spiky brown grass puncturing the icy snow like hair brush pins.

It was as desolate a place as Sam could remember. Untouched by the heavy hand of humans. She couldn't keep her eyes from it.

The carriage rattled some more, and the train, which was already travelling very slowly, ground to a halt. Sam put her head against the cold window, her breath catching the glass with condensation. She tried her best to look forward, to see what was happening, but the track curved away from her and all she could pick out was the end of the single carriage and the start of the locomotive. She knew that behind them there was a long line of container wagons – she hadn't counted; but there were enough of them for the train to struggle to make any speed at all. Everywhere else she looked there was tundra. Tundra and a perfect sky.

If she moved over to the other side of the carriage she could probably get a better view – maybe pick out the rigs in the distance. But the four seats opposite her were occupied by two big Russian men, both catching up on their beauty sleep. She really didn't want to wake them.

The train was due into the oilfields at 7am. In conversation with the two men last night, they had shrugged their shoulders when Sam had asked if 7am was an accurate arrival time. 'It depends,' was all they could manage.

Even before the train had set off, both men had tucked into a packed meal of dried meat and bread, and shared a bottle of vodka, drinking alternatively from the bottle. The larger of the two, although that was a tough call, offered some to Sam; he wiped the top with the tail of his shirt. After the rubbish of the previous week it had been a hugely welcome gesture. Sam, not wanting to appear ungrateful, had taken a swig. She'd declined further offers (as she valued her soft palate), and soon the two men had settled into the seven-hour journey, making themselves as comfortable as they could. Once asleep, they serenaded Sam by snoring at a strength of around gale-force eight.

At least she had felt safe. So much so, she had managed to sleep (on and off) – although her right thigh, which had taken the brunt of two makeshift para-rolls in under a week, nagged her that all was not well below her pelvis.

In between snoozing, she reminded herself of where she was.

They were following her, whoever they were. That was immutable. They had clocked her getting onto the plane in Moscow. Either mechanically, by tailing her to the airport (although she'd followed every procedure in SIS's Ladybird book of 'losing a tail' to ensure she was clean), or by having an e-alert on the booking of her flight. She assumed the latter. That didn't help her narrow down her list of likely enemies: SIS, FSB and, she guessed, Sokolov's team, could all manage that.

Sam was confident that nobody on the plane was assigned to her. It was a four-hour flight and she'd been to the loo three times to check the passengers out. The plane, which was a 737-600 Next Generation, carried 120 passengers (she wasn't a plane spotter, she read the detail from the on-board information leaflet). Sam had counted 57 on board. None of them seemed interested in her. Her recollection of the passenger of the black Mercedes 190 in Salekhard didn't seem to match anyone on the plane.

So, she had been met on arrival. Which was a neat trick.

Which organisation had agents on call to meet a rogue SIS operative who, without warning, catches a plane to the least likely destination in all of Russia?

Sam discounted SIS; certainly not in any official capacity. The FSB may well have that sort of reach, but having worked with them for six months, she struggled to believe they could be that efficient. That left one conclusion, which sort of worked for Sam. The two men were in the employ of Nikolay Sokolov. He probably owned half of Salekhard, with all the oil kicking around. And the two tailers didn't appear that effective – that is, not FSB-level effective; otherwise they wouldn't have let Sam get away.

Before she rejoiced in the certainty of that conclusion, she reminded herself of Rich's comment, mixed in with Vlad's advice: *everyone's telling me to be careful*. Why would an FSB agent tell her to be careful? Was he talking about the way she conducted herself around his colleagues in Lubyanka? Not to press too hard? Or was it something wider, something about what she was up to now? If that was the case, maybe the FSB *were* party to this. And Rich's suggestion of a mole? Was someone in her organisation warning off Sokolov?

What *was* she onto that was so important they'd be prepared to murder an SIS operative? As far as she knew, the last time an MI6 agent was killed by the opposition was in the days of the Cambridge Five – in the 50s. Were the stakes that high? Or were east-west relation so poor that no one cared anymore?

That left the key question: who could she trust?

The good news was that she appeared to have got on the very slow train from Salekhard to the oilfields without further incident. She didn't think she was followed through the station. And the train had only one passenger carriage. There were 15 of them making the journey further north – she was the only woman. Having wandered around the carriage, Sam would have bet a month's wages that none of them were assigned to her.

She was being tracked, that was for sure. But she may have stolen a short march on her pursuers; bought herself some time.

The next complicated bit was what to do when she got to the oilfield? She was determined to get to see Jim Dutton. That's why she had come. If he were there, she would persuade him to see her. She could do that.

But, by exposing herself at the oilfield she would become a target again. How long did she have? How far did they reach? Sokolov owned the oilfield. Did that mean everyone at the field was looking out for her? She was hardly inconspicuous.

She had to get onto the oilfield. She had to see Dutton. Once inside the perimeter, she'd turn her mind as to how to get out. Something would crop up.

The train chugged and lurched forward, the movement catching her off guard and forcing her back against her seat. It clattered and clanked for a further ten minutes and then the station came into view: a concrete and block platform, a carriage and a half's length long. There was the screech of brakes and the train stopped.

The carriage erupted into a slow frenzy of oil-worker movement. Most of the men had big rucksack and holdalls which, with bangs and scrapes on the narrow thoroughfare, followed their owners to the exit.

Sam waited for all the men to get off. Then she picked up her Osprey and, now wearing a black woollen hat she had bought at the station (which, when added to her uber-warm black army softie, made her look like an SAS groupie), she stepped out into a whole world of unknown.

She stood on the platform, surrounded by a new type of cold – one which mixes low temperatures with a dampness from the sea; she took it all in. First, she looked for a welcoming party of Sokolov's hoods, ready to wrap her in a blanket and throw her down one of his wells. No one. Just a couple of minibuses, 14 oil workers and her: a 5' 6" Michelin woman in Doc Martens. There was a large, industrial siding behind her. It was already breaking into activity as trucks, men and cranes started to work on the containers their train had brought with it.

Beyond the minibuses, in the middle distance, she could see the field and rigs. They were maybe a kilometre away, and were clearly large industrial complexes. But, as the rising sun glinted off one of the towers, Sam could see that even they were dwarfed by the enormity of the Russian tundra.

Sam's 'what next?' question was interrupted by a *peep* from a horn. The platform was now empty; all the train passengers having squeezed into the minibuses.

The driver from the first wound down his window.

He called out in Russian, 'Where do you want to go, lady?'

Sam came to immediately.

'Rig number seven, please,' she shouted back.

'Rear bus.' The driver used his thumb to indicate where Sam should go.

Seconds later, stood at the bus's sliding door, she was pleased to see that her two large, vodka-drinking Russian friends were heading in her direction. One of them tried to move his holdall so she could find a seat. But the bus was too full, and it stayed where it was.

'No worries,' Sam said, working hard to sound colloquial rather than fluent. 'I'll sit on the bag?'

The man nodded, and Sam plumped her bum on his holdall.

'Why have you come to the rig?' the Russian asked.

'I'm a relative of one of the workers. I've travelled all

the way from England to give him some good news.'

'Who's that?' The directness of the Russian's enquiry didn't faze Sam, she was used to their lack of pleasantries.

'Jim Dutton. The QA on number seven? I'm his cousin.'

The Russian man's face, which was already white and blotchy, changed colour markedly. The whites became more translucent and the red of the blotches sharpened – he now had the face of a poorly made-up clown. He didn't respond to Sam's comment. He stared straight ahead.

Sam paused, immediately on edge. What have I said? *What's the problem with Jim Dutton?*

She pressed on.

'Do you know Jim?'

The Russian, seemingly unable to reconcile her question, ignored Sam and stared straight ahead.

What the...? Sam bit her lip.

The minibus was at the front gates of the rig a couple of minutes later. There was a perimeter fence and a gate guard; their bus was waved straight through.

I'm in.

The minibus stopped outside what looked like an administration building. Sam was first out. She was clueless when it came to oilfields, but recognised a tall Eiffel Tower-like construction which she assumed was built on top of the well. There were countless pipes and gantries, a good number of large, towering cylindrical constructions and 20 or 30 shipping containers lying about in an orderly fashion. One or two looked like they might be offices or accommodation.

The admin building had a short step up, a single metal door and an official sign: *ExtraOil Rig Number 7, Yamal Oilfields. Site Manager and Chief Engineer: D C Berezon MSc BEng.*

The men had all headed off to various locations on the site, carrying their oversized bags. The minibus drove into the depths of the oilfield. Sam was left feeling a bit nervy; all alone. It was just her. On an oilfield. In northern Russia.

She turned to face the entrance to the admin building. She shook her head, as if to say, 'What have I got to lose?', took the single step and opened the door. She was immediately met by a small cubicle and a second door. An air lock. To keep the heat in. *Makes sense.* She opened the second door.

Inside was an unremarkable, open-plan office with assorted desks, only one of which was occupied – by a woman; she was sat in the corner of the office, her workspace decorated with tens of photos of the soap opera, *Lyubov Kak Lyubov*, a Russian favourite. To the left, a doorless corridor led away; to Sam's right was a glass partition and another door. Behind the glass was a more ornate desk and a TV on the wall. She guessed it was the chief's office.

'Hello, can I help you?' The woman had stood and was making her way over. In the heat of the office, Sam was beginning to feel overdressed; she took off her hat and stuck it in the pocket of her softie.

'Yes please.'

The woman was much like Sam; the same sort of age. Mid-height and build, but with mousy hair which she had managed to streak purple. She wore heavy cotton cream trousers, a simple white blouse with a strange brooch (which Sam couldn't make out), and a green cardigan. The similarities stopped when it came to body piercing. Sam had had her ears done when she was a kid. The woman, who wasn't unattractive, had decided to pierce her nose (twice) and her bottom lip. On reflection, Sam thought it sort of went with the purple hair.

She smiled at Sam, a simple smile, as though having a strange woman arrive in the northernmost extremities of Russia was an everyday occurrence.

'I'm a cousin of Jim Dutton's, who I think is the QA here – on the rig?'

The pierced woman, who had almost made it to where Sam was standing, stopped dead in her tracks. Like the large Russian in the minibus, her face also changed colour. Hers turned completely white – a mirror of the snow outside.

'Ehh, OK. Umm…'

Something's definitely not right.

'Would you like a coffee?' It was a blurt rather than a sentence. Words to cover an embarrassment – *or something else?*

'Yes, maybe in a while. Is there a problem with my cousin?'

The woman then visibly collapsed, somehow managing to remain on her feet by placing her hand on a nearby desk. Sam spotted tears forming.

'I guess you haven't heard. I am so, so sorry.'

'What?' Sam immediately checked herself. She felt rising anger, but knew that grief would be the emotion of choice when the bad news came. Bad news that was due at any moment.

Sam put out a hand and placed it on the woman's elbow.

'Please tell me.'

The woman, who had been staring at the floor, now looked up at Sam. A hint of makeup was being degraded by a steady flow of tears.

'Jim is dead. I'm so sorry.' The word 'dead' flicked a switch in the woman's demeanour; she broke down, sobbing and sobbing. All of a sudden she looked very young; pathetically immature.

'I haven't cried since the accident. I'm so sorry,' she blubbered some more. 'You must be more upset than me.'

Sam was upset. That was definitely an emotion she was experiencing. Upset – yes. But anger was a stronger feeling. And really 'effing' frustrated. She searched for anxiety – even fear. She found neither. Just now she was furious. That was two people dead – and the professor on his way to a modern gulag.

She wanted answers. And she wanted them now.

Calm.

She gently brought the woman to her and held her; a sisterly hug.

'How did he die?'

The woman stayed in Sam's arms, her shoulders gently rocking.

'It was an accident on the site. He fell from a gantry when he was checking some equipment. It's all very odd. He was such a careful man.' She sobbed some more. 'Such a nice man; so generous.'

Sam wanted to squash the woman. To hold her so tight, she'd struggle to breathe. To release some of her own tension.

Somehow, she resisted.

'I see.' She took a deep breath and then, squeezing her eyes closed as tight as she could, she found some tears for effect. Sam gently pushed the woman away from her. She looked a mess.

You look a mess.

At this distance Sam could make out the brooch. It was more of a badge: *I am a Member of the Lyubov Kak Lyubov Fan Club.*

Oh dear.

'You were a friend of Jim's?'

The woman snuffled, using the sleeve of her cardigan to wipe her eyes.

'Uh-huh. He was most people's friend. But we were close. No one here believes that he's dead.'

I do.

You were close? How close?

'Are you sure it was an accident?'

The woman sniffed and looked at Sam as though she'd asked the most stupid question in the world.

'Yes? Of course!'

OK.

'Where's Jim body?'

'The undertaker came from Salekhard yesterday by train. They took the body away yesterday evening. I understand that his family have asked for a local cremation? That's what the chief had said.' She sniffed again and then added, 'I'm so sorry you didn't know. What a wasted journey for you.'

Indeed – much more than you could imagine.

'Look, is there any way that I could see his room, maybe his personal effects? I could take something home with me?'

The woman stuttered, still overwrought.

'I think his belongings have all gone – they were immediately boxed up and dispatched. I'm not sure where to, though…'

How convenient.

Sam was rushing through all the possibilities. How could she rescue something from this disaster?

'Could you take me to his room anyway?' She made a further attempt to look grief-stricken. 'So, I could get a feel for his last few days?' She sniffed. She was a rubbish actor.

'Yes, yes. Of course. I'll get my things. First, I'll just phone the chief and tell him that I'll be out of the office. He likes me here first thing so I can make him his special coffee.'

Bless him.

As the secretary did what she needed to do, Sam had a look round the office, trying to find something that might help piece the jigsaw together. But it was in 'oil-speak': indecipherable charts and instructions. It was completely lost on her.

The secretary, who seemed less upset having now thrown on a thick woollen coat and a knitted hat, led Sam back out into the cold. She carried a set of keys.

Three minutes later they were outside a silver and white shipping container; it was the third one along, on the bottom level of an identical block of ten containers – two high and five long. There was a metalled mesh walkway joining the entrances to the top five containers, with a set of steps which rose from the far end. Jim Dutton lived on the bottom floor. Sam wondered if that was a privilege.

The secretary, who had introduced herself as Lucya on the short walk across from the admin building, opened the door and motioned for Sam to go in.

She couldn't. She froze. It wasn't that she was entering the room of a dead man. That wasn't it. It was that the last time she was in a shipping container, she was being held captive by terrorists; two days in a freezing cold, blacked-out metal box. Two days that very nearly killed her. The experience had left a permanent mark on her subconscious: shipping containers were to be avoided. At all costs. To Sam they stank of fear and death.

The wind picked up as Sam prevaricated. But the temperature didn't stop a bead of sweat dribbling down Sam's back.

Sam bristled. She knew she had to go in. To see if she could find a clue. Some ammunition that she could use to unpick what was happening. To help stop the death.

'Give me the key.' Sam was beyond trying to display grief. And had run out of pleasantries. She had to have the key. No matter how irrational. She had to have control of the door. Of the lock.

Lucya gave her the key, but accompanied the exchange with a withering look.

Sam offered Lucya into the room. Her second precaution. She wasn't going to leave anyone outside who might close the door; to lock her in. In the metal prison.

Sam followed her and, just as Lucya was about to close the door, said, 'Leave the door open. Please.' The 'please' an afterthought.

She took a deep breath and steadied herself.

At first glance, there was nothing of Jim left in the room. A single window, a bed, fitted with a mattress, a bedside table, a larger table and two chairs, a wooden wardrobe and a tall metal locker with a tiny key in it. And a door leading through to a small en suite.

It took Sam five minutes to check out what she could. Everything was empty. Everything was clean.

The place had been professional exorcised of Jim Dutton. It was an empty shell. There was nothing. Nothing.

Shit.

She stood in the middle of the room, her mind short of answers; full of futility. Frustration welled up inside her. She was lost. Five hundred miles from the safety of her office – if it were safe; 5,000 miles from her home country – not that she had much to call home.

What the friggin' hell am I doing? What am I up against?

Sam knew the red mist was coming. She knew that, when it came, she could go one of two ways. Either she'd become an automaton, like yesterday in the taxi. Reflexes would take over. Adrenalin would replace the blood coursing through her veins.

Or, she'd lose it. And then nothing was safe. Everything was a weapon. Anyone was a target.

Shit, no.

But it was too late. Her brain chose option two. The closest object to her was the metal locker, which she'd just inspected. The closest weapon was her foot.

Smack! She kicked it with all her might.

Shit, that hurt… Her bruised thigh joined her foot in the 'don't do that again' club.

Lucya instinctively drew back, her arms hugging her shoulders, her head bowed in self-defence.

Smack!

Sam kicked the door again, a size five dent now very

evident in the locker door. She was snorting, blood in her ears amplifying the sound. She didn't care.

Fuck you!

Sam changed tack. She slammed the top of the door with her fist, it rocked backward an inch until it hit the wall, and then fell back to its original place. In defiance to Sam's assault.

Clunk.

A soft sound of something falling inside the locker. Something different from the rage-induced noises coming from Sam's efforts to do damage.

She was panting. She had no idea where Lucya was. Nothing in her peripheral vision registered.

A clunk? What was that? What the fuck was that?

Sam slowed her breathing. She un-tensed her fists, her hands dropping loosely by her side. She started to regain control. The mist cleared – a little.

She focused on the lock in the door. *Unlock it – now.* She did as she instructed herself. After an effort to prise it open (it had been bent during the assault), Sam peered in.

Nothing.

Shit.

Hang on.

She looked in the bottom compartment, where, she guessed, cousin Jim used to keep his work boots.

And there it was.

A small notebook, A5 size. Hardcover. With

masking tape on its underside.

Stuck to the roof of the compartment. Hidden.

Clever Jim.

She reached for it, and suddenly remembered that Lucya was in the room.

Sam furtively looked inside the notebook. She felt Lucya moving to her side, but she was too late. Sam had a photographic memory. She had seen what was written on the first page and had reconciled the detail already. Sam snapped the book shut.

She had seen the first page; therefore, she had read the first page. She was that quick. She could remember it word for word. If subsequent pages contained the same sort of information, she now knew why Jim had had an 'accident'. He knew too much.

Far too much.

'It's a notebook, erm, full of love letters.' Sam grimaced a smile. She was back to herself now. The adrenalin was pretty much spent. 'It's personal. We… ehh, we had a relationship. Which is not great between cousins. I didn't love him. It was a fling.' She was lying again now. It was a rubbish lie. She ploughed on.

'That's why I came to see him. You see, I'm pregnant.' Sam pointed at her stomach. *Idiot.* 'And I couldn't, ehh, tell him on the phone. I had to tell him face to face. You understand?'

Lucya was shaking her head and nodding at the same time – her piercings a silver blur against a canvass of white flesh. She looked dazed. Sam guessed these situations came up all the time in *Lyubov Kak*

Lyubov. But when it happened to you…

'Look, I'm sorry for the damage.' She raised the notebook to Lucya. 'I'm glad I've found his notebook. I can leave now. Content.' Sam was showing Lucya to the door. She gave Sam a wide berth.

Sam's mind was in overdrive. The book was dynamite. She needed to find space to read it from cover to cover. In private. *Where? When?*

Her thought process was interrupted by the sound of an *ExtraOil* Mi-8 helicopter landing about 500 metres away off to her right.

As Lucya locked the container door, Sam watched two men get out of the passenger door of the helicopter. They hadn't waited for the blades to stop spinning. They were in a rush.

Shit. It was impossible to be sure at this distance, but Sam was pretty certain that the one of the two men walking across the pad was the one she remembered from the Merc. They were headed for the administration building.

It all made sense. They had come here for one reason only.

Think.

'Lucya, you and Jim were close?'

Lucya nodded, sheepishly.

'Look, I don't have a problem with that. He was easily loveable. But, for his sake I need you to do me a favour.' Sam looked back across to the two men. They were 300 metres from the administration building and closing.

Lucya nodded again.

'I need time to read this – in peace.' Sam raised the notebook for effect. 'I need maybe a day. You see, I came into the country illegally,' *How long can I keep this drivel up for?* 'and the police are after me. I fear prison, which I probably deserve. But I need time to come to terms with Jim's death. Do you understand?'

Would anyone believe that?

Lucya nodded again.

'Can this be our secret – two of Jim's lovers?'

Lucya paused for a second and then nodded slowly. Her world of Russian soaps was probably now a little too close for comfort. Or maybe she was thrilled with the drama of it all? Sam couldn't tell, nor did she care. She just needed to buy some time.

'Yes, of course.'

'And, is it okay if I have a quick wander around the site?' Sam waved an arm about. 'To get a feel of where Jim spent his last days?'

Sam glanced back toward the two men. They were being met outside the admin building by a third man. She didn't wait for an answer from Lucya and moved off, leaving the secretary with her pierced mouth hung slightly ajar, as if expecting to be fed.

Sam headed away from the administration building. She walked around the back of the accommodation block and immediately saw what she wanted. Beyond multiple pipes, but with a clear path between the entrance and the back of the site, was a vehicle yard. She jogged the hundred metres or so to an ungated internal compound, where there were two Toyota Hiluxes and a Nissan Navara. All three were decorated with *ExtraOil* livery, and all three were in good nick. She looked into the cabs. No keys. Off to one side was another container. The *ExtraOil* notice displayed 'Transport Pool'.

Sam tried the door. It was open. Obviously up here nobody stole anything – there was nowhere to take it to. The office was unoccupied. The digital clock on the wall read 7.47am. Sam guessed work would start pretty soon. She needed to get a move on.

There was a key rack hanging on the wall, next to clipboards full of schedules. She picked out the one with a Nissan fob, and then turned to leave.

Ahh!

On the back of the door was an *ExtraOil* waterproof coat and a safety helmet, decorated with the company's logo. The coat was far too big for her, but it would do. As she left the container she checked in the jacket's pockets. A small bottle of vodka. *Oh well.*

Now wearing a jacket and hat, and every bit an *ExtraOil* worker – albeit shorter than most, Sam jumped into the Nissan. She adjusted the seat and fired her up. *Three-quarters of a tank. Perfect.*

She drove slowly, but purposefully, out of the oil field – past the security guard who waved at her. On the way out she got within 20 metres of the administration building. The two men from the helicopter were having an animated conversation with the third man.

Tick. Tick.

She had both faces. Indelibly etched.

Behind them was Lucya, who had stopped on the entrance steps and watched as the Nissan left. Through the rear-view mirror Sam thought she saw her shake her head in disbelief.

Chapter 7

Double Coffee, Vuktyl, Western Siberia, Russia

Sam chewed on the end of the biro that the waitress had lent her. She read the lines of Cyrillic she'd written on the back of the postcard. It had cost her 75 kopeks – which included an internal stamp – from the kiosk in the small mall in central Vuktyl.

Dear Lucya, thank you for looking after me. I'm so sorry for your loss. Time is a good healer - I have first-hand experience of what you are going through from a long time ago. Keep the faith and thanks again. Sam - Jim's cousin xxx

She filled in the address, a vague: *Lucya, Chief's Secretary, Oilfield Number 7,* ExtraOil, *North of Salekhard, Russia.* Her experience of the Russian mail system was that it was efficient. The postcard would reach its intended recipient. Her thank you to Lucya, the over-pierced, purple-haired, soap lover, would get there.

Eventually. She had one last look at the photo on the front of the postcard: it was a babushka doll. Lucya may not notice, but what caught Sam's eye was a strip of tartan tied around the doll's waist. Jim would be pleased. In any case, it was either a card with the doll, or choosing one from a set which included: dull, local administrative buildings – or hunters, equipped with guns, stood with their feet on a slaughtered wildlife. *No thanks.*

Lucya got a thank you card with a tartan doll on the front; Sam knew she owed her a good deal more than that. She was sure the secretary had kept her pursuers at bay.

Sam had made best possible speed south from the oilfield, on the dirt and gravel 'road' that was the only way out. The track was raised about half a metre from the surrounding tundra, giving it some air from the ice-logged landscape. She drove quickly and competently, the Nissan expertly following her lead. If she ever needed to buy a 4x4, she had just found a new favourite in the Navara.

The track was broken in a couple of places; she had to go off-road to find favourable ground before rejoining it further south. A small bridge had been washed away, but previous trucks had left their mark, leading to a shallow ford 30 metres downstream. None of it was too much for Sam. She had driven a Land Rover in the army for five years, and the Navara displayed a level of grip and determination well above the hugely competent Land Rover. And the heater worked, unlike the Land Rover; the latter still used a system designed in the 50s – when men were men, and heaters an afterthought.

She knew she had a head start on the Sokolov's men; she was pretty sure that's who they were. Unless she broke down or had an accident she didn't expect to be caught on the 100-kilometre trip to Salekhard – unless one of them was *Mika Häkkine*.

However, they did have an Mi-8. Every moment of the two-and-a-half-hour journey, she'd expected to hear the *wocker-wocker* of the helicopter's blades cutting through the cold morning air. Sam had turned her work phone off, so if it were being tracked they wouldn't know exactly where she was. But with only one route, and driving a 4x4 in livery that shouted, 'I'm over here!' she would be easy pickings for anyone.

In the end, nothing happened. The journey was incident free and, after about half an hour, she really started to enjoy herself. It was like a big game of kids' hide and seek; cat and mouse in muscular vehicles. She loved it. However, the accompanying adrenalin rush which remained topped up until she got to the outskirts of Salekhard and took some minor roads, had taken its toll. By the time she'd hit the centre of the town and found a covered carpark, she was shattered. And hungry; a coffee also high on her 'must have' list.

Actually, what she really she needed to do was read Jim Dutton's notebook. And then formulate a plan – much more than she needed to be fed and watered; but she was ambidextrous. She would manage both.

Walking quickly, she'd found a cafe a few blocks away, and ordered the biggest, sweetest coffee on the menu, some toast with cured meat, and a sickly-looking cake. She knew she didn't have much time and couldn't afford to hang about in Salekhard.

Eat and read (together) – then scat.

After ten minutes of using the cafe's WiFi, accompanied by mouthfuls of food and slurps of coffee which somehow made it to her mouth, she had a way ahead. Jim Dutton's notebook didn't have any more OMG moments after the first page – but there were lots of very interesting notes, covering investigations into Sokolov's businesses. It was nothing that any half-competent person with a computer couldn't have unearthed, but it was a couple of weeks' worth of really helpful and enlightening investigation that she now didn't need to do.

The impact of Sokolov's illegal and highly dangerous venture in the Salekhard oilfields and beyond, had wide-ranging and far-reaching impact – exactly how far, Jim hadn't been able to fully uncover. From his notes, Sam focussed on one of Sokolov's other oil fields, a fracking site, in the eastern Urals; near a village called Arbat. Sam had never heard of it. She Googled it and, after the usual Wikipedia and TripAdvisor entries, found a report from two days ago. It was linked to the *Médecins Sans Frontières* website in Moscow. The report was signed Dr Sabine Roux. Her address block tied her to Arbat at the same time as the report. Jim would have been dead before the report had been published.

Sam picked out the bones of the report which was titled: *Cas médicaux insolubles – Arbat, Russie*. Her French was not great, but she got the gist: MSF were working in two villages in the eastern Urals; both were crammed full of unexplained illnesses; at least three deaths had been reported; at present there was no obvious medical explanation.

Sam had one.

It was on the front page of Jim's notebook.

She found Arbat on Google Maps and did a time and motion assessment. She couldn't fly; well she could, but she'd expect to be met at Moscow airport by an unwelcoming party. She had a vehicle. *A very good vehicle.* But it was hardly inconspicuous. She could hire a car, but that would mean using one of her aliases, which she assumed were compromised. Finally, she could take a train and/or bus. But she really did want to get somewhere – soon.

Time check: it was 11.35am, Sunday morning. She'd email M later and throw a sickie for tomorrow. That gave her a day and a half to do what she had to do, and then get back to Moscow.

Moscow was 800 miles away down half-decent roads, southwest. She'd be spotted in the Nissan, unless she took a circuitous route which would add to the journey. Arbat was 500 miles due south. On less-than-promising roads. But they wouldn't be expecting her to travel south? And there was a provincial airport at Nizhny Tagil, close enough to Arbat; they flew to Moscow twice a day. *Sorted.*

Oh, and she'd been using her phone. If someone in SIS were interested, they'd now know where she was. Time was therefore pressing.

And that's how she now found herself in Vuktyl, four hours' drive south of Salekhard. Penning a postcard to Lucya, whilst drinking her second dark, sweet espresso in the unimaginatively named *Double Coffee*. She was exhausted and needed sleep. The Nissan's satnav reckoned she had another 496 kilometres of partially tarmacked road before she got to Arbat. At her current pace, she reckoned she could make that in seven hours. It was 4.35pm. There was an early morning flight from Nizhny Tagil to Moscow, which she knew she couldn't make. Not without propping her eyelids open with matchsticks. The afternoon flight was at 3.30pm. *Get to Arbat for dawn. Have a chat to the good doctor. Drive the 100 kilometres to the airport. Book in at the last minute. Back to Moscow for early evening.* That might just work.

That gave her about four hours' leeway – to get her head down. She'd do that in the Nissan, which was parked in a two-storey carpark a block away. Although, she really did need a shower. *And a post box.* She might not manage the shower.

Ping. It was her phone. *Bugger.* She'd not turned it off having just had a quick check of any messages.

It was an email.

From Vlad!?

Sam opened the secure mail, and before she read it, swiped to settings and turned data roaming off.

Hi Sam, hope all is well. Like me, you're probably having a tough weekend.

More than you could imagine…

I thought you might like to know that we are pulling together a short-notice operation for early next week. It's concerning the movement of ammunition (will explain in more detail when I see you). And there could be a Nikolay Sokolov dimension, who I believe you are interested in?

What? What does he know? Chrissake…

We're hoping to meet late Monday once we have further intelligence. I'm persuading the team here that we need SIS input. And they owe you.

Let me know.

Have a good Sunday.

Vlad

What the flaming hell was going on? Why would Vlad know she was interested in Sokolov? Was this why he was telling her to be careful? Did the FSB have a file on Sokolov (*of course they did*), and was she now on that file? Is that how he knew?

And what ammunition?

She had enough intelligence in Jim's book to wrap Sokolov in irons and throw away the key. And Sam was convinced there was more. Much more. If this new FSB op added to the case against him, then all the better.

She turned her phone back on and selected 'Reply' to Vlad's email.

Vlad, things okay here. Getting lots of fresh air to sort out my head. Definitely up for the Op. Will need to clear my lines with the boss. Have a busy day on Monday. May be late for the meeting - but will make best endeavours to get there.

Thanks for thinking of me. Sam

She pressed 'Send' and switched data off again. She'd make that meeting, even if it killed her. Before then she had an unscheduled meeting with a doctor, and, just now, she had to find a post box. And, if possible, some hot water.

40°44'41.9"N 28°07'59.3"E, in the Sea of Marmara, South of Istanbul

She'd never felt so lonely, so without contact. It was getting dark and she hadn't seen *that* woman all day. There had been no lunch. No tea. By now she would normally have had three sumptuous meals – all served on a silver platter by *that* woman. Feeding her, making sure she was in good health for the daily ritual.

He'd be coming soon. Wouldn't he? In some ways, she longed for it. For the certainty that things hadn't changed; that they hadn't got worse. That she wasn't being left to wither away; or punished for having her period. Or something her mind didn't want to comprehend. She could cope with the brute coming at her if it meant that things were as they were.

She'd even made the bed. *That* woman had taken away the bottom sheet, but had left her with the top one. So, she had carefully made the bed. She had also covered herself by wrapping a towel around her middle so, if she bled, it wouldn't get on the sheets — she'd try very hard not to stain them again.

Click.

The sound of the lock in the door being turned.

It was him? It would be early for him — and initially she felt sick, her knees involuntarily pressing tightly together. But, if it were him, it would bring *certainty*. Which is something she longed for more than anything else.

And then the real horror started.

It wasn't the brute; it was the two men who had picked her up from Athens in the first place. They burst into the room carrying ropes and sacking.

Are they taking me somewhere? Maybe they're going to tie me up and put me ashore? Leave me to be found! Yes, that's what's going to happen.

How wrong could she have been?

They did tie her up. Roughly. The ropes on her bare skin were so tight she let out a yelp. And then they threw an old hessian sack over her head, pulling it down so it hung around her waist. They then strung a further rope around her neck.

Gasp! She struggled to breathe. The rope was so

tight!

Help me! She couldn't call out. She was fighting for air. Words were an impossibility.

Gagging, she was flung over one of the men's shoulders and, in the partial darkness that was her world inside the hessian sack, she thought she was taken up some stairs and then outside onto the deck. She could smell the fresh sea air, a cooling wind played with the naked flesh of her legs.

Someone was fiddling with the rope at her feet. Tying something. Attaching something.

Oh God! No!

She didn't have time to think through what was going on – it was all happening too fast.

No! Please, no!

She screamed through the throttling rope; her shallow cry lost as her body was flung overboard, the gym weights that were attached to her feet immediately followed. Then, as they both hit the water, the weights pulled her down to the bottom of the Marmara Sea.

As the foam on the water dissipated, one of the men took out some snuff from his pocket and snorted a pinch. He remained by the chrome railings of the superyacht, staring out across the water at the lights of Istanbul in the middle distance – the six, tall slim towers of the Blue Mosque lit like sandy-coloured space rockets prior to lift-off. It was an awesome sight, especially at night, looking across from the sea.

'Bring on the next one,' he said in perfect English.

Apartment 14B, Spiridonyevskiy Road, Moscow, Russia

Simon Page was irritated. And when he was irritated he had to do something. Share his frustrations. He'd phone Richard Warden, the ex-copper. Throw some smoke. But before he did that, he'd pour himself another scotch – it was probably one too many, but he was beyond caring. It was late, past 11pm. Too late, probably, to call one of his team – on a Sunday. But he needed to take his angst out on someone. And with his wife now back in the UK staying with her mother, he had no other targets.

It had been a fascinating, but deeply frustrating weekend. One, in the end, that he couldn't fathom. Green had hopped onto a plane to Salekhard (of all places), taken the train north to the arse-end of the universe, and then driven due south as if her next stop was Tehran. OK, so she was static now, but her trajectory looked forever downwards.

What the fuck was she playing at? She'd got involved with that reporter, messed up a perfectly workable FSB drugs smuggling op, and was now gallivanting around the Russian hinterland as if her arse was on fire. He'd kept an eye on her because that's what he was being paid to do. And it had been amusing to watch the fool for a while. But now, it was dull. He had no answers as to what she was up to. He really didn't. It was all a bit of a mess. And, as the Section Head of Her Majesty's very Secret Intelligence

Service, he felt emasculated. By an ex-sergeant – from the Intelligence Corps! She didn't even serve in a proper Regiment, like The Guards.

And she'd had the audacity to text him earlier to say that she wouldn't be in tomorrow – as she wasn't feeling too good. *Stupid cow*. What did she take him for? He'd give her what for when he next saw her. He would.

Of course, ordinarily, he'd know what she was up to. She'd be working on an op, or running an agent; there'd be an agreed plan. If things weren't quite right, she'd be in touch. By now he, or one of his team, would have called her. They would know exactly what was happening. The fact that he didn't know made him feel inept. Stupid. He didn't do stupid. He couldn't afford to do stupid. Not now. Not at this time. Not when he was getting close to finishing. Completing both his contracts.

He walked across his fine Persian rug to the beautiful mahogany drinks cabinet that was in pride of place in his sitting room. He picked up the bottle of Fortnum and Mason select, ten-year old whiskey – one of three delivered every month from London. It was almost empty. He poured the remnants into the cut-glass Waterford crystal tumbler, the brown liquid naturally finding its place a third of the way up the glass. He raised it to eye level and studied it mindlessly. It was definitely one too many. He knew that now. That was his weekends: ones too many.

How long did he have left with SIS? Two years. Twenty-three months to be precise. He could probably get out of Moscow six months before that. In its current state, his mind struggled to do the maths. Seventeen or eighteen months? And there was the other thing. Could he really keep both going for that long? Did he have the stamina? The resolve?

He had no choice. He had nowhere to go. He had to stay – to see it through.

And that was fine a couple of months ago. Before the lesbian Green turned up and started doing her own thing. He had to get a grip of her. He really did.

Page picked up the phone and sped-dialled Richard Warden. The man would pick up. That what spies did when heads of sections phoned in the dead of night.

'Hello M. Is there a problem?'

'What's Green up to?' He didn't have the energy for pleasantries.

There was a pause on the line. In the old days, there'd be some clicking or bleeping to let the callers know the phone was, or was not, secure. That didn't happen nowadays. It was all secure – and all perfectly natural. Not a hint of delay as the encryption algorithms did their work at lightning speed.

'I don't know. Having a weekend off after a pretty difficult couple of days?'

Simon scoffed, and then took a sip from his glass.

'Well, I thought you were a close buddy of hers? Apparently, she's not feeling so good. Probably time of the month…' That was the whiskey talking.

There was another pause. Was the copper in cahoots with Green? Were they a team? His befuddled brain was concocting all manner of scenarios which, in a sober moment, would have been rationalised out before they surfaced.

'Ehh... I don't know. I did see her on Friday night. She was upset, but looked well enough. I'm not sure what's happened over the weekend.'

You saw her Friday night – you dirty old...

He had to get a grip before he said something that he would later regret.

'She's called in sick. Won't be in tomorrow. Pop round and see her first thing, would you? You know, just to make sure she's OK. And let me know how that goes. Heh?'

That'll be difficult for you, if you know where she is. It's a long way to the Urals. He smiled at his quick thinking.

'Ehh, okay. Is there anything else M?'

'No, no. That's all. Have a good night.' He knew he slewed his last couple of words. Would the man know that he'd been drinking? Who gives a shit. What he does in his own time is his own business.

Wasn't it?

Arbat Village, Eastern Urals, Russia

So, this was it. Arbat. A hamlet of a place, blistered to the side of a rising escarpment with higher hills in the distance. Ignoring the church, with its light blue, peeling plaster and flaking, gold, onion-shaped dome, it was a bleak place. If Sam hadn't spotted old-style power and telephone lines coming into the village from an adjacent field, and a couple of 70s cars (one of which was a yellow and rust Lada Niva; the other she didn't recognise, which frustrated her — she'd have a look at some point), it might have been a scene taken from any of the previous three centuries. Most of the houses were wood-framed and clad, big, half-trunks of old forest and corrugated roofs; windows with glass, but only just. One or two were brick built from the bottom, but the upper stories were constructed of wood. The whole place looked like it might blow down in a mild breeze; but had obviously been standing for years.

She parked up in a crumbling tarmacked square, next to a school-shaped building with a small front garden, enclosed by a fence that needed a good coat of creosote. She got out and stretched. Everything ached. Her legs, her back — her eyes. Other than a three-hour stopover at Vuktyl, a further pee-break in the trees on some desolate strip of road, and an unscheduled stop to fix the Navara, she'd driven throughout the night. The 4x4 had performed perfectly. It was she who had let the side down. At o'Christ-thirty hours she had fallen asleep at the wheel and found herself in a ditch still doing 30 miles an hour. Her reactions had been sharp and had saved her from a looming one-on-one with a pine tree, which doubtless would have come off the better. Somehow, with Sam's help, the Navara had slewed out of the ditch and made it back onto the road. She threw on the brakes and waited for a minute as her heart gradually made its way from her mouth and back down into her chest. She was shaking – and she couldn't stop. She looked at her hands in the half-light of the dashboard LEDs; they wouldn't stop jumping about.

And then came the tears. It was shock, that was for sure. But it was also culmination of so many things, so much rubbish that had filled her days recently – the enormity of what she had taken on: her versus the oligarch, with no one to turn to. Tiredness, beyond understanding. And now, another near-death experience caused by her own stupidity. She hated the tears. Hated them. It was a weakness – a weakness she had no control over. But still they came.

The madness was that she knew from experience that when her body had had enough, it shut down – without her permission. She'd fallen asleep at the wheel before, back in her army days. Then, thankfully, her passenger had been awake and saved them from leaving a German autobahn well before their planned exit.

Stupid, stupid, stupid.

When her pulse rate had returned to something sensible, she'd got out of the Navara and had a look around. Even though tall, black fir trees pressed onto the track as if to reclaim the it for their own, a half-moon gave her enough light for a cursory inspection of the Navara. The passenger side was bashed and dented, and the front-right headlight was out.

And, *shit*, she had a puncture.

At that point Sam had screamed at the top of her voice: 'Fuck, fuck, FUCK!' That had helped. A bit.

She wiped the dampness from her eyes and dribbling nose with the sleeve of her favourite Lowe Alpine fleece, and got to work. She found the spare and the jacking equipment. In poor light, and at temperatures hovering around freezing (and suffering from monster exhaustion), she managed to replace the wheel. It had taken an hour.

Back in the driver's seat, she looked at herself in the rear-view mirror. Already in desperate need of a change of clothes, she now looked like a car mechanic after a long week in the inspection pit. There was more carbon and oil on her hands, sleeves and trousers than there probably was on the whole of the rest of the truck. And her face and hair was a complete mess. She looked like she'd applied camouflage paint and was going to into the bushes to hide for a year.

In this state, she still hoped Dr Sabine Roux would take her seriously. That is, if she were in the village at all. In that respect, it had been a bonkers idea to drive all the way to Arbat. She could have gone to the MSF offices in Moscow and spoken to someone in authority. But, something told her she wouldn't have been listened to. And, in any case, she'd ruled out driving to Moscow just in case she been tracked down by a predatory Mi-8.

Sabine Roux would be here. She would.

An elderly woman carrying a packet of pills shuffled out of the school building, picking her flowery dress up with her spare hand to prevent the hem from getting muddy. She smiled at Sam and nodded her head.

'Good morning! A lovely day?' Her voice was a

croak, and she dragged her left leg. But she was stoically polite.

'Yes, it is,' Sam replied in perfect Russian, mimicking the woman's accent. 'I'm guessing this building is the doctor's surgery?' She already knew, but thought the woman would want to help.

'Yes. The doctor is in, if you need to see her.'

'Thank you.'

Thank you.

Sam smiled. She then reached into the cab and took out her rucksack.

She jogged over to the only door and entered. There were five people sat around on infant chairs, a man kneeling next to a young woman having a conversation, and in the far corner of the undecorated room, was a door. Stood in the frame was a short, slim woman, more western than everyone else. She had soft, attractive features, dark hair tied in a bob, and from this distance, she looked as exhausted as Sam felt.

That'll be Dr Sabine Roux then.

Sam raised her hand in a half-wave.

When she caught a glimpse of Sam, the doctor's expression changed from 'will this line of patients never end?' to one of, 'who the heck is that?' She hesitantly waved back. And then beckoned Sam over.

Sam knew that she looked like she'd just come off the set of *28 Days Later*, and that she'd probably need all her persuasive powers to get through to Dr Sabine Roux. But she had the professor's notebook in her rucksack, and SIS delivered the best negotiation training of anywhere in the world. If she could coax a local to turning informant, she could persuade the doctor that she knew what was causing all of these people to become unwell. In any case, what did Sabine Roux have to lose?

'Hi, I'm Sam Green. Can we have a chat, Dr Roux. Please?' Sam spoke in English. She was shaking the doctor's hand.

The doctor's face didn't shift from bewilderment. How could this scruffy English woman, Sam, know her name?

'Ehh, look, I've another six patients to see this morning, and then I've got to get across to the other village. Anyway, who are you?' The accent was unmistakably French. And gorgeous. Sam let the tone ring in her ears for a split second.

'Can we talk in your office?' Sam pointed to behind the doctor. 'I read your report over the weekend, and I think I can help with your predicament – the, erm, number of unexplained illnesses you have here.'

That was enough for the doctor. Sabine turned sharply and walked into the room. Sam followed, apologising for the way she looked; something about driving through the night and having had a puncture. Sabine didn't bat an eyelid. She was an MSF doctor; she'd obviously seen worse.

Sam closed the door behind them. They both sat.

'Look, I really don't have much time. Please tell me what you need to, and then let me get on with treating my patients.'

'Okay.' Sam took a deep breath. 'I understand that you have assessed the village's water sources?'

'It's actually nothing to do with you, whoever you are. But, yes.'

'High in chlorine – from the purification tablets?'

'Yes. And that's perfectly normal.' Sabine looked puzzled, which was turning to anger.

'But you haven't checked...' Sam paused, not for effect, but to summon the energy for the multitude of questions that would follow, 'for radioactive isotopes?'

There wasn't a reply. Just a stunned silence. Sam was sure she could hear cogs turning in Dr Sabine Roux's head.

The silence remained unbroken. That surprised Sam; she was expecting an onslaught. The doctor stood up and turned to stare out of the window.

'Bien sûr! Comment pourrais-je être aussi stupide?' she said under her breath.

Sam managed to translate without asking for help.

Sabine turned back, sharply.

'How do you know? From where? And, who are you?'

'This may take a while. I'm Sam Green. Sit down, please, and I'll explain.'

'No. First I must tell Dimitri to hold the patients. I will tell him to give us half an hour. Yes, we need that time. Would you like some coffee? We only have instant, I'm afraid.' She was on her feet, her sentences pouring out without punctuation; Sabine was in a rush.

She wanted to know more – now. Sam had underestimated her. She knew Sam was right as soon as she had heard the word 'radioactive'. It all made sense now. She didn't need any persuading.

Over two cups of steaming coffee, Sam took half an hour to explain what Jim Dutton had uncovered in Salekhard. Sam didn't mention people's names, nor that of the oil company, but added gravity to the story by showing Sabine her British Embassy ID card. They had both had a laugh at her photo, compared to what she looked like now. At that point Sabine had offered her kettles of hot water, and the bathtub, once they were finished.

The engineering was complicated, but Jim had explained it well using a couple of line diagrams. Sam did her best to explain what she had learnt from the notebook; there was a lot of hand gesturing. She remembered everything. She could have made an exact copy of what Jim had drawn, and recited every word.

Sam explained that most oil from a conventional well naturally rises to the surface, as it's under pressure below ground. This mixture that comes out is called 'formation water', which is a combination of crude oil and all manner of other liquids and particulates. Once the oil is separated, what is left is known as 'produced water'. In older fields, where the pressure in the seams has dropped, fluid is pumped into the well. In these cases, more 'produced' water is returned. Much depends on the geology of the rock, but nearly all 'produced' water is contaminated, and most is laced with traces of radioactive material – although levels are low and generally safe. Normally these traces are dealt with by separating the solids, which include the radioactive elements, from the liquid – and digging the remaining sludge back into the soil in an agreed, environmentally safe location.

The radioactive materials are mostly: barium, strontium and radium; the latter is more likely to stay in solution, so is often more difficult to purge. Sam didn't need to explain that all three elements were harmful to man.

So far everything Sam had mentioned was normal, legal practice. She made that point to Sabine who nodded vigorously.

'Now, let's come closer to home. There is an oil fracking site just over the ridge of the escarpment behind you. About 20 kilometres away.' Sam pointed aimlessly toward the hill.

'I didn't know that. I'm not sure I fully understand the difference between normal drilling and fracking?'

Sam closed her eyes. She was shattered. *Come on, almost there.*

'Fracking is like well-drilling. But the oil, and often gas, is suspended in minute seams in the rock – normally in horizontal layers of shale, rather than reservoirs. It is not naturally under pressure and needs to be helped out of the ground. Since the mid-50s, the US, who lead the world, has been extracting oil and gas by drilling down to shale, and then, working horizontally, forcing highly pressurised fluid into the rock. The fluid cracks open, or fractures, the seams of shale and displaces the oil and gas – which returns by a separate well back to the surface. What comes out is pretty much your average 'formation water' and is dealt with in the normal way. The difference is with the fluid that is used to do the fracking. It contains a 'proppant': silica, sand and sometimes bauxite, which stays in the cracks in the shale preventing them from closing when the formation water has been extracted. Like props down a gold mine?' The last line had just come to Sam and she thought it painted a simple enough picture.

'And the fracking fluid contains additional additives, such as acids, salt, polyacrylamide, ethylene glycol, borate salts and other things – these reduce friction and turbulence of the fluid, help clean the fissures and prevent scale deposits in metal pipes. Fracking fluids are not that cheap to manufacture. And the whole process is more expensive than normal land-drilling; costs add up.'

Sabine was transfixed. Sam took a sip of her coffee, which was starting to get cold.

'The problem with fracking, and the one which environmentalists and protesters cite more than others, is small earthquakes. These are "allegedly" caused by the fractures closing – the silica being crushed by the weight of the earth.'

Sabine was ahead or her. 'But that's not the problem here – well, not the main problem?'

'No. Another issue is water contamination, but the environmentalists have struggled to make a coherent case – anywhere. There's always been another explanation if water quality is poor near a fracking site. However, in Arbat, the scale of the problem, as you have found out, is in a different league.

'What the oil company has realised is that the "produced" water from their northern oil site is an incredibly efficient fracking fluid – proppants and everything. In fact, the radioactive materials, which are all metals in their own right, work as friction reducers and allow pumps to work at higher pressures. And there's a lot of radioactivity – radium in particular, that is associated with the northern fields. Levels are dangerously high in the Arctic circle.'

Sabine finished the story, her French accent entrancing Sam. 'The oil company pumps highly-radioactive fracking fluid into the watercourse here at Arbat. The village is supplied by relatively new fresh water, which falls as rain. The permeable chalk layer that forms the escarpment, supplying wells at its base where chalk meets impermeable clay. We covered this in geography when I was at school. So here, the rainwater mixes with the radioactive fluid, and the mixture pours out in abundance as springs; there are two in the village. And, as a result, we are all drinking radium-flavoured water?'

Sam could see the lights turning on behind Sabine's eyes.

'Worse than that, I'm afraid. The fracking process also dislodges its own radioactive material in the local shale – so your villagers get a double whammy: radiation from the fracking fluid, and radiation that naturally comes from your local geology.'

'And the oil company know this?' Sabine's face was turning from one of enlightenment, to one of anger.

'Oh yes. They benefit twice. They don't have to pay to produce an effective fracking fluid. And they don't have to fork-out to get rid of their higher-than-normal radioactive "produced water" from their northern wells, other than transport it the 800 kilometres to get here. It's a cheap and effective alternative.'

'*Les enfoirés!*'

Sam looked confused.

'The bastards.' Sabine translated.

'Is it only happening here?'

'No. there are at least two more sites in Russia where the oil company are using the same process – as far as I am aware. But, my understanding is that the geology at those two sites make the emergence of radioactive water a much longer-term process – by which time the radioactive material may have...' Sam repeated for effect, '*may have*, dissipated.'

What Sam didn't add was that Sokolov's oil interests were spread much wider than just the boundaries of Russia. And that Jim Dutton had just started to piece together a scenario which would impact on considerably more people than a small hamlet in the eastern Urals – with much more devastating effects.

Headquarters Secret Intelligence Service, Vauxhall, London

Jane Baker had a lot on her plate. The Syrian situation was testing her teams to the limit. She had only six case-officers in country. Four of them worked alongside the SAS and Special Reconnaissance Regiment (SRR) – it wasn't a job for the faint-hearted. Their role was to evaluate the efficacy of coalition airstrikes against Daesh/IS, and report on the intent and damage caused by the joint Russian and Regime's bombardment. Whilst the army members of those teams had eyes on, and designated suitable targets with laser markers, SIS staff worked hard to recruit local agents and informants to get their information. Jane pretty much operated with a blank cheque. But, even so, there were limited opportunities to find help on the ground. Finding Syrians who weren't too shell-shocked to be effective, or so scared that any amount of cash couldn't recruit them, was nigh on impossible.

A fifth member of her in-country team was based in Damascus, overseeing an agent in the national government and two senior officers in the Regime's army. Finally, a sixth worked alongside the rebels, providing intelligence support and advice, which was collated daily by her multi-agency team based here in Vauxhall.

As the Middle East lead she also ran operations in Iraq, Yemen, Iran, Jordan, Israel, Palestine and the whole Saudi Peninsular: 72 case-officers on the ground and 30 analysts and support staff here in Babylon. It was the biggest desk in the building – and she loved it. If anyone thought that SIS operated with a woman-proof glass ceiling, she was evidence that that wasn't the case. Today, the only thing that mattered was getting results – which, for Area Leaders, required a basket of skills. These included: operational planning;

the ability to hold onto multiple briefs; a thorough understanding of the gathering and exploitation of data (and all its sources); leadership acumen to get the best out of among the brightest young minds in the country; risk analysis; tact and diplomacy, for dealing with staff from the Foreign and Commonwealth Office (FCO), GCHQ, Special Forces, the Met, the Anti-Terrorist squad, MI5... She could go on.

Being of a particular gender wasn't on that list. Indeed, nor was transgender. SIS didn't care what your sexual orientation was, unless your preferences made you susceptible to blackmail. So, you were encouraged to come out – leave nothing in the locker, so to speak. Recent history showed that more members of SIS were asked to leave the Service for financial impropriety above any other indiscretion. Insurmountable debt was easily the most effective way to turn an agent. She should know, SIS played that card all the time when recruiting informants.

She had a mountain of a day ahead: back briefs from three teams; a meeting with the Chief concerning the clearing of the deployment of another operational team to Syria; and a session across the Thames with Joint Intelligence Committee (JIC). Her in-tray was overflowing.

And, on top of that, she had a thick, 'pink' (designated SECRET) file on the corner of her desk. It had been there since she had called for it on Thursday. All its contents, some of it going back to the 70s, had been scanned and were available on SIS secure cloud. But, Jane found it so much easier fingering through a wodge of paper, rather than scrolling down document after document on her LED screen. And, when there were this many papers and folios dating back 40 years, holding all that history in a single file added further weight and context to the subject matter.

The file was titled 'PIERROT', the single word typed on a white sticky label. It was held together by a thick, red elastic band. Hanging from the band was a piece of scarlet-card, about four inches wide by two inches deep; a marker. Typed on the card were the words: *Very limited Signatories: Special Handling Required*. A secret file with a secret marker. Red: the highest level of classification within SIS's security hierarchy.

Jane was the custodian of the file. That responsibility weighed as heavily on her as the safety of all of her in-country teams in the Middle East. It was a responsibility that had been passed to her by her previous boss, David Jennings, just before he retired – he could have given it to anyone, but for some reason had chosen her. And it was one of the nation's most closely-held secrets. The full file was only available to four people: the chief, the prime minister, the permanent secretary and her. A thinner file, without the Pierrot title and with chunks of vital intelligence expurgated, could be accessed by appropriately authorised SIS staff. But even that file, which was only available in e-form, was 'marked' with an orange label: *Special Care – Authorisation Required*.

She'd called for the file on Thursday because an alarm algorithm had alerted her to the fact that someone had accessed the lesser e-file earlier in the day. She was always alerted when a member of staff opened the e-file; or contributed to it. And, last

Thursday, that someone was Sam Green. Sam had not added to the file, she'd just read it. And knowing Sam Green as Jane did, she would have read it from cover to cover, memorising it all.

What was Sam up to? She was a case-officer in Moscow (and not a very effective one, if you listened to her boss). And whilst the Russian connection was clear, what was Sam's interest in Nikolay Sokolov?

Jane could pick up the phone and speak to Sam direct, or get Simon Page to back brief her on what was going on. Neither of those really suited – the last thing she wanted to do was to set some hares running; not all over the Pierrot file.

What to do?

She thought for a second.

That's it, I'll get Frank to chat to Sam.

'Claire!' Jane raised her voice so that her PA would hear her.

Claire poked her head round the door.

'You could always use the intercom.' There was a hint of a smile.

'I know. Sorry. Look, could you ask Frank to come and see me before close of play today?'

'Yes, of course.'

'Preferably before I walk over to the JIC. And, could you be a darling and make us some coffee?' Jane grimaced – she hated asking Claire to run domestic errands for her. She waved her hands at the mountain of work on her desk.

'Us being you *and* me?'

'Indeed.'

'OK.'

As Claire walked out, Jane reached for the pink file and started to remove the red elastic band.

DISINTEGRATION

Chapter 8

Outside the Lubyanka Building, Moscow

OK – let's do this. Sam strode purposefully toward the main entrance of the Lubyanka. She and Vlad had exchanged texts earlier in the afternoon; they'd arranged to meet at the front desk. The meeting was due to start at 5.15pm and she was already 30 minutes late. In her defence, it had a very long day – and it wasn't over yet.

Since lunchtime she had been dressed like a lumberjack's daughter, having discarded her oily clothes at Nizhny Tagil airport. She replaced them with some 'too big for me' jeans, a light brown, heavy cotton shirt with more button-up pockets than was necessary, and a red and black-checked padded jacket – all of which she had bought in the airport lounge. The shop was called '*Hunting Attire*', or the Cyrillic version of the same. It was the only clothes shop in the building. The upside of wearing this lot was that she looked somewhat in disguise – if Sokolov's men were waiting for her at Moscow, they wouldn't be looking for an undernourished wild boar stalker.

She'd spent another 15 minutes with Sabine, looking over patients' notes, before having a strip wash in the surgery's bathroom and then heading straight to the airport. Sabine had agreed not to mention Sam's visit, but to let MSF know that she had come to the radioactive water solution herself – by process of elimination. Sam had assured her that she would follow up on the oil company (and she would). All MSF needed to do was to come to the right medical conclusion, make some noise, and then let the authorities follow the logic.

Hopefully *ExtraOil* would come a cropper. But Sam had a feeling that Sokolov's influence was stronger than some minor MSF protestations; there would probably be a cover-up.

At least the villagers would now be safer than they had been. Although, as Sabine had pointed out, radiation poisoning was difficult to reverse in some, impossible in many.

So, Sam needed to follow through with the *ExtraOil* investigation. She knew that the company had global operations that might be using the same processes. If they were, then more people would become sick and some would die. She had to put a stop to that.

She jogged up the ten or so steps to the main entrance of the building. Vlad was waiting for her at Reception on the other side of the metal and substance detector. When Sam passed through without a beep, he looked at her as though he was seeing her for the first time.

'Did you bag any?' Vlad asked.

'What?'

'Any deer. Or bears?'

Very funny.

'Very funny, Vlad. No, and it's a long story. Which, at some point in the future, I might share with you.'

'OK.' He smiled. 'We'd better get going.'

Vlad led them upstairs to the fourth floor, but to a different operations room. The team was the same, but had expanded. There were two more Russians in the room. They all acknowledged each other – the Russians seemed cautious, as though having a member of SIS in the same room cramped their style. After the pleasantries, Sam sat down on a spare chair facing a screen. The slide displayed was a bunch of photos of Arab-looking men, all but one taken at odd angles, clearly without their permission. Only one, a 'red-carpet' shot, had an accompanying name: Prince Kahlid bin Fahd. Next to the screen was a large-scale map showing most of middle-Asia and the Saudi peninsula. The map was devoid of supplementary markings.

'Welcome, Miss Green.' It was the usual Russian lead, Matvei Popov. If he felt any contrition for the recent failed drugs op, he didn't show it.

He pressed a button on the remote a couple of times; the slides flew backwards. The resulting image was of a Russian naval captain (Sam recognised the badges immediately).

'Captain 1st Rank Mikhailov,' Matvei started. 'He's an ex-submariner. Commanded the nuclear-powered

TK-202, a boat which has recently been decommissioned.' Popov was looking directly at Sam. She was having her own catch up slide show.

The Russian pressed his remote and an image of the submarine appeared on the screen. He paused, letting the information sink in.

Sam decided to show off, just to make a point.

'It's a Typhoon-class, or Akula using your terminology; a ballistic missile boat. Commissioned in 1981, laid down at the Sevmash military shipyard in Severodvinsk, probably, in 1983. They carry 20 SLBN ballistic missiles, each with ten multi-launch nuclear warheads. They are powered by two nuclear OK-650 pressurized water reactors. Your navy built six of them. This is the last boat to be decommissioned, I think, in the same shipyard.'

Take that, you arrogant bugger.

There was a pause.

'Very good, Miss Green.' The congratulations came from one of the new men. He leant forward and introduced himself.

'My name is Nestor Abrahamov. I am a Captain 3rd Rank in the Russian navy, also a submariner. Captain Mikhailov was my boss. I was his warfare officer. My colleague here,' he gestured to the second new Russian to his right, 'is from the Rosatom, the Russian State Atomic Energy Corporation, based in Moscow.'

He sat back his chair, making himself more comfortable.

Still facing Sam, he asked, 'How come you know so

much about our submarines?' It didn't come across as a pointed question.

'It's my job, I guess. I'm ex-army. But you all know that – it's in my file. Anyway, that led to me having a particular interest in military equipment from around the world. And I have a good memory. No more than that.'

'I see.'

Matvei brought them to order.

'We need to move on. For you Miss Green, some further background. Captain Mikhailov went missing two weeks ago. He has not been found. The initial assumption was that he had taken himself into the woods and decided not to come back. Submariners are a particular breed. Hard-working, intense, loners, who are often uncomfortable in the wider world – later in life they have a propensity to "disappear".'

'Do you mean suicide?' Sam asked.

'Yes, and no. Once they've commanded a boat, the pinnacle of any submariner's career, a few feel there is nothing left for them. Apart from, maybe, a crate of vodka and a long stay in the forest. We did expect the captain to surface at some point, maybe with an excruciating hangover. Or, someone would find him whilst walking their dog, with a shotgun in his mouth and missing the back of his head.'

Sam glanced to her right. Captain Abrahamov was slowly nodding his head. He knew how the captain might be feeling.

'Except, we now believe that he is not in the

woods.' Matvei pressed his remote. A map of the Saudi peninsula appeared. 'We understand that he's currently in Saudi Arabia. Exactly where, we're not sure. We had the briefest of tails on him. Unfortunately, after he attended a party led by Osama bin Fahd, the third son of the Saudi Prince Kahlid bin Fahd, we lost him. And he hasn't surfaced. Yet.'

Sam was slowly putting the picnic together. But she was short of some chicken legs.

'So, he's having a knees-up with the unacknowledged fundraiser and quartermaster of al-Qaeda, who's based in Riyadh. I'm guessing you people know that?'

'You're very well-informed, Miss Green. Yes, we did know that. But we don't know much more than that. That's why we've asked you here today. The British have very close links with the Saudi government and, as I understand it, your network is strong in the country. We are better placed in Iran and Syria – as you know. But if Saudi Arabia is central to this operation, as we think it is, we all need to pool our resources.'

That's an admission. Although, Matvei, I wouldn't discount our reach in both Iran and Syria.

'Go on,' Sam pressed.

'Ordinarily, a rogue naval captain, rubbing shoulders with a lesser member of the Saudi royal family would be interesting, but not critical to the FSB. However…'

Matvei pressed his remote again.

The new slide was of the shipbuilder's yard at Severodvinsk.

'This image just paints a picture. As you may be able to tell, it's the yard at Severodvinsk, in Arkhangelsk. They have the responsibility for decommissioning the TK-202. A job they were doing adequately until Pavel here,' Matvei acknowledge the Russian from Rosatom, 'carried out a periodic inspection last Monday. Pavel.'

Pavel leant forward so he could see Sam.

'One of my jobs is to check the dismantling and decommissioning of the reactor – the nuclear reactor that powers the boat. There are hundreds of checks that must be carried out, one of which is measuring the weight of the 32 spent fuel rods – to ensure that all of the radioactive material has been accounted for.'

Sam now had the whole picnic; including a gingham rug.

She didn't mean to be a smartarse, but couldn't stop herself.

'And, when you weighed the rods, even after you discounted minor mass loss due to thirty years of nuclear fission, you found that some of the highly radioactive Uranium 235 and other isotopes were unaccounted for.'

'Exactly. And I checked the fuel rods three times. And had a second inspector flown in from St Petersburg to redo my calculations.'

'How much is missing?'

'Thirty kilograms.' Pavel opened his eyes wide and

tipped his head feigning his own surprise.

'Almost not enough to notice, if you were casual with your inspection.'

'Exactly.'

'And nowhere near enough to make a nuclear device.'

'No.'

Sam was on a roll.

'But more than enough to make a dirty bomb.'

'Precisely.'

Sam leant back in her chair. There was constant discussion in the office concerning the movement and loss of Russian nuclear fissile material from weapons silos, and even power stations. But no one had ever been able to verify a lead.

Until now.

'Our view is that Captain Mikhailov has created an opportunity for the uranium to "disappear". And that he has established contact with al-Qaeda in Saudi Arabia, with the intention of selling the material for subsequent use. After some pressing, naval intelligence has informed us that Captain Mikhailov has a penchant for small boys and cocaine. It's an expensive habit which exceeds his meagre salary. He has to pay for it somehow.'

Sam raised her hand to her head. She was so tired, and the heavy cotton of her new hunting shirt was rubbing under her arms. It was going to make a very fine duster.

Pushing her weariness to the back of her mind, she ignored the naval officer's disgusting habits, but focused, instead, on the theft of the radioactive material.

'Thirty kilograms of radioactive uranium wrapped in, let's say, low-grade, mining-quality, PE 4 – which you can pretty much buy off the shelf. Apply a detonator. Load it into the boot of a car, and you have the third-worst imaginable terrorist weapon,' Sam said.

'What are the other two, Sam?' It was Vlad.

She turned to him.

'A nuclear device, first. A biological suitcase, second.'

Sam knew all about the second one. She and Henry Middleton had prevented an Ebola attack on central London five years ago. If the Ebola had been released, initially thousands, and then thousands more, would have been infected.

She turned back to face Matvei.

'Do we know the intended target?'

'No. Pick any major European city. Park up, and then explode the device, showering everything within half a mile with nuclear debris: shrapnel with a radioactive half-life of 700 million years. Leave aside the initial casualties, the lasting effect would be to close a significant portion of a major city for years. Maybe decades. Pick Frankfurt's Bankenviertel. And then "*Boom!*"' Matvei used his hands to demonstrate an explosion. 'The whole of the European mainland's financial sector goes into meltdown, if you'll excuse the pun.'

It was one of the most terrifying opportunities for any terrorist. And much easier to pull off than Sam's first two scenarios. There was no known terror cell anywhere that had the wherewithal to build a nuclear bomb. If it were that simple, Iran and North Korea would both have one by now. And, whilst it had been attempted in London, keeping a biological agent alive prior to release was incredibly difficult to do.

However, blowing up some nuclear fissile material was easy – if you could get your hands on a small amount of used nuclear fuel, and you could find someone who was prepared to work with it. Anyone spending more than ten minutes near the uranium would be sick for a week. Half an hour and they would likely die a premature death. But, as suicide bombers were two-a-penny on streets of Kabul, Damascus and Baghdad, finding a volunteer for this sort of work would be easy.

'Where do we think the missing pieces of fuel rods are at the moment?' Sam asked.

'In Russia, we believe. But we don't know where,' Matvei answered.

That's a pretty big place to start looking.

Over the next two hours they discussed opportunities and responsibilities. Sam was tasked with engaging with SIS in Riyadh, to see if they could piece together any of the jigsaw. London would also get involved, and that would mean speaking to Jane. Finally, they all agreed that, for the moment, this would be a two-country op. No other nation would be involved. Sam didn't need to press on why the FSB hadn't involve the CIA at this point. It was a pride thing. The US-Russian relationship was in a bad way. And whilst the Europeans were hardly flavour of the month, the FSB were prepared to deal with countries like the Brits when there was an overwhelming need to share intelligence.

They agreed to keep in touch and meet again in 24 hours.

Finally, Matvei announced the op was to be called Op Samantha. Initially he'd kept a straight face, but a smile cracked open on his lips when Sam stared him out with a 'what the blazes …' look.

'Think of it as an apology, Miss Green.'

That had made her feel better.

At the end of the meeting Vlad showed her to the main entrance. Just as she was about to leave, she turned to him and asked, 'In your email you mentioned Sokolov. But his name wasn't part of our discussions upstairs?'

Vlad smiled.

'Between you and me?' He used a finger, pointing at both of their chests in turn. 'Absolutely close hold? No one else – spies' honour?'

Sam smiled and nodded at the same time.

'The head of the FSB thinks Sokolov is bankrolling the exchange for a heavy slice of the profit. The problem is, Sokolov and the Premier are very close and, before anyone casts any aspersions, we need to be absolutely certain of his involvement. To be clear, no one else other than the director has this piece of intelligence, apart from me.' He stopped and then added, 'And now you.'

'Why are you telling me this?'

He almost said something, but stopped himself.

'Just be careful, Sam. Please.'

And with that, he turned on his heel and walked back toward the lift.

The Grand Bazaar, Istanbul, Turkey

Holly Mickelson was in her element. She loved the Grand Bazaar. It was everything she had imagined. A spider's web of tall, tunnel-shaped avenues, the gothic-arched ceiling a decoration of peeling yellow paint, dark blue tiles, small, arched windows and mosaic-styled friezes. The walls were shop after shop, squeezed side by side, their wares bursting out onto the tiled floor from within brick-arched vaults: the gold quarter; the leather quarter; the spice quarter. There were plenty of touristy stalls selling bangles, necklaces and other holiday wares. But, intermingled with these, were serious boutiques offering fine handbags, exquisite porcelain, beautiful jewellery and fabulous, multi-coloured glass lampshades. The colours were all primary; the smells all entrancing; the noise, at times, deafening. Tourists may have been put off by the earlier carnage of the Daesh terrorist attack at the city's airport, and deadened further by the coup with its ensuing 'Westerners are no longer welcome in Turkey' feel, but the Bazaar was still crammed full of people.

It wasn't just the colour, the smell, the energy, the tactility of the whole place – it was its furtiveness, its exoticism, the ever-present element of danger. And that wasn't just because Turkey was in the throes of the greatest change to its geopolitical landscape for over a century – whilst outwardly secular, it was turning inwardly Islamic. Neither was it because nearly all the shopkeepers were men – their dark, oily skin, even when dressed in western shirts and slacks, setting them apart from their American equivalents. It was what all bazaars had been for millennia. A battle; a tussle – even today. Trader versus purchaser. The language was uncompromising, but laced with charm. The shopkeepers forcing themselves on the innocent browser, sometimes grabbing their arm and tugging them gently into their stalls.

It was alive. Tempting. It wasn't the front line of one of the many broken countries in the world, but it was as close as Holly was going to get at this moment. She had her Lumix on hand and was taking picture after picture.

Holly was out with a new friend of hers, one of the junior liaison staff in the Consulate; a 'buddy' assigned to her by the protocol officer (with whom they had cleared their evening itinerary). They would start with a meat kebab and chips at a small, inexpensive restaurant in the student quarter up from the Bazaar. Then, they would take in the Grand Bazaar, and finish with a drink on the Galata Bridge, spanning the Golden Horn, looking out across the Bosporus. It was Holly's first night of freedom after her induction, and she was loving it.

After the coup, all US staff had been warned only to go out at night in pairs. It wasn't a rule the Consulate enforced rigidly; the staff were adults and could do as they wished. However, it was mandatory for new single staff and interns; essentially, anyone under 25. In addition, Holly guessed that the protocol officer was probably under strict instructions from the Ambassador in Ankara to ensure her safety. It wouldn't do for the daughter of one of the Democrats' future presidential hopes, to be let out into 'dangerous' Istanbul on her own. If any harm came to her, the poop would hit the fan.

'Hello, miss! Gorgeous, miss. Your boyfriend is the luckiest man in the world!' The call, similar to so many she'd received so far, was accompanied by a smile that would melt the hearts of the prudest of women. The man, probably in his early 30s, was gorgeous. The drop-dead variety.

Until now Holly and her companion had resisted the hard sell, but this tradesman had a gift.

'Ehh,' Holly could feel herself blushing; she blamed the heat of the night which, inside the Bazaar, was close to 30 degrees, 'I don't have a boyfriend, actually.'

It was the lamest of retorts. She could have kicked herself.

'I cannot believe that.' It was that smile again. She

felt her knees give a little.

'Where are you from? England? Australia?'

In the noise of the Bazaar it had been difficult to hear some traders as they trotted out the clichéd, 'I have the best price, just for you', line. This time it was different. Holly could pick out every word from the latest salesman. It was as though they were the only two people in Istanbul.

She flinched an answer. 'The US, actually.'

His face lit up; his good-looks amplified by its openness.

'I love the US! I spent some time in Washington with my father. He was a diplomat, working for the Turkish government. Now he owns this shop – quite simply the best rugs in Istanbul.' He gracefully swivelled around, using his extended arms to highlight a window full of Turkish hand-woven rugs. 'You see? Aren't they beautiful.'

Holly was being drawn closer, managing to switch her gaze from the man's gorgeous features to the window and then back again. He was right – the rugs looked fabulous.

'Would you like to come inside and have a look? I'm not good at the hard sell – I prefer to let the rugs do their own talking.'

Holly quickly glanced over her shoulder and found the back of her companion, who was over the other side of the tunnel, fingering some coloured, scented soap.

'Jaz!' Her friend didn't reply. 'Jaz! I'm going in

here.' Her words lost against the background hum of the Bazaar.

The man had her hand, holding it gently, his hands soft, his gravity unforgiving. With one last glance back to her friend, Holly entered the shop.

Inside it was smaller than she expected. There were beautiful carpets everywhere: hanging from the walls, on the floor, slung over the counter. The colours were vibrant, but subdued. Dark reds and browns; blues and mild creams. She touched one of the carpets. It felt like silk.

'Do you like them?'

The man was inside her personal space. So close she could smell his expensive aftershave. He was taller than her, piercing green eyes, fuller than average lips, high cheekbones and dark, glossy, but beautifully-styled, hair. He wore a very expensive light woollen suit and an open-necked, brilliant white, collarless shirt. He was looking down on her, but she didn't sense power. She sensed passion. It wasn't overtly sexual (although she couldn't persuade her libido of the case), it was sensuous. It was as if the man was plugged into the mains – he was electric, and her body tingled in response. This man could do what he wanted to her. When he wanted. She knew it wouldn't last; that men like him took women like her, used them and moved on. Their charm was a weapon; a hugely powerful one. It was entrancing, hypnotic.

But who cares? This was her new life, her free life. She was in control, and out of control, all at the same time. And she wanted this man more than she ever wanted anything else in her life.

'Yes, they're, wonderful.' She caressed one of the rugs whilst looking directly into his eyes. It was hopeless. She was lost.

'I have some more out the back. They are better still. For *special* customers. Discerning customers. Would you like to see them?'

Holly didn't answer. He was already leading her through a door in the far wall. She was simply an unwitting follower.

The chloroform-soaked rag was a surprise, but such was her bewitched state, Holly didn't fight. Just before she passed out, she thought that maybe this was all part of the act; he was a drug – like the Turkish shisha, hubbly-bubbly pipe, which she and Jaz had agreed to try later when having a drink on the bridge. It was a precursor to something special?

She was out like a light in a couple of seconds.

'Get her out the back quickly.' The man's tone had changed markedly. He was no longer charming. Now he was ruthless – efficiently so.

'Yeah, all right mate.' A non-Turkish, hard, London accent. 'We've got her now. You go back out front and make sure when she's missed, her friend thinks she's moved on.'

As the Turk moved back into the shop he hissed in his native tongue, 'Fucking infidels.'

THE INNOCENCE OF TRUST

4th floor, British Embassy, Moscow, Russia

Sam had taken Vlad at his word when leaving the Lubyanka building. It was way past 7pm and dark. She had walked in the direction of the Metro, only to pick a taxi at random to drive her to the Embassy. When she was on her feet she had used all the skills taught during training: altering her pace; doubling back; surprising herself with her route choices; and keeping a close watch for the enemy. She was good at that. It helped having 20:20 vision, but in particular she had that sixth sense when it came to people who weren't doing things they suggested, when what they were really doing was tailing her. Folk dawdling when walking home; or not looking in shop windows when buying stuff; or not sweating when jogging.

Sam could spot them, provided she could see them.

As a result, she'd beaten the tail at every session during training at Portsmouth. That had frustrated and surprised her instructors; it was as though she had some inner track to the Main Events List (MEL) – the detail of the day's exercises, which wasn't to be shared with students. She hadn't; she was just very good at it.

Walking was a safe way to get about the place – provided you followed the rules. Using the Metro, however, could be more problematic. It channels and restricts, and there are plenty of dark spaces to get lost in – and not resurface.

Hailing a taxi, on the other hand, was OK. Pick a random one, ideally one travelling in the opposite direction to your intended movement, and the outcome for the tailer can be catastrophic. You have gained time, speed *and* given the wrong indication as to which way you're heading. So, this evening, Sam had walked the 'SIS walk', and then hailed a taxi. If she were being pursued, she had lost her stalker.

The office was empty except for Rich and two other case-officers. Sam was glad to see that M's office door was shut and that his PA had gone home. She would catch up with the inevitable bollocking tomorrow.

She waved at Rich, who swivelled his chair and waved back.

'Hi Sam. Have you been to your apartment?'

'Ehh, no.' *Another odd question?* 'No. I did as we discussed on Friday and only got back into Moscow earlier this evening. I've been to the FSB this evening. Another op has come in. Looks like it's going to be interesting.' She let the conversation trail off having made her way to her desk. She sat down and started to boot up her desktop. It required fingerprint unlocking via a separate pad.

She opened her mail. She knew there was an email from Frank; it had arrived during her briefing at the Lubyanka. The UK was three hours behind them, so Frank's mail had been sent late afternoon. *I wonder what he wants?*

It read:

Hi Sam,

I hope everything is OK. I took the liberty of keeping an eye on your trace (the SIS's colloquialism for the track of a mobile signal of one of its case-officers) *over the weekend. Unless you'd leant your phone to an Inuit, it seems like you've had one hell of a journey.*

Whatever. Jane asked to see me today - her call. We discussed you and Sokolov. I told her what you had given me: Bogdan Kuznetsov and the Tesla. And Iosif Ergorov aka Blue Suit. I also told her I was worried about you. And that was before you buggered off to the Arctic Circle for the weekend. I remain worried.

She was circumspect. But, wants to know everything you have. And has instructed that you leave Sokolov well alone until you have spoken to her. His file's orange marker is a clue. In short, you do not have authorisation to continue to investigate - not without further clearance. I said I would pass that message to you.

She did say that you and she could discuss the access issue when you talk - if you had a problem with it.

That's all. Good to see your 'ping' back in Moscow this evening. I guess it was the Inuit returning your phone.

Keep in touch. And be safe.

Frank xx

Sam leant back in her chair, her hands resting behind her head. Her mind spinning with all manner of theories. *Jane doesn't know about ExtraOil. No one does apart from Rich. And now Op Samantha? How can I possibly give Sokolov a wide berth?* She'd speak to Jane tomorrow.

She checked her watch. It was 9.35pm. She had so much to do and was so tired. Her body would give up soon. Thankfully she wasn't driving.

'Hi Sam.'

It was Rich.

'Hi Rich. Look, I've got a mountain of stuff to do before I pass out at my keyboard. If it's a "how are you?", then the answer is "I'm fine". Can we talk tomorrow?'

If Rich was offended, he didn't show it.

'Sure. Just be aware that M asked me to pop round to see you today; to make sure you were OK. He was poking at something, which I couldn't put my finger on. It was an unusually generous gesture from him. Mind you, he did ask me late last night when he was obviously pissed.'

'What the hell does he want to know about me for, on a Sunday night?' Sam's tone was uncompromising.

'Dunno. He may have been checking on your trace, for some reason? Saw that you weren't sick, but gallivanting around the Arctic Circle? Or maybe he has a soft spot for you?' Rich smiled.

That wasn't funny.

'What did you tell him?'

'Pretty much the truth. That I couldn't raise you. That you were probably at the doctors. But, that I wasn't worried.'

'Do you think he looked at my trace?'

'I'm not sure. I think I would have done. But, you just don't know with him. Anyhow, I'll leave you to it. It would be good to have a gas about the weekend, you know, if you wanted to unburden yourself.'

'Thanks Rich. Maybe tomorrow. And thanks for looking out for me.' She smiled again and touched his arm. He smiled back.

She turned her attention back to her machine. She had four things to do: use Cynthia to photofit the two thugs who got out of the helicopter – that would take about half an hour; knock up a briefing note to M about Op Samantha (but not mention the Sokolov connection?); email Frank with a bit of an update; and arrange a call to Jane tomorrow.

It took Sam 25 minutes to get exact likenesses of the two men she had seen in Salekhard. She started the run of their ugly mugs through Cynthia's database; it would take an hour before she had any results. She would probably have to leave the search running overnight, otherwise she might be sleeping (involuntarily) in the office with her face plastered to the keyboard.

She had just enough energy to reply to Frank:

Hi Frank,

Thanks ref Sokolov. Could you let me know first thing when it's best to call Jane?

I'm fine. Probably best that we talk through the weekend rather than me spend too long typing stuff. It's a Sokolov connection to do with one of his companies called ExtraOil. *Mostly, it's about radioactive pollutants which, after today, I think I might have sorted (as far as I can) here in Russia. I'm going to abuse an analyst here tomorrow to consider* ExtraOil's *reach outside of Russia. I think they operate in Alaska and possibly mainland US - but this is internet search stuff only. If I don't get anywhere here, I might have to come back to you.*

In addition, I've attached 2 photofits of 2 more thugs who I came across at the weekend. I'm working the machines hard here, but could you spread the net wider and see what you get?

There is also something cooking here with the FSB about a major international terror plot that's going to keep me busy for a while.

It's all go.

Hope all is well with you.

Sam xxx

She decided not to expand on the detail of the terror plot, and certainly not to mention Sokolov. Vlad was clear (*why her?*): Sokolov's involvement in Op Samantha was on the closest of holds.

And for some reason she trusted Vlad more than anyone else at the moment. He seemed to deserve her trust, so she wouldn't undermine it.

Shit! Briefing note for M.

Sam glanced at the digital clock on her screen: 10.45pm.

She needed to get home. M would have to make do with a verbal brief tomorrow morning. Why was he interested in her? Was he watching her trace? Did he know that she was away from Moscow at the weekend? If he did, would tomorrow be her last day in the office?

What the hell. If so, so be it. At least she had unpicked why Alexei had been killed. She had kept her promise to the beautiful reporter. And that made her feel half good.

Flat 17, 3125, Prechistenskiy Road, Moscow

It was 11.50pm by the time Sam got back to her apartment. She'd taken a taxi after following the usual protocols, and fallen asleep in the back. If someone had been tailing her with a view to abduction, she'd now be in a cellar somewhere, wrapped up in chains with her fingernails being yanked out with a pair of pliers.

The taxi driver had woken her with the retort, 'You're home, Tchaikovsky girl.' She was flattered. She assumed it was reference to Sleeping Beauty. But equally it could have been a poke at his 1812 Overture; she being a very tired French girl accompanying Napoleon's long march. She hoped the former.

Idly, she took the lift and, at her front door, she stretched before reaching into her pocket for her keys. The door was triple-locked and had a biometric entry system using her iris. The kitchen window might let in a gale, but the security was good.

The door clicked open.

Straight away Sam was on her guard. She didn't know why. She couldn't understand what had set her on edge. But something was different. She didn't turn on the hall light.

Any tiredness had evaporated. Her pupils dilated to let in the correct amount of light. Her pulse quickened, but not so it ran out of control. And her breathing was shallow – allowing her ears to work without interference.

She stood perfectly still and listened.

Nothing.

A minute passed.

Still nothing.

She knew every inch of her flat. It was both the burden and the beauty of being wired up the way she was. She saw; she registered; she remembered.

It was very dark in the hall, but not pitch black. She'd left the lounge door slightly ajar and a sheath of yellowy, grey light peeked in, its origin probably an outside street light making its way through a gap in the curtains.

Sam reached for a bookend which was on top of the shelf in the hall. She gathered it using one hand, arming herself, whilst pulling the bottom of the end book toward her, ensuring the line of books stayed upright.

On her left was a door into her bedroom. It was windowless – it would be devoid of light. She opened the door, it pushed inward. But she didn't enter. She let the door hang open and waited for a reaction from inside the room.

Nothing.

She walked four paces forward, her steps as soft as a ballet dancer's – her breathing easily the loudest thing in the flat. On her left was the door to the bathroom. It would also be dark, but the dull light from the lounge door would provide some illumination.

She opened the bathroom door. It creaked. *Grrr.*

Sam didn't go in. She waited.

Nothing.

Now the lounge door. If pushed, it would swing open until stopped by a fake fireplace.

Standing as far back as she could, she kicked it with her foot. A sharp kick, aimed at sending the door swinging to the fireplace. If there wasn't anyone behind it, it would clatter, wood against fake marble. If it had a soft landing... she'd need the bookend.

Clunk!

Nothing.

She waited.

Was she mad? What was it that had set her off? Was it the tumultuous weekend: the taxi chase; the train journey; the purple-haired secretary and her woeful tale; Sokolov's two thugs (their images still running with Cynthia); the escape, the crash into the ditch, and then her emotional meeting with Dr Sabine Roux? Or was it Frank's email and the fact that she had made her mind up to lie to Jane tomorrow about Sokolov's involvement in the dirty bomb? That was hers and Vlad's secret.

She held her breath.

Nothing.

She stepped into the lounge. From what she could

see in the low light, everything was as she had left it. As she expected it to be.

She turned on the light.

Nothing. Everything normal.

She breathed out and, at that point, tiredness almost overcame her. Her knees gave a little shake and she almost collapsed onto the floor.

Come on!

Sustenance. That's what I need.

She'd have a glass of milk and get to bed. If she were lucky she'd make four hours before her alarm went off. That would be enough for today.

Still holding the bookend, Sam dropped her rucksack on the sofa and made her way into the kitchen. She switched on the light.

And what she saw stopped her dead.

It was a small thing. Probably, to begin with at any rate, unnoticeable to a casual observer.

But Sam spotted it straight away.

Her fridge door. Two postcards from her huge selection of friends.

And her letter magnets – not quite a set, the number of letters had dwindled over the years. Normally arranged haphazardly, or displaying an expletive which she had picked out to express what she thought of Moscow.

Not now.

Now they read:

carful wot you wish 4 samanthe

Sam closed her eyes. And then opened them, hoping that what she had just seen was an apparition – a joke played on her by her dulled senses.

No, the words were still there. *Careful what you wish for, Samantha.* Who calls her Samantha? *The FSB? Oh God!* Or someone else throwing a different scent?

The writer had used most of the letters on the fridge door. Hence, she guessed, the lack of spelling. Whatever, her heart rate was now out of control. The red mist was back. Strike and flight was the overriding sensation. Hit out. And get out.

She reached for her knife block and drew one with a six-inch blade. She gripped it tightly. She now had knife in one hand; bookend in the other.

She had already turned and was facing the lounge door.

Who's first? Come on, you bastards!

She stomped around her flat. Noise wasn't an issue for her now. She wanted whoever was there, whoever had been there, to come out so she could release her pent-up energy. Strike and then run.

Blood pumped round her head, which darted left then right. Searching. Looking for an enemy. The thing that had broken into her flat. Violated her space. Messed with her fridge alphabet.

The bastards!

How could they have broken in? With biometric entry? It didn't make any sense.

What did Rich say? 'Have you been to your apartment yet?' What was that all about?

She couldn't keep this up for much longer. The surging adrenalin was running its course. The spike of alertness was blunting. She knew she would come down soon. She had used all her spare capacity. Her batteries were flat. If she didn't sleep soon, her body would do it for her.

Think! Could she stay here? Could she? Where else would she go? Rich was the only friend she had – but was he her friend? *Go back to the office?* No. She had to get some sleep. In a bed. Be prepared for tomorrow. For the next assault.

Stay here. But better armed.

She walked back into the kitchen. She took all the knives from the block and two more from a drawer. She then systematically walked around the apartment placing weapons at key points. If she had another visitor, they would never be more than four feet away from a knife in the chest. Along with marksmanship, that was another facet of hers that she'd displayed during training that had surprised her instructors. For a mid-sized woman, she had proven to be effective at close combat. Red mist and good reflexes: worked a treat.

Last of all, she made it into her bedroom and put the last knife on her bedside table.

Then she fell on the bed, fully clothed and slept like a baby.

Chapter 9

Basement Gym, British Embassy, Moscow

The sweat was stinging Sam's eyes. She glanced down at the running machine's display. It read: 5.22km; 14.2km/hr. That was close to ten miles an hour; as fast as she had ever run on a machine. She couldn't keep it going for much longer.

The beauty of running on a treadmill was that you could fight it. It wanted you to press the 'stop' button, or fiddle with the speed toggle and reduce the running rate. Its job was to break you. There were little men inside the apparatus who were programmed to mess with your head. Sam knew they were there and she was determined not to slow; determined to beat the machine. Blow one of its fuses if necessary. It struggled at over 16km/hr, most half-decent running machines did. And, whilst she couldn't run at that speed for any sensible period, she was determined to run 7km at over 14km/hr. She wanted to hear the little men ask for forgiveness. For the machine to beg to be shut down.

Come on! You can do this.

It was either her or the machine.

It was going to be her.

Think of something else – let the rubber belt do the work; you just keep up.

Her mind wandered as the pain receptors in her legs, and the alveoli in her lungs, reminded her that she was very close to overdoing it.

It had been a remarkable morning, one which didn't include her getting the sack – which was a surprise and, on the face of it, a good thing. She had a plateful of work that needed her attention.

Before M had made it to the office, she had tasked Debbie (one of a pool of SIS analysts on the fourth floor) to look into *ExtraOil's* conventional drilling and fracking business. She hadn't mentioned her trip at the weekend, but had given Debbie all she needed to explore as to whether the oil company was removing 'produced water' from vertical wells and using it as 'fracking fluid' at fracking sites. Sam gave Debbie Jim Dutton's notebook as a guide. He'd already made loose references to a conventional site in Alaska and a planned fracking site in California. There were probably others.

Sam didn't have the authority to directly task analysts without an operational code, which M would assign. As things stood, even after the briefing note that she'd prepared for M at the end of last week, no code had been allocated. It was all very tiresome.

'Do you need an op code from me, Debbie?' Sam had asked.

Debbie smiled, a warm smile. 'No Sam, don't worry. When you have one I'll put my hours against it. In the meantime, this looks like a lot of fun. Anything to have a go at big business.'

Sam got on well with all the junior staff on the fourth floor. And that was the norm nowadays. Not many years ago, case-officers would look down on analysts; sort of an 'officer versus an other-ranks' division, as was the case with the Army in the olden days. Sam got the impression that in Moscow there was still a bit of that, probably not helped by the fact that M seemed to encourage it. She'd been an analyst. She knew what it was like at the end of the food chain.

'I'll have something by the end of the day. And then we can talk some more about where else you'd like me to "drill down".' Debbie had made a turning motion with a finger, pointing to the ground. She giggled at her pun.

Sam nodded and smiled.

'Thanks Debbie.'

That had been one job. Next was her meeting with M. His PA had come across to Sam's desk as soon as she had delivered her first cup of coffee to the boss. She looked flustered, as if she'd run to work and not had chance to have a shower. *Bless her.* It must be tough working for the idiot.

'M would like to see you straight away, Sam.'

'Sure, I'll be right there.' Sam picked up her

notebook and pen and followed the PA back to the door of M's office.

'Go right in.' The PA motioned.

'Thanks.'

Sam had decided to be combative. She had helped solve an insoluble medical issue in the eastern Urals, and was now central to a joint FSB/SIS op to track down a dirty bomb. M should be pleased with her – rather than scolding her.

'You wanted to see me, M?'

'Yes, Green. How are you feeling after your day off?'

Was that laced with sarcasm?

'Fine, sir, thanks. And you?'

Confusion spread across M's face. He quickly dismissed her question, waving his hands about.

'Look, what's on your plate at the moment?'

Does he know about the weekend? I am going to have to tell him.

'Two things. First, I have established why Alexei Orlov was murdered. And second, the FSB has included me in an operational planning team looking at, possibly, a dirty bomb destined for a European city.'

M looked confused and surprised at the same time.

'A dirty bomb? And who's Alexei Orlov? No… got it. He's the reporter fella you thought was taken out by the Chechen bomb. I read your brief.'

Bravo.

'Yes, sir. That's correct.'

Sam went on to tell M about the weekend, including last night's episode with someone entering her apartment and leaving a threatening message.

At the end of her diatribe, M said, 'Sit down, Green.'

And continued. 'Okay. I hear you with the Sokolov oil thing. And you may be right. But, I think that's unlikely. MSF have left-wing tendencies…'

That was too much. His patronising tone; his lack of respect for her work. Something snapped. *The red mist was on its way.* Sam lifted her bum off the seat as she spurted out, 'You don't believe me? Do you have a problem with my work? My role as a case-officer here? Do you trust any of your staff?' She'd lost it and stepped over a line. The end was near.

'Stay in your chair, Green, and listen to me.' M was firm, but not angry. In fact, he was remarkably controlled, which was equally frustrating. 'You have been here for 20 minutes, with little to show for your efforts thus far. I have seen the likes of you come and go over the decades and I am telling you – and you need to listen – that organisations like *Médecins Sans Frontières* have agendas. They are anti-capitalist; and, here in Russia, they are anti-regime.'

Sam went to contradict M, but he put up his hand.

'Your problem is that you're bright. And quick. And I take my hat off to you for following up on this Alexei whatshisname issue – although I am placing you on a six-month disciplinary report for operating without authority, and for travelling away from Moscow without permission and necessary cover. You put your life and the reputation of SIS in jeopardy. *Capisce?*

Sam nodded as she gritted her teeth. This was not going to plan.

'Your problem is that you think in black and white, when you should be looking at the greys. You want to sort everything out, now. When, actually, the best plan is often to let things find their own way; keeping an eye and reacting to developments. In short: you are naïve, Green. And impetuous. And, with your energy, I can't see that changing anytime soon. So, along with you disciplinary six-monther, I'm putting you on a competence six-monther. My PA will sort out the paperwork, and I suggest you read the fine print. Now, what about this dirty bomb?'

Flabbergasted was an understatement. Not that she had been put on a dual report – after her outburst she expected worse. But that the man had done all of it without batting an eyelid. He'd shown none of his usual agitation. He was *too* calm. He wasn't clever enough to be this calm. That really riled her.

Sam hadn't finished. She slowed her speech and forced her bum into the seat. M had taught her a lesson on winning by not reacting.

'I'm sorry, but I don't take your line about the MSF. I discovered the radioactive water connection. MSF are just working with it. I'm confident that this is wider than a Russian operation. This morning I tasked Debbie to look into *ExtraOil's* overseas subsidiaries to see if they were using the same processes in, say, the US.'

M put his hand up again, taking a resigned deep breath as he did.

'What is it with you, Green?'

Sam thought she saw a spark of anger behind M's composed demeanour. *That's more like it.* 'You know you can't task analysts without an op code. So, why do it?' He shook his head. 'No, don't bother answering the question. Just get Debbie off the case. And note that this sort of indiscretion would lead to immediate dismissal under the rules of both six-monthers. I'm prepared to ignore this one, this time. But leave the whole thing well alone. Do we understand each other?'

What could she do? *Poke at him – cleverly.*

'Do you want a brief from the weekend? My notes on Sokolov, *ExtraOil*, Dr Sabine Roux – all of it?'

M thought for a moment. He wasn't fazed.

'No. Don't worry. I won't read it. Just let this thing run for a while. If you believe the whole radioactive water theory, then any report from the MSF will reach the authorities and they will deal with it.'

Yeah, like that's going to happen, with Sokolov's friends in the Russian government.

'Now, tell me about the FSB op and the dirty bomb.'

Initially fuming, but eventually calming down, Sam spent a further 15 minutes talking through what had been discussed at the Lubyanka the previous evening. She purposefully didn't mention the Sokolov link. And she purposefully failed to mention that the op was titled 'Op Samantha'. She knew she'd be laughed out of the office by the idiot if she had. And, the way she felt at the moment, that might elicit one of two reactions: uncontrolled anger, or tears. She really didn't want either of those to surface in such a confined space.

'That's interesting,' M said at the end of her brief. 'Okay. I'll email an operational code for you. You can certainly task Debbie on this. And deal with London. Should you need any more horsepower, then let me know. This could be your redemption, Green.'

Sam ought to say 'thanks', as that would have been polite. But she didn't want to give the idiot any sense of reconciliation.

'By the way...' M was on his feet. The meeting was over. 'What have the FSB named the op?'

Sam hesitated. 'Ehh. They haven't given it a name yet. I'll let you know when we have one.'

M scratched his chin. 'That's odd. Okay, drop me an e-brief by the end of the day. Good luck, Green.'

That had been the second part of her morning; that, and briefing Debbie on Op Samantha (at least she'd smiled at the name). Debbie had wanted to continue to look into Sokolov's oil business, despite M's 'stop' order. 'I'm interested in it.' Sam didn't dissuade her.

In addition, she would engage GCHQ and ask around the building to see if there was any emerging int. on Osama bin Fahd. Sam would talk to Jane later, who would inevitably then brief the staff at Vauxhall to see what London had. She and Debbie would touch base again at 3pm and compare notes. The next FSB meeting was at 4.30pm; that would work.

Her third job had been a confusing conversation with Jane. Sam had given her the same brief she had provided to M, including the earlier stuff about Alexie's murder and the hit and run. She got a diametrically opposed reaction.

'Wow. Good work, Sam. That's impressive. What are MSF going to do next?'

'Just report their own findings and see whether the authorities will look into *ExtraOil's* and Sokolov's wider businesses. I'm concerned about his global oil interests. Apparently, *ExtraOil* is drilling in Alaska under a different name. And they have secured the rights to frack in California. It doesn't bear thinking about?'

It was at that point that things got a little weird.

'Sam, Frank has been keeping me in the loop about the whole Sokolov thing. Do you really think your life's in danger?'

'Well… yes. I told you about the Tesla incident. Being pursued in Salekhard. And now the message on the fridge.'

There was quiet for a moment.

'And you've briefed M?'

'Yes. This morning. The outcome of which was two coincident six-monthers. He asked me to lay off the oil thing. Let it drift for a bit.'

There was another pause.

'I think that's sound advice.'

What?

'You think I should let MSF push the issue and

hope that they have enough clout to get the wider authorities to look into *ExtraOil's* reach overseas? I'm sorry Jane, but it doesn't make sense. There'll be a cover-up. And there are people's lives at risk here.'

'I know.' Jane paused, and then, almost in a resigned tone, continued, 'OK. We'll deal with it here. Has Frank got all the details?'

This doesn't make sense – it's my op.

'Ehh. No. But I can bring him up to speed.'

'Do that Sam. Please. Now, what about the other thing you wanted to talk to me about? The dirty bomb?'

'Hang on, Jane. You want to take the *ExtraOil* thing from me? I'm not sure I'm prepared to let it go that easily.'

The line went silent for a few seconds.

'Sam. You know that Sokolov's file has an orange marker on it. There are reasons for that which I'm not prepared to go into. You're going to have to trust me on this.'

And what about Sokolov's involvement with the dirty bomb?

Sam sighed. She wasn't convinced. She'd seen the anguish in Dr Sabine Roux's eyes. Sensed her passion for the villagers. Had had a look at the list of patients and their ailments. Felt the death. And learnt of the dying mayor of the next-door village.

She really wasn't convinced.

In answer to Jane's question about the dirty bomb, Sam ran the same briefing she'd given to M. She was getting bored of talking and not acting.

'Good. Good work, Sam. This is huge. Do you have the right manpower in Moscow?'

'Yes – we do.'

'Good. I'll brief Frank. Use him as you point-man here. Ask for anything you want. And copy me in on your briefs to M. I'll have a chat to the DA in Riyadh and see what he has on Osama bin Fahd and the prince.'

And that had been the end of a shitty and incomprehensible morning. M acting almost reasonably. And Jane the latter; not jumping up and down on the *ExtraOil* conspiracy thing.

Sam didn't get it.

To compound the rubbish as she left for her beasting in the gym, she'd opened an email from M which was addressed to all case-officers in station:

Just to remind you that you are all expected at the reception tonight for the Foreign Secretary: 7-9.30pm. It is a three-line whip. No excuses. And, unlike last time, I do not expect to be the last man standing. Girls - wear something revealing. The Foreign Secretary likes a bit of flesh. M.

It wasn't the last line that had made Sam want to reach for a razor blade – although it had made her stomach turn (*the idiot*). It was the fact that she had to put on something smart and make small-talk to people she really didn't like, and didn't find interesting. She was hopeless at it, and always felt like a prune. She would need to drink heavily. Even before she got there.

She glanced back down at the running machine's display, which was covered in her sweat. It read: *6.95km, 14.2 km/hr.*

50 metres to go.

She held on for the last couple of seconds…

Done!

Sam smacked the 'Stop' button. The machine wound itself down quickly – in as much need of a break as she was.

She staggered off the running belt, bent double, holding onto one of the machine's arms to steady herself. Her chest was heaving and her legs were crying out for a warm bath. Her meagre breakfast was trying its best to escape northward.

What a day. What a rubbish day. She still needed to brief Frank on *ExtraOil* and Op Samantha; and see what Debbie had been able to unearth. Maybe the Saudi DA had something, or the SIS team in Riyadh?

Oh shit! I've forgot to check the photofit results of Sokolov's two thugs from Cynthia. She'd do that as soon as she'd showered.

Then it was off to Lubyanka for the Op Samantha meeting. After that, a quick change, and for her the worst nightmare of all: the formal reception. She was bound to say something out of place, or use the wrong knife. She hated it when people laughed at her – especially when she would be trying so hard.

As she dried the sweat from her face, she looked up at the gym's main TV screen which was showing the BBC News channel. There was no sound, a couple of the gym's occupants preferring the heavy beat of some hip-hop music to accompany their spin session. The screen showed a photo of a young, attractive woman – all teeth and smiles. The red title block showed the words 'Congressman's daughter goes missing in Istanbul.'

At least she wasn't having that sort of day. Small mercies.

4th Floor, British Embassy, Moscow

Simon Page was struggling to get the end of the whole baguette into his mouth. Too much ham. As he squeezed the bread together, a dollop of mayonnaise escaped from the side of the sandwich and fell onto his suit trousers.

Fuck! He hated it when that happened.

The morning had been a trial. But he had to congratulate himself. He had stayed calm with the lesbian Green in the room. Calm was what was needed. He couldn't afford to push her over the edge. And this was not the time to get rid of her. If he had, Vauxhall would doubtless have taken her back for a period of reconciliation. And then, who knows what stories she would tell? He needed her within reach. To control.

And he needed her to lay off Sokolov.

He had done a good job. In fact, if she pulled off this dirty bomb op with the FSB, there could be accolades all round. *Simon Page CBE*. That sounded the business. He would help her with that. Certainly.

After Green had left the office, he'd briefed his contact on the details of her weekend jaunt.

When she had booked the original flight from Moscow to Salekhard on Friday, he'd placed a call; he'd sensed surprise on the other end of the line. It was as though no one had any idea what she was up to. He certainly didn't; but that was often the case. He reported and carried out specific instructions. He wasn't given the bigger picture, unless that helped him task assets effectively.

It wasn't until Green had briefed him that he was able to put the pieces together. It now all made sense. He had to hand it to her. She was a very good, if maverick, agent (he hated the relatively new term 'case-officer', the original term 'agent' had a satisfying Ian Fleming ring to it). He didn't think there was anyone in the building who could have put together the *ExtraOil* conspiracy as quickly and efficiently as she had. And then brought the Russian piece of it to such a neat and successful conclusion. It was impressive.

Obviously, he wasn't going to tell her that.

Now, she did need to leave well alone – for her own good.

But also for mine.

If she came to heal and survived long enough, she

could be a useful asset. And if she pulled off the dirty bomb thing, it wouldn't do any of them any harm.

Yes, he would certainly help her with that.

He wiped his mouth with a paper napkin. What else had his PA ordered from the very good Embassy kitchens? He searched his desk.

Ahh! An apple and strawberry tartlet; with cream.

That would do nicely.

Ballroom, British Embassy, Moscow

Sam was stood on her own, just to one side of the 'great fireplace'. She held a tumbler of gin and tonic in both hands, cupping it as though it emanated warmth. She looked across at the huge grandfather clock that stood to one side of the main exit from the ballroom. The big hand was pointing to the '5' and the small hand just beyond the '8'. It was, she thought miserably, just 8.25. There was another hour to go before she could leave without fear of incurring the wrath of her boss. Not that she cared about that. For her it was about 'doing the right thing'. Following orders. It was her military training.

She looked down at her gin and tonic. The ice had melted, but a slice of lemon still floated on the surface – the only thing in the drink that was good for her. *Who gives a shit?* It was her third, and she wasn't counting the glass of red she'd wolfed down in her apartment. And the Embassy didn't serve half-measures.

A stonking run in the gym, a day without a glimpse of a let-up, an inconclusive and ultimately disappointing meeting at the Lubyanka, and, with very little to eat (apart from some fruit for lunch and now a couple of 'devils on horseback'), the alcohol had surged unopposed into her bloodstream and was now playing havoc with her inhibitions. If the reception had had a karaoke, she would have been ready to barge to the front of the queue and belt out, 'I Will Survive'.

She could do that as well as the next woman.

Unfortunately, the only music came from the sinuous warblings of a string quartet, playing something 'background'. And there was no microphone.

Oh well…

She hadn't been alone for the whole all evening. Rich had found her after about half an hour and they had chatted about this and that. She had tried to reconcile how she felt, but no matter which way she looked at it, she couldn't trust him. Someone was keeping a very close eye on her, alerting Sokolov's henchmen, and he was an obvious suspect?

Why him? She couldn't say. But he certainly had the 'how'.

She gave Rich a watered-down version of the weekend's activities and decided not to tell him about the break-in at her flat. He had gently pressed her on the 'dirty bomb' op, and she had given him a brief outline.

To change the subject, she had asked him what he had been up to. His story was that he ran a couple of Russian government agents and, unsurprisingly, three members of the Russian state police. He was leading an op which he hoped would expose endemic election fraud under the control of the Russian government. Nobody was sure if anyone would do anything with the findings. But, it was the sort of information that might be leaked to the OSCE (the Office for Security and Coordination in Europe; often called to oversee national elections to ensure that they were 'free and fair'). That organisation would then expose the Russian government and, just maybe, Russian democratic activists might be encouraged to bring down – what was now agreed to be – the current dictatorship. It sounded interesting.

Rich had fetched Sam her second large gin and commented, in a benign way, on the way she looked.

'You scrub up well, Sam. The Doc Martens suit you, but you also look good made up to the nines.' He'd smiled apologetically, to cover up any perceived patronising or sexist slant to his statement.

Sam glanced down at what she was wearing.

Post the earlier meeting at the Lubyanka, it had all been a rush. She had made it home in 20 minutes, employing limited decoy tactics while sprinting for a taxi. She had showered, held her shortish, scraggly auburn hair back with two grips, applied the simplest of make-up, thrown on her just-below-the-knee black dress and slipped on a pair of matching, kitten-heeled, shoes. The crowning glory was her grandmother's exquisite gold chain suspending a drop-pearl, complemented by a pair of pearl-stud earrings her mother had left her.

Sam wasn't a clothes horse – she was more Claudia Winkelman than Claudia Schiffer. But she also knew that she wasn't unattractive. She had no boobs to shout about ('A handful is more than enough,' her mum always used to say when Sam complained about how flat-chested she was), but she did have a bum.

The 'little black number' had nothing to do with her; the dress and the shoes were Jane Baker's choice. At the end of training, all the team were bussed up to London for a formal dinner at SIS headquarters. She knew it was coming and she didn't own anything that would do for a dinner where the blokes were wearing black tie. As the day approached, she titled closer and closer to a flat spin, and in a moment of panic had phoned Jane. Jane had been privately educated at a school in the southwest somewhere – she would know what to wear, and have wardrobes full of the stuff.

As a result, they'd spent an afternoon in London choosing outfits. The dress came from L.k. Bennett, and the shoes from Russell & Bromley. She'd not been into either of the shops before and was flabbergasted at the price tags: she could have bought a very decent alpine walking jacket for the price of the dress; and some top-of-the-range Gortex trekking boots for the cost of the shoes – which were made with less leather than a couple of cow's ears.

But it had been a fun afternoon.

On the way into the reception an hour before, she'd caught a glimpse of herself in the huge mirror in the entrance hall of the Embassy. She had done all right – for a council house girl.

She looked up at Rich. He was waiting for a reply to his rather back-handed compliment.

'Thanks Rich. I'm sure you understand when I say that I'd much rather be wearing my Patagonia fleece, walking trousers and a, pick-any-colour-you-like beanie.' She played with the end of her hair, pulling a curly strand and then letting it go. 'You look fabulous in your penguin suit, by the way, but I guess you'd rather be dressed more casual-like.'

Rich laughed.

'How right you are, Sam. How right you are. Anyhow, there are a couple of the lads I'd like to have a chat to. You happy if I make a move?'

'Be my guest.' Sam half-curtseyed. Rich, smiling, bowed. And then took off.

That was 20 minutes (and another trip to the bar) ago. And she was still stood on her own – like the prune she'd known she would be. Still holding her tumbler of gin as if her life depended upon it; her legs crossed at the ankles, her shoulders hunched a touch. She couldn't give off any more 'leave me alone' vibes if she tried.

She emptied her glass, and burped a small womanly burb, discreetly holding one hand to her mouth. The grandfather clock, which thankfully was still in focus, struck 8.30pm. The string quartet played another incomprehensibly dull, but genuinely pleasant piece of classical something or other.

And then the course of her history changed.

It wasn't a cataclysmic event, like paralysis after a bad car accident. Or falling head-over-heels in love with a complete stranger, marrying him six weeks later, and then mothering a six-aside football team. *The flippancy had kicked in.*

It was the final twist of a screw. A screw that had bored its way into her life over the past ten days. A screw that had tapped into her emotional core, playing havoc with it.

The final twist of a screw that would send her on a journey that could only end in tears. Or worse.

The Foreign Secretary's party were late arriving. There had been an earlier rumour that the talks with the Americans and Russians, over the brokered ceasefire in Syria, had taken longer than anticipated. So, they had taken a break to come to the reception, and would reconvene later in the evening.

M was with the main man, directly opposite where Sam was standing; small clusters of 'cocktail party' groups partially obscuring her view. There were three other men with him: the ambassador, the Foreign Secretary, and a third, who had his back to Sam. He was big. Tall and broad. He towered above the other three.

M was in his element. He was a social animal; never afraid to mix with the high and mighty. Sam thought he had probably just finished recounting some witticism. The other three men laughed, the big man with his back to Sam, touched M on his elbow. It was a gentle gesture; one possibly exchanged between two friends.

She was just about to head left to the bar, and inadvisably grab a fourth G and T, when the big man turned his shoulders, and then his head, and looked directly at Sam. He made some comment to the group and left them, heading in her direction.

She knew who it was instantly. She had seen at least a dozen photographs of him. She knew he was tall, and broad. But he was much bigger than she had imagined. He looked incredibly composed as he strode the six or seven steps it took to join her at the fireplace. The black dinner suit and the white, golf-ball fronted shirt, couldn't have suited him better. He was too big to be Sam's type, but the power and confidence he exuded was magnetic. This was a man who didn't understand barriers. Who could get anything done that he wanted. Nothing got in his way.

But, as he approached, Sam spotted something that had not come through when she had read his file. His face was strong; his features chiselled. He was blond, but not Danish blond – more somewhere between Aryan and mouse; attractive, not shocking. His eyes were blue-green; penetrating. His mouth was wide, his lips thin. The perfect combination for an orator. People would listen to his words and not be put off by the movement of his mouth.

But there was one feature that, unless you were a casual observer, was striking. The right side of his face, around the eye socket, was motionless. He smiled as he approached Sam, but his right eye didn't respond. She spotted his left eye blink; but his right didn't follow suit. If he didn't look so composed, so complete, Sam would have said that he had suffered from a stroke that had affected that side of his face.

She couldn't stop staring.

'Hello, Samantha Green.' Perfect English.

Sokolov held his hand out.

Sam, still bewitched by his right eye (*I must stop staring*), didn't take it. She couldn't shake it.

Sokolov was everything she detested about the current state of the Russian system. Power and money. And men.

The previous communist system had always been morally bankrupt. It showered a lavish lifestyle on those at the top of the tree, and incarcerated and murdered those who stood in its way. But, and it was a huge but, it also provided something for ordinary people: a job; some regular cash; a bit of dignity; self-respect. And that just about worked.

The problem with today's Russian elite was that they didn't give a shit about the proletariat. They were too busy buying up London's most expensive properties; allowing their wives to fly first-class to Shanghai once a month, to be detoxed with tiger bone. And paying for their children's uber-expensive British public school fees with gold bars.

Sam thought that today's Russian politics redefined the adage that 'absolute power corrupts absolutely'. That was written when people aspired to become part of a defined political elite, and when they got there, the smell of power perverted even the most resolute of men. The problem in Moscow today was that power could be easily bought; there was so much money sloshing about, it was swapping hands like cigarette cards. For these people, new to riches beyond their dreams, they were surprised by their new-found influence. Money could buy you a Bugatti Veyron in any first-world country. Here, in Moscow, it could buy you a seat at the top table. No matter who you were.

You didn't need to be a politician to yield power. You just had to buy one.

Sokolov was one such man. And his influence was at the highest table. He was bright – Cambridge educated, and then back to Russia to join the KGB where he befriended the current premier. Rising quickly through the ranks, he was in a position of considerable influence when the Iron Curtain fell. And with a degree in economics, he had seized failing Russian industries that had come to the market cheaply as the country denationalised its precious assets. Like most oligarchs, he dismantled what he had bought, keeping the prizes, depleting and discarding its loyal workforce, and then selling what was left. Commodities were his thing: gold, precious stones, oil and gas, bauxite, iron and coal. His file gave a conservative view of his wealth at $25.9 billion. He had property in London, Berlin, Shanghai, New York and Aspen. And a superyacht berthed at Sevastopol. He was on his third wife, who was a 29-year-old Slovakian supermodel. It was all in his file.

And now he was attempting to shake Sam's hand.

She stared impassively at him. Nonplussed. The alcohol had deadened her senses. She felt safe here. On British soil. Stood next to, probably, the second or third most important man in Russia. The man who, via some thugs, had pursued her. And, at least once, had tried to kill her.

No, she wasn't going to shake his hand.

He withdrew it, but didn't show any sign of being put out.

'Well, that's not very friendly, Samantha Green.'

Why has he got to keep using my full name?

He continued. 'Look, I'm busy at the moment.' He glanced over his shoulder. 'I have to get back to your Foreign Secretary. He's a nice man, if easily charmed by younger women – maybe you and he should get together?'

Sam stared at him. Not a word.

'Sorry, how rude of me. That wasn't called for. I should get back. My friends and colleagues may think it strange that I am spending so much time with you; a simple case-officer with Secret Intelligence Service.'

Still nothing. Impassiveness was currently Sam's middle name.

Sokolov sighed.

'Well, I know you've had a busy weekend, visiting here and there. And I know that you think you've done some good.' He let that hang for a split second. 'If I might offer some advice.' Sokolov's face changed at that point. The charming, if slightly lop-sided, facade broke. All his features hardened. His lips became so tight that Sam thought they might crack. He teeth were clenched, which made his cheekbones lift.

He's on the edge?

'You don't understand what you are messing with, Samantha Green.' He lowered his voice and brought his mouth close to her ear. Her head moved slightly away in protest, but she didn't flinch. He smelt of expensive cologne; his breath mint fresh.

With one hand in front of her face he whispered. 'You have this one chance to pull back. Any more interference and I will snap you in two.' He clicked his fingers – *easy as that*. 'And don't flatter yourself that anyone would care. You are worth nothing.'

Sokolov pulled back.

He was smiling again now. Composure regained.

'Be careful what you wish for, Samantha ...'

And then he was gone.

Sam stayed calm. She watched Sokolov make his way through the double doors on her left, in the direction of the bar. She looked across to where he had started his journey – to the small group, which included the Foreign Secretary. M was staring at her, a look of consternation on his face.

Sam didn't alter her flat expression. She closed both eyes in a slow blink, as if to wake herself up from a dream. And then she quickly made her way to the ladies' loos.

She picked the first available cubicle, went in, closed the door, and threw up in the bowl; then she retched again.

She reached for some tissue, wiped her mouth, opened the door and found a basin. A woman she didn't recognise looked at her sympathetically.

'Bad prawn,' Sam uttered as she patted her stomach.

She gargled some water to get the taste of vomit from her mouth. It was hardly ladylike, but she was beyond caring.

She took out her work mobile and opened her secure mail. She pressed 'Compose', and typed 'Vlad' into the 'To' box. Vladislav Mikhailov's email address filled the space. She typed:

Vlad. Can we meet first thing tomorrow? After today's meeting I don't think we're being proactive enough with regard to Op S. I've had nothing positive back from London, but I do have some thoughts on how to proceed. Let me know. I can be with you by 8am. Sam

She pressed 'Send'.

Chapter 10

4th Floor, British Embassy, Moscow

Sam was back in the office by 6.30am. She'd agreed to meet with Vlad at the Lubyanka at 10.30. And she had a lot to do before then.

The rest of the evening had been a blur. Regardless of M's edict that all his staff should stay until the final whistle, her one-sided exchange with Sokolov had done for her. She had walked out of the front door of the Embassy, taken the first taxi she had come across, waltzed into her apartment, and then had thrown up again when she reread the threat on her fridge door. Thankfully the kitchen sink was close by.

Feeling slightly better, she had put a cheese sandwich together, made a promise to herself that she wouldn't drink again (*until the next time*), showered, brought her alarm clock forward to 5.30am, and slept soundly until it woke her.

No one was in the office this early. That was good.

She needed some time to bring everything together. She had to meet Vlad with a plan. Her text to him last night said that she had some thoughts about how to proceed. She hadn't; she needed a deadline to provide focus to the whole project. Vlad had replied in the early hours of the morning (she was flat out; *what was he doing up at that time?*) – he'd be free at 10.30. And, yes please, they really needed some inspiration.

Sam collected a pad of A2 paper from the stationery cupboard and laid it out on a large table in one of the organisation's meeting rooms. She started to sketch out in big writing what she had:

- <u>*Fracking*</u>.

- *MSF report yet to be seen. Must look out for it. <u>Action</u>: Me and Debbie.*
- *Debbie chasing* ExtraOil's *non-Russian businesses. Looking primarily at Alaska and California. <u>Action</u>. Debbie.*
- *Frank waiting for* ExtraOil *brief from me. Jane promises London will look into detail. <u>Action</u>: pen brief for Frank today.*

- <u>*Sokolov*</u>.

- *Orange marker on file. Operates with impunity. Both Jane and M instruct layoff. (These two are <u>not</u> in cahoots. Their ambitions are different? Jane protecting Orange maker? M and Sokolov close after scene last night?)*

- *Threat widespread. Bogdan Kuznetsov works for Sokolov - Tesla hit and run? Iosif Ergorov (US most-wanted list) aka Blue Suit. Murdered Alexei Orlov over* ExtraOil *connection. Me too?*

- *Two thugs in Salekhard. Nothing from Cynthia. Nothing yet back from US/Interpol via Frank. Has he let up after direction from Jane? <u>Action:</u> Must check with Frank.*

Sam drew a goose egg around the word *ExtraOil*.

She continued.

- *Who has the capability track SIS case-officers and enter their apartments. SIS link? Rich?*

At that point she realised she was casting aspersions in the very offices where she thought there might be illicit support. She dashed back out to the stationery cupboard and grabbed herself a black whiteboard maker. In no time at all '*SIS link?* and *'Rich?'* had been expurgated by its thick ink.

It was a good thing that she had. At that point, Rich stuck his head round the door.

'Hi, Sam. Early doors?'

'Yes, Rich, you know how it is. Still buzzing from last night's fabulous party.'

'How's your head?' He asked playfully.

'It would be better if you happened to be making some coffee.'

He took the hint and disappeared.

She had a quick glance down at what she had so far. Nothing inspiring. Just as she was about to continue, Debbie came in.

'Hi Sam. Is this something I can help with?'

Sam didn't need to think for long.

'Of course, Debbie. Come in and take a seat. Let me explain what we have so far.'

She talked Debbie through the diagram.

'Happy?'

'Yes. And I have something from the US on *ExtraOil*. Do you want to hear it now?'

'Sure. I'll scribe on the paper – here.' Sam pointed to a space right of the Fracking title. As Debbie briefed Sam, she summarised:

- ExtraOil *owns US start-up* CleanDrilling *(CD). CD has rights to drill in Beethal, W Alaska.*

- CD *also has secured rights to frack in Crestline, NE of Los Angeles. Preliminary bores have been sunk. Federal Energy Regulatory Commission (FERC) due to inspect sight later this month. Industrial fracking could begin as early as three weeks.*

'And there are no other equivalent projects in the US?' Sam asked.

'No, I don't think so. I've had this checked out by a senior oil exploration engineer at Imperial College, London. It's where the best of the best in the UK go to study. He reckons that *CleanDrilling* were lucky to get the authority to frack that close to the major conurbation of San Bernardino, a suburb of LA.'

'So, we have about a month before a good chunk of the LA watercourse could be polluted with radium?' Sam asked.

'Possibly. I asked the chap in Imperial if he would expect higher levels of radium, and similar, to be a by-product of drilling in Alaska. Like they have at Salekhard. He phoned me back late yesterday afternoon. He wasn't conclusive, but it seems likely that the geology of Arctic Alaska is equivalent to that in northern Siberia.'

'Wow. Great work, Debbie. Thanks. We need to decide what to do with this.'

Sam scribed a huge '?' next to Fracking.

Rich came in with Sam's coffee. He stopped and looked at the A2 sheet.

'Coffee for Debbie as well, please, Rich. Thanks.'

He raised his eyes to the ceiling and wandered out again.

Surely, he's not the one dobbing in on me?

'Now the big one.'

On a new sheet of A2, Sam scribed again.

- *Op Samantha*.

- *30 kg of Ur 235 etc missing, stolen under the orders of Capt Mikhailov. Whereabouts unknown.*
- *Mikhailov in likely deal with Osama bin Fahd, 3rd son of the Saudi Prince Khalid bin Fahd.*
- *Target - European city?*
- *…*

Sam stopped herself. Without comment to Debbie, she folded the original paper and placed it on a chair.

Rich came back in with two cups of coffee.

'One for you, Debbie. And one for me. Carry on, Sam.'

She continued.

- *Nothing from London on Saudi connection. <u>Action</u>. Check with Frank first thing.*

Sam checked her watch. It was 7.25pm. Frank was unlikely to be in for another hour and a half.

'Debbie, did you get anything yesterday from GCHQ?'

'No, nothing of use. They tell me that "listening in" on the Saudi Royal family is very sensitive. I've tasked them using the op code you gave me. My pal there has said that he would need further clearance either from M, or Jane Baker, before he went to work. I spoke to M yesterday evening, just before you lot went off gallivanting; he gave me his signature for this. We might have something back later today.'

'Brilliant work, Debbie.'

Sam looked across at Rich, who was sipping his coffee. She paused. Her pen wavering above the paper.

She left a gap and started scribing again. As she did, she said, 'Let's put ourselves in the minds of the terrorist.'

Target - Maximum Impact.

- *Germany: Berlin, Frankfurt, Bonn.*

Rich spoke. 'Stick down Hamburg and Köln.'

Sam did as he asked.

- *France: Paris, Marseilles, Toulouse, Nice, Lyon.*
- *Poland: Warsaw.*

'Why Poland?' Debbie asked.

'Because, if the bomb is being moved by vehicle, they'd want to carry it as short a distance as possible. Less chance of detection at borders.' Sam raised the top of her pen to her mouth and chewed on it absently, 'That's a point. Let's have another go at this.'

Sam pushed the piece of paper to one side and took out another. From memory she quickly drew a pretty accurate map of Europe and western Russia. She marked in the capital cities of the major countries. She, again freehand, drew five concentric arcs from Moscow, spreading out across Europe. Warsaw was easily the closest capital. Next were: Berlin, Prague, Vienna, Budapest and Bucharest.

'Which one of those would you hit?'

'Berlin. An obvious choice,' was Rich's reply. 'The centre of the European project, with a Chancellor who is struggling to maintain unity in her country. Bomb Berlin and the far right in every country in Europe would take to the streets. The EU would collapse. It's one helluva target. And, by the way, you've forgotten Helsinki and Stockholm. They're within the first arc.'

Sam let Rich's point sink in.

'I'm not convinced by a Scandinavian target. But I take your point about Berlin.' She underlined it twice. 'What about the next closest bunch: Amsterdam, Brussels, Bern and Sofia?'

Debbie raised her hand by way of interruption.

'Go on Debbie.'

'If they're going to go for a European capital, then Berlin is the only choice. It ticks impact and distance. If we have limited resources, we should focus on Berlin. However, I like a previous comment from you Sam, about Frankfurt: the Bankenviertel. Irradiate Europe's banking hub and the fall out, excuse my pun, would be huge. That's close enough, and a second choice. But if we're after maximum impact, let's think global, rather than European. Shouldn't we be looking at religious targets?'

Sam breathed out. Rich scratched his head.

'You mean Jerusalem?' Sam said.

'What about the Vatican?' Rich added.

Sam tapped her pen on the paper in thought.

'OK. both good choices, although both would be a struggle to reach by vehicle – especially Jerusalem – there are too many borders, fences, and men with guns... They'd have to get through Turkey, Syria and Lebanon.' She loosely pointed at the route with her pen. 'But, of course, if 9/11 is anything to go by they could just fly it in – crash the plane on a site of their choosing.'

'Although,' Rich added, 'if you wanted to guarantee success, I'm not convinced you'd risk an air assault. This is easily the biggest attack since 9/11, the event which prised open this holy war. Crashing planes into cities isn't as straightforward as it used to be.'

Sam interrupted. 'Not in a commercial airliner. But maybe a Lear? The Saudis have squadrons of those?'

'Still not guaranteed,' Rich added. 'And an aircraft leaves a trace, no matter how disintegrated it is. If I were the terrorist, I'd want a cast-iron target with a cast-iron approach. And if there is a Saudi connection, I'd be very keen *not* to leave my fingerprints on it. A truck or car is best for that.'

'OK.' She'd got enough for now. She then scribbled down:

- *How to steal and transport some Ur235.*

'How did they do it; and where would you keep it?'

They spent the next 15 minutes talking through the opportunities and possibilities. It felt good to have Debbie and Rich working, literally, off the same sheet of paper. She was just about to bring the whole thing to a close when M walked in.

They all went silent.

'Don't stop for me, you lot. Carry on.'

Sam summed up where they'd got to.

M took the stage.

'Good work. As you say, key to this is establishing and then exploiting the Saudi connection. That includes finding the submariner – as, according to you Green, they were the last people to see him. He may lead you to the bomb. And, second, getting close to the Fahds – and the al Qaeda connection. Someone there knows the intended target. Conventionally, you and the FSB have little chance of finding the uranium in Russia. Nor catching it as it crosses the border. Unless you are very lucky. Chase the Saudis. They're the key.'

Sam couldn't fault M's logic (although she was put off by him playing with something in his trouser pockets. *Yuck.*). She supposed that you didn't get to become head of section without knowing a thing or two about intelligence gathering and how terrorists operate.

'Are we onto Riyadh?' he asked.

'Yes. Both via our Embassy and GCHQ. I think we should also press Kabul and Tehran to see if they have anything,' Sam added.

'Do that, Green. Do that.'

At that point M seemed to lose interest and left the room, his hands still thrust deep into his pockets. As he waltzed through the main office, Sam could hear him whistling 'They're changing guards at Buckingham Palace'.

Huh?

'Thanks a lot, both of you; that really helped. I'm meeting with the FSB in...' Sam checked her watch, 'just under two hours. I'll speak to Tehran and I have a pal in Kabul. Keep thinking. Debbie, can we get together at 9.45am for a quick update on where we are?'

'Sure, Sam, sure.'

All three of them went back to their desks, Sam clutching the paper she had scribbled on.

There was no doubt that tasking whatever assets they had in Saudi Arabia was an essential slice of this. Jane should be onto Riyadh; GCHQ were on the case via Debbie. In the next half hour she'd talk to Julie in Kabul, and the appropriate desk officer in Tehran. They might have something. This was very much the British avenue – and the thing she'd been asked to pursue by the FSB.

For their bit, the FSB would be scouring their huge country for a chunk of highly radioactive fuel, small enough to fit into a large suitcase. And tracking down an errant submariner.

There was one further approach. The Saudis knew the target, and the delivery method. The Russians were searching for the material. Currently, no one was looking for the gauleiter. To Sam, Captain Mikhailov was a pawn. On the face of it, he had secured the uranium; he had the opportunity, the shipyard connections and the motive. He was also the ideal front man in Saudi. The Saudis respected military rank as much as they did money.

But he couldn't have pulled this off without a kingpin. A puppet master. Someone with vision, reach, confidence. And political influence. Sam understood military rank. And she'd been in Russia long enough to know how much clout a Captain 1st Class had in their own country. It wasn't much. He might just be able to secure a table at *The Turandot* – provided he booked early enough, and didn't mind a spot by the kitchen. There was no way he could have pulled off the heist of the decade – not without leaving traces of radioactive material leading all the way to his dacha.

He did, however, have some nasty and expensive habits. He could be easily bought. The ideal frontman for an operation that would be worth, who knows how much money? Tens of millions. Maybe much more. And he was the perfect fall guy if things went wrong. Cut the strings of the puppet, and let it fall.

No. Sam was clear. Someone was ultimately running the show And, as Vlad had intimated – this had Sokolov's fingerprints all over it.

So, that's where she intended to look.

44° 58' 09"N, 31° 18' 44"E, Somewhere in the Black Sea

Holly couldn't stop poking at her broken tooth with her tongue. It ached. She'd drunk some of the orange juice that had been brought in with breakfast on the silver tray this morning. The shock of the cold drink on the exposed nerve had made her eyes water. She hadn't cried though. She wasn't going to give these people the satisfaction of seeing her cry.

Last night was more horrific than she could have ever imagined. When she had come around from, she guessed, the chloroform (that's what they used in the films?), she hadn't been so groggy that she couldn't lash out. By the time they'd taken the straps from around her legs, the guy who spoke perfect English had got a knee in the groin; he was bent double for a bit. The other guy, who didn't say anything – but who looked more Turkish, or at least Balkan, than properly western – had wrestled her to the ground and tied her up again. She was gagged so couldn't make any noise, but she certainly wasn't going to come peacefully.

They had manhandled her onto a small rib, and the next thing she knew they were moored at the back of a superyacht out in the Bosporus; the boat must have been over 200 feet long. With her hands and legs tied, she made what protestations she could, but it wasn't enough to prevent the Englishman from throwing her over his shoulder, carrying her on board, and then unceremoniously dumping her in one of the forward cabins, removing her constraints. It was opulent, there was no doubt about that. Her daddy knew some people with large motorboats, and she'd been lucky enough to be asked on one for lunch last summer. That was grand – but this was palatial.

After she had attempted to open the doors and the porthole (with no success), she sat on the luxurious king-sized bed and had tried to piece together what was happening. Were they after money? She thought that unlikely. The boat must be worth $100 million – her daddy might be a congressman, but he'd just struggle to find $1 million, and that's only if they sold the small family home in Tampa. Were they hoping to pull some political lever? Unlikely. Whilst it infuriated her, Congressman *Chad Mickelson* stood for the middle ground. Everything from the gun laws, to abortion, and even the invasion of Iraq, Congressman Chad somehow or other managed to please both sides of the debate. She wasn't here because her daddy might force a bill through the House.

But soon it all became clear. Crystal clear.

Not long after the men had dumped her, a woman resembling Berta from *Two and a Half Men*, but with a sharp, unpleasant Russian accent, came into the cabin. She ordered Holly to undress. Holly had refused. The woman had tipped her head to one side, as if to say, 'I warned you,' and then with strength that Holly couldn't fathom, had stripped her of her clothes. At one point, Holly had managed to get her fingernails into the woman's arm and drawn blood. In reaction, the woman had held her down with one hand, and swung her free hand into the area of Holly's kidneys. The pain was excruciating. She was a flaccid doll after that.

Between then and when she had eventually fallen asleep, the ensuing horror was too acute to recall in any detail. The man who raped her was big – ugly, almost deformed-looking with bent teeth, a wonky eye and jug ears. And strong. She had fought him with all her might, but it had been hopeless. Whatever she tried to do to resist, her actions only appeared to excite him more. He wasn't on top of her for very long, but it seemed like forever. Once finished, he picked up his clothes and walked to the door.

Holly sensed an opportunity. Even though she was naked, and devoid of strength which had been sucked out of her by the abuse, she launched herself at his back. If she could get past him, out through the door and up the stairs, she might be able to throw herself off the side? She was a strong swimmer. Even in her current state, a mile would be well within her abilities.

Smack!

He must have sensed her rushing toward him. He turned quickly for a big man, his fist finding the centre of her chest, stopping her in her tracks. She spun round, falling uncontrollably in the direction of a white and gold dressing table. Her mouth hit the corner of the furniture and she heard a *crack* as one of her incisors broke in half. The fist to the chest had forced the wind from her lungs and her heart went into spasm. She lay gasping for air on all fours, blood pouring from her mouth and onto the cream, deep-pile carpet.

He turned to walk out.

'You bastard!' It was a quiet call, between shallow breaths. Blood projecting with the words, spreading red splatters on the carpet further than the initial pool between her hands. It was all she could manage.

The man turned back and faced her. He held his clothes in front of his groin, like an embarrassed schoolkid on his first day in the boys' communal changing rooms.

He looked confused. Exposed. Weak.

And then he turned back toward the door and left, the crunching of the tumblers in the lock a clear indication that there was no way out.

'He's no more than a child?' Holly said under her breath. A pang of sympathy momentarily floated in her mind – she couldn't stop herself. And then it was gone.

She had washed thoroughly in the huge bathtub and was presented with some biscuits and cocoa at about 10pm by Berta; the whole thing was incredulous – too bizarre to contemplate. Berta, who was carrying a tray, stopped where the blood had stained the carpet. She looked across at Holly and sighed.

'Don't fight. You won't win.' The accent was horribly harsh.

After a second bath, she had slept fitfully, and woken with a clear determination to find a way out; or at least communicate with the outside world. Berta had brought in breakfast, some cleaning fluid and a cloth. She had made Holly get onto her knees (still naked) and mop up her own blood. The carpet was remarkably easy to clean. It was obviously very expensive.

While she was scrubbing the pile, Holly had tried to strike up a conversation. Asking Berta simple questions like 'what's your name?' and 'who do you work for?' Nothing was forthcoming. And then she left, leaving Holly, still naked but well fed, sat on a bed dressed with clean, satin sheets. Playing with her broken tooth.

It was strange, but the abuse, while unmentionable, didn't register. Her brain had shut it away somewhere. She knew she hated every second of it and felt violated beyond words. But she didn't dwell on it. And she wasn't scared. All of it made her stronger and more determined. She was surprised at how together she felt.

She had to think of a way out. If this was going to be the way it was, then an opportunity would present itself. She was intelligent; more intelligent than the delinquent who was using her as a sex toy. And probably brighter than Berta.

All she had to do was think. And plan. And then act.

4th Floor, British Embassy, Moscow

Sam had finished the email brief on the *ExtraOil* op and had sent it to Frank. She added Debbie's contribution reference *CleanDrilling*, and had taken a couple of photos of Jim Dutton's notebook, showing all the key bits of info. She'd finished by asking Frank if he had any results on the two mugshots she'd sent. She pressed 'Send', leant back in her chair and thought for a second.

I wonder if London will do anything with this? She'd keep an eye. If they didn't, she had a contact at Langley: a CIA pal of hers she'd met during training. Both organisations run similar agent training – and every year, one or two lucky staff attend the sister course in the other country. It helped breed cross-agency understanding and friendship. Jodie, her SIS-trained CIA mate, would be all over *ExtraOil* and *CleanDrilling* like a dose of measles if Sam asked her. That would do the trick should London decide not to pursue.

Whilst tucking into a pasta salad she'd made last night – it was only 9.05am but it felt like lunchtime – she phoned Julie in Kabul, and then the duty officer in the Tehran. Both agreed to look to their al-Qaeda agents and informants to see if they had any leads. Currently there was nothing on their radars.

She then metaphorically rolled up her sleeves and went to work on what she loved most. Image analysis. It was technically Debbie's role, although the boundaries between the posts had blurred over time. Sam had spent eight years as a photo analyst in the army's Intelligence Corps, and two years doing pretty much the same job in Vauxhall. Once an analyst, always an analyst; and she was pretty good at it.

It was, as it was with all intelligence, a matter of spotting the missing piece of ordinary. What should be there, but wasn't. The trick was not to look for something that shouldn't be there; if your enemy is good enough, you won't see what they don't want to show you. But they might well forget, or ignore, the everyday. In photos, don't look for disturbed earth;

look for where grass should be growing, but wasn't. Don't search CCTV for a missing person; look at the video footage for where the person should have been, but wasn't – and then track down the others in the shot. And, always question a perfect set of company accounts; nobody makes that much effort.

It was all degrees of subtlety. And subtlety was what Sam did best.

How long did she have? She checked her watch again. *Thirty minutes before my meet with Debbie.*

She needed to order some satellite imagery.

The UK got nearly all its satellite imagery from the US. They were easily the world leaders. With over 8,000 satellites orbiting the world, and 100 more joining the throng every year, there were more than enough people taking pictures of the earth. But even with that many, it was a fallacy to believe that you could get real time imagery of anywhere on the earth, at any time. It was also a fallacy if you believed that you could read a paperback held open in someone's hands from space. Cameras weren't yet that good.

However, there were cameras up there that could read the headlines on a broadsheet. Resolutions for still photos, especially after digital enhancement, were now down as low as two centimetres for monochrome shots (ten times larger if you wanted colour); about the size of a thumbnail. Civilian firms, such as GeoEye and DigitalGlobe, could get close to that granularity, but they weren't allowed to sell images with a sharper resolution than 25 centimetres. If they did, the US government would shut them down. And their CEOs would go to jail. Without passing 'Go'.

As for real time, you needed a good slab of luck – that is, the satellite needed to be overhead when you wanted a shot. Or you had to wait for a second or third pass (around every three to five hours, depending on the satellite), and then only after the controller had tweaked the bird's path.

It wasn't yet like *Mission Impossible*.

SIS could task the US for imagery and get 'very recent' photos to two-centimetre resolution within six hours; they held a 14-day old depository that could be accessed that quickly. In the vaults at Langley, they also held satellite imagery from as far back as the 60s, shot on celluloid by the first viable reconnaissance satellite, HEXAGON – or colloquially known as Big Bird; it was the size of a school bus. This satellite took outstanding photographs from 370 miles up, to resolutions in the order of 60 centimetres. The rolls of film were ejected from the satellite, and fell to earth, landing softly in the Pacific Ocean near Hawaii, via the aid of a parachute. It is said that HEXAGON's work during the Cuban Missile Crisis had saved the planet from World War 3.

Probably in deference to its success, the US still referred to their current satellites as 'Big Birds'.

In short, if you wanted a decent, near time overhead, the US would deliver (in SIS's case, via Langley). It cost about $100 for one US mile square, but Sam had an op code, which meant she had a budget. With a credit limit that made her eyes water.

Of course, Op Samantha was an FSB op. And the

Russians had their own reconnaissance satellites. But, as was the case with most of their high-end equipment, it was neither up-to-date, nor well maintained. They would have photos; but they wouldn't be as good as the ones Sam could get.

When dealing with the FSB Sam was also stymied by rules. The US provided detailed imagery to the UK on an 'EYES-ONLY' basis. This meant that Sam couldn't share the high-res photos with Vlad, or any member of the FSB. But she could share the intelligence she had gleaned from the images, and use less resolved photos to paint the picture. She'd procured US images for Op Michael, the drugs op. She'd found the alternative route, which the drugs had eventually followed, by initially analysing the high-res imagery from Langley. However, when she was fruitlessly explaining her findings to the FSB team, she had shown them a grainier image. She wasn't surprised when the line, 'Can't you see what I'm seeing – look, here?' got lost in the poor quality of the photographs.

She'd need to apply the same approach with the images she was just about to order. It was a cross she'd have to bear.

Sam opened the mapping app on Cynthia. She zoomed in on the Sevmash military shipyard in Severodvinsk. She acquainted herself with the layout, swiping her screen left and right so she could take in the size of the establishment. She picked out Number 2 Shed where the TK-202 was being decommissioned. She then highlighted ten grid squares and opened a drop-down box. She needed to get the timings right. She checked her notes from yesterday's meeting.

When was Captain Mikhailov declared missing? *Got it – two weeks ago Monday. Now, let's select every day, mid-afternoon, for the previous 21 days.* That might throw up an anomaly.

Next to Sokolov. She knew she couldn't open his file – an alert would sound somewhere and she'd be on the first plane home. But, she didn't need to open the file. She remembered it all.

Using the map app again, she found his residences in central Moscow, his dacha in Novo-Ogaryovo, his office complex in Moscow's White Square, his Park Lane apartment in London and… – she scratched her chin as she searched her memory for the detail – the berth of his 230-foot superyacht, *Cressida*, in Sevastopol. It wouldn't have surprised Sam if Russia hadn't annexed Crimea just so Sokolov's floating gin palace could be berthed on Russian soil. *Maybe they'll invade Latvia next?* She knew he had an ocean-going mega-yacht being built in Hamburg, Germany. Every oligarch worth his salts needed a permanent Russian-owned berth on the Baltic Sea. And, as St Petersburg was so 'last-year' for the nouveau-riche, Vilnius might just be the next best thing.

She also had the addresses of Bogdan Kuznetsov, the Tesla hit-and-run man. He was a known Sokolov associate. She bagged an image of those as well.

Timings? When do I want these overheads?

As close to now as you could get it, would be a good place to start. And taken just before dusk (she checked dawn and dusk timings on Google); every day for the past 21 days – as per the shipyard. *Perfect. Hang on*. And, as for the future, every eight hours from 4pm today for the next seven days. The night-time shots would be taken with an infrared camera and the pixel resolution would be much poorer. But it would give them something.

Sam topped and tailed the e-requisition form, including adding Debbie to the distribution, and pressed 'Send'. She received an immediate email alert from Langley telling her the photos would be with her within around six hours. Cost = $14,450.

Bargain.

She sensed Debbie at her shoulder.

'Hi Sam, it's 9.45. You wanted to meet?'

'Yes, thanks Debbie, pull up a chair. What have you got?'

She opened her notebook.

'Nothing on *ExtraOil* and *CleanDrilling*. I'm assuming you're leaving that to London now?'

Sam nodded.

'GCHQ have come back. They have a team of three SIGINT analysts looking over all the recent tapes they have from the section of the Saudi royal family that we're interested in. They have also managed to put an intercept bubble on Prince Khalid bin Fahd's estate, in a suburb of Riyadh – where Capt Mikhailov was last spotted. As at 7am this morning, there were 397 separate mobile traces in the space the size of half a football pitch. They're monitoring those. They don't think they can do any better than that, unless you have a specific number.'

'No, but that's a point. I wonder if the FSB have Mikhailov's mobile number, although he'd be an idiot if he's using it? I'll check with Vlad when I see him. Anything else?'

'No. You?'

'No. Since I sent the *ExtraOil* brief to Frank, I've spoken to Kabul and Tehran. They're on the case. And I've ordered some imagery, actually $15,000 worth of imagery – from Langley. I've granted you access to the lot. Now…' Sam drew her breath. 'I've got some photos coming of the estates/residences of Nikolay Sokolov and a man called Bogdan Kuznetsov. The latter works for the former. You've heard of Sokolov?'

'Yes, of course! Rumour has it, that Robbie William's track *Party Like A Russian* was inspired by him. Doesn't everyone know that?'

'Oh dear…' Sam raised her eyes to the ceiling. She was feeling old, even at 34.

She continued. 'Don't ask any questions. Just trust me when I tell you that there might be a linkage here to the op. And, please don't have this discussion with anyone else; nor analyse the images when someone might be looking over your shoulder. Are you happy with that? If not, I can take you off the distribution.'

Debbie looked perplexed.

'Am I going to be breaking any rules by looking at the photos?'

Sam thought for a second.

'No more than you were when you continued to investigate *ExtraOil*, when I had been pulled off the case.'

Debbie smiled.

'I like you, Sam. You're easily one of the best case-officers in the building. And one of the nicest. If you think this is important, then I'll do it. What am I looking for?'

'30kg of Uranium 235.'

Sam slapped her forehead with her hand.

Bugger! We missed that off the list this morning.

'Actually, that's a point. Get in touch with Porton Down. Get one of their boffins on the case. What would a dirty bomb look like if you had that amount of spent fuel rod to detonate? How would you mask it? How much explosive do you need…?' Sam stopped talking. Debbie had the 'do you think I'm an idiot?' expression on her face. 'Sorry Debbie. You know what we need. But let's get them to prepare some images. And if PD don't play game quickly, and I'm not in the building, get into M's office and ask him to press them hard. We need to know what we're looking for by close of play today. And keep Frank in the loop.'

Debbie was taking notes again.

Sam looked up at the clock on the wall. It was 10.05. She needed to shoot.

'Got to go. Sorry. Keep in touch, please.'

Debbie stood to get out of her way as Sam picked up her rucksack and made a dash for the door.

Chapter 11

The Lubyanka Building, Moscow, Russia

Sam kept an eye on possible tails as she weaved her way to the Lubyanka. Walk-taxi-walk. She knew this was the way it was going to be until, either, she was tied up in a cellar somewhere, or Sokolov was behind bars.

So be it.

Vlad was waiting for her at reception. It took a minute or so to book in. They then made their way up to the fifth floor to a pokey office; it had room for just a desk, which was placed against the far wall, a filing cabinet and a couple of chairs. If there were a view from the only window, you wouldn't know; it needed a good clean.

'Coffee?' Vlad asked.

'Yes, please.'

Behind the door there was a small fridge, a kettle and

some containers. The fridge, the kettle and, what looked like Vlad's computer and screen, were all powered by the same socket. Sam looked for smoke detectors. There were none. It was a catastrophic fire waiting to happen. Such was her attention to detail, that if she wasn't a spy, she'd make a great health and safety inspector. No wonder she didn't have many friends.

They made small talk as the kettle boiled, and then they both sat down, their knees almost touching as the chairs struggled to find appropriate space. Vlad's desk was small and covered in paperwork. But it was tidy. The screensaver was a selfie of him, Sam guessed his wife, and two children. There was sea in the background.

'The Black Sea?' Sam pointed at the screen.

Vlad lowered his mug and turned to look at what Sam was pointing at.

'Yes. Last year. That's my wife, Alyona, and our two kids. It's Volkonka – on the coast. A great holiday – nowhere near long enough. It's always the case, don't you find?'

That wasn't a great question. Sam didn't do time off well. In the short break between finishing her language training in Lithuania and her arrival in Moscow, she'd revisited the island of Mull in Scotland; and, in particular, the island of Iona. There, five years ago, two ex-CIA thugs had set fire to her campervan and what remained of her meagre existence. Since that point, her life had been a rollercoaster – with many more downs than there had been ups. Actually, a rollercoaster was an inadequate metaphor. More like a game of snakes and ladders, with a handful of three-rung ladders, and a vipers' nest full of genetically enhanced snakes.

Mull had been a mistake. She was hoping to find some final closure to the death of Chris, the only man she had ever loved; stolen from her by a Taliban mortar round what seemed like an eternity ago. There was no closure. Just a load of recurring, rubbish memories: Sierra Leone; the Ebola incident; Uncle Pete's death in the Alps; and she and her German colleague, Wolfgang, being chased around Europe like a pair of pheasants on a Sunday morning shoot in the Cotswolds.

She hadn't stayed long in Scotland.

Instead, she'd spent the rest of that break in London with an old Army pal of hers, Linda, watching far too many West End musicals and drinking a bit too much red wine. But, she had kept herself fit. Running across Clapham Common every day, purging the alcohol, and some of the memories. By the time she got on the plane to Moscow she was level again. Just.

She envied Vlad. Probably more than anyone else she knew. He had a decent job. He seemed happily married, and had kids. He even went on holidays to the seaside. What was wrong with her? Why wasn't she married with kids? When was the last time she went to the beach and ate an ice cream?

Vlad seemed to sense that, albeit briefly, Sam was a bit lost.

'You OK?'

Sam looked at him.

Godalming Library

Customer ID: ****069

Items that you have borrowed

Title: Minute I saw you
ID: 11233234
Due: 29 October 2020

Total items: 1
Account balance: £0.00
08/10/2020 10:12
Borrowed 1
Overdue: 0
Reservation requests: 1
Ready for collection: 0

Thank you for visiting us today

At that point, more than anything, she wanted to open up to this kind Russian. A man, who, on more than one occasion, had told her to 'be careful'. Was he the only person she knew who was looking out for her?

Then Sokolov's face burst into her psyche. She smelt him again; that cologne – the mouthwash. Clean – but filthy at the same time. Her stomach gave an involuntary lurch and then it settled.

Sam touched Vlad's knee.

'I'm fine. Thanks Vlad. There's a lot going on up here…' She pointed to her head. 'Not all of it is a great deal of fun.'

'You should take a break?'

Sam smiled.

'No, Vlad. We have 30kg of uranium to find. And, if I get my way, an oligarch to depose.'

It was his turn to smile.

'OK, Sam, what have you got.'

She explained what she, Rich and Debbie had spent the first part of the morning pulling together. She was waiting for potential SIGINT from GCHQ looking into Saudi connections. And that SIS were squeezing their agents in the same country, as well as Iran and Afghanistan.

After his previous suggestion that Sokolov might be part of this, she outlined her theory of Sokolov's involvement. And then expanded on Captain 1st Rank Mikhailov's role as his aide to procuring the spent nuclear fuel. Of the captain being the frontman in

Saudi, and the fall guy if things went wrong. And, on the back of those presumptions, that she had ordered some imagery of Sokolov's and Bogdan Kuznetsov premises, as well as multiple shots of the shipyard.

'We think the likely targets are Berlin, Frankfurt and, if you use a Lear Jet, Jerusalem and the Vatican.'

Vlad thought for a second. He looked at Sam over the rim of his coffee mug.

'Good work. But strike off Jerusalem. The Al-Aqsa mosque in the city is the third holiest Sunni site after the al-Haram in Mecca and the al-Nabawi in Medina. It's a stone's throw from Temple Mount, which I'm guessing you might think is a target. The terrorists couldn't afford that sort of collateral. In any case, Al-Qaeda wouldn't risk an attack on Temple Mount, because, whilst it's the centre of Judaism, and thus a spectacular target, it is also a celebrated Muslim mosque. Sorry, I'm just not convinced. But, I do agree with your choices of Berlin and Frankfurt. Our list also included Vienna. It's a tourist hub, and the right wing are very strong in Austria. It wouldn't take much to set them off.

'Also, we've found Mikhailov's mobile. It had been retrieved from a ditch at Moscow airport by a passer-by, who thought all his Christmases had come at once – it was an iPhone 6. They had started to use it. Unfortunately for them, they got a visitation from friends of ours at the SVR, who tell me that they won't be paying for his new front door. Anyway, it seems likely that the phone had been discarded by Mikhailov before he got on a plane to Riyadh. So, we are no further forward in tracing him.'

'Are you covering your borders?'

'Yes. We have the major ones alerted and our border guards have Geiger counters on hand that should pick up stray radiation. Their instructions are to check every fifth car and every second truck. It's a long shot, made longer by the fact that any self-respecting terrorist would use a lead car and alert the carrier to any checks at the border. If I were them, I'd keep probing crossings until I found an open one. We also can't discount the bribing of border guards, nor high-level political influence – allowing packages to cross unchecked. It is the way it is here, I'm afraid.'

Vlad had a resigned look on his face.

Sam helped. 'By close of play I should have a mock-up of a potential bomb; images, the lot. At least then your people will have a better idea of what they are looking for.'

'Do you think the device will be assembled in country?'

'Likely, don't you think? If it's a Russian-based op, the expertise and infrastructure would be in-country. If I were the Saudis, I wouldn't buy a bomb that was in multiple parts. I'm guessing we're talking a price tag of $10-15 million. I'd put my best man on the inspection, to make sure I was getting what I was paying for. To me, that smacks of a job that needs to be done here.' Sam pointed to the ground to make a point.

'What's the timeframe?' Vlad asked.

'I'm not sure. Let's see what our people in the UK come back with, as to how they would make it. We've lost at least a week already. It may take a further week to build the device; a week to ship it? We have a couple of weeks, probably less – if they work to a tight schedule. If not, who knows?'

'OK, thanks. My team have already got pretty decent satellite imagery of Number 2 shed over the past 14 days. It's periodic, not complete. But it's something. We have analysts looking at that now to see if we can pick up any clues. And, yesterday, our small detachment in Severodvinsk interviewed most of the staff that were involved with the decommissioning – so far there's nothing in the transcripts that gives us anything to work with.'

'Do you have the question set?' Sam asked.

Vlad turned to his keyboard and, after a couple of keystrokes, what looked like interview transcripts appeared on the screen.

'Help yourself.'

Sam moved the keyboard so that she could use it.

With a speed that seemed to alarm Vlad, she scrolled quickly through the first set of interview notes. Then the second.

She stopped.

'How can you do that?' Vlad asked, the incredulity undisguised in his voice.

'What?' Sam was confused.

'Look at, maybe, 40 sheets of notes in less than a minute and expect to make sense of it all?'

Sam smiled. 'It's a knack.' She didn't elaborate. 'Look, Vlad. These are the wrong questions.' She paused. 'Sorry. These aren't all the right questions.'

'What?'

'Sure. You have to press the people on the ground for any accounting discrepancy during the decommissioning process. Look for links and fissures between the staff and Mikhailov. Accomplices. But, having read two sets of interviews, there is nothing here to go on. Either: they know nothing; or, the few that are involved are well rehearsed and covering each other's backs.'

Her assertions had knocked Vlad back. He didn't look overly happy.

'So, what questions would SIS ask?' He spat it out.

Sam realised that she had been too pushy. Too forthright. She'd have to work harder with her one key ally.

'We're focusing too much effort here on the wrong man – Mikhailov. This isn't a bank robbery. It's not been undertaken by a bunch of gangsters, who broke in in the middle of the night and stole some gold bars. If it was, your people would have found something already. This is top-down fraud. Organised and affected by people, or someone, with the highest authority. Mikhailov is key because he knows his ship inside out. He's lived in it for...?'

'Five years.' Vlad completed Sam's sentence.

'But, authority to release the fuel has come from outside the organisation via the very top of the shipyard. From Sokolov, or someone on his bankroll. Of course, the interviewers need to ask if anyone has seen some furtive folk wandering around, slipping uranium into their coat pockets. But, we need to put pressure on the top men – the ones who have the real authority and reach. The shipyard's director – and his second-in-command. Establish a link to Sokolov. Check bank accounts; look for family connections; find which ones of them go to the same parties. Belong to the same club. Which member of the senior team in the shipyard has been on the *Cressida*?'

Vlad looked confused.

'Sokolov's superyacht. Berthed in Sevastopol.'

Sam stopped and let Vlad's cogs turn. She knew she was right. Pressing the decommissioning team hard may throw up a clue as to how the uranium had been stolen – but it was gone now. Establishing the hierarchy behind the crime, and following that route, would give them so much more that was current.

'OK, Sam. That makes some sense. I can get some people onto that now. But I must be careful. In the same way that I was telling you to do the same. Not only is pushing at Sokolov a highly dangerous pastime, we may only have this once chance of nailing him. And I am under strict instructions from the director not to mess this up. We have to have watertight evidence. Otherwise we will have more than Sokolov to answer to.'

Sam stood up. They had talked enough.

'What are you up to?' Vlad asked.

'I want a quick look at your photos of Number 2 Shed, please. I shouldn't need any more than 30 minutes, maybe an hour. That should give you time to get some things together.'

'Things? What things? What are you talking about?' Vlad was on his feet now.

'Overnight things. Hear me out. It's going to be another six to eight hours before we have anything from Saudi, and another couple of hours before my analyst will have had a decent chance to look at the photos I've ordered. The mock-up of the dirty bomb should also be available later, but possibly not until early evening. And I can access all of that on my SIS secure Nexus.' She held up her ruggedised, secure, eight-inch tablet. 'I guess your team can be tasked by phone to get oversight of the senior staff at Severodvinsk?'

Vlad nodded. He was struggling to keep up.

Sam continued as she put her Nexus in her rucksack.

'I don't know about you, but I'm catching the first flight up to the shipyard. Let's waltz right in and start poking around. Get access to the director's office – without him finding the time to rehearse any responses. And press him hard. Then shake the chief finance officer, or whatever his title is. Start at the top and work down. Let's make someone squeak.'

'But, if we assume a Sokolov linkage, the moment we walk out of their offices, he's going to know!'

'Exactly.' Sam stopped and looked at Vlad, and then stared almost through him, to the smudgy window and out to what was a grey and cold autumn day.

She spoke quietly, almost in a whisper. His face had lost some of its previous colour.

'I met him last night. He singled me out at an Embassy party. He walked straight across to me.' She was now looking directly at Vlad; eye to eye. She knew her face was expressionless, as though all feeling had been sucked from her.

'Without flinching, he threatened to kill me – under his breath, but still in front of a hundred people. He was charming – utterly. Except for a few seconds. When our faces were so close they almost touched. Just then, for just a couple of moments, his facade broke and I sensed his weakness. He's clever – yes. Smart – absolutely. Incredibly well connected. And with money that can buy the most influential of favours. But he's arrogant. Cruel. And vicious.' Sam hadn't blinked. Her words were monotone, but were coming straight from her heart.

'Above his expensive aftershave, I could smell anger. Hatred. And with it, fragility. I'm guessing he has never lost anything in his life. He's always been on the winning team. Now, he feels threatened; only a touch. But threatened nonetheless. If we put our finger in the wound, he won't be able to stop himself. He'll lash out.'

She broke the trance. And half-smiled.

'And it's then, just then, when we will be able to access his deepest secrets.'

Vlad didn't say anything for two or three seconds. Sam wasn't sure what was going on in his head. Maybe he thought she was mad – which wouldn't be too far from the truth. Maybe he cherished his current life more than a potential duel with the devil. She got that.

But he needed to tell her.

'I can't just leave the office.' He threw his arms out wide. 'I need authority. I have to sign for a credit card, so I can book flights. I need to tell my family.' He looked fidgety. Unsure.

Sam tipped her head one side. *I'll take that as a 'yes' then.*

'I have a firm's card which has unlimited credit on it; and no restrictions on how I spend it.' (*Actually, I need to account for every penny...*) 'In my book, that means all you have to do is tell your family. And you can do that when you pop home and get your overnight bag. But not before you show me where the photos are.'

Vlad shook his head.

Then he picked up his car keys and wallet from his desk, and led Sam out into the corridor.

Who was this woman, Sam Green? Vlad had absolutely no idea where she would eventually take him. The trip to the shipyard made sense, and he'd go with that – although Alyona would be disappointed by him being away from home again.

But Sam's thing with Sokolov? Or, just as important, his with her? It had obviously become personal, and she'd need to guard against her emotions skewing her many abilities.

She was very good, there was no doubt about that. When she had been posted to Moscow, they'd read her file: the Ebola incident; saving the German chancellor's life; and bringing down the *Kirche des*

Weißen Kreuz. All on her own, if you believed everything in the file. She was immediately placed on the FSB's 'to watch' list.

So, they couldn't believe their luck when she had been assigned to the FSB – rather than be free to poke her nose into their other business, where they'd rather not have SIS company.

He knew that Sokolov had tabs on Sam, and had had for over a week. It was Vlad's job to know as much about Nikolay Sokolov as could be known – without unsettling him. His key informant was a man in the oligarch's inner circle. It was he who had mentioned that Sokolov may have had a part in the theft of the uranium. But he couldn't share that among his team. Sokolov was on 'close-hold'. The file was Operation Magpie; it was available to just Vlad and the director. A file that was potentially bigger than a dirty bomb, or any other illicit activity that Sokolov might have his fingers all over.

So, when he'd been tipped off by his informant that an SIS case-officer was creating waves in Sokolov's pond, he had quickly found the cause: Sam Green. What infuriated him was that he wasn't able to work out what Sam was onto last week. He could, maybe should, have had Sam tagged. Maybe she'd tell him in due course?

Whatever, Sam had a thing for Sokolov; and he her.

That was a good thing.

Both he and the director had agreed that she was key to Magpie. They needed someone pliable in the British Embassy with a link to Sokolov. Someone to force the British's hand. Only then could they hope to find the key piece of intel which would close the Magpie case.

It was clear then. He needed to earn Sam Green's trust. And to do that, he'd stick by her. Whatever.

'Here we are, Sam.' Vlad led them into a larger room, in the centre of which were four desks. Each desk was equipped with two large LED screens, and each had its own operator; all of whom were wearing headphones. He could hear the shrill of music coming from the nearest analyst's headset. That was allowed. Anything to improve concentration. Running along the wall, under the two windows, were a series of tables with maps and satellite photographs strewn across them. The walls were plastered with charts and more imagery.

'All of these analysts are working on Op Samantha.' The four operators, now aware of the pair's presence, looked up and then immediately got back to work. 'Follow me.'

Vlad led Sam around the set of tables to the operator on the far side of the four. It was Evgeny. He was the youngest of their analysts and easily the most attractive.

Here we go.

If Sam thought she could take control of Vlad's life without a bit of mischief coming her way, then she was wrong.

'Evgeny. This is Samantha Green. She's a liaison officer from the British Embassy. She has complete authority to look at any of the Op Samantha slides.

Please let her study what she wants. By the way, her Russian is better than yours, which I know isn't difficult as you're a Cossack. So, try not to be rude. I'll be back in 40 minutes. Happy?'

Evgeny, who was the coolest dude in central Moscow, didn't bat an eyelid. He half turned to Sam and gave her the biggest smile his face could manage – the one that all the secretaries in the building hung about in corridors hoping to get a glimpse of.

'Pull up a chair, Miss Green.'

Vlad smiled to himself.

Smooth as silk and pure chocolate. Take that, Sam Green.

Up until that point Sam had a soft spot for Vlad. Now she hated him more than a plateful of broccoli. She got straight away what he was up to. And she knew that vengeance would be sweet. *I don't know how, I don't know when…*

Evgeny was gorgeous. But knew it. And that would normally have been enough to put Sam off. But, even so, it was going to be impossible to concentrate. It was like being offered a seat next to David Gandy, and then being asked to thread a needle.

They shook hands. He moved his chair to one side, but no so far that, when she pulled a seat next to his, the notion of personal space was a lost sensibility.

She took a deep breath and asked a couple of access questions. Evgeny, all elbows and thighs, showed Sam some folders which were date-marked. And then which keys she needed to use to enlarge the photos. Using an overhead of one of the docks, he demonstrated how to further manipulate the image. Throughout, his face was far too close to Sam's for comfort. He did smell nice.

But she couldn't concentrate.

I've had enough of this.

'I'm a lesbian.' She raised her eyebrows in a, 'that told you' sort of way.

He checked back, and smiled again. Her knees weakened.

'Seriously. You are an attractive man and your attention flatters me. But, I prefer my partners with breasts and without the dangly thing. Now, can we please get to work?'

'Sure.' He tutted in a fabulously sulky way.

Sam clenched her teeth. And her knees.

God, how I wish I had better control of my libido.

Once her pulse had settled, it took Sam 15 minutes to get her general search of the 220 monochrome images down to three – all of Number 2 Shed. A little over three weeks ago, a Saturday, a Sunday and a Monday – taken at 15.00; 15.35 and 15.47. The change of times, Sam assumed, was due to the obliqueness of the satellite orbit. Whilst Sam was poring over the images, the supermodel had been dispatched to make them both coffee. He may have been God's gift, but the brown sludge he returned with was rubbish.

Sam had the earliest photo on the left screen and,

reduced in size, the latter two on the right. She enlarged all three separately, and then reduced them again. Pixilation began at 40 centimetres and, due to the lack of enhancement software, when the image started to blur she had to zoom out again.

'Leave these three,' Sam barked at Evgeny. She stood up and walked to the window, staring out through the grey for inspiration. Drops of rain had started to splatter the glass. She hated the run up to winter. In any country.

She came back again and sat down. Evgeny was looking intently at all three.

'What can you see?' he asked.

Sam took hold of the mouse and used it as a pointer.

'It's not what I can see, it's what I *can't* see that's important.'

On the left screen, she hovered the pointer over a small light-grey rectangular splodge with a line down the middle of it.

'What's that?'

Evgeny leant forward and stared at the screen, its reflection creating a mosaic in his fabulously blue eyes.

'Not sure. Using the scale, it's probably two metres square. Looks like a tent.'

Sam flipped the mouse between screens. She pointed at the same place on the top photo on the second screen.

'And that?'

'It's the same thing – it's not moved. Whatever it is.'

'And here?'

Sam had moved the pointer to the lower photo and paused in exactly the same place where the grey splodge had been before. It had gone. It was replaced by a smaller, darker grey, chequered square.

Evgeny looked confused.

'Something's been moved? Whatever was there before has gone?'

'Exactly. What should be there, but isn't.'

'What does that mean?' Evgeny asked.

Sam leant back in her chair and put her hands behind her head. She didn't mean to push her modest chest out, but Evgeny couldn't stop himself from catching an eyeful. *Bless him.*

'I'm not sure. And I need to do some work on this. I think the first two photos of Saturday and Sunday show a workman's tent.'

Evgeny finished her thought process.

'And the third, Monday, shows the work complete. Possibly leaving a manhole cover.' Having taken his eyes off Sam's breasts, he was now looking back at the screen. 'Just about 30 metres from the main shed. And…' he used his finger to point at the date of the photo, 'about the time we think the piece of fuel rod went missing?'

'Or, pieces. This could have been going on for some time.'

'That's genius. They could have been stealing the

uranium and getting the fuel out of the shipyard via the drainage system.'

'Correct. So, the next step is?' Sam tested Evgeny.

'Get a copy of the drainage plans and see if we can establish a route that takes us out of the boundaries.'

'Right answer. Can you do that?'

Evgeny reply was curtailed by Vlad's return; he was carrying a black carry-on case. He raised his eyebrows at Sam playfully.

Sam smiled, a knowing smile and touched Evgeny's forearm.

'Brief the boss, Evgeny.'

Which is what Evgeny did. He used 'we' rather than 'Sam', but she really didn't mind. Hopefully he'd learnt a few things today: how to be a better photo analyst; and how to treat women with more respect.

No, he'd never learn the latter.

'That's great work. What now?'

On a normal day, Sam would have let Evgeny continue, but they needed to leave. She'd checked flight times before she'd left the Embassy. They had 90 minutes. The next flight to Arkhangelsk was five hours later – it would be too late.

'Evgeny's going to check out the drainage system. I want my team to look over our own images using the same logic. And we need a Geiger counter.'

Vlad scrunched his face up as though the last sentence had hurt.

'I have a couple in my office.'

'That's Russian sarcasm, isn't it?' was Sam's response.

'Yeah.' He thought for a second. 'I guess we're in a rush to catch the 12.45? I checked on the way over.'

Sam was on her feet now, collecting her things. And nodding at the same time.

'Evgeny. Get hold of the appropriate department at the university. Have them blue-light a Geiger counter to the airport. They have an hour.'

Vlad finished the last sentence as he and Sam rushed out the door.

In the air between Moscow and Arkhangelsk

Sam and Vlad had managed to get seats next to each other on a packed flight from Moscow. The flight was scheduled to take three and a half hours; they'd be landing at Arkhangelsk, the closest airport to the shipyard, at about 4pm. Vlad's team had got a Geiger counter to them just before they boarded the plane. He thought it might be dangerous air cargo, until Sam pointed out that it was just a metal cylinder with a high-voltage tungsten wire running through its middle (the power supplied by a medium-sized battery). Her mad physics teacher used to spend an hour with the class making one from old bits of throw-away rubbish. So she understood how they worked: a plastic cap at one end allows radiation to get into the tube; it affects the gas inside, sending bits of it to the tungsten. This causes a pulse of electricity, which then makes a sound. Lots of bleeps means lots of radiation. It was perfect for their needs. Especially as the latest ones were small enough to fit in your pocket.

Whilst taxiing, Sam had drafted and sent an email to M, Debbie and Rich. It read:

The FSB have asked me to accompany them to Severodvinsk. We have caught the 12.45 from Moscow (SVO) to Arkhangelsk (ARH). Aim is to undertake further interviews/investigations at the shipyard.

Notes:

1. FSB have added Vienna to the target list, and removed Jerusalem. I agree.

2. Possibility that Ur could have been removed from shipyard via drainage system. Debbie: look to sat photos of Number 2 Shed over the 3 days, three weekends ago (Sat to Mon), at a distance of 30m SW of shed, east wall, bottom corner. In Lubyanka we found poss workman's tent on the Sat/Sun, then only manhole cover Mon. Might be key. We will physically investigate drainage whilst we're there, unless instructed otherwise.

3. FSB have limited border coverage, but view is device being put together in Ru - and still here.

4. FSB looking into files on senior staff at shipyard. Debbie, dig out wiring diagram and give me anything we might have on those staff. Looking for high-level political influences and ambitions. (Sam wanted to press Debbie to look at senior staff links to Sokolov, but couldn't mention his name.)

5. Forward int from GCHQ and PD as soon as you have it.

6. I will liaise with Riyadh and Tehran separately.

Thanks. Will be in touch and hopefully return tomorrow.
Sam.

In the spirit of bipartisanship, Sam let Vlad read the email before it went.

He then showed her his instructions to his FSB colleagues to also look for linkages between the key shipyard staff and Sokolov. And, just before the air hostess told him off for using his mobile during take-off, he'd tasked the Severodvinsk FSB team to expect the pair of them, and to meet them at the airport – they were also to let the shipyard boss (Semyon Bukhalo – they had Googled the name in the taxi on the way to the airport), know that he was to be available for interview before close of play today. That is, whenever they got there.

The in-place FSB team were nervous about the second instruction. Bukhalo was a big-cheese in Severodvinsk and wouldn't necessarily take kindly to being ordered about. Sam was impressed with Vlad – his retort was along the lines of, 'when the director of the FSB asks you to be available for interview, you're available for interview.'

Simple.

The pair of them had compared further notes for the first hour and a half, but had got no further. They then agreed the interview question list; Vlad would interrogate – Sam would observe. (She thought she might struggle with a supporting role – but would do her best to keep quiet.) After that, they played with the in-flight video before being fed. Sam had pushed the food, which was greasy meat and dumplings, around the tray. Vlad had wolfed his all down as if it were his last meal. They both declined alcohol and, after coffee, Vlad had fallen asleep, his head leant back on the headrest with his mouth slightly open. As he sat there, oblivious to the world, Sam felt a real pang of affection for this middle-aged FSB agent. She was so glad that she was taking on the likes of Sokolov with someone as grounded and experienced as Vlad.

And on that floating thought, she too fell asleep…

Chapter 12

CEO's Office, Sevmash Military Shipyard, Severodvinsk, Russia

'This is outrageous. First, you order me to stay behind after office hours, as a result of which I will be late for my son's birthday party. And then you bring a British Embassy official in here, as though it was the most natural thing in the world!' Semyon Bukhalo, the CEO of the shipyard was not happy. Not happy at all.

Vlad, who was stood in front of the CEO's desk, was beyond caring. Bukhalo was just an ex-Commodore in the Russian navy, and now promoted to two-star equivalent in the civil service. Two-stars were ten-a-penny in his book.

The man, across the desk from him and also stood, was blotchy, overweight, early 60s and due a heart attack. Bulging veins showed up on his forehead. If he carried on like this, they'd be administering CPR to him on the worn, paisley carpet – in his worn brown office. Vlad thought that would probably best be a job for Sam.

He looked across at her. She sat impassively on a chair in the corner of the office, her hands together on her knees. Prim and proper.

Bukhalo was bent over his desk, supporting his torso with straight arms, ranting some more. Vlad let him run out of steam. There was silence for a short while.

'Please sit down, Commodore Bukhalo.' Vlad used his rank. They liked that, these ex-military types. It played to their previous status. On the way from the airport he'd received his first int. update from Evgeny – there was half a page on the CEO. At first take, Bukhalo seemed clean. He was an ex-naval engineer, whose last military job was senior engineer on the *Admiral Kuznetsov*, one of their huge navy aircraft carriers. His background, and the fact that he had served as a submariner before moving onto carriers, made him the obvious choice to oversee the shipyard when the post became vacant two years ago. He didn't have an FSB file, and his police record was clear. Evgeny had more to do to uncover his political affiliations and personal connections. That would come. From what he had, though, Vlad thought it unlikely that he was Sokolov's man.

Bukhalo sat down, the redness of his face dissipating a touch as he did.

'As you know, 30 kilograms of spent fuel rod is unaccounted for from the decommissioning of TK-202. Our local FSB staff have interviewed the pertinent personnel involved with the decommissioning process.

We are widening our interviews to include all senior shipyard staff. My British Embassy colleague and I will stay in Sevmash for as long as that takes. And I am here with the full authority of the director. If you wish, you can phone him at any time. Miss Green,' Vlad acknowledged Sam, 'is a specialist in nuclear material theft. She is here under that capacity.'

Vlad couldn't see Sam – but guessed she had a surprised look on her face after being presented with her newfound area of expertise.

Bukhalo moved in his seat. He had a resigned look on his face. His son would have to wait.

Vlad pulled up a chair and interviewed the CEO for 30 minutes; the transcript was picked up by a voice recorder, which he'd placed on Bukhalo's desk. The questions included: the CEO's role; his knowledge of the decommissioning process; previous unreported loss of fuel rods (there were none); and how he thought the uranium might have been removed. Further questions included his view of likely suspects and motives; to which Bukhalo didn't add anything to the sum of all knowledge.

Then Vlad changed tack, as he and Sam had agreed.

'What are your political affiliations?'

The redness in the CEO's face returned.

'What sort of question is that?!' He voice was somewhere between talking and shouting.

'Can I remind you that 30 kilograms of nuclear waste has disappeared on your watch? *Your* watch.' Vlad didn't need to use his finger to make a point; but he did anyway. 'Just answer the question.' Vlad thought he probably sounded as bored and frustrated as he felt.

'I am a loyal *United Russia* party supporter and a paid-up member. I have been for over a decade. You can check my voting slips, if you haven't already.' Bukhalo's response came out as an affronted bluster.

Vlad looked across at Sam. She was still sat there, hands on knees.

This isn't going anywhere.

Then, against their agreed protocol, she butted in.

'Do you have a relationship with Nikolay Sokolov?'

Vlad shot Sam another glance, which he hoped would stop any supplementaries. Sam's question was not one they had agreed.

Bukhalo looked confused.

'What? No! He's an oligarch, and a prime arsehole. He's everything I hate about the current Russian system. Last year I refused a permit to let him berth his massive yacht in this yard.' Bukhalo's venom wasn't far beneath the surface.

No love lost there, then. I'll let you have that one, Sam Green – not a bad question.

There was a prickly silence.

'OK, Commodore. That's enough for today.' Vlad checked his watch. It was 6.35pm. 'We have your Chief Operations Officer (COO) to see next. And I understand your Chief Finance Officer (CFO) is back from annual leave tomorrow? We will see him and your contracts and technical leads first thing. Please make sure they are available from 8.30am.'

Vlad looked across at Sam. His look beckoned any further questions. Almost imperceptibly, she shook her head.

Vlad stood and leant forward, offering his hand to Bukhalo, who took it.

'I hope you son has a delightful birthday party.'

Their interview with the COO followed the same pattern. Almost exactly, although his response to Sam's question about Sokolov was less damning. But, as with Bukhalo, she thought both were telling the truth. Unless the two were very good liars, neither appeared to have a connection with the theft of the fuel rods.

Sam was already thinking that perhaps her impetuosity was currently her least reliable weapon. She had always followed her nose; always gone where her inclination had led her. And that had worked. Maybe this trip was going to prove that rule – or blow it out of the water?

As they left the two-storey, flat-roofed, red-brick headquarters into the dark, cold evening, Sam's phone rang. She checked the screen. It was Julie; Kabul. Secure.

Sam held her hand up to stop Vlad. And, as she pressed the green 'Accept' button, she moved into the lee of a large metal shed to shelter from the sleety rain which had begun to fall.

'Julie. How's it going?'

'Good. And you?'

'I'm up at the shipyard with an FSB colleague. It's where the fuel was stolen from. So far, nothing to report. And you?'

'Well, it's interesting. We have nothing concrete here. Except, and this is very odd, some low-level chatter heard by one of our local informants. He's an older, always Taliban, man – been around a bit. He described it as similar to what he remembered in 2001, just before 9/11. That sort of unplaceable, excited murmur. Like people knew something big was going down, but nobody had a clue what it was. Do you remember the post-9/11 wash-up lecture the retired CIA bigwig gave us during training? He spoke of the same – which they picked up in the summer of 2001 at Langley. A hum of rumour that was unspecific, untraceable, but it was strong enough not to ignore. They'd never heard of the likes of it before, but couldn't find anything. So, in the end they had to ignore it? It's folklore stuff – you had to be there to believe it, sort of thing. My boss thinks this is similar. And, if you hadn't alerted us to the potential attack, we probably wouldn't have recognised the hum. Not yet anyway.'

'Wow.' Sam would need to repeat the gist of the conversation in Russian for Vlad, once she and Julie had finished. 'Can your local man press for anything more?'

'Yes, of course. But our view here is that this is not Afghani based. As you suggested, probably Saudi. It seems unlikely that we will unearth anything specific. But we're onto it.'

'Thanks Julie. Great stuff. Is there any correlation between the level of hum and the timing of the attack? Big hum equals imminent threat?'

Julie seemed to be in thought for a second.

'It's a fair point, but no. Even if we were to do some stats, they would be so unreliable as to be misleading. I think we're going to have to wait for a known piece of intel.'

Or a uranium primed explosion rocking the centre of a European city?

'OK, Julie, Thanks. Anything else?'

'No, that's it, Sam. Keep at it.'

Sam closed the call and recounted the conversation to Vlad.

'That's good. At least it seems we're heading to the end of the right rainbow.'

They walked out into the sleet, Sam pulling up the collar on her Mountain Equipment waterproof jacket to protect her neck.

'Let's have a look at the manhole cover. And then I'll call the local boys to take us to the hotel?' Vlad suggested.

'Good idea.' After gravy for lunch, Sam was famished. And cold. They hadn't got the drainage plans yet, so couldn't follow a potential escape route to beyond the fenced boundary – if there was one. But they could check out the entrance and see if there was any radiation noise. Then Tweedledum and Tweedledee, her pet names for the two short and addled local FSB men, could pick them up and take them somewhere warm.

A couple of minutes later they were standing in the area of where the manhole cover should be. Initially, they couldn't find it. It was dark, wet and the ground had collected a covering of sleet. They were going to struggle in these conditions.

Thinking along the same lines, they both got out their phones and switched on their torches. Vlad started kicking at the sleet with his feet. From what Sam could see, he looked despondent. And in a thin, black jacket and just a pair of jeans, he looked cold *and* despondent.

Sam stood still. Turning her head, she found the corner of the huge Number 2 shed and another, smaller building she'd remembered from the satellite photo. She triangulated her position and, as Vlad continued aimlessly to kick snow about, she walked out 20 long paces. Then, shuffling her feet, she marked out a circle. Vlad was outside the shape, shoulders hunched, still pushing white stuff around.

'In here.' Sam used her torch to highlight the circle she'd made with her feet. 'Walk extending chords from one point on the circumference.' Sam drew a zigzag motion with her torch's beam explaining what she meant. 'You start from where you are. I'll go from here.' Her torch marked her spot.

Vlad grunted. Then, a minute of clearance later, shouted, 'Got it! I am a genius!'

Sam smiled inwardly at the success of a basic military reconnaissance method. She strode the few metres to Vlad's position. He had already cleared most of the snow.

It was a rectangular manhole cover; bigger than the average you'd find for domestic use. It looked heavy and, no matter how hard they tried, they couldn't open it. To compound things, as neither of them had gloves, their hands were beginning to protest loudly.

'Try the Geiger counter,' Sam suggested.

Vlad was a bit finger and thumby, but he soon had it working. He scanned the edge of the closed, metal hole and got a few background clicks, but nothing else. He and Sam looked at the accompanying blue-lit dial. It showed a reading of 80 counts per minute.

'It's normal,' said Vlad. 'Nothing here.'

Sam thought for a second.

'No, it's not as simple as that. The snow and the wet will have dampened any reading. And it's been days since they may have used this route. We need to get inside where the conditions are more benign. Maybe see if there is a constriction where what they were carrying scraped along the wall. We'll do that tomorrow?'

Sam could pick out Vlad's face in the half-light of their torches and a nearby streetlamp. He didn't look impressed. *Bless him*. He probably needed a drink.

'Call Tweedledum and Tweedledee. I owe you a drink. And...' Sam touched his arm, 'trust me. We're doing the right thing.'

Am I sure about that? She really wasn't convinced —

not after their two disappointing interviews.

Vlad grunted and swiped at his phone, turning off the torch and accessing his keypad.

Lost in thought and struggling with the cold, Sam stared ahead at the huge decommissioning shed. It looked big enough to hold a zeppelin. Which shouldn't have surprised her. The TK-202 was the biggest submarine ever built. It weighed 44,000 tons and was now an enormous piece of scrap metal. The size of it was overwhelming.

Overwhelmed? That was an apposite word.

What were they on the periphery of? How big was this thing they were chasing? Were they missing something; running down the wrong leads?

Had she led them on a wild goose chase? Pursuing a man for all the wrong reasons? Was it a vendetta? Was she thinking straight?

Who did you think you are Sam Green?

It was a good question. At that point, the wet snow that was accumulating on her shoulders added to the burden she was carrying. All of a sudden Sam felt very tired. And very lost.

This time, it just might all be too much for her.

Nordsky Hotel, Severodvinsk, Russia

By the time Sam and Vlad had showered and made

it downstairs for a pre-dinner drink, it was 8.35pm. They put the round on Sam's bill and rushed into the restaurant before it closed for the evening. Vlad was always hungry, but after an hour or so in the sleet, and after an already fairly testing day, he was ravenous.

Sam seemed lost as to what to eat – it was essentially different cuts of pork, potatoes and root vegetables, although they did have a cheeseburger on the menu.

The waiter floated to the table.

'Cheeseburger please,' Sam asked.

Why wasn't Vlad surprised?

He ordered pork chops in a local sauce, dumplings with carrots and swede.

They chatted for a bit about the cold, and the state of their pretty average hotel. It could have been a converted block of flats, such was the care taken with the design. *Maybe it was?* But it was warm. And they served pig and beer. What more could you want?

The food arrived quickly. The chef was obviously in a rush to get home.

As Vlad swigged his drink and tore off chunks of pork, smothering them in potatoes and gravy, he could sense Sam judging him.

'What?' he demanded.

'Nothing. Just interested in what the man about Severodvinsk eats nowadays. Does Alyona feed you this at home?'

Vlad paused his fork halfway to his mouth. Looked

at it lovingly, tipped his head to one side, and ate it anyway. Between chewing he said, 'No. That's why I'm making the most of what's on offer today.'

Sam, who was obviously making a point, only ate the meat and cheese of her burger, and a couple of chips. She finished by placing the napkin to the side of her plate.

'I've had some stuff through from Moscow.' She looked around the room; Vlad thought she was checking that no one was listening. 'Our boffins in the UK have designed a bomb for us. With explanatory notes. What they've sent through has surprised me.'

Vlad was finishing off. He took another swig of his beer, caught the waiter's eye and ordered a second. Sam declined.

She moved from her chair onto the bench seat so that they sat next to each other. She opened her work's tablet and showed Vlad the pictures.

It was incredible what her people had done. Vlad doubted their science team, based in separate building in Moscow, could have produced a piece of work of this quality without very clear instructions. And certainly not in under 24 hours. He would have struggled to get something by next month.

There were five diagrammatic images, almost cartoon-like, and a couple of pages of notes – bomb-making for idiots. His written English was poor, but the pictures were worth more than a thousand words.

The first image showed how the pieces of fuel, which were shown as egg-sized pellets, might have been removed and taken elsewhere. It seems that when reaching the end of their useful life, and after a considerable period of cooling, the fuel can be separated into small balls. The experts showed the pieces being carried away in simple glass or metal jars, with the radioactive material suspended in brine. Next to the container there was a label: 'WARNING – VERY HOT!' Vlad understood that piece of English. Obviously, the fuel still retained its heat.

The second image was an overview of the bomb-making equipment. As well as 30kg of spent fuel rod (Vlad reminded himself that that was the equivalent of 30 bags of sugar), the team had drawn in 60 kilograms of explosive – the easiest to procure was quarry-ready plastic explosive. They also showed four industrial detonators, and five ten-kilogram bags of sharp sand. Finally there was a metal container, a pig's trough with a lid, or similar.

The third image was a straightforward, internet-available, priming and detonating kit. It consisted of two lithium-ion laptop batteries, a Raspberry Pi children's programmable circuit board, two mobile phones and a lot of speaker cable.

The fourth image showed the constructed bomb. What surprised Vlad was that the glue which held the bomb together was the plastic explosive. The explosive was inert until set off by separate detonators, and pliable like Plasticine. The uranium fuel and the sand was layered between the explosive in the container – like a series of Victoria sponges. Key, however, seemed to be an inner core of explosive, about 20 kilograms worth. The rest was moulded around the sand and uranium in the container.

The fifth image showed detailed circuitry, which was lost on Vlad, connecting one phone, the Raspberry Pi and the four detonators. As Vlad finished off taking it all in, Sam pointed to the lines of Python code on the accompanying notes that would need to be programmed into the Raspberry Pi; these were to ensure that the mobile phone signal sent the right messages to the four detonators.

'Assuming that we have hundreds of fundamentalist volunteers lining up to drive this baby into a city centre somewhere, why are your people suggesting that the device is remotely detonated by mobile signal?' Vlad asked.

'The collective wisdom is, I think, that even Islamic fundamentalists are human. In the old days of the IRA, the terrorists used to tie locals into cars or lorries which were rigged with explosives; they kept their loved ones as hostages. They then ordered them to drive to the target, and detonated the bomb remotely. This is,' Sam pointed at the final image, 'no great stride forward. Humans are unreliable. Mobile communications are not. I think it's as simple as that.'

'But, this is just a suggestion?'

'Yes. That's true. It would be simpler to have a car battery with two crocodile clips on the passenger seat. Your suicide bomber drives up. Stops. One terminal is already connected. All he or she needs to do is touch the free crocodile clip to the spare terminal. And boom!' Sam showed her childlike side by describing the explosion with her hands.

Vlad couldn't stop himself from laughing.

The waiter appeared. Vlad was about to order another beer when Sam butted in.

'Two coffees please.' She smiled at him, and moved back to her chair. When she was settled, he looked across and scorned.

'And why the sand?' Vlad asked.

'That's what surprised me. The notes say that it does two things. First, it helps keep the radioactive material cool. The pellets of fuel, even if they've been allowed to cool for a couple of years – which is where we are with the TK-202, can still be too hot to handle. The sand acts as a heat barrier. Second, it's a sort of radioactive shrapnel. The explosion will be huge – blow cars over at 100 metres. The sand, and the outer casing of the bomb, will be radioactive. First, by dint of the fact that they've been in contact with a highly radioactive material for maybe a couple of weeks. And, second, because the uranium will be vaporised by the explosives – which will transfer a good deal of its radiation to the sand. Think of it as radioactive sand-blasting.'

'The sand will pepper and lodge into building facades and ensure that they remain radioactive for longer?'

'Exactly. Decontamination will be much more than just washing down walls with whatever it is they use nowadays – in my day it was fuller's earth. They'll have to knock down buildings, tear up tarmac – everything will have to go.'

'So, what do we tell our people to look for?'

Sam looked beyond Vlad as if trying to find some inspiration.

'This is 150 kilograms of bomb. Most cars will need beefed-up suspension to carry this in their boots. Small vans: look for ones that are down on their back axle. Medium-sized vans – you won't be able to tell. So, for them and anything bigger, it'll have to be Geiger counters at dawn.'

'That's not helpful. Without an early lead, the moment the bomb's on the move, it be like looking for Osama bin Laden in the suburbs of Islamabad.'

It was Sam's turn to laugh now.

She had a sip of her coffee and continued.

'So, we have to either find it now, during construction, or prevent it from detonating when it gets to its target – statistically, as you probably know, more devices are found by intelligence services in the very late stages of deployment, than in their development. All we need to do is reduce the number of targets, and then be very alert.'

'How do we prevent it exploding? Even if we find the vehicle in the final stages of deployment and stop it before it gets to its target, it will be nigh on impossible to prevent it from being detonated remotely. And a radiation bomb going "kaboom" in, say, the suburbs of Berlin, would create as much mayhem as the same thing happening at the target. Say, the Brandenburg Gate?'

Again, Sam stopped the conversation by not replying. She daintily scratched her chin, her slim fingers a distraction. He sighed inwardly. Thankfully, Sam Green wasn't Vlad's type. She was cute. Sure she was. And she was one hell of an agent. But he preferred his women more, well, "womanly". With some flesh on the them. If she put on about 50 pounds, she'd have pressed a few more of his buttons. Not that that would have forced him into action. He'd never been unfaithful to Alyona – and knew he never would be. But every man could dream – couldn't they?

'We turn off the mobile towers. So, they can't transmit the detonation signal.'

'Can you do that?' Vlad wasn't sure if that would be possible in Moscow.

'We did it once in London. Five towers. It prevented a car bomb detonating in the City area. Made the bankers livid for a couple of hours, but it did the trick. We have that authority in the UK. And our mobile operators, if they're given a couple of hours' notice, will comply.'

'What about Germany?'

'I'm not sure. Everyone thinks the Germans are efficient. And they are. But their security services don't have the reach of the UK's, or the US's. They could probably manage it if you gave them a week's notice.' Sam was in deep thought again. She was mulling something over.

'I'm giving away state secrets, and should probably be locked in the Tower. But we have people with equipment who can block signals across the complete mobile signal frequency range. We'd need to get the equipment to the target. But once in place, and we have it up and running, mobile phones wouldn't work. Period. Until someone politely asked us to turn off our gear.'

Vlad was impressed.

'Range?'

'In the city centre, probably a kilometre square. In the country – three by three?'

They both remained quiet for a while as the waiter brought the coffee.

'Do you have anything else from Evgeny?' Sam asked.

'Yes – sorry, should have said. I have a set of lat and long coordinates for where the drainage tunnel surfaces outside of the boundaries of the shipyard – it seems to be in another yard. We can have a look at that tomorrow. It's about 100 metres from the manhole cover we found today. And Evgeny has also sent through the actual tunnel map.' He took a sip of his coffee. 'And, I have provisional files on the CFO, the chief tech and the contracts man.' Vlad was feeling pleased that he had something useful to offer.

'And?' Sam asked.

'Looks like both the techy and the contracts bloke might be clean. But…' he paused for effect, 'the CFO has a police record.'

Sam motioned for Vlad to continue.

'S&M prostitution; and heroin usage.'

'And is he married?'

'Yes. Devotedly so. Three children across the age range. The middle girl is at a specialist music school in the UK. Fees of £20,000 a year. Apparently, she's a good cellist?'

'And there's no hint of wider family income?' Sam asked.

'No, it's all self-made, apparently. And he's loving it. Drives a BMW 7 series with all the bells and whistles. Wife stays at home, no income, while he makes a huge amount of money as CFO of Sevmash Military Shipyard.'

Sam added, 'On a wage of, probably, no more than 2,200,000 roubles – say £30,000 a year?'

Vlad nodded. The sums didn't add up.

'And we're seeing him first tomorrow?'

'Yes. He and his family have just come back from two weeks in Thailand.'

'Perfect.'

Indeed it was. They might just have their first break.

'And you, Sam. Anything else?'

'No, sorry. Nothing from GCHQ from the Saudi intercepts. And nothing from Tehran.' She was distracted again.

'What, Sam?'

She leant forward, her chin resting in her hands.

'Why do you think Sokolov is pulling this together, Vlad?'

He wasn't surprised by the question. It had played on his mind as he'd got dressed after having had a shower.

'I'm not sure. You?'

'My logic is this. You set off a dirty bomb in the

middle of Berlin. Germany implodes – there's a snap general election, the far-right get into power, anyone who even looks like an immigrant is persecuted. The same thing happens in one or two more countries in the EU – and that bloc disintegrates.' She tipped her head to on side. 'Who's the winner?'

He thought for a moment.

'Russia, I guess. Although I'm not convinced we're up for full-scale colonisation of our satellite states again. I think people here are too well informed to stomach that sort of nationalism.'

'I agree with you. And I don't see Sokolov as a nationalist. He's not an idealist. He's not a politician. But he *is* a businessman. A hugely wealthy, and ultimately greedy, one. So, let me ask you again, who wins?'

Vlad had it. He could see her logic. In some very perverse way it all made sense.

'Sokolov. Him. Himself. His empire. Set the world alight and what happens to commodity prices? They go through the roof. As they always do when there's a crisis. Everything he owns will double, triple in value. He's the winner.'

Sam was nodding.

'I think that's it, Vlad. I really do.'

Chapter 13

CFO's Office, Sevmash Military Shipyard, Severodvinsk, Russia

Vlad had finished the standard set of questions. If he stuck to the script they'd rehearsed over breakfast, he was now going to take Abram Stepanov on a more difficult journey. So far the man had been unflappable; as smooth as silk. It was the analytical mind of the accountant. They had the ability to think fast – getting ahead of the interviewer.

Stepanov's looks matched his demeanour. He was one cool customer, that was for sure. In comparison to the drabness of the shipyard, he seemed out of place in his grey-blue, pinstriped woollen suit, a light pink cotton shirt with a cut-back collar, and a dark blue and white polka dot tie. The last time Sam had seen someone dressed so yuppily was on TV – at a Conservative Party conference.

'You have a police record, Mr Stepanov?' *Good – this is where things should get interesting.* Vlad was aiming to draw the first blood.

If the CFO was unnerved by the question, he didn't show it. Instead, he smiled a self-satisfying smile, as if fondly remembering his wedding day.

'That's correct. 2013. I was caught during a brothel raid in Moscow. Unfortunately, Miss "Whiplash", I think that was her name, was high on heroin – there was some in the bathroom. I couldn't tell, mind you, I was wearing a mask at the time – and tied to the bed.' His smile turned to a chuckle, which he quickly stifled. But the smile remained. 'The police set me up with both charges, to which I pleaded guilty *in absentia*. They fined me 50,000 roubles, which I thought was a bit steep.'

He was enjoying himself. There was something of a piece of theatre about him. Sam knew his type. It was all about him. He had to be in the middle, surrounded by an adoring throng. She didn't get why wives stayed with men like him – especially after a hooker sting and a slab of heroin. Mind you, she was hardly an expert.

Some men…

'You seem quite proud of yourself, Mr Stepanov?'

He feigned bashfulness.

Sodding man.

'No. Not at all. But we all have our vices, Mr Turov?'

Sam saw Vlad tense, as though he was preventing himself from launching across the lounge lizard's desk and throttling him.

He didn't. Instead he asked the next penetrating question.

'How do you account for your lavish lifestyle, on wages of 180,000 roubles a month? Your recent family holiday to Thailand, for example, couldn't have been cheap?'

Stepanov smirked. He reached across the desk, picked up an expensive fountain pen and played with it.

'I'm an accountant, Mr Turov. I manage my finances well.'

'Well enough to send your middle daughter, what's her name – Bepka, to an English boarding school?'

Stepanov's mouth tightened. Not much, but just enough for a bit of colour to drain from his lips.

'We have family money. My grandparents left me some from their farm.' He was back to his charming self now, but not quite so self-assured. A tiny crack had appeared.

Sam's patience had run its course. She couldn't stop herself.

'What's your relationship with Nikolay Sokolov?' She interrupted, against the agreed flow of questions. She wanted to break him – to see him squirm.

Stepanov's gaze drifted in Sam's direction. She knew he was the sort of man who didn't expect to be asked questions from a woman – unless they were fawning secretaries offering to make him a coffee; or soliciting prostitutes suggesting something slightly darker. He stroked his nose with an index finger, and then looked back at Vlad. He clearly wasn't going to give her the time of day.

'Mr Sokolov and I are acquaintances.'

Sam could see the cogs turning. Quickly. Stepanov knew he was talking to the latest version of, what had been, the KGB. Three letters that struck terror into the heart of any Russian. If they didn't yet have access to all his inner secrets, they would – sometime soon. By any method. He needed this to be good.

'We belong to the same club in Moscow. I don't know him by his first name, but we have bumped into each other. I admire him.'

'Enough to assist with the theft of 30 kilograms of spent fuel rod?' As Sam said it, she noticed Vlad tense. A question that wasn't in the order they had agreed. But she was on a roll.

Stepanov ignored her, his gaze fixed solely on Vlad. A gaze, behind which, Sam sensed a rising anger.

Good.

'I used to have the greatest respect for the FSB, Mr Turov. But it seems to me that things are not what they used to be. Especially, as now, you have to rely on the British Secret Service for support. I'm disappointed.'

Vlad stood up, raising himself to his tallest height. He picked up a brass paperweight that was on the CFO's desk and casually inspected it. Then, with a speed that surprised Sam, he reached across Stepanov's desk and grabbed hold of his wrist. He then slapped the man's hand to the table and, before the CFO could stifle a scream in submission, had smacked the paperweight onto the CFO's fingers. The crunching sound of brass, bone and sinew made Sam flinch.

Vlad held the man's hand in place for a second, and then let go.

'Fuck! You bastard!' Stepanov was staring at the back of his hand, which, from where Sam was sitting, looked slightly deformed. And very red. *How many fingers are broken?*

With both elbows on his desk, he thrust his head into his spare, unbroken hand, and closed his eyes. His damaged fingers were pulsing like a minor human lighthouse. He rocked from side to side.

'Answer my colleague's question Mr Stepanov.'

Sam lowered her head slightly, twisting her neck so she could see at least some of the CFO's face. Tears of pain were dripping from his cheeks, pooling on the wooden desk.

'I don't know. I really don't.' It was a mumbled response.

Vlad took the man's wrist again and, just as smartly as before, went through the motions on slamming the paperweight down on the exposed fingers. Sam really thought he was going to go through with it, but Vlad stopped just short.

'STOP! Stop. Please.' Stepanov's mumble had turned to a blubber, his face staring up at Vlad's – tears of horror streaked across his cheeks.

Job done. He was a broken man.

Sam was surprised that she didn't feel uncomfortable with Vlad's methods. It had shocked her, but only because it was unplanned. The whole torture argument was one they had discussed at length during training, with no definitive answer; it was as though SIS could never condone torture, provided that they didn't actually administer it themselves.

But Sam was clear. If all Vlad had to do was lift the paperweight again to illicit responses to some penetrating questions, then a few broken fingers were probably worth the effort of attending any future board of inquiry.

And he hadn't yet let go of Stepanov's wrist.

'You don't know him. He'll have me killed.' More blubbering. Then, as if a lightbulb had come on, he lifted his head and asked, 'Can you protect me? Take me into custody? You know, like in the movies?'

Sam felt her shoulders drop. It was pathetic. Men and their fragile bravado. Strong when they can be. Weak when put to the test. She thought that Sokolov was probably the same, although there may be a screw loose somewhere. That would make him much more difficult to predict.

'Just answer the question,' Vlad replied without emotion, the paperweight still hovering menacingly.

Stepanov's moment of lightness evaporated. Submission returned.

'I set up a meeting between the captain of the submarine…'

'Mikhailov?'

'Yes, that's him. And Sokolov. At our club. And then all I did was ensure that the shipyard could be accessed on two weekends, three weeks ago, I think. That's all. Other than security staff, who wouldn't react if the captain and I were guiding people in and out, there would be no one here. I just opened the doors they wanted opening. I had no idea what they were up to!' He almost shouted the last sentence. Sam thought he was probably telling the truth.

'And how did they get the fuel out?'

'I really have no idea. They couldn't have got the stuff out through the front entrance – the area is protected by a radiation detection loop. Anything radioactive would send the alarms crazy. They go off every so often when the staff working on the reactors drive out to go home. It's a nightmare.'

Vlad looked at Sam. She nodded. They had what they needed. For now. There was more. Much more. You don't live Stepanov's sort of lifestyle without being corrupt to the core. She wouldn't be surprised if the shipyard's accounts were full of extremely well-hidden, financial anomalies.

'My local team will be interviewing you later today. I expect you to answer their questions thoroughly and honestly. Do you understand?' Vlad was still standing next to Stepanov, paperweight in hand.

'No protection, then?' the CFO asked meekly.

'Not from me. Sorry. Maybe ask your paymasters?'

Vlad put the paperweight back on the table and nodded to Sam.

They were done for the day.

Outside Number 2 Shed, Sevmash Military Shipyard, Severodvinsk, Russia

The pair of them had quickly agreed to hand over their two scheduled meetings, with the senior technical and contracts officers, to the local FSB lads; Vlad made a quick call. They'd now try and establish whether the nuclear fuel had been removed from the shipyard via the drainage system.

As they walked out of Stepanov's office, he had tasked the CFO's secretary, who was looking fidgety and uncomfortable, to get a foreman to meet them outside Number 2 Shed as soon as possible. The poor girl picked up the phone immediately and started making a call.

Outside, most of the overnight sleet had disappeared. But it was still damn cold, even if the sun was making an appearance. He crossed his arms to hold in some warmth. He shouldn't have packed in such a rush. With more time he would have found a fleece, or a heavier jumper. He blamed Sam Green. She had a lot to answer for.

As they walked to the space where, last night, he had found the manhole cover, a man wearing dark blue overalls jogged over to meet them.

Vlad extended his hand.

'Hi. My name is Vladislav Turov. I'm an FSB agent. I need this manhole cover opened as soon as possible.'

'OK, Mr Turov. I'm the foreman. I'll go and get a crowbar.' The foreman disappeared back in the direction of the decommissioning shed. Vlad looked across at Sam. She was playing with her phone.

'Anything?' he asked.

'Nope. Still nothing from Saudi. Although GCHQ have narrowed the mobile phone search down to just ten. They're hopeful. But's that's it. I'm just penning an email to Debbie – an update.'

A few seconds later the foreman returned with a crowbar and took the cover off the manhole. Inside, there was a drop of over four metres; access into the abyss was granted via a set of simple, vertical metal steps, to the left of which was a single handrail. From where Vlad was, he could only just make out the bottom. There looked to be a couple of inches of water down there.

'What's this for?' Vlad pointed to the hole.

'Entry to the feed pipe, between two of the dry docks and the sea, and some overflow capacity. It's fed by a couple of Archimedes screws that are located in that brick building.' The foreman pointed vaguely toward a building in the middle distance.

Vlad tried his best to picture the layout from the diagram, the one Evgeny had sent through last night. If he remembered correctly, it was a straight route of about 60 metres away from the hanger, a left at a T-junction, and then a further 30 metres before an access hatch outside of the grounds. It seemed an extraordinary oversight to have allowed the tunnels to exist as they did, breaching the shipyard security. Although Evgeny had put a circle around a notation on the plans, which identified a security mesh halfway along the tunnel. If that had been breached, then they'd know they were looking at a possible escape route for the uranium.

'Leave the manhole cover open. We'll be half an hour,' Vlad barked.

The foreman nodded.

Vlad offered Sam to go first. She returned a look of 'do you really think I'm that stupid?' Vlad huffed, and then dirtying his jeans on the wet tarmac, made his way down into the access hole. When he reached the bottom, he turned his phone's torch on and looked up. Sam's bum wasn't far behind him.

'Get the Geiger counter out,' Sam ordered.

Vlad did as he was instructed.

The back-lit, blue dial read 65 cpm. Normal.

And then Sam was off, her torch leading the way.

'Hang on, hang on!' Vlad shouted, as he chased after her.

'What?' There was a touch of desperation in her voice.

'I need to take some readings.'

'And I need to spend as little time in here as possible. There's a constriction 50 metres ahead, where the security gate is.' She signalled down into the darkness to their right. 'We can check again there.'

She'd only glanced at the plans last night? How does she remember all of this?

Vlad couldn't really see her face – the only decent

light they had was from their torches, and he didn't want to shine his in her face. But, from what he could make out, she looked ashen. Almost panic stricken.

'Is this your Achilles heel? Confined spaces?' he asked, trying to be as tender as he could.

'This, and spending time in a drainage tunnel with a pork-eating, Russian spy. Now come on!'

They both moved as quickly as they could, restricted to a fast walk by six inches of water and limited visibility. Vlad's feet were soaking. His Nike pumps would be ruined. Another wardrobe oversight – Alyona would kill him. After three or four minutes Vlad caught a glimpse of the remnants of a set of crossed metal bars which, if they had been intact, would have prevented them moving forward. Someone had taken them down. After a quick look at the raw metal edges, it must have happened recently.

Success.

He took the Geiger counter out of his jacket pocket.

And then they froze. Sam turned to Vlad, both their torch lights throwing a ghostly shadow across her face. At any other time it would have been comical.

Clunk. Whirr. Clunk. Whirr. Whirr!

The noise was unmistakably mechanical; and it came from the direction of where they started. The distant circular grating sounded like the turning of a huge drill. Metal against metal. As it got quicker, the sound got louder. Within a few seconds there was an accompanying waft of stale air. Followed by the terrifying noise of gurgling water.

It needed no explanation – it was the screws. The only decision they had to make was whether to head backwards to the open manhole; or run forwards, and hope that they could get out of the second opening.

If it were open.

The rising water and strong current made the decision for them.

Sam grabbed Vlad's arm, breaking his semi-trance, and pulled him away from the oncoming deluge. Their original fast walk now became a heavily laden run, the tunnel lit by bouncing torch light and accompanied by the fearful smell of rising salt water.

As he struggled to keep up with the mad woman who was tugging at his sleeve, he reminded himself of the layout of the tunnel.

Maybe… 30 metres… T-junction… Turn left… God, the water's up to my knees!

The muscles in his legs ached, his heart was beating as though it was trying to escape from his rib-cage, and his lungs were red-raw. If he ever got out of this, he would make much better use of his gym membership.

They hit the T-junction and were met by a wall of water that was now over his waist. Sam, who seemed to be swimming and running at the same time, dragged him left; immediately the water level dropped back down toward their knees, the initial surge split in two directions.

Shit!

He stumbled on something underfoot, and fell forward. But Sam still had hold of his arm and, with strength he couldn't comprehend, she helped keep him upright. And kept him moving.

Then, to his immediate front, all was dark.

К черту! My phone! It was gone, in the stumble. *Idiot!* Lost in the swirl of water which was easily traveling faster than he was. *Why don't we just surf it to the end?*

But Sam was still on her feet, using the water to gain momentum but somehow not allowing it to take control. And she still had her phone – it lit up the tunnel ahead, glancing left and right above the water which was up to his middle again. The original mechanical noise was now lost in the cacophony of water sloshing against the brick sides of the tunnel.

And she was still pulling at his arm.

The bitter cold of the water now mixed in with his sense of dread. If they didn't drown, the would surely die of hypothermia.

Sam stopped abruptly; they were there. It all happened in a rush. Sam stuck her phone in her mouth and, with her now free hand, held onto a railing which seemed to come down from a black heaven. She placed his hand on the first step above the water.

'Goonegh!' The word was undecipherable through a mouthful of mobile and the immense noise of the rushing water.

It took him an instant to realise that they only had a few seconds left before the current took them away; Sam was hanging onto the rail with both hands, her body almost horizontal.

Vlad worked as quickly as he could, pumping his freezing cold legs to get his body out of the water and up into the darkness. Once his feet were clear, he moved more quickly.

After a few seconds his head struck metal with a *'clunk'* that reverberated around his brain; a wave of dizziness came over him.

Shit – that hurt!

The manhole cover.

He looked below him and saw a pair of eyes illuminated by a torch just below his feet. Relief washed over him for a second. But it didn't last long.

He couldn't shift the cover.

With his head bent, he pushed his shoulders against the metal and forced his body upright. Nothing. He took another step on the metal ladder and, still holding the railing with his left hand, he used his right arm to add some more leverage. And pushed.

Still nothing.

He pushed again, his strength draining away. Nothing.

One more go.

Fucckkk yoouuu!!

The cover lifted a fraction and he quickly shifted his stance to the left; he felt a muscle twinge in his lower back. The cover followed his movement, its edge now resting on the ground outside. A shaft of light. A sign from heaven. *Thank you.* He'd go to the gym every day.

And church on Sundays.

'Get on with it, you wuss!'

Sam had obviously managed to get her phone out of her mouth and was now able to offer encouraging advice.

He took a deep breath. And pushed. And shifted – the huge metal slab following his movement. His back twinged in protest. He pushed some more. Soon there was lots of light. And a minute later there was a gap big enough to crawl through. They both struggled out onto the wet grass, lay back on the ground and stared up at the sky.

'The fuckers tried to kill us,' Vlad panted.

'They did.' Sam took a breath, her words staccato, between chattering teeth. 'But they didn't. Result for us.' Lying prostrate on the ground, she thrust a thumb in the air.

'You sound cold.' Vlad turned to face her, he could hear her teeth rattling from where he was lying.

'Fr... freezing.'

Vlad got up, stretching his back as he did. *Christ, it was sore.* He reached for Sam's hands and helped her to her feet, grimacing as he took her weight.

'Come on, let's go and get somebody arrested.'

She didn't say anything. She was looking around – Vlad sensed her analyst's mind at work. They were in a small compound with rusty, sheet metal walls, and a heavy steel gate off to their right. There was a lone portacabin, a few piles of old metal, and a couple of dozen wooden pallets. Apart from that the place was empty.

On the side of the portacabin, in Cyrillic, was a sign. It read: 'Nation Industrials', with a telephone number underneath it.

Sam was on her keypad.

'What are you doing?'

'Shut up.' She stuttered; she was still shaking with cold. As she prodded deliberately at her phone, Vlad took off his jacket and placed it tenderly around her shoulders. Sam smiled at him.

He heard her mobile ringing. She offered it, so they both could hear.

'Hello. Nation Industrials. How may I help you?'

Sam shot a glance at Vlad.

'Hello.' She was working hard to control her chattering teeth. 'I'm writing an article for Russian Life Magazine – we're doing a piece on successful, worldwide companies, and your firm has been mentioned. Could you tell me, who is your CEO?'

Sam screwed her face up. It was a long shot.

There was a slight pause. Vlad thought the woman at the other end was establishing whether this was a hoax call.

'Why, it's Mr Bogdan Kuznetsov. Can I ask who's calling?'

Sam dropped the phone from their ears and ended the call. Vlad noticed that her teeth had stopped chattering and some colour was returning to her cheeks.

'Who's Kuznetsov?'

She had that faraway look in her eyes. He recognised it. It was the one where her brain was spinning.

'He works for Sokolov. And he drives a maroon Tesla. Use my phone. Get hold of one of the Tweedledum or Tweedledee and get them here fast – before both us lose what little body warmth we have left.'

Vlad took the phone and punched in a number.

'Hi, Abram. It's Vlad.'

'Hi Vlad.'

'Look, I know you're interviewing, but one of you needs to get a car round to…' Vlad found the sun that was peeking through the clouds, 'the southwest corner of the shipyard. Look for a metal fenced compound about as big as a couple of tennis courts. The company is called Nation Industrials. We'll hopefully be waiting for you outside.'

He had no idea how they were going to get out, although the gate looked climbable.

'Sure, Vlad, I'll do that now. And, I have some news.'

'What's that?'

'The CFO, Stepanov, who you interviewed this morning. And you asked us to follow up?'

'Yes, go on.'

'He's gone. Scarpered. We went to arrange a meeting with his secretary and she was all at sea –

sorry to use a naval pun. She's says he disappeared about ten minutes after your chat this morning. Told her to cancel all of his meetings. And then pushed off.'

'Great...'

Now, why doesn't that surprise me?

4*th* Floor, British Embassy, Moscow

Simon Page was feeling restless. Six of his case-officers were out of the building doing what they did. Five of them were on top of their game. Only one was potentially at risk of messing up his day. The lesbian, Green. What was she doing up at that godforsaken shipyard? What did she think she could achieve up there, that a couple of local FSB agents couldn't? Her time would be much better spent back at the hub, pressing GCHQ to get more intel on the Saudis.

What did they teach them at Portsmouth nowadays?

She was a thorn in his side, and always would be.

He'd go for a wander around the office. Pick on a couple of the younger ones. Spread his largesse – and hope to impress.

Who to go for first? Ahh, Debbie! She was a well put together girl. If she played her cards right...

Hands thrust deeply into his suit pockets, he was at her desk in no time, moving quickly between the cabinets. At one point he nearly knocked over a potted plant that was on the corner of a desk. *Whoopsie-daisy.*

'Morning Debbie, how's it going?'

He had startled her. She was attentively studying her two large LED screens. The left screen showed an overhead of a piece of the shipyard – the front end of grey warship, surrounded by dark blue sea, giving it away. The right looked like a residential property – could be anywhere.

'Good, sir. Good.'

M couldn't be sure, but Debbie seemed to be uncomfortable with him looking at the right-hand screen.

'What have you got?'

She played nervously with a notebook on her desk. M saw that she had written 'SAME VEHICLE?' in capitals across the pad.

'Eh, nothing really, sir. I should get back onto the shipyard. Sam emailed me this morning to say that she and her FSB colleague were going to tackle the drainage system...' She reduced the screen with the residential property on it, and then, with some quick clicking of her mouse, deftly displayed a photo of Number 2 Shed. 'Here.' She pointed at a grey manhole cover a short distance from the shed.

'Is that how they think the fuel was removed from site?'

'Yes. I've not heard from her since, but the FSB have drainage plans which show a connection between the manhole here, just outside Number 2 Shed, and a second manhole, outside the compound, here.' She was now pointing at the left-hand screen. The juxtaposition of both the images was making his head hurt.

'It seems pretty preposterous to me – there must be easier ways of getting the stuff out than via a tunnel? It's not a Nazi prison camp.' M was shaking his head.

'And what was on the photo you just reduced?'

'Eh, nothing. Another preposterous notion of Sam's. I'm going to leave it now.'

Something's not right here.

M was just about to give the girl a piece of his mind for being elusive, when his mobile rang. He looked at its screen: the caller was *Gravytrain*.

'Shit,' he said under his breath.

'Are you OK, sir?' Debbie bleated.

'No. Yes. Just get on with your work. And I want a full explanation as to what you were looking at here when I come back in a couple of minutes.' He wasn't sure if the girl heard the last bit – he was rushing to his office.

He pressed the green 'Accept' button as soon as his door was closed, tentatively raising the phone to his ear.

'Yes?' He was sheepish.

The phone was secure, but they still didn't use names. Just over two years ago, when the liaison kicked off, he'd provided Nikolay Sokolov with a works phone. As the boss, M could get whatever he wanted. And he wanted a spare phone. So 'Q', the

Embassy's quartermaster, delivered one.

He had quietly passed it onto his new acquaintance.

Simon Page was paid in cash. Monthly – $25,000 a time. It wasn't a huge sum of money, but over three years – that was the contract they had both agreed – it would be close to $1 million. With his SIS pension, it would easily be enough to see him through his retirement. He saved every dollar into a Polish bank account, which he'd set up in Krakow when he'd visited Auschwitz a couple of summers ago. He went back there twice a year, and deposited the cash in a lump sum. No questions asked. His wife thought he was going there on business. She was blind to most things; *stupid cow*. She had left him at Christmas citing nothing more than that he was a miserable sod; 'not a jovial bone in your body'. Well, when he pushed off to the Bahamas with $1 million dollars in his back pocket, then she'd see who was miserable. And it wouldn't be him.

Sokolov didn't ask for much, and Page was happy that what he handed over was hardly undermining national security. It was simple things like, and this was a good example, the itinerary of the recent visit by the Foreign Secretary. He guessed the FSB would have that sort of stuff covered – so he didn't feel that uncomfortable about passing it along.

Recently Sokolov had been interested in Green. At his meeting with her on Monday, he had discovered why. The dead reporter, and then Green, had pieced together a conspiracy to do with oil drilling. With Sokolov's business interests he understood why he would want the story squashed. On Sokolov's order he had tracked Green's phone, under the clear assumption that no harm would come to her. He may be bent, but he wouldn't be complicit to serious injury. Or murder. Not of his own kind.

As a result, he had felt a little uncomfortable when Green had been knocked down by one of Sokolov's associates – thankfully she was only bruised. He'd assumed that they were trying to scare her. But, because Green had the skin of a rhino, it didn't do the trick. So, against their agreed protocol, he'd phoned Sokolov and told him he would frighten Green himself. And then order her off the case.

Sokolov had agreed.

He'd broken into her flat and left a message on her fridge. Then, the next day, he'd made it clear to leave *ExtraOil* well alone. Job done. And, thankfully, the dirty bomb op had come along to divert her attention.

The last time he'd spoken to Sokolov was at the Foreign Secretary's reception. He'd told him what he had done, including what he had written on the fridge (which he thought was very *Nightmare on Elm Street*). He was on top of her. She was under control. And he was very pleased with himself.

Sokolov's parting comment was that they should give each other a wide berth for a couple of weeks, and let the whole thing calm down.

So, what did he want now?

He held the phone an inch or two from his ear. He was nervous, and he didn't understand why. Very soon, it all became clear.

'Green is in Severodvinsk. Digging about in something which she shouldn't be.'

What?

Page's brain went into spasm. Surely there wasn't a linkage between the submarine, the missing nuclear fuel, and Sokolov?

Surely?

His mouth went dry. He had nothing to say.

'Get Green back in Moscow and off the case. Do this now – by the end of the day. If you don't, then she will meet with an accident. And you don't need that sort of paperwork. Do you?'

Page couldn't believe what he was hearing.

How could a simple relationship, based on a transfer of small snippets of intelligence, in exchange for a minimal amount of cash, spiral so badly out of control? What had he got himself involved with? Sokolov and a dirty bomb? *Really?* His team were among the best employees in the UK. They were working at the edge of the envelope. Putting themselves at risk every day. It wasn't an exaggeration to say that, every year, they helped unpick plots and actions by governments and terrorists that, if left to come to their own conclusions, would inevitably have led to the death and injury of scores of innocent people. They were stars. His stars.

'Page!'

They'd never used names over the phone before. Never.

This is some serious shit.

'OK. I'll do it. But nothing else. I can't do anything else. I can't work for you at this level. I'm no longer comfortable with our relationship.' He felt pathetic. Drained. Panicky.

There was no immediate response from Sokolov.

Then, almost in a whisper, 'You get this done, Page,' he flinched at hearing at his own name again, 'and you will do anything else I ask of you. We have a contract. Remember?'

And then the phone went dead.

Simon Page was sweating, which was odd, as his mouth was so dry his tongue stuck to its roof.

He staggered to his desk and went to sit down. But didn't. Instead he turned, and wearing a face of complete resignation, he dragged his feet across to his filing cabinet. He opened the bottom drawer, pulled out a bottle of Fortnum and Mason whiskey and a cut-glass tumbler. He filled the glass to just below the rim and took both over to his desk. This time he did sit down.

Flop.

He filled the chair. His centre of gravity sat as low as possible, as if his body was boneless. He was spent.

He looked at his mobile. He slammed it onto the green leather topping of the large oak desk, a desk shared by all previous 'Ms' at the British Embassy since the First World War.

What a legacy. All those brilliant men.

And me.

He took a long swig of his drink.

And then swiped his phone open, accessing the secure MMS App.

He typed in Sam Green's name in the 'To' box, and, using his thumb, placed the cursor on the 'Message' box.

He picked up his drink with his spare hand and stared at the brown, silky liquid as it gently rolled and swelled in its glass prison. He took another long swig. As the whiskey slipped down his throat, it warmed him. Soon the alcohol would be in his bloodstream, adding to that warmth. Then he would be able to take on the world. Green. Sokolov. His wife. All the fuckers.

All the fuckers.

He typed.

Green. Get back here now. By close of play - without fail. I want a full report on my desk by 7 am tomorrow morning. You are off the operation. The FSB will now work independently. M

Simon Page's finger paused above the 'Send' button.

What the hell am I doing?

He drank the final third of the glass.

And then pressed 'Send'.

Chapter 14

41°23'27.0"N 29°16'46.3"E, Short of the Bosphorus, Black Sea

Holly stared out of the single porthole. It was Thursday; just after lunch. She knew that. And she knew that she had been abducted on Monday night. In Istanbul. Those were the certainties of her current life. In among which a secondary pattern was emerging: wake – eat – rape – sleep.

Repeat.

Almost three days of horror. If the regime continued, Berta would be bringing in lunch any time soon. It would be fabulous. And Holly would eat it. She was ravenous. She had no idea where her appetite was coming from. She didn't normally overeat; that's how she'd kept her figure. But the ordeal (that's the word she was using for it) had triggered some primeval reaction which was making her want to scoff anything that Berta brought in on her silver trays; store energy to be used later.

In the gaps in her routine she was trying to find an escape opportunity. Looking for a weapon. Watching Berta's movements. Where she kept her keys. How the door locking system worked. Trying to see if there were an opportunity that she could exploit.

And she thought she was making some progress. The door was both biometrically and physically locked. She knew it was physically locked because she heard the cogs turning when either Berta or the oaf entered the room. Once in, they didn't seem to lock the door – only after they left; she thought the keys were probably on the outside. To get out, Berta looked into what Holly presumed was an iris-recognition camera, to the left of the door. Holly'd tried it – looked at the camera and pressed a button on the wall which was at waist height. The camera seemed to move, as if focusing, and then nothing happened. It wasn't recognising her eye.

The only way for her to escape was to wait until either Berta or the oaf were in the room, disable them (*how?*) and then use one of their eyes (*which one: left or right – did it matter?*) to open the door.

How am I ever going to incapacitate either of those two? Both must weigh over 200 pounds.

Then she'd need to lift them to full height so the scanner could recognise their iris? And press the button? All at the same time?

It was hopeless.

But not as hopeless as the fact that she hadn't seen land since yesterday evening. Escaping from her fabulously appointed, waterborne cell was complicated enough. Getting off the boat and onto dry land was another matter. Yes, she was a strong swimmer, but she'd need to have shore in sight before she even thought of trying to make a break.

She'd almost completely lost the geography. She had a pretty good idea of what the eastern Mediterranean was like. Istanbul stood astride the Bosphorus, a narrow channel joining the huge Black Sea to the eastern Med. That was Monday night. They'd left during the night and sailed, what she thought was northward (*the sun rises in the east and sets in the west* – she'd remembered that from high school). They'd moored up somewhere that evening – Tuesday: a big dock with lots of industrial-sized boats – not pleasure cruisers like this one; she thought she'd heard an Eastern European language being spoken on the dock. They'd stayed there for a day (that was Wednesday), and left early hours the following morning. She'd kicked herself when she thought that her best opportunity to escape might have been the full day in the port yesterday.

Yeah, like that was possible.

And now they had sailed south. Back across the Black Sea? Back to the Bosporus? If she were right, they'd be an opportunity to escape when the boat was sailing back through the channel.

Or, what if they moored again, offshore in Istanbul? That would be a chance.

That might work.

And then, naked apart from a wrapped sheet, she saw it through the porthole.

Land. Off in the far distance. Miles away, but closer

than not being there at all.

Clunk, clunk.

The door lock was being opened.

Lunchtime. Berta. Silver tray. A blunt metal knife and fork.

And dry land. *How far – ten miles?*

Berta came into the room exactly as Holly was expecting. One hand on the door knob, one holding a tray carrying lunch suitable for the President. She looked across at Holly – her face was devoid of emotion. She let the door close.

Holly watched it inch toward its resting place – the door frame. Berta, who moved effortlessly for such a big woman, walked into the cabin. Everything for Holly was in slow motion. Door closing; Berta stepping forward, slightly unbalanced; a full tray in one hand, nothing in the other.

Land. In sight. Miles. *But swimmable?*

Go!

Holly threw herself into the centre of the room – on a direct path with Berta. Berta moved, the tray tilting from her hand. As it fell to the floor with a resounding smash and clatter, Holly met Berta's half-turned mass – and connected. It was a shoulder barge, as she'd seen American football defence players apply to a sprinting quarterback.

But it was Berta who was defence-sized. And Molly, much less than a quarterback.

She bounced off Berta and fell into a heap on the

floor. Berta wobbled, stepped back and steadied herself with a hand on the wall, clearly unsettled by the experience, but not overcome.

Holly twisted around on the floor, trying to get some traction with her hands and knees on the carpet – she wanted to launch again. As she lifted her head, she saw Berta with her back to the wall, still on her feet, squaring up to face Holly.

Where's the knife?

A coffee pot! There was a silver blob with accompanying brown stain on the carpet.

Metal. Solid. Hot. A weapon.

As Holly scrambled forward to grab the pot, Berta met her with a foot.

Smack!

It didn't take much. Berta's foot hit Holly just below her ear. The noise was tremendous, the ensuing ringing unbearable. The dizziness was uncontrollable. Her sight went, her arms gave way and she flopped to the floor.

All her fight was gone.

She had spunk – she knew had. She was a fighter; *no*, she was a protester – she had moral courage. The courage to do the right thing. To fight for what was right. But, she now knew she wasn't cut out for physical violence. Two attempts in three days – both abject failures.

Colour returned. The lights went on. Things came back into focus.

Berta. The big blob that was Berta. Her gaoler. Her preparer. Her nemesis. She was as guilty as the delinquent. She hated her.

Berta, who was rasping, had leant forward. She was picking Holly up by her under arms. Over her shoulder. And then dumping her onto the bed. She left Holly where she was, opened the door, went out, and seconds later returned carrying a pair of handcuffs.

I should have guessed.

Berta, still breathing rapidly – like a smoker who had been for a run, sat her large backside on the bed, took hold of Holly's right wrist and cuffed it to the bedstead. When she'd finished, she placed the key in her pocket.

Holly assumed that, at that point, her bid for freedom and the resulting punishment was over. Her head throbbed and her ears still rang. She'd learnt that lesson. It was rescue, or nothing. She wouldn't try again.

But… Maybe if she treated them both with kindness? She might win them over? And then there might be a chance? Her mind was chasing other opportunities.

What!?

Holly might have thought the punishment was over – but Berta hadn't. She hadn't finished making a point.

She grabbed the little finger of Molly's cuffed hand, and, in one swift movement, brought it back on itself. The finger bone popped out of its socket, and Molly heard the sound of sinew or cartilage breaking. Berta kept hold of the finger.

Molly screamed. And then howled.

Berta was staring straight at her. Holly's eyes were filling with tears. Her mouth wide open, sounds of disbelief occupying the void.

With their eyes still locked together, Berta wrenched the finger back in place – the second movement equally as painful as the first.

Holly squeezed her eyes shut, but the tears still came. She'd managed to stop the squealing noise that had filled the room for a few seconds. But she could do nothing about the tears.

She panted. Short breaths. Her eyes still closed. How she wished it would all go away. That she'd not gone to Istanbul – had listened to her daddy.

'Don't do that again. Otherwise it will be your arm next.'

Berta let go of Holly's throbbing finger. She stood up, made her way to where lunch had spread itself over the floor and started to clear up.

CEO's Office, Sevmash Military Shipyard, Severodvinsk, Russia

Sam had her phone in one hand and her second cup of steaming coffee in the other. The CEO was fawning about the place. Ordering lunch, a change of clothes, some more coffee. What with the water she'd swallowed in the tunnel and now the gallons of coffee, if she didn't pee soon, she thought she might burst.

'I'm so sorry for this. I have no idea how it happened. Sorry, so sorry.' Ex-Commodore Semyon Bukhalo was clearly very sorry.

He and Vlad were jabbering, much of it Sam filtered out. They were talking about the CFO, Stepanov, and where he might have gone to.

Bill and Ben – *No, come on girl*, Tweedledum and Tweedledee – were sat on a couple chairs in the office, looking uncomfortable. After all, it was on their watch that a senior FSB officer and a member of the British Embassy staff had almost been flushed down the pan and out into... wherever it was the water would have sluiced them to. Or maybe drowned, forced up against the metal meshing in the tunnel.

She shivered. She wasn't sure if it were the remnants of the cold, or the thought of a watery death.

Everyone was trying to be as helpful as possible. And so they should.

But none of that was of any interest to Sam. Two other things were on her mind.

She tried to put them in order of importance.

This would do.

First, Debbie had sent through two photographs. The detail wasn't great on Sam's Nexus, but she was able to see what Debbie had seen. The first image was of the southwest corner of the shipyard. It took in Number 2 Shed and the Nation Industrial compound. It was three weekends ago, a Saturday – that was one of the weekends Stepanov had opened the yard for the fuel theft. The workman's tent was over the manhole cover.

In the compound, outside of the shipyard, was a vehicle – a white VW transporter; Sam couldn't make out the series, but it was either 4 or 5. When she enlarged the image, it pixelated. She'd need to be back in the office to get the detail.

The second image was of Bogdan Kuznetsov dacha, south of Moscow. Dated the following day. The light was poorer, but the picture was still manageable. There were four cars in the tarmacked area in front of Kuznetsov's house. One, unsurprisingly, looked like a maroon Tesla Model S saloon. *Tick*. With this level of detail, she couldn't make out the designation of the other three. Except one was definitely white; and definitely a small-sized van. *A VW T4/5?*

Sam couldn't tell if they were the same vehicle – not without Cynthia's image enhancement software.

But Debbie could. And had. She had attributed a 90% probability that both vehicles were identical. A white VW T4, probably 2002; with a small dent in the rear left of the roof panel. On both vehicles. *Gotcha!* That was good work. With this, they were making progress. Proper progress.

The second thing of interest was a secure SMS from M. She was being ordered back to Moscow, and off the case. She had no idea why and, still recovering from another attempt on her life, was beyond caring. She really was. She'd have this out with him when she got back. He was an idiot.

But his message poked at her.

He is an idiot. He was.

She'd fight him on this decision. Absolutely. They were getting close. Nothing would stop her. Not now.

But, and it was a lingering 'but', there was clearly something going on here. Sokolov's friendly touch on his elbow at the Embassy party. Her every move being easily shadowed – only someone in SIS could do that. The note on her fridge door – again, an easy job for someone on the Embassy's 4th floor.

Something was going on.

It may well be him. Could it be? It was too big to contemplate. And she was too frazzled to think about it. So, she didn't. It would wait.

But it nagged.

In any case they were flying home to Moscow this afternoon. Vlad had just booked the flights. They would be back by the early evening. Would there be time to give Kuznetsov's place the once over? See if there were a white, radioactive, VW T4 van hanging around? There might be. She'd need to talk to Vlad – who was still being fawned over by Bukhalo. A trayful of sandwiches had just arrived. And some more coffee.

God, I need a pee.

4th Floor, British Embassy, Moscow, Russia

By the time Sam got into the office it was 7.45pm. Debbie had agreed to stay on and bring her up to date with what she had. Sam was also keen to confront M. She didn't know what a confrontation meant, nor where it would end up. But she had an armful of evidence stacked against Bukhalo and Sokolov. And they now knew what vehicle they were looking for – thanks to Debbie. It was real progress.

He must keep me on the case?

At the shipyard, she and Vlad had decided not to visit Kuznetsov's place after they had landed; it would almost certainly be too late. Instead, whilst eating his seventeenth sandwich (she wasn't counting), he tasked the local police to get a warrant and make an entrance into the dacha as soon as possible. If the VW were still there, they were to seal the boundaries and wait for further instructions. His phone had 'pinged' as soon as they had landed. Disappointingly, but not unsurprisingly, the place was clean. Kuznetsov's wife had told the police that her husband was away on business for a few days, but should be back after the weekend. She had no idea where he'd gone. It was, according to his wife, a common theme. He was away a lot.

Whilst they were in the air, the police had also followed Vlad's second instruction, which was to start stopping and searching every white, 2002, VW T4 in the country. The border guards were to be especially alert.

When they'd got off the plane, Sam had given Vlad the once over. He looked exhausted; his back was still giving him a good deal of pain – all that sitting about in rubbish seats on an aircraft. She'd persuaded him to go home. He would pick her up from her place at 7.30

tomorrow morning and, Geiger counter in hand, they'd make their own trip to Kuznetsov's place and have a poke around. They didn't have a specific warrant, but Vlad explained that the FSB had 'special powers'.

Powers that included smashing a paperweight into a suspect's hand? Obviously...

He'd reluctantly agreed, and went home.

She caught Debbie's eye and gave her a wave.

'Hi Debbie, thanks so much for staying behind.' And then, in much lower tones, 'Is M in?' She pointed in the direction of his office.

'No. He went home after lunch. His PA said that he wasn't feeling himself. She reckons he'll be in tomorrow.'

Bugger. The confrontation would have to wait.

'Great work on the T4. The whole of the Russian security network is now scouring the country for a white VW van with a dent in its roof.'

'Was there anything at Kuznetsov's place?'

'No. Vlad and I are going to visit it again tomorrow, first thing. The man's away "on business".' Sam used her fingers to demonstrate speech marks. 'According to his wife, anyway. But we'll give the place a once over. Anything from London?'

'Yes – some news from GCHQ. I'm not sure if it's good, though.'

By now Sam was at her desk and had booted up her desktop. She dropped her rucksack and walked over to

Debbie's station. She pulled up the chair from the next-door desk.

'Frank was on the phone earlier. They've put together a report which has just come through. It seems that there's been a verifiable intercept from Prince Fahd's compound – the phone is unattributable, but they have the number.'

'What's the gen?'

Debbie paused, looking a little downcast.

'Come on!' Sam didn't have the energy for Debbie to prepare her for bad news. She just wanted news. Good or bad. She smiled to cover her frustration.

Debbie skewed her left-hand LED screen so that Sam could read it. She then double-clicked on a secure email from Frank. It read:

Debs,

We spoke. Decoded transcript from GCHQ is as follows:

Timing: 28.1317.Local

Compound (Saudi cell phone): Is it in transit?

Currently unknown location (Russian cell phone): Yes. Moving now.

C: When can we expect arrival?

U: Monday. As agreed.

C: Good. We will have delivery vehicle available as planned. Will coordinate within 6 hours of arrival.

U: Payment?

C: As agreed. You should see first transaction within 2 hours. God is great!

The Saudi cell phone is still active and in the compound. The Russian cell, which GCHQ managed to triangulate to within 100 kms of Moscow, is now off air.

Assessment.

1. Call refers to Op Samantha. Russian/Saudi link is the trigger.

2. Movement of device is taking 4 days. Options:

- by vehicle. Distance: within 3,000 km of Moscow. Any European city east of, and including, Paris.

- by train. Probably less distance: 2,000 km. Any European city east of Berlin.

- by air. Discounted. The language doesn't match to air delivery.

3. Notice to attack. Monday/Tuesday next week.

Jane believes we now need to inform all other security agencies. She's going to get C to discuss with FSB Director. Leave that with us.

Give my regards to Sam.
Frank.

Sam took a deep breath. They had four days, maybe five, before a nuclear contaminated device rocked a major European city. They were chasing a white VW T4, one of the most ubiquitous small vans in Europe. Two of their three leads had disappeared. Kuznetsov was away 'on business'. And Stepanov had left his office this morning and vanished. The FSB lads had visited his house this afternoon and found nothing, other than a distraught wife.

Sokolov was key. And he could be found – he wasn't the shy and retiring type. But he had the air of someone who was invincible. Protected by a force field, which was supported by, none other than, the Russian premier.

And he was clever. *Very clever.*

It was him. *It was him.* But Sam was convinced they would never be able to prove it. He was too well protected. And, after what Vlad had said last night at the hotel, she wasn't sure that his boss could find the authority to haul him in for questioning.

He was safe. *Unless.* Unless he exposed himself – riled by their poking around. Too proud to sit back. Wanting to take control.

In the meantime, they had one avenue: find the T4.

And that would start tomorrow, first thing, at Bukhalo's place. Between now and then she needed to write a very persuasive report for M, get home, bathe and sleep. Preferably in that order.

There were busy days ahead.

THE INNOCENCE OF TRUST

Flat 17, 3125, Prechistenskiy Road, Moscow

Sam had decided to walk to her flat from the Embassy. She'd got away by 8.55pm and reckoned, at a lick, she'd be at her front door by 9.30pm. She needed the exercise. Last night's hamburger still sat uncomfortably somewhere in her middle, a lump which had been compounded by three and a half hours of misery in an economy class seat on an Aeroflot internal flight. A brisk walk would do her good.

For the first 15 minutes she'd applied evasive techniques. Sensing nothing, she then walked straight home. At the corner of her block she checked out her apartment. She did a double-take.

Did I leave a light on?

Sam's mind ran through the series of events from yesterday morning.

No, she'd didn't think so.

What now? She was caught. Turn back. Where to? Phone Rich? Phone Debbie? *Phone Vlad?* Or, assume that she'd left a light on and everything was OK?

Think.

She plumped for the most likely option (but the one that she didn't believe): she'd left a light on.

She took the stairs two at a time, turning left down the hall to her front door. As she got close, she slowed. Then stopped.

Her front door was ajar. Only an inch or so, but it

was ajar.

Shit!

And then, bizarre of bizarres, the sound of James Blunt's *Goodbye My Lover* wafted out of her front door and into her brain.

That's my Back to Bedlam *album!*

What the fuck is going on?

She was curious now. Not scared. Alert – yes. Frightened – no.

She edged forward, pushing the front door open far enough to see in.

There was a light in her lounge at the end of the hall, the door, again, was ajar. James Blunt had moved onto *Out of My Mind*. No amount of reconciliation was piecing this together. It didn't make sense.

Sam reached over to the bookshelf on her right and found the kitchen knife that she'd hidden there. She was now armed. And felt reasonably dangerous.

She walked forward slowly, a short step at a time, until she reached the lounge door.

Now!

She kicked it open, stepping back as she did – knife poised ready to strike.

Come and get me, you fuckers!

Nothing happened. Then she gawped. Dumbstruck.

There, sat in her TV chair, was M. AKA Simon Page. *AKA 'the idiot'.* He was slumped, almost horizontal. His hands were resting on the arms of the chair. One held a tumbler. The second gripped a bottle of Famous Grouse.

My Grouse!

She blinked. He looked at her, through glazed eyes. He slowly shook his head.

'Don't be so sodding dramatic, Green. Come in. Sit down. That's an order.' His words were slurred, but comprehensible. He was drunk.

And then she noticed the pistol. An SIS issued Glock 17, 9mm – short recoil, semi-automatic. It was sat on his lap like a toy dog. He looked at her, looking at the gun. He followed her gaze.

'As I said. Sit down. We need to have a chat.' He hiccupped.

Still armed, and very much on edge, Sam sidestepped to the far end of the sofa – keeping a good six feet between her and Page; M; *the idiot*. In her head she couldn't settle on a name. Not now – not when he'd broken into her flat (*again?*) and was, sort of, threatening her. Still holding the knife, she took off her rucksack, placed it beside the sofa, and sat down.

'What are you doing in my flat? Did you break in last time and write that note on my fridge?'

Page lifted the glass to his mouth. He almost missed, a dribble forming on one side of his mouth and then making it down to his chin.

'The problem with you, Green, is, *hic*.' He metaphorically steadied himself for a second. 'You just don't know when to stop. You so full of shit. So full of do-gooding. Of making the world a better place. You make me sick.' He wasn't looking at her. It was almost as though he wasn't speaking directly to her. He was staring at the wall to her left, his eyes focused on the middle distance.

'Do you know what fucking trouble you've caused me? With your gallivanting off to the fucking Arctic, and then to the bloody shipyard. Do you?' He was looking at her now. His eyes focused on her with some effort. Sam couldn't work out whether the look was one of anger – or fear. There was a lot she wasn't getting tonight.

She decided not to answer. Not yet, anyway.

'Of course not. *Hic*.' He attempted to fill his glass with what was left in the bottle. Half of it splashed on the armrest – she'd need to get the covers dry cleaned.

'Of course you don't.' Melancholy now. 'You so full of shit. You. And Rich – the fucking copper. And that tart, Debbie. All of you.' His words tailed off.

Sam thought he was about to fall asleep. James Blunt was doing his stuff. She gently made to stand.

'Sit down!' Any sign of slumber was immediately gone. In a single movement, he let go of the bottle and reached for his Glock. The bottle fell to the floor, but didn't break. Sam watched it spin, a small amount of the whiskey sprayed out of the opening until the turn lost its momentum.

Sam's eyes were back on the pistol. Her heart rate had risen, but there was no red mist. She felt in control, as if she were about to engage a jumper from a ledge.

How is this going to end? Is he really going to kill me?

'Did you break into my flat before? Write the message on my fridge?'

Page smiled. A self-satisfying smile.

'Yes. I thought that was rather good.' His left eyelid was drooping. He was never far from passing out. The barrel of the pistol lowered a touch. If she kept him engaged, he might just drop off.

And then what?

'And you've been tracking me. My trip, Salekhard and the Urals. You've been following the trace on my phone?'

He smiled again.

'Yup. That was me!' He suppressed a giggle. And then, with massive concentration, farted. 'Excuse me.' He smiled again.

Gross.

She changed tack.

'Why is there an orange marker on Sokolov's file?'

Page stared at his knees, concentrating. His face grew harder. His chin pushed out. He looked back up at her, their eyes met. Again, Sam couldn't tell if it were fear or anger. Had she just pressed a button of Simon Page's that was best left alone? Especially as he had a pistol in his hand.

But she had to know.

'I've no fucking idea. It's been there since the beginning. London's call. Perhaps you should speak to your "friend" Jane?' His tone made it quite clear that he assumed her friendship with Jane was more than platonic. 'She's another fucking dyke.' Under his breath this time.

Sam should have been more horrified, but wasn't. All Page was doing was cementing his stereotype. She felt sorry for him. *On second thoughts, maybe not.*

'And Sokolov. Is he a friend of yours?'

'What the fuck has it got to do with you!' He was shouting now, spittle following the trajectory of the words; he was almost out of control. The pistol pointed directly at her head; his firing arm straight, outstretched – but wobbly; his eyes wide, and bloodshot. Sam thought he was moments from pulling the trigger.

She raised her hand, dropping the knife as she did.

Calm. Submission.

She really didn't want to die here. Not now, having survived so much. And certainly not by the hand of this man.

'Sorry. Sorry. Look, I'm not sure why you're here, but maybe I can help you? Can I make you a coffee? Or a sandwich.'

Page looked confused. Upset. The concentration on his face broke, the tip of the pistol dropped a few centimetres.

And then Sam could see dampness in his eyes. A single tear formed in his left eye. She watched it as it took its own course down his face, hitting a fold in his cheek, and then dropping into his lap. Any anger was gone. His mood switching like a faulty neon tube.

'Listen to me, Green. I've done some things I'm not proud of.' A second tear formed from the same eye, and made the journey south. 'But it is what it is. I can't undo the things I've done.' He sounded more sober – more in control. He concentrated for a second, leaning forward slightly. 'Your job is to get the bastard Sokolov. Bring him down. You understand me? You get the fucker. He's up to his arms in all this shit. Bring him down.' Tears now fell from both eyes.

Sam wasn't sure where this was going. Or what an adequate response should be.

But none of that mattered. She didn't even have time to scream, 'No! Don't!' as she watched Simon Page place the pistol in his mouth and, without any ceremony, pull the trigger.

The noise, in the small room, was deafening. Piercing. Her ears rang as her eyes tried to take in what she had witnessed. She didn't see where the back of his head went – she must have blinked. But when her eyelids allowed her to see, the sight was pitiful.

Page was sat just as he had been, but with his head pivoted back; his Adam's apple thrust forward. One hand still had a grip on his glass, which looked surprisingly steady on the armrest. The other had fallen beside his leg, his hand now only loosely holding the pistol. Still completely mesmerised, she watched the weapon untangle itself from his hand. And then it fell.

Clump.

She glanced up. There was blood all over the ceiling, and, as she followed the splattered trail, there were spots on the walls. And the top of the chair. It was a mess.

She wanted to move. But couldn't, not initially. She thought she needed to throw up – she knew that was her stock reaction when things overwhelmed her. But her stomach hadn't lurched. In fact, she was surprised at how together she felt. The more she thought about it – the more she took in Simon Page slumped dead in her chair, the calmer she felt; even with a dribble of blood now forming at the corner of his mouth.

But she must throw up? *Surely?*

She tried again to stand; this time her body responded. She gave Page a wide berth and walked into the kitchen. She made it to the sink. She bent over it. And waited. No vomit. Nothing.

As if in a trance, she took hold of the kettle. She picked it up and moved it from side-to-side to check it had water in it. It did. She put it on. And then reached for a mug. She put a teabag in. It was ready for the hot water.

She stopped.

What am I going to do between now and when the kettle boils?

It was a tough one. She had a corpse in her sitting room. The neighbours must have heard the gunshot. Somebody would have called the police. They would be here soon. She had nothing to worry about. She had nothing to hide. She just had a void to fill. She looked at the kettle. It was making gurgling noises.

What should she do? Whilst the kettle boils?

She closed her eyes.

Get some milk.

She turned to the fridge and froze.

There was another message. From M.

sory get sokolov 4 me

Her mouth was open. The past 20 minutes flashed before her. Those vile 20 minutes.

And then she threw up. Thankfully she made it to the kitchen sink. She took a couple of short breaths. And then threw up some bile.

That did the trick; her head had cleared.

Phone Jane. At last. She had herself back.

As James Blunt did his falsetto thing to *No Bravery*, Sam took her phone out of her pocket. She speed-dialled Jane, who picked up on the second ring.

She was halfway through explaining what she thought had just happened when police sirens entered her consciousness from some far-off place.

They would be here in a moment. Here to mop up Simon Page's body.

What a mess.

Chapter 15

Outside the British Embassy, Moscow

Sam checked her watch. It was 9.50am. Vlad was late. They'd spoken earlier and agreed to meet outside the Embassy at 9.45. He'd been called in to see his director, an appointment he couldn't miss, so she guessed that was running over. They'd already abandoned the 7.30 start, after the suicide 'incident' – she couldn't describe it as anything other than that.

He'd be here soon.

Last night, post the 'incident', was a blur. She'd opened the door to the local police just before they'd broken it down. She'd been pushed against the wall, spread-eagled, her phone still in her hand and still connected to Jane. She talked at them in perfect Russian – lying, in order to find space: 'it was her flat'; 'she'd was heading up the stairs and heard the shot'; 'this is how she'd found him'; and, 'yes, she knew him'.

Just before the police had stormed the building,

Jane had made it clear that they, SIS, needed to keep a lid on this – 'control the news.' She wasn't asking much, especially as Sam now had the local plod stomping all over her place, asking difficult questions, like, 'who do you work for?' None of that was going to help.

As soon as they had released her from the wall, she'd hung up on Jane and phoned Vlad. He had been flat out to the world when she called, but quickly came to and assured her that he knew what to do. Ten minutes later one of the three policemen had a call on his radio. Sam picked up bits of the exchange. The FSB would be there in 20 minutes; leave the girl alone; the crime scene would be their jurisdiction. Most of all: don't mess this up.

After that, they were gentle with her.

Vlad and the deputy head of section (M2 – Sam always found that amusing; somebody's title was the same as a very dull motorway between London and Dover) turned up within minutes of each other. Sam explained to both of them what had happened, but left out the bit about Sokolov; she might have that conversation with Vlad at a more convenient time, if it helped them find the device. She'd already told Jane everything – that's probably as far as it needed to go within the organisation. From her lips.

It was getting on for 1am by the time they had agreed a way forward; before then, two security staff from the Embassy had arrived and had started dealing with the scene – shooing the three of them into the kitchen. After quickly mixing up M's message on the fridge door, Sam made them all some tea (it was just about all she could manage – that and irreverence) whilst Vlad and M2 agreed that the scene could be designated 'British Sovereignty', as though the crime had occurred in the Embassy itself.

Having agreed what they needed to and finished their tea, they walked back into the lounge where a third man, Sam suspected the Embassy doctor, had arrived. There was more plastic sheeting lying about than she'd seen in a *Christo and Jeanne-Claude* wrapothon. And she spotted a body bag. *Yuck*. The doctor was playing with the top of Page's head, as if he were performing surgery. Sam presumed he knew that M was dead.

As Vlad left, he said to Sam, 'I assume first thing tomorrow is off. Call me when you're ready. We can then discuss our next move.' Sam had nodded compliantly. It was all she could manage. At that point M2 took a call from Jane. When that was done, he explained to Sam that Jane would be flying over first thing to 'take control'. She expected to be in Moscow by midday.

And then he added something which surprised and frustrated her.

'Jane has made it clear that you are not to continue your investigations regarding Nikolay Sokolov, not until she has had time to talk to you. I'm not sure why that's the case, but I'm convinced you're going to want the morning off? You can brief Jane on her arrival, and then move on from there?'

I don't want the blooming morning off.

Sam had a VW T4 to find. But she didn't argue

with the man.

'Where do you want to stay tonight?' M2 then asked.

The question caught her off guard. She hadn't thought about it. Could she sleep?

'Ehh, here. It's fine. Providing this lot don't make too much noise.'

'You could come and stay with my wife, Bev, and I?'

Sam was flattered.

'No thanks, sir. I'll be fine here.'

'OK. Well, we won't expect to see you until lunchtime. And if you need more time, then that would be fine.' He paused on his way out. 'Oh, and if you think you need some support, the Embassy has a counsellor. And a padre.' He smiled.

Another surprising comment.

Sam had had her fill of psychiatry and counselling. To overflowing: after the Camp Bastion mortar attack in Afghanistan; in the early days as an analyst with SIS, post-Sierra Leone and the Ebola incident; after Berlin and *Köln* – two days in a freezing container accompanied by more death. If she never had another one-to-one with a shrink it would be too soon. No, she could cope, thank you very much.

Can I?

'No thanks. Sir. No, I'll be fine. I'll be in tomorrow. You go home.'

And that had been that.

She had slept, and slept well. Dreamlessly. She'd woken with her alarm at 6.30am, got up, wasn't surprised to see a security man still in her flat stood by the front door ('We thought it best, miss.'), showered, made a quick breakfast for two – the security guard was delighted, and then took the metro to work, checking her tail as she did.

She'd called Vlad as soon as she was in, and he'd told her about his appointment with the director. They agreed to meet at 9.45am and then drive to Kuznetsov's dacha. Kuznetsov wasn't Sokolov, so she wasn't really disobeying any edicts from on high. *Not really*. It was good enough for her; it had to be.

In the interim, she had busied herself avoiding everyone in the building, especially M2. She and Debbie had popped to the staffroom to share a cuppa. Sam had quickly routed any question onto Op Samantha, rather than more complicated ones like: 'So, M topped himself in your apartment – are you OK?' and, 'You think M was on Sokolov's payroll – how does that work?' Debbie had agreed to keep in touch with Frank and, on Sam's behalf, phone an oppo in every Embassy in countries where al-Qaeda had a presence and press them for any leads. She wanted to widen the field.

'Oh, sorry. I almost forgot. Ask Frank to get in touch with Defence Intelligence. Tell them, and use the Samantha op code, to get one of 14 Signal Regiment's Light Electronic Warfare Teams on suitable standby. He'll know what I'm talking about. They'll need to be able to deploy to any city in Western Europe ASAP.'

'Sorry, Sam. For my education, what are you talking about?'

'It's an Army team of four men; a mixture of Royal Signals and Intelligence Corps personnel. They deploy anywhere – at any time. They can intercept and triangulate enemy radio equipment, and they also have the ability to conduct mobile jamming.'

'What, you mean like blocking signals from radios?'

'Yes, but specifically in our case, mobile phones.'

'Got it. It's the detonation signal for the device. You think it's going to be set off by mobile – like in the diagrams from PD.' Debbie was on it.

'Yes, I think so.'

'OK. I'll do that. And what are you going to do – wait for Jane?'

'Yes. Well, no. Not exactly. Vlad and I are going to Kuznetsov's place. He's a bit delayed. But I'm off there…' she looked at her watch, 'in ten minutes. Sorry, Debbie, I'd better dash.'

And that was that.

And here he was.

A dark blue, Mercedes E-class. Probably 2008/9. The W211 version with the ridiculous oval front lights – four of them. *What were Mercedes thinking?* It looked like a Mr Chad – all that was missing was a bit of urban graffiti down its side: *Kilroy was Here*. By the sound of it, it was a diesel, probably the E220 Cdi – the smallest version. Whatever, her chariot had arrived.

'Really sorry about last night. I'm so sorry you had to go through that. Did he give any reason?' Vlad didn't know where to balance the questions. He obviously needed to show his sympathy, whilst discovering what the hell was going on. The suicide of the Head of Mission of the UK's second largest SIS detachment was huge news. And in such odd circumstances – *in Sam's flat*? Could it have anything to do with Op Magpie? He really needed to find out.

Especially after this morning's meeting with the director. The boss had previously been called to the Kremlin and told, in no uncertain terms, that he was to leave Sokolov alone. There was no problem with chasing the 'dirty bomb', but Vlad's actions had caused a stir at the very highest level of government, and Sokolov wasn't on the menu.

'Find the VW – stop the bomb. Do that, and use the team to help. But, if we both value our jobs, Vladimir, and we don't want to be wearing grey overalls and carrying a pickaxe for the rest of our lives, steer clear of Sokolov – for the moment. But, press your girl, Green. This suicide has something to do with it. I'm convinced there's veracity behind Op Magpie. Convinced of it. Green is the answer. Press her hard, and she will force the UK's hand.'

The director had flinched when Vlad had told him he intended to visit Kuznetsov's dacha this morning with Green. Kuznetsov worked for Sokolov, so there was a link. But, he was chasing the last known location of the VW van. Was that a problem?

The director had thought for a second.

'No, Vladimir. That's fine. Just keep Sokolov's name out of any conversation.'

He had the greatest respect for his director. The man was KGB/FSB through and through. But he had none of the tainted history of many of his colleagues. He was a Russian – impeccably so. But he wasn't a fanatical nationalist. He wanted what was best for his country. All of his country. Not just the rich elite and the senior politicians. That's why he was pushing the Sokolov operation so hard. Op Magpie was central to what the director stood for. And Vlad felt humbled to be, as far as he was aware, the only FSB agent working with him on it.

Sam wiggled in her seat uncomfortably, and then played with some of the dials on the dash. She wasn't going to answer his question.

'Has it got heated seats?' she asked.

Vlad was perplexed.

'Ehh, yes. Electric everything.'

'We could have done with these when we got out of the sewer yesterday.'

She found the appropriate button, and pressed it.

'I didn't see you as a Merc man?'

'Well, I am. They're very reliable and make me feel important.'

Sam flashed him a smile.

'You need all the help you can get.'

What can you do with her? He tried to revert to the original question.

'Do you want to talk about last night?'

'Nope.' Sam was fiddling with something else now, down beside her. It was the electric seats. She moved slowly up and down, accompanied by an electronic whirr.

Vlad was then clear that she wasn't going to talk about M's suicide.

'Anything else on the op?' he asked.

Sam stopped playing with the buttons and stared straight ahead. She breathed out heavily, her cheeks puffing out. Vlad thought she must be exhausted. Almost drowned in a tunnel in the morning; watch a man blow his head off in the evening. Not a great day for even the strongest of stomachs.

'Sorry, Vlad, in all the excitement I forgot to tell you about the intercept we've had in. It's from an exchange between a Saudi and a Russian mobile that was within 100 kilometres of Moscow.'

'Go on.'

'D-day is Monday, or Tuesday…'

Vlad had to stop himself from slamming on the brakes.

'What? That quick?'

'Yes. The transcript of the call said four days travel from yesterday; and a day to prepare. London reckon anything east of Paris – including Paris. Jane, a senior hood at Vauxhall, she's my ex-boss I told you about – the one who's flying over today to "take control"… Anyway, she's going to speak to her oppo at your place and send this thing global.'

That made sense. And better the Brits do it for Europe. They'd have more credibility than if the FSB tried. Having a continent-wide search for the bomb would help.

'Let's hope we find something at Kuznetsov's dacha. If not, we're stuffed,' Vlad continued.

'Won't your director haul Sokolov in and grill him?'

'Not possible. Not at the moment. My meeting this morning was about laying off Sokolov. My boss had his collar felt at the Kremlin. We're to leave well alone for the moment.'

Actually, it was about more than that – but that's all I can tell you.

Sam was quiet. She'd stopped fiddling with all the buttons and switches.

'Why is there this reluctance to pursue Sokolov?' Sam asked.

'Political influence from our side, Sam. We know he has the ear of the premier.' He wasn't going to let this lie. 'What about yours? Why did M call you back?'

She was in thought again. She had information which she wasn't prepared to share – he knew it. How could he get it out of her? *How could I make her trust me more?* The irony of his last thought wasn't lost on him.

'Sam?'

She looked across at him with eyes which said, 'I want to tell you something, Vlad, I really do. But I can't.'

She broke the impasse.

'How long before we get there?'

He checked the road signs and then looked at his Satnav.

'A couple of minutes. Just around the corner.'

They travelled in silence for the final kilometre or so.

Kuznetsov's place was stood back from the main road, surrounded by trees. A high, concrete-based, metal fence declared its boundary; a large, automatic gate prevented immediate access.

Vlad pulled up, lowered his window and pressed on the intercom. It buzzed.

They waited a few seconds.

'Who is it?'

'Vladimir Turov. I'm an agent with the FSB. Is that Mrs Kuznetsov?'

'Yes.' The reply was tentative.

'I need access, please, Mrs Kuznetsov. And I want to ask you a few questions about your husband.'

'But I spoke with the police yesterday, Mr Tupov.'

Vlad sighed. *It's Turov.*

'I'm FSB, Mrs Kuznetsov. Please let me in.'

There was a buzz. And then the gate opened.

Mrs Kuznetsov met them in front of the two-storey, white house. It was modern and angular, with big picture windows and a flat roof. But, perhaps typically for a newish Russian house, if you looked hard enough you could see that it wasn't well finished. Kuznetsov may work for Sokolov, and he might own a dacha on the outskirts of Moscow, but Vlad didn't think he was on oligarch's wages. Maybe if they pulled off the dirty bomb?

There was only one car on the gravel in front of the house; it was a Citroen, probably the wife's car. Vlad looked for a garage, but couldn't see one.

He shook Mrs Kuznetsov hand.

'We're just going to have a look around. The local police tell us that you saw a white van here, about ten days ago?'

'Yes, that's true. It was only here for a couple of hours. Then it disappeared.'

'Who was driving it, Mrs Kuznetsov? Your husband?'

She laughed.

'My husband. Driving a van? No, Mr Tupov. It was a man I've never met before. Yesterday, the police asked me to recall what he looked like, but I was hopeless at it. He looked like, well, a man. He never came into the house, but stayed with the van. I do remember that he was wearing a red and white sweatshirt – it had an emblem on the front. Probably a football team. But I can't be sure.'

That's helpful.

'Was there anything odd about the van?'

'No. Not that I recall.'

'Do you remember exactly where it was parked?'

Mrs Kuznetsov looked confused, her hand to her chin.

'Over there.' She was pointing.

Sam was already over in the area where the wife had indicated, crouched down. She was studying the tread marks. She had her phone out and was taken photos.

'Vlad, have you got the Geiger counter?' Sam asked.

Vlad jogged over. He took the Geiger counter out of a small daysack he was carrying. He turned it on and stuck the nose to where Sam was pointing.

It went mad.

'550 counts per minute.' He moved it left to right. The further he moved it from Sam's spot, the weaker the signal became.

'What did you point at?' Vlad asked.

'Between the two rear wheels. Where I would carry a heavy load.'

'Well, we know it was here. That's something.'

Vlad turned off the counter.

'Mrs Kuznetsov, do you know where the van went to?'

'No, I'm sorry. My husband doesn't share his business interests with me.'

Sam joined the conversation.

'You and your husband own this dacha, a small flat in Moscow, and your husband works out of offices, which are also in Moscow. Is that correct?'

'Yes, Miss?'

'Green,' Sam continued. 'Do you own any other properties, Mrs Kuznetsov?'

The wife thought for a second.

'No, not really.'

'What do you mean, not really?' It was Vlad's turn now.

'Well, my husband and his brother own a log cabin-cum-workshop about 30 kilometres south of here, on Lake Shishkino. It used to be their father's, and when he died, they kept it. They use it for fishing and boys' weekends away. I've not been there, I'm afraid. I've never been invited.'

'Do you have the address?' Sam asked.

'Yes, I do. Shall I get it for you?' she replied.

'Yes please. And, Mrs Kuznetsov, when was the last time you spoke to your husband?' Vlad continued.

She smiled again, a knowing smile.

'We don't speak when he's away. He likes to have his own space. I'm happy to give it to him.'

And with that, she disappeared into the house.

Five miles short of Lake Shishkino, South of Moscow, Russia

Sam's phoned pinged. It was a secure SMS from Debbie. As she opened it she checked the time on her phone: 11.45am. The text read:

Hi Sam. From Reuters. Russian head of MSF resigned. Cites political differences with regime. Nothing else on ExtraOil *from anywhere across the media spectrum. Jane due in in 60 minutes. Will you be here?*

'Was that anything exciting?' Vlad asked.

Sam didn't reply. Instead she typed.

Thanks. And no. Am moving onto new location SE of Moscow. Sam

She'd need to do something about the whole *ExtraOil* affair. She was thankful that Debbie had stayed on the case. She'd lost it in the noise of the all the other rubbish that had been going on.

She glanced across at Vlad, who looked very comfortable at the wheel. Behind him, a small snapshot of the massive forest they were driving through, flew by.

He was an interesting character. Tenacious, a skilled agent, at times ruthless and, clearly, extremely keen to get to the bottom of the whole Sokolov/dirty bomb affair. And Sam trusted him. He had looked after her from the beginning; had followed her lead without flinching. Any normal person would have spent much more time questioning her maverick approach, instead of following her wild leads that had, she admitted thankfully, so far worked in their favour. He obviously trusted her. And that felt like a really good place to be. Especially as Sokolov wasn't done with them yet.

Did she trust him enough to share M's semi-admission? That he was on Sokolov's payroll? Would it help them find the bomb? Or just muddy where they were?

Probably the latter.

'What are you expecting to find at the cabin?' she asked.

Vlad was tapping his fingers on the steering wheel. He had put the radio on, tuned into Capital FM 105.3. It sounded like Russian heavy-rock. Even if the lyrics had been in English, whatever it was wouldn't have been on her playlist.

'We're assuming that Kuznetsov and the van driver bought the T4 to the lake. If it's as secluded as it looks like it's going to be,' he waved a free hand at the dense trees rushing past, 'I'm guessing this would be a good a place as any to bring together all the ingredients and turn them into a bomb. Mrs K spoke of a "workshop" – that sounds promising.'

'And if the T4 was there, but is now gone? The Saudi intercept said the device was in transit.'

Vlad looked across at her. He smiled and raised his eyebrows indicating an 'I haven't a clue' look.

'Let's hope they've left enough evidence behind to point us in the right direction.'

It took them another 15 minutes to make it to the cabin. The approach was along a half-kilometre, tree-lined, gravel and grass track. As they got close, the wood thinned, leaving an open area just about big enough for a medium-sized, all-wood cabin and, to its left, a garage/shed affair; wood and corrugated iron. Sam could pick out the lake just beyond the cabin. She looked left and right. There were no neighbours. It was a perfect place to escape to if you wanted to find some peace and quiet. Or, if you needed seclusion to conduct some nefarious activities.

There were no vehicles – and no sign of life. Sam stole a look upwards. The tree canopy almost covered the open area to the front of the cabin. Even if they'd known about the place, normal satellite photography wouldn't have been able to show much. They might have got somewhere with infrared (IR) cameras, showing hotspots – which the US could do.

But that didn't matter now. They were here in the flesh. And so far, it didn't look promising.

Vlad was out of the car. He walked over to the shed and played with the double doors. They were locked. He'd got the Geiger counter out. He shouted across at her that the reading was normal.

Sam was looking at tyre tracks by the front of the cabin, just off the broken tarmac. She had taken a photo of the T4's rear tread, but didn't need to look at it. She'd know a match when she saw it.

Nothing here.

'Have you got anything?' Vlad asked from across by the shed.

She didn't answer.

She moved left, still staring at the ground. It was

wet – the rubbly tarmac right up to the edge of the wood. No chance of any tyre tracks.

Hang on?

There was a patch of mud toward the track they had come in on; about a metre square with a small puddle in the middle. Still half-bent over, staring at the foliage as she moved, Sam made her way to the area of mud. She stared intently at it.

That's it.

'Vlad!'

He was using the Geiger counter to take readings at the front of the cabin.

'No Sam, come here. There are raised readings here. 180 counts per minute.'

'That might still be within the normal threshold. Bring the machine here. I think I've found the T4's tracks.'

Vlad jogged over.

'Here.' Sam pointed to an area of mud a couple of feet to the right of a smudgy tyre mark.

Vlad pressed the 'Read' button on the Geiger counter.

210 cpm

'Inconclusive?' Vlad asked.

'In a court of law. Probably, yes. As are the tread marks just there. But good enough for a strong hunch. I'll snap a photo just in case we need it. I'd probably bet a month of your wages on it being the T4.'

Vlad snorted a laugh.

'Typical. I'll go and try the front door.'

Sam snapped the muddy area whilst Vlad had a go at the front door. It was locked. He peered in.

'Looks deserted to me.'

Sam joined him, looking round his shoulders. It did look deserted. And there was something about the place that gave her the creeps. The T4 had been here – she couldn't prove it, but she knew it. And this cabin held the secrets as to what they should do next.

'Let's go round the back.'

The cabin was about the size of a small house. It looked to be made straight from chopped pine trees, the corners of the building an intertwined set of two perpendicularly stacked tree trunks. Sam could easily make out the growth circles of each tree, where they had been cut with a chainsaw. There were a couple of windows on the side, and two more and another door on the back. A path led from the rear of the house directly to a ramshackle, wooden jetty, which poked out into the lake. A canoe was tied up to one of the jetty's piles. It all looked pretty idyllic.

Sam felt a small, but hungry insect bite into her neck. She slapped it away.

Maybe not that idyllic.

As they shuffled slowly along the back of the cabin, Sam was sure she heard the muffled sound of people talking from inside. The voices were high-pitched; it could be the radio? Or TV?

Vlad put his hand up to stop Sam. He was looking in through the back door, which was half-glassed at eye level.

He beckoned her forward, putting his finger to his mouth as he did.

Be quiet.

Sam looked in through the window, under Vlad's arm.

There, in what she assumed was a kitchen-diner, was an armchair. Beyond the armchair was a TV. It was on. Sticking out from the top of the chair was the back of a head. A man's head?

Her heartrate was up. Her mouth drying.

Vlad used his hands to make signals. Sam translated: *me, open door; you stay here; me go inside.*

OK, Vlad. But don't expect me to wait outside whilst you tackle the man in the chair.

Vlad gently tried the door. It was locked.

He looked at her, raising his eyebrows in resignation.

He then took a couple of steps back and launched himself at the door.

It gave way, not at the hinges, but at the frame. As it fell, so did Vlad. Both he and the door ended up on the floor in an almighty clatter.

Sam, sensing the man on the armchair might well have been distracted from the TV by the noise (*OK, so that was sarcasm*), jumped over Vlad and reached for the nearest weapon – a pan that was on the kitchen table.

As she took it, she turned to face the armchair.

I really must sign out one of those Glock 17s the next time I do this.

She was poised ready to strike when…

…Nothing happened. Just the sound of the TV – reverberating with pictures and sound a few feet away.

Is he dead? Is that the news? What's that smell?

Vlad was on his feet, brushing himself down. They both looked at each other. Sam inched her way round between the man in the chair and the TV. The smell was repugnant. It wasn't death – she'd been there before and would recognise it. It was more putrid than that; a much stronger version of the smell she'd remembered when she'd visited her dad in the nursing home. Very old and infirm people?

She looked at the man. She now understood the smell.

Vomit, pee and excrement.

The man was alive.

But only just.

She could see that. A vein in his forehead pulsated away, very slowly. His eyes were half-open. Sick dribbled down his chin, the remnants of whatever he had previously eaten was staining his red FC Spartak sweatshirt. A pee stain spread out from his crotch. His mid-blue jeans a darker shade around the zip area. The smell of excrement was overpowering – like a baby's nappy. Sam knew that he was sitting in his own.

But none of that compared to the state of his head.

His face was blotchy, sharp whites, rosy reds and some blue, *like bruising*? His eyes, what Sam could see of them, were lifeless – his irises colourless. And his hair was falling out in clumps. Big chunks of it joined the vomit on his chest.

Vlad was at her side. He hand was covering his mouth and his nose.

'Take a reading. Try his hands first,' Sam said.

Vlad, still using one hand to protect his senses, took out the Geiger counter. He switched it on and pointed it at the man's right hand.

It went ballistic.

810 cpm.

They both took a step backward.

'Leave him. He's as good as dead,' Sam said – but then abruptly stopped herself, realising that the man might still be able to hear her. She stepped forward, crouched down, looked him in the eye and tenderly touched his hand.

'Sorry fella.'

Vlad was already in the room next door.

'Sam!'

She jogged in to join him.

And there it all was. The remnants of exactly what Porton Down had described – the packaging of everything you needed to make a dirty bomb. There were a stack of glass containers that Sam assumed had been used to bring out the uranium from the shipyard. There were empty bags of sand and gravel strewn about the place. And, on a table to one side, the distinctive oily, white wrapping of maybe up to 50 sticks of plastic explosive. She picked one up.

'Russian military grade PE4. There's a date mark of Nov 15, here.' Sam was pointing at a designation on the packet.

Vlad had the Geiger counter out, sticking it near bits of the discarded equipment. They were used to hearing clicks from the machine. Noises like a couple of dolphins: that would be a normal background radiation. The reading from the man's hands sounded like a couple of pools of the mammals had got together for a party. The noise from one of the glass jars was a high-pitched whine – the clicks all squashed together in protest.

Vlad read out the score. '2800 cpm. Shit! We can't afford to stay here long, otherwise we'll end up like the Spartak supporter next door.'

Sam wasn't listening. She was ahead of him; searching. They were a step further along the bomb's journey. Now they needed to find out where it had gone to next.

And she was looking for a clue.

'Sam!'

She turned. Vlad was holding up packaging for a Motorola mobile phone.

'There are two of these here. And a couple of empty laptop battery containers.' He held up one of those as well; looking very pleased with himself.

Good. But where next?

She knew they didn't have very long. Within 30 minutes they'd both start to feel nauseous. Any longer and having Mr Right's children would be in jeopardy – and she valued her uterus as much as her hair, which would fall out in clumps next week if they hung around.

But, they couldn't leave here empty handed. They had to find something.

They both poked about for a further five minutes. Sam found the packaging for an automatic stop button – the big red variety – as fitted at each end of an escalator. Confused by her latest find, Sam went back into the kitchen. Unsurprisingly the man hadn't moved.

'Vlad, phone for a decontamination team and an ambulance. They might be able to provide the man here with some dignity,' she yelled.

'OK,' was the call from next door. 'I'm going upstairs for a quick look.'

Sam needed to think. She sat at the kitchen table. Dirty dishes lay strewn around.

The TV was still on. It was showing Russia 1. The news.

Something caught her eye. The guy on the TV was stood next to a Stars and Stripes. The caption underneath it read: *Henry Clarke – Deputy Director FBI*. She tuned in. The man was speaking, subtitles turning the English words into Russian for the home audience.

'…We can confirm that the body discovered on a beach on the Greek island of Crete, is that of the missing American teenager Kelly Jameson. Her hands and feet had been tied together before, we believe, she was thrown into the sea. And there's still no news of the missing 21-year-old American woman, Lizzy Jefferson. She was abducted in Larnaca, Cyprus, five weeks ago. Nor is there any news on the missing Congressman's daughter, Holly Mickelson. What we do believe, is that the murder and abduction of these three vulnerable women is part of a pattern of crimes. For example – all three women were young; all three were blond. And all went missing from a port on the east Mediterranean coast. We are liaising with other police forces to see if they have reports of other abducted innocents.'

The interviewer, who was off screen, asked a question.

'Do you have any leads?'

'Only ones that naturally come to mind. For example, as I've said, all three women were abducted near major ports: Larnaca, Athens and Istanbul. The women could have been taken by a ship that does business in these ports. We are following this lead, among others.'

Sam stopped listening. She tuned out.

Think.

Four days. Four days of travel between yesterday, and the day of delivery. Thursday to Monday. Four days. That's a long time.

By van. Or train.

Or ship?

Who would use a van, when you had so many

borders to cross? Or a train, which restricts flexibility?

Her thought process had nothing to do with the poor girls. But the report had triggered something. Sokolov had a ship. A big one. Berthed in Sevastopol on the Black Sea. Maybe 800 kilometres south of here? No distance at all. And then the open sea. To where? Tel Aviv? Alexandria? Athens? Istanbul? Trieste? Venice? Rimini? She was running out of eastern Mediterranean ports that she could remember.

Many of those were too close for a ship capable of 20 knots. Not in four days – unless it dawdled.

Think further.

Venice was good. Trieste, also.

Good – but great? Spectacular?

Probably not.

Naples? *No?*

Rome? One of their targets; Rich had suggested it. Home to the Vatican – the centre of the Catholicism. Residency of the Pope. Now that was a spectacular target. And Rome had its own port: Civitavecchia. Where all the cruise ships stop. Sam had seen it on afternoon TV. Only 30 kilometres from Rome?

Could they make it to Rome from Sevastopol in four days? She did a quick calculation. 20 knots – that's quick for a boat, but not impossible for one like *Cressida*. Multiply by 100 hours. Around 2,000 miles in four days. How far was it from Sevastopol to Rome – by sea? She didn't know. Less than that, surely? Through the Bosporus and then onto the Strait of Messina, between the toe of Italian mainland and

Sicily. It might be tight. Would they need to refuel?

Hang on. There was a website where you could track all ships and boats in the ocean – via their Automatic Identification System (AIS). They'd played with it during training at Portsmouth. What was it? '*www.vesselfinder.com*'. *That's it.* Every ship and boat, even 30-foot yachts, have one of these fitted – by law. The AIS gave out GPS location information by a VHF radio signal, or a satellite system – if they have one fitted. *Cressida* would be fitted with one.

Unless they'd decided to turn it off.

Would they?

Sam heard some clumping about upstairs. She was too engrossed to be bothered with the noise. It would be Vlad thumping about.

She opened her phone and Googled 'vesselfinder'.

Her phone laboured using the slow data signal from a far-off mast.

And there it was. A map of the world's seas and oceans covered in coloured dots and arrows – all of them designating a boat or a ship.

She typed in *Cressida* in the 'Locate' box on the website, and pressed 'Return'.

Three boats of the same name automatically appeared in the drop-down box. She tapped on one. Up came a photo of a massive oil tanker, with coordinates somewhere in the Atlantic. *Nope.* She returned to the main screen and pressed on the second.

Before she could see the outcome, her ears tuned into an unwelcome noise. Tyres on gravel.

Shit!

They had company.

She put the phone away and ran into the next room, keeping away from the window, but close enough to get a view.

A dark red Ford Mondeo. Latest version, the Mark 4. Both the front doors opened. Two men got out.

Gotcha.

They were the same two men who had got out of the Mi-8 at the oilfield. The taller of the two reached into his jacket and pulled out a handgun. Sam couldn't see what it was at this distance. Short-barrelled, 9mm – very likely. Accurate at 25 metres, if you stood still and took aim. Useless at a moving target, unless you were lucky. Really handy at close range.

They were here on business. No doubt about that.

She jumped as Vlad touched her elbow.

You frightened the life out me!

'I don't suppose you're armed?' he whispered.

'Only with my wit,' she replied.

'Oh well. I don't even have that.'

'Let's get out of the back door and make a run for it. Maybe circle round, come back and collect a car? Or not?' Sam was making it up as she went along.

One guy was already at the front door. It was being unlocked.

'Good idea.'

They both went together, Sam was first to make it through the door into the kitchen…

…Where her heart leapt out of her mouth.

Stood there, so close to the frame of door that she couldn't get past without knocking into him, was the man from the armchair. It was like coming face-to-face with a zombie. Bloodshot eyes, irregular clumps of hair, a complexion of a man with the plague, and dried vomit on his chin and all the way down his front.

Sam recoiled and screamed, a truncated scream of a woman who was struggling with the choice between staying quiet for fear of being shot by a 9mm slug; or grappling with the walking dead. It was an instinctive, girly reaction. And she hated herself for it.

As she stopped and ducked in the door frame, Vlad smacked into the back of her. The man wobbled and started to fall, and the three of them became one mass of bodies: legs, arms, vomit, and the foul smell of excrement.

Crack!

Sam knew the sound, as she guessed did Vlad. It was the sound that followed the trajectory of a low-velocity bullet. Likely 9mm.

Vlad's body, which she felt pressing against her, became inert. He'd been hit. *Shit*. The three of them fell through the door into the kitchen.

Think! Most 9mm magazines hold at least eight rounds. The man had fired one. There were plenty left for her. But Sam wasn't prepared to wait to discover the nomenclature of the weapon; nor how many rounds the magazine held. And she really did want to turn to Vlad. To administer first aid. To get the bastard who had shot him.

But hanging about wasn't going to save him.

Getting out of there alive was.

Reluctantly, but efficiently, she pushed Vlad's body away from her, and with strength she only ever found when her life was truly in danger, she stood – grabbing the zombie-man's arm, lifting him and half-dragging him behind her.

She was using him as a shield. She knew that. And at that point she had crossed a line – and was now as reprehensible as the men trying to kill her. But she had to get out. To get the message about the ship to Jane. And get help; to try and save Vlad's life.

She was at the back door, turning to go through it.

Crack! Crack! A double tap.

The man's dragging body became limp. He had done his job, and he was gone. And now he was useless to her. Dead men weigh more than live ones. It's one of nature's known unknowns.

She dropped him and made it out of the cabin. As she ran, she was faced with a choice. Car – left? Woods – ahead? Water – right?

Woods won.

It was the wrong choice. There was no obvious path, and the bracken was high. Her run petered out. A sprint became a jog. She hopped between gaps in the undergrowth. Trying to weave. Trying to become a more difficult target.

Five metres. Ten. Fifteen.

Crack!

The explosion in her right shoulder spun her round as if she were dancing the tango. As she dropped, she picked out one of the men from the Merc. He was stood at the back door. Feet spread apart, one slightly further forward than the other. Both hands outstretched, one holding the weapon, the other supporting the firing hand and the butt of the pistol. It was a good shooting position. The best. Just before she hit the floor and all went black, she judged the distance. *Could be 25 metres?* That was a really good shot.

Or a lucky one.

Chapter 16

4th Floor, British Embassy, Moscow, Russia

Jane Baker was still wearing her coat. She'd called Debbie into M's office. She needed a much wider brief on Op Samantha than Gerald Masters, the section's deputy, was able to provide. His job was more on the admin side and so he wasn't up to speed on the op – other than what Sam had told him last night. That was one of the reasons Jane had got on the first flight out. The place needed getting a grip of.

The whole thing was a mess. The suicide of the top man. And Sam Green stomping all over the Pierrot file.

Where the hell was she?

The fact that Sam had pushed off, back out into the field, didn't surprise Jane. She knew Sam well. They, were, as far as former boss and employee were concerned, as close as you could get. Sam was an exceptional analyst; but probably not tied down enough to be a wholly effective case-officer. That was

Jane's view. There were too many loose wires. Too much emotional baggage, when, what you needed was considered thought – and measured decisiveness. She'd been surprised when her old boss, David, had put Sam forward for case-officer training. But, the girl had passed the course. And passed it well. You couldn't take that from her.

After last night, Jane couldn't see Sam taking a morning off. Or hanging about in the office, basking in the glory of a truly newsworthy event. No, Sam Green would be out somewhere, poking around – or down some dark hole; turning over stones and making mischief.

She certainly didn't want her poking around or making mischief with Nikolay Sokolov. No matter what he was up to. If there was mischief to be made there, she was the only one in the building with the authority to do so. That was immutable. And she was disappointed, but not surprised, that Sam still hadn't managed to get that message.

'Where is she, Debbie?'

Debbie Wiltshire, mid-height, mid-build, and with a pretty, rounded face, was, by all accounts, a decent analyst. Jane had never met her before, but SIS, at just over 2,500 strong, was a small business. Most people knew, or knew of, most other people.

'The last I had was a text from her and Vlad, he's her FSB oppo. It said that they were "heading for a new location southeast of Moscow". I have no idea where.'

'Have we got a trace?'

Debbie was shaking her head, her hands raised in a 'didn't think it was my job' stance.

'Where had she been?' Jane was logging into M's desktop as she spoke.

'Kuznetsov's dacha. On the outskirts of Moscow. I can find the address if you want it? The police visited there yesterday. They were following up on the last known location of the T4.'

Jane looked up from the screen. She was expertly removing her coat without being distracted from the job in hand.

'Gerald. Coffee please. Black. Debbie – do you want one?'

Debbie shook her head. M2 didn't bat an eyelid. He clearly knew his place. He disappeared from the office.

'If I read last night's section's sitrep correctly, that's the white van you spotted from the air photos? And the van the local police didn't find when they visited the dacha, yesterday?'

'That's correct, Jane. Yes.'

Jane was tapping away, accessing the Cynthia's mobile tracing app. She didn't look up.

'Who else is on the case?'

'Just me, although Rich has been on the periphery of this operation.'

'Rich who?'

'Richard Dixon. He's an ex-policeman…'

Jane knew him. A good case-officer.

'Yeah, yeah... I know him.' Jane hadn't got time for unnecessary detail. 'Get him in here. Please.'

Debbie scooted off.

Jane opened the tracing app and typed in Sam's number. She knew it from memory.

A dialogue box sprang up:

Device not found.

Jane typed in the number again. The same dialogue box appeared.

Something is not right.

Where are you, Sam Green?

Debbie returned with Rich, M2 following on with a cup of coffee.

'Hi Rich.' Jane put her hand up to stop him from replying.

'Debbie – what's Sam's number.'

Debbie didn't need to think. She regurgitated it without a pause. Analysts were good at that.

It was the same number that Jane had already used.

Jane sat down. She'd come to Moscow to oversee any media fallout from M's suicide. To provide the section with support during a difficult time – although, knowing Simon Page, she couldn't imagine there would be many of his staff completely overcome with grief. And to get a grip of Sam and refocus Op Samantha on finding the device, and not pursuing Sokolov – that wouldn't happen without her authority.

Instead, it looked as if she'd need to divert all their

efforts to finding an errant case-officer.

'Device not found.' She pointed to her screen. 'Has this happened before on the machines here in Moscow?' She was looking at Gerald.

'No. Never.'

'So, Sam's phone is off. Or broken? Run out of batteries? Out of signal? Possibilities? Rich?'

'Broken – unheard of. Out of signal – Moscow is notorious for providing decent mobile coverage. Turned off – why? She's always taken my calls. Debbie – and yours?'

Debbie nodded.

'And I don't think, even in her state from the past couple of torrid days, she's of the mindset of not charging her phone. That just wouldn't be her.'

Jane agreed with Rich. Sam Green didn't forget to charge her phone. In the same way most people don't forget to breathe. She stared beyond them to the wall, focusing on a portrait of the Queen. *How Simon Page*. Jane wasn't a republican and she had a good deal of time for the old girl, but she didn't think she'd ever have a picture of the Queen on her wall – pride of place.

'I don't suppose anyone has the Russian, Vlad's, number?

Nope – Debbie and Rich shook their heads.

'Any other ideas?'

There was a lot of fiddling of fingers and not much else.

Then Rich broke the silence.

'Do you know that she was threatened – knocked over by a car? It was something to do with oilfields and an oligarch named Sokolov. We can't rule out that she's in danger. Who knows what's happened to her.' Jane was surprised by the sensitivity in Rich's voice. He obviously had a soft spot for Sam.

But Jane already knew all of this – what she hadn't heard from Sam from the other day on the phone, she'd got from Frank. Sam was definitely in danger, especially now M was dead. Sam's disclosure that Page was very likely to have been on Sokolov's payroll, and was controlling Sam on his behalf, was a huge revelation. But, from Sam Green's perspective, that had been a good thing. Now, with M gone, there was no one to control her. For Sokolov, that could only mean one thing: Sam Green would be terminated.

And Jane didn't have the power to stop that.

The only answer was to find Sam and bring her in. Now.

'OK. Here's what we're going to do. Rich: get hold of someone in the FSB and find out where Sam's oppo is. They must know. Call him. If he doesn't reply and if they haven't the technology to immediately trace his number, then get it from them. We can do it in ten minutes via GCHQ. Debbie: warn GCHQ that a Russian mobile number might be on its way. And get them, Priority 1 – use my name, to triangulate Sam's number to its last known location. And check her browsing history; both her phone and her Nexus. You can look at her desktop as well. Let's see what she's been up to.'

Jane hoped she had overegged the pudding. Sam's phone was down. Vlad would answer his. They would be having lunch in a local bar. She'd get Sam back into the Embassy by teatime. And all would be well.

Really?

Probably not. Something wasn't right – she knew it. This was Sam Green they were talking about.

She looked at her watch. It was 13.50.

'Let's meet at 15.00 and see what we have. Both of you, keep trying her phone. And get a trace map up on a screen somewhere, so if her phone gets turned on, or we receive a signal, we know exactly where it is.'

They both looked at her.

'Come on. Let's go!'

Rich and Debbie left in a rush. Gerald stayed where he was. Jane guessed that he didn't think he was included in the latest instruction.

'OK Gerald. Let's have ten minutes on what we're going to tell the media about Simon Page.'

Kuznetsov's Log Cabin, Lake Shishkino, South of Moscow, Russia

Vlad slipped in and out of consciousness. When he was awake, he was joined by a new friend of his: excruciating pain. He couldn't breathe. That is, he couldn't breathe deeply. His chest hurt more than he could bear, even without any unnecessary expansion and contraction. So, he took shallow breaths and tried to work out what was going on.

He was with Sam? *That's right*. In the cabin. There was the man in the chair. And then he was in front of them? They were escaping. And then the noise of the gunshot. He'd been hit. Chest wound by the feel of it. He listened for his heart. That was beating. Rapidly, but regularly. His brain was working. He'd have an entrance wound. And maybe an exit wound? Two places where he could lose blood – externally. And then there would be all the veins (and arteries?) in his chest that had been ripped open by the slug. He didn't think an artery had gone, otherwise he wouldn't have woken up – he'd be pushing up the crocuses. But he would have lost a lot of blood – that was for sure. And he needed to stop that. How much could he lose? A litre and he'd be unconscious – well, he'd just been there. Two and a half and he'd be dead. *That's right*.

He tried to open his eyes. *Nope*. That didn't work. He tried again.

He blinked.

And then the smell came. It was as though by opening his eyes he had rebooted all his senses.

The smell!

Vomit. Urine. Excrement. And a fourth smell, which he couldn't quite register. Like a petrol station? Not sure.

Whatever, it was putrid.

His stomach involuntarily lurched.

Блядь! нет! The pain was too much. His eyes closed again. Squeezed tightly closed. Pushing out unstoppable tears of pain: falling from the eye closest to the ground, straight onto the wooden floor; and dribbling over the bridge of his nose from the other eye, falling to join the pool.

He couldn't remember the last time he had cried. It must have been when he was a kid.

Let's try again.

He opened his eyes, and blinked, clearing the tears.

That worked.

Everything was at 90 degrees to the normal. It was an odd perspective.

He didn't move his head, but swivelled his eyes. He was ten feet from the back door. Or a hole where the door used to be. Vlad remembered knocking it down.

He could see the man; he was sort of in a bundle, a little way away from the door.

That was his escape route. It was too far.

How do I to get out then?

Use your mobile – *идиот*!

It took him two attempts to try his pockets. On the first try, he passed out from the pain. He had no idea how long he was gone for. Could have been minutes. Or hours.

His mobile wasn't in any of his pockets.

Voices!

Quiet at first.

'OK. We've got all the stuff in the right place?'

'Sure. What about the Mercedes?'

Then louder. Two men walking round the cabin.

'Let's get the cabin alight, and then we'll torch the car. Happy?'

'Sure.'

One of the men stepped in through where the back door used to be. Vlad checked that his eyes were closed. They were. *Look like death.*

'He hasn't moved. He's not going to. Anyway, it'll all be over in ten minutes or so. Come on, let's get going.'

The man stepped back out through the hole in the kitchen wall. There was more talking which grew quieter as the men moved away.

Get the cabin alight. Torch the car.

That was clear. The smell. It was petrol. Gasoline. A ring of fire.

Shit!

He had to move. *I have to move!*

But he couldn't. Not without that pain, and then passing out.

Crackle. Crackle.

But, he had to move. If he didn't, the pain of being burnt alive would easily surpass the bullet in his chest.

Crackle. Crackle. The smell of burning wood was getting stronger.

Move. Move! Now. Stay low. The smoke will kill you before the flames do.

He lifted his torso. *Fuck!*

Change of plan. His legs felt good. Use his legs.

He moved onto his back, dizziness almost overcame him.

He breathed. Then he brought his knees up, dug his heels in, and pushed. Pain. Lots of it. But movement. He did the same thing again. And again.

I need to rest. He couldn't rest.

He pushed again. Excruciating pain. And pushed again. Dizziness.

Stay awake.

He forced himself around the bundle of the man, knocking over a kitchen chair as he did so. The smell of burning was all pervading. The heat from the outside wall was tremendous. Looking up, he saw clouds of acrid, dark grey smoke building up above him. Parts of the ceiling were glowing orange. The fire had taken hold upstairs.

One of those beams could drop at any moment.

He tipped his head backward, like a backstroker just about to push off from the wall of the pool. He could see a burning hole behind him. Splodges of green between the black smoke and orangey flames. The outside. First a fire hoop – like the circus. Then freedom.

Almost there. Four more pushes should do it.

One! So much pain. God, no. Not again.

Two! Dizziness. *Stay awake!*

Three. His torso was out of the building. *Result. Come on!*

To his horror, in slow motion he saw the lintel above the door crack. It was alight. It was falling.

Four!

4th Floor, British Embassy, Moscow, Russia

Debbie had Cynthia's tracking app running on her left screen. Sam's number was active – but there was no trace. Rich had already been across to tell her that the FSB had tried Vlad's number, but the phone wasn't connected. They weren't concerned about him not being in touch, and had no idea where he was. But they had reluctantly provided Rich with the number. GCHQ now had it. Debbie was waiting for them to get back to her. She'd promised to let Rich know as soon as she had anything.

She'd already been through Sam's browsing history on her SIS desktop and found nothing of interest that she wouldn't have expected. She'd also accessed all her recent files, and, again, there was nothing there that gave any clues as to where she might be now.

She checked her watch. She had 15 minutes before she and Rich were due to see Jane. GCHQ needed to get their skates on if she were to have anything to take to the meeting. In the meantime, she'd look again at the recent satellite photos she had from the US. She'd ignored those of the shipyard. Those images had done their job. However, they were still getting photos every eight hours of Sokolov's residences and Kuznetsov's dacha. It was one of the Kuznetsov photos that had thrown up the matching T4. She was quietly very pleased with herself about that.

What about Sokolov's places? Her previous reviews had shown nothing anomalous. But, as an analyst – no matter how good you were – you never quite saw the whole picture. She would look at them again. *How many were there?* Sam had ordered photos of Sokolov's Moscow residence, his dacha, his central-Moscow office, their house in Park Lane, London, and the berth of the yacht in Sevastopol. New sets of images every eight hours; the ones taken at night would be infrared. Over the past three days that gave them 44 images. The next five were due in an hour and a half. So, 44? Not a problem for her.

She'd start with Sevastopol and get it over with. Cressida hadn't been in her dock since they'd started taking the photos, and there was nothing around her berth that looked out of place. Begin there – and quickly move onto Sokolov's dacha.

She had just opened all five images of the berth, when her phone rang. It was GCHQ; almost certainly Tim, the desk-officer she spoke to at the Doughnut (the new build, all concrete and glass, was a shaped like one).

'Debbie, here.'

'Hi Debs, it's Tim.'

'Hi Tim, what have you got?'

'I'll back this up with an email which I'm finishing off as we speak – you'll need the details. First, the last known location of the SIS number you gave us was from an area of woodland, southeast of Moscow. The lat/long will be in the email. Which, hang on… I've just sent to you.' An email alert popped up on Debbie's machine. She opened it.

'We've got the location down to about one square kilometre. It's the best we can do. Coverage from the local towers is average, but, importantly, it's uninterrupted over the past 12 hours. So, it's not the telephone company's lattice coverage that is at fault, it's the phone that's not pinging. Last comms between Tower K/12D4 and the mobile was 12.45 today. The Russian number gave us pretty much the same result. It's last ping to the same tower was at 12.57. They both appear to have stopped communicating with the tower within minutes of each other.'

Debbie held the phone in one hand and rested her forehead on the other. She was concentrating – working the options, whilst staring blankly at a paperclip.

'OK. That's not great. We better get there asap. Sorry, Tim. Anything else?'

'Yes. This is odd. You asked us to look at SIS's phone's browsing history. The detail is, again, in the email. But, the phone's data was active until 12.45. That is, the browser was open when the phones stopped responding. And the latest web address was "*vesselfinder.com*".'

What the hell is that?

'Debbie.' It was Rich at her shoulder. 'It's time.' He was pointing at M's office.

She nodded at Rich.

'Thanks, Tim, I've got to go. And thanks again for that.'

Rich had walked off in the direction of the office.

Debbie highlighted and then copied the lat and long coordinates from GCHQ, and then pasted them into Google Maps. A pin dropped on the digital map. It was an orange pin in a mass of green, next to some blue – *forest and lake*. There were a couple of dotted white tracks which led from the pin to a yellow road.

Darkest nowhere.

Debbie scrolled out. *However, it's only about 30 clicks southeast of here*. With the coordinates cemented in her consciousness, she scrambled after Rich.

M's PA showed them into the office. Jane was surrounded by files. She looked up and put her pen down.

'Any news?'

Debbie gave Jane what she had from GCHQ, about both phones being down, and that she had a lat/long of their last known location.

'How long will it take us to get there?' Jane was one her feet, reaching for her coat.

'Half an hour, traffic dependent.'

'Let's go. Rich, sign out a firearm. Debbie, get us a

firm's car. I'll meet you round the front in five minutes.'

On the Edge of Lake Shishkino, South of Moscow, Russia

The rough track they had taken from the minor tarmacked road had led them to the lake's edge. The section's four-year-old Vauxhall Vectra was just about man enough for the job, and Debbie had driven well. She might struggle to turn it round, though, in the small clearing they had driven into.

The three of them got out of the car.

Trees and water. No sign of humanity. Nothing.

This doesn't make sense?

Jane soaked in a bit more of the scene. It was beautiful. And tranquil.

'This isn't right,' Rich said as he kicked the bracken to one side looking for something.

'Can you smell that?' It was Debbie.

Jane took a deep breath.

Smoke. Wood fire.

'Look, over there!' Debbie was pointing off to Jane's right, through the forest, along the lakeside.

Jane bent down slightly so she could see under the lower layers of the pine trees branches. About 400 metres away there was, what looked like, the remnants of a fire. A pretty large one.

Oh my god...

She blanked. She knew Rich and Debbie were waiting for instructions. She was at least three ranks senior to them – that meant you took charge. She dithered.

She'd been here before. Chasing Sam, and her UN friend Middleton, across Sierra Leone. Dragging them from a burning hostel, in a little shanty town called Kenema. Minutes from death. That building had been upright. It still had its roof. They'd made it just in time. No permanent damage done.

If the fire through the trees was what was left of a building, it no longer had a roof. It was an ex-building. They wouldn't be pulling anyone alive from that.

'Jane!' It was Rich.

She still stared, rooted to the spot.

She always expected the worst. She planned for it. It was in her nature, and it had fared her well. Sam Green was in that fire – she sensed it. And Jane hadn't protected her. She hadn't saved her, from herself. She'd been too busy with Sokolov. Too busy keeping an eye on the Queen's friends and enemies. She felt sick.

Rich's voice cut the impasse.

'Debbie, bring the car round. Jane...' He was at her side. 'You're coming with me.'

And they were off, running down the edge of the forest, a small gravelly beach strewn with large rocks and the odd low branch. They'd be at the fire in less than two minutes. The exercise was purging her anguish, her heart pumping blood into her brain – making it work again.

Jane was easily keeping up with Rich. She was fit. Jogging and yoga. A small run in the woods was well within her ability. She and Sam used to do yoga together, until Sam had left for her language training…

Stop it!

As they got closer, the smell became more acute; and the scene started to unfold. It was a building: black and brown charred logs, and heavy, half-burnt cross beams, rising out of a smouldering mass. There was the odd lick of flames, but mostly there was just smoke. It got hotter as they got close, but not unbearably so.

It was a cabin of sorts…

…And a body! There!

Rich reached it first, but only just.

A man's body was lying on the grass, about three metres from the embers. He was on his back, his head furthest away from the fire, his knees brought almost to his chest, trying to get them as far from the heat as he could. Even so, his training shoes were burnt, the plastic unbearably moulded to his feet. And his jeans were singed; red, exposed flesh peeking out through black-edged holes. Above his waist he looked OK. A black bomber jacket, covering a chequered shirt.

But he looked dead. Smoke inhalation?

'There's a pulse.' Rich was on his knees next to the man. 'And very shallow breathing. Second or third degree burns to the legs. I'm going to put him in the recovery position. Jane, call the Embassy. Get an ambulance.'

'Sure, Rich. I'm OK now. Sam was a very close friend of mine.'

Rich looked up as he was about to put the man on his side.

'She's not dead yet, Jane.'

Jane accepted the admonishment – she deserved that.

She took out her phone and was in the process of tapping in the Embassy number when she heard the man on the ground 'grunt' in pain.

'Fuck.' Rich took a breath. 'Sorry, Jane. Gunshot wound to the chest. Entrance is through the back. He still bleeding. I'm going to have to stem the flow. And we need a drip. He's lost a lot of blood.' Rich's hands were covered in it.

Just as the Embassy switchboard picked up the phone, Debbie arrived in the car.

'Get the emergency pack from the boot!' Rich shouted.

There was a distant 'OK' from the car, 20 metres away to their left.

'Hi. Who's this?' Jane asked.

'It's the duty officer. Is that Jane Baker? Her number has come up.'

'Yes. Listen. First triangulate this phone. Second, get onto the emergency services and have an ambulance here as soon as possible. We have at least one casualty. Gunshot wound and second degree burns to the legs. And, when you're sure that's all working, get a link-up call with the director of the FSB. Now. Understand?'

'I'm not sure I can…'

'Do it!' Jane tone was both loud and menacing.

Debbie was now with Rich. He had his jacket off; the residual heat from the cabin still pumping out like a thousand bar fires. They had a shell dressing on the man's back, tying the attached bandages carefully round his chest. The man was out for the count. And Rich had pulled the man's sleeve back and was looking for vein, pushing on the man's forearm with his thumb. He had a needle in his hand, and Debbie was holding up a saline drip which was attached to the other end.

Jane wandered to her right, keeping a good couple of metres from the cabin. Was she staying away because of the heat? Or for fear of seeing something she didn't want to.

Was Sam Green in there?

The odds fell that way. The guy on the ground looked mid-40s and fit. That would be Vlad. Sam was with him. She would have stayed with him. Probably pushed him out of the door first. That was her way. She didn't make it out of the fire.

Stop! She had to keep a clear mind.

Round the front of the house there was a burnt-out car – it looked like a Mercedes E-Class. There was another smaller building off to one side. That had also been razed to the ground. Its fire was almost out. It seemed unlikely that Sam would be in here. She leant forward and peered in at the charred remains. Burnt tyres, and what looked like a fridge. A metal bedstead. Nothing of import that she could see. They'd have to get the forensic boys down here. Or, should she say, the FSB would need to get *their* forensic boys down here. This definitely wasn't her jurisdiction.

She was round the far side of the cabin now. Nothing obvious. But she still didn't want to look too closely at the cabin. She didn't want to see what might be in the remains.

Then back round to the rear. Rich and Debbie were still working on the man. He was in very good hands. Every SIS vehicle carries a very comprehensive medical emergency pack. And all SIS case-officers spend a month in a local accident and emergency unit prior to deployment; this was following on from two weeks of intensive first-aid training. They're definitely not doctors, but they're good at patching up. Debbie was standing by the man, holding the drip.

'Anything?' Rich asked.

Jane had her back to the cabin. Better that way.

'A car round the front. And whatever forensics can pick out of that mess.' She signalled over her shoulder with a flick of her head.

She still couldn't look. She couldn't.

Rich nodded and walked over to the edge of the cabin.

Jane stared at the trees, and then glanced to her

right, hoping to find some solace in the calmness of the lake. A white stork had settled on one of the posts of a jetty.

'Jane.' Rich's tone was quiet. And flat.

'What?' She didn't turn.

'There's a body in here. About a metre in. I can't make out much more than that.'

Jane instinctively turned and looked directly at Debbie. Debbie raised her free hand to her mouth, her eyes welling up. Still expertly holding the drip which didn't budge, she turned to one side, her head nodded to the beat of accompanying tears which had begun to flow.

A rage swelled in Jane. From the pit of her stomach, rising slowly.

Random, self-loathing thoughts filled her head.

She had let Sam Green down. Her country had let her down.

Just now Jane wished she hadn't been promoted. Wished so much that she hadn't had to carry the burden of the Pierrot file. So wished that she'd stopped David from pressing Sam into the ranks of the case-officers. She should have called Sam back to the UK when they'd spoken to each other the other day. She could have done that.

There were so many things she wished she had done.

She hated herself. The anger was focused on her. She was to blame.

Suddenly her phone rang. It was welcome relief.

She fumbled as she collected it from her pocket. It fell to the floor.

'Fuck!' A quiet, female *fuck*.

She picked it up. It was the Embassy.

'Yes.'

'It's the duty officer, Jane. The ambulance is on its way.' He paused. 'And I have the director of the FSB. Shall I put him through?'

Jane looked for a place to speak where she couldn't be heard. The jetty. Thirty metres away. She could talk there.

And then she would throw herself off.

She walked as she talked.

'Yes please.' There was a click. 'Hello. Director?'

'Yes, Jane Baker?' Perfect English with a Russian clip.

'Yes, sir. I'm the…'

'You don't need to tell me who you are, Miss Baker. I think I know you quite well.'

Of course.

'Of course. We have a situation here. I'm on the side of Lake Shishkino, South of Moscow. Do you know it?'

'Yes, I do. But not well.'

'We were tracking down one of our case-officers, Sam Green. I think she came here with an agent of yours, a man named Vladimir?'

'Yes. Go on, Miss Baker.'

Jane was reaching the end of the jetty. She was staring out into the lake. Her anger simmering just below the surface. She had to watch what she said. She was on very thin ice. She also knew that she had to keep her anger under control.

Could she?

'There's been a fire. I think your agent, if it's him, was caught up in it – after he'd been shot. A couple of my staff are looking after him. He's hanging on. We have an ambulance on its way. I think it will be touch and go, though. I'm sorry.'

The director was silent for a while.

'That's unfortunate. And your woman Green?'

Of course he knows about her.

'We can't be sure, but there's a body in the remnants of the fire…' Jane didn't want to finish that sentence.

Further silence.

'That's also unfortunate. I'm sorry, Miss Baker. I believe they were onto something – pursuing the radiation device.'

Jane took in a deep breath through her nose; her teeth tightly clasped together.

Here goes.

'You can stop this, Director.'

Another pause.

'How is that so, Miss Baker?'

'We both know that Nikolay Sokolov is behind this. You can get him stopped.'

The director chuckled.

What's so funny?

'I have no control over Mr Sokolov, I'm afraid, Miss Baker. He is, as you westerners say, "above my pay grade".'

Jane thought she understood. Sokolov was as close to the Russian premier as any man could get. Any case against him would have to be completely watertight, and, even then, he might walk away unscathed. The director of the FSB undermined by an oligarch? That's where Russia stood right now.

'You could stop him, Miss Baker.'

What?

'I'm not sure I understand, Director.'

There was a pause.

'Yes, I think you do, Miss Baker.'

Jane looked to the sky. She didn't need any inspiration. She just needed to get away from here. From the responsibilities that she carried. From the stench of burnt corpses; from the expectations of her staff. From Nikolay Sokolov. From everything.

She now knew that the director of the FSB was onto the Pierrot file.

Or… he *thought* he knew about it. Because if he had been absolutely certain, no amount of protection could save Sokolov.

What had he just said? 'I have no control over Mr Sokolov... he is above my pay grade.'

So – he *wasn't* completely sure. There was doubt.

And she wasn't going to elucidate.

'I have absolutely no idea what you're inferring, Director.'

Chapter 17

36°52'37.2"N 23°36'38.1"E, The Aegean Sea.

Where am I? Shit, that hurts – my shoulder is throbbing like hell. Come on, open your eyes!

Sam opened her eyes. And immediately closed them again. The light was too bright. Instead, she lay still and listened to her body; felt her environment. She was on something soft, probably a mattress. Her heart was beating regularly – maybe 75 beats per minute, quicker than her usual resting rate of 54, but at least it was a steady rhythm. Her shoulder ached like there was no tomorrow – *I was shot, that's it. I remember.* As she was running in the woods? She couldn't picture the detail. It was something like that.

She felt really groggy.

Keep checking. She tensed the muscles in her legs. They worked. Breathed in deeply. *Ouch!* Her shoulder didn't like that. There was no smell, other than something clean? The whole room was swaying, accompanied by a slapping sound – *hull on water?* And she needed a pee.

OK, let's do this.

She opened her left eye. She blinked. Closed it. Opened it again – and blinked again. This time she managed to keep the eye open. She was in a small room, lying on top of a mattress on a metal-ended bed. No sheets, or blankets. The room was mostly white, and some shades of blue. It looked completely sanitised. Like a plastic pod you could wash down with a hose in a couple of minutes. The bed, which was up against one wall, took up most of the room. On the far, narrow wall, was a door. It was funny shaped, oval at the top. There was no door handle. But, at eye height to its left, there was a biometric iris reader accompanied by a simple, dull-chrome button – she knew what they looked like. That told her something.

She opened her other eye. Stereoscopic vision. Brilliant. But it was still the same pokey, whitewashed room. She lifted her head; the pain in her shoulder ramped up a couple of notches, but not so much that she couldn't bear it. Beside her was a metal shelf, riveted to the wall. A wall which curved gently outward as it followed the hull of, what Sam assumed was, a pretty big boat. And beyond that, opposite her, was a door-shaped space leading into a simple en suite. A metal toilet bowl, which didn't seem to look like it had a seat; a metal sink; and she thought she saw the edge of a shower.

There were no decorations. No signs. A bed, a sink, a loo, a shower and no space to swing a cat. No porthole. She was in a compact, comfortable room, which doubled up as a cell? Or maybe the other way round? At least it wasn't a shipping container. She shivered at the thought.

She was on a big boat?

Cressida?

Sam slowly lifted herself up, using her good arm – her left – to steady herself, and swung her feet off the bed. She looked at what she was wearing. Dark blue coveralls. No underwear. Give her a white hard hat and some mirrored shades and she could understudy for the Village People. She poked at her right shoulder. Padding, under the coveralls. A dressing. She lifted the collar and had a look. Competently done. No signs of blood. She wanted to put her finger under the bandage and have a look at the hole. She assumed she'd see a big gash – an exit wound. She wouldn't see the entrance wound without a mirror. She leant forward and peered into the en suite. No mirror. The whole place was devoid of anything that wasn't riveted down. Except for her.

Definitely a cell.

She'd leave the dressing alone. It was doing a good enough job.

She studied her feet. White slippers, the sort you get given in an hotel. No shoelaces. She wouldn't be hanging herself from the rafters any time soon then.

Sam attempted to stand, but needed two goes. The pain in her shoulder nagged like a decaying tooth. She waddled across to the en suite. As she thought: a metal shower, a metal sink and a metal bowl. Nothing to be used as a weapon.

She carefully undid the press studs on her coveralls and sat down. The seat was cold against her bum.

As she peed, the sound oddly comforting against the metal of the pan, she tried to remember anything she could about the last... how long had she been out for? She had no idea. They had taken her watch and her phone. There was no porthole, and, therefore, no sun. The only light was artificial, neon strips imbedded in the ceiling with the metal surrounds riveted in place. Was it morning? Her stomach rumbled. *I'm hungry.* So at least one meal time later than when she was last awake. Saturday morning? *Possibly.*

She remembered being shot. *Think, what else?* She closed her eyes, the vision of the man with the gun coalescing into her consciousness. Then what? Boot of a car? Did she remember the smell of rubber? A spare tyre? And... it was no use. Her memory had failed her. Maybe they had drugged her?

Try the here and now.

She was on a boat. A big one. Very likely to be *Cressida*. She hadn't seen the satellite photos that had come through of the berth. But, what was in Debbie's report of Thursday night? *The berth had been empty on all images.*

Was it in transit somewhere – carrying the device?

That's right. She'd just opened *vesselfinder* when the two goons had arrived at the cabin. She had been trying to establish where *Cressida* was.

No. That didn't make sense. Why would anyone put a radioactive bomb on a, what had Sokolov's file said? A £100 million superyacht. She and Vlad – *God,*

Vlad! How could I forget? I wonder how he is? Her heart started to sink. All of a sudden, she was in freefall. She tried to banish the thought.

Stop!

She couldn't banish the thought. Her world started to crumble at the edges. She felt anguish closing in. He was down; she had tried to get away. *Without him!* Both of them shot. Was he dead? Her bottom lip wobbled. The thought was too much for her. She squeezed her eyes tightly shut. No tears. She couldn't afford tears. Flippancy had been uprooted and been replaced with pain.

Come on, girl. None of this was helping.

She shook her head. Her shoulder reminded her that that wasn't necessarily a good plan.

Get with the programme!

Now!

Good.

She breathed out heavily.

Where was I?

She sniffed.

She and Vlad had agreed that Sokolov was doing this for the chaos that would ensue; and what that impact would have on commodity prices. But, even so, you wouldn't spoil a £100 million yacht for the chance that that *might* happen. Would you?

She wiped herself – there was a loo roll on the floor next to the pan. But there was no soap and no towels. Showering was going to be a lot of fun.

Clunk.

The door. Sam quickly stood up and pulled on her coveralls. Her shoulder protested. She poked her head into the bedroom.

It was a woman. A big woman. Not hugely fat, although she carried plenty of spare flesh. Big, though, as in rugby prop-forward big. She wore grey joggers, a black hoodie with a zip down the front and two pockets, and a pair of white Asics sneakers.

She was carrying a plastic tray. Various bits of cold food were chopped up on the tray: cheese, ham, chunks of bread, whole baby tomatoes. And a plastic beaker with, she could smell it, coffee. The woman placed the tray carefully on the bed.

'Eat this. I will be back in ten minutes to pick up the tray and the mug.' Her English was unpolished, but comprehensible.

'Thank you.' Sam came back in perfect Russian. She chose a Muscovite accent.

The woman didn't flinch.

'How is your shoulder?' English again.

Compassion?

'Fine, thank you.' Russian.

She reached into a pocket and pulled out a couple of green and red pills.

'Take these.' Still English.

'No. Not until you tell me what they're for.' Sam continued in Russian.

'Please yourself.' English. She put them back in her pocket. 'Ten minutes. Then I'll be back. Enjoy.' The woman put her right eye (*check*) up against the reader and pressed the button. The door opened.

The perfect waitress. It could have been an exchange in any cafe in Paris.

Sam paused for a second. And then ate the food on the tray as though she hadn't eaten for a week. She left the coffee until last, sipping at it, savouring every drop.

4th Floor British Embassy, Moscow, Russia

Debbie had a hangover. She didn't normally drink, certainly not in quantity. But last night had been an exception. She was an SIS analyst. That's all. She wasn't trained to operate in the field. To assist with saving the life of a man who had been shot – and burnt. To discover that someone she knew well and liked a lot, hadn't survived a fire. To be at the scene where all of this had happened.

She didn't begrudge being involved. On reflection, she wouldn't have had it any other way. But it had knocked her sideward. Taken the wind out of her sails. And every other appropriate cliché she could think of.

And it had led her to drink. Too much.

The three of them left the scene after about two hours, once Jane had handed over to an FSB agent. Throughout, Jane was pensive; fretful. But in control.

Rich was fantastic. He had been so good with the poor man who had been shot. She assumed that Jane was equally qualified in first aid. Perhaps all case-officers were? Debbie certainly couldn't have done what Rich had done. The man wouldn't have survived a minute in her hands.

When they'd got back to the Embassy it was almost 5pm. Jane had sent her home. It was an order she was glad to be given. She'd been tearful in the car on the way back thinking about poor Sam. She couldn't handle seeing her yesterday sat at her computer, and then not seeing her today. Even though they were just metres from each other.

If she'd have got back behind her desk, she wouldn't have managed to do anything meaningful. Being sent home was a blessing.

She'd drunk a whole bottle of red wine – thick stuff; gorgeous. It was the one she had won in the raffle at the staff Christmas party. She was halfway down the bottle before she'd decided to cook. And then she had been too fuzzy to make any sensible decisions, so had had some toast and ham. She then drank the other half, trying hard not to go over the events of the day. At about 10pm she had showered and, rather wobbly, made her way to bed.

She'd made it to Saturday – and she didn't have to be in work. But she needed to purge the alcohol and get away from being alone in her apartment – thinking. And, she needed to complete what she had started yesterday – with Sokolov's yacht. For Sam's sake.

Both Rich and Jane were in when Debbie arrived.

Rich was onto the FSB, waiting for any forensics to come back from the fire site. Jane was in M's office. She had no idea what she was up to. It was quiet and sombre.

Start.

Coffee and paracetamol in one hand – mouse in the other. Head throbbing.

After yesterday there were now eight photos of the berth in Sevastopol: five daylight shots (10am and 4pm Thursday, the same for Friday and 10am this morning), and three night-time infrared shots (2am Thursday, Friday and, again, 2am this morning). Langley had failed to deliver the first shot that Sam had ordered – Wednesday 4pm. They hadn't managed to get their act together.

It had taken her 30 minutes to look at all the photos in detail. There was only one anomaly: it was on the 2am Thursday infrared (IR) shot. IR shots are notoriously difficult to read. For a start, the quality is nowhere near as good – around 80-centimetre resolution, as opposed to ten centimetres for daylight images; but you work with what you have. The real complication is that normal photographs show light and shade, which is what the brain naturally recognises (and the ones she had were monochrome, giving the very best possible resolution). IR images, on the other hand, display hot and cold (again, monochrome). Hot is white. Cold is black. Shades of grey in between. You had to think differently. For example, providing it had been driven recently, an IR car isn't car shaped. It's just a hot engine – a 'hotspot', with warm tyres heated by the friction of rubber on tarmac. Its windows, which reflect IR, are dark grey or black. It doesn't look like a normal car; it looks like an IR car. If you have experience, you can pick out make and, sometimes, model. It was a skill. And Debbie was good at it.

The anomaly on the Thursday 2am IR image was a particularly bright hotspot on the quayside. It was rectangular, although a bit fuzzy at the edges. Debbie did some calculations: it was two metres by one metre. And it was ten metres away from the berth – which was empty. *Cressida* still wasn't in any of the photos.

She looked at the next image, that from an overhead at 10am, Thursday morning. Even though there were some clouds, the quayside was as clear as anything. There was nothing where the hotspot had been eight hours previously.

All images can throw up distortions; light-sensitive electronics have a habit of doing their own thing sometimes. IR was notorious for it. This was probably one of those? But she'd be thorough. She looked at the next image in sequence; 6pm Thursday. Nothing. And then the next – another IR shot: Friday 2am.

That's odd.

In exactly the same place as the previous IR image, there was a faint replica of the original hotspot. She put one image on one screen, and the second on the other. Two IR images side by side. She glanced from one to the other: hotspot – trace. She looked again: hotspot – trace. She didn't get that at all. She almost called Rich over for a second opinion. But thought better of it. She would come back to it.

Debbie was about to move onto Sokolov's dacha,

to look over the old and recent images, when she remembered what GCHQ had said about Sam's mobile browsing history. The last page she'd looked at was *vesselfinder.com*.

She reduced the images and opened the website. The opening page was a map of the North Atlantic and a dialogue box: *Search by Ship name/IMO/MMSI*. She typed in *Cressida*. Three ships were immediately displayed in a drop-down box. She opened the first, it was a huge oil tanker. Position: somewhere in the Caribbean. Debbie thought probably coming into or going out of The Panama Canal.

Nope.

She hit the jackpot with the second.

CRESSIDA
VESSELS>>YACHTS AND SAILING VESSELS

There was an accompanying photo of a 230-foot-long, brilliantly white, super yacht. It shouted luxury and opulence. The app gave its current location as 44.616N, 33.525E, and it had yesterday's date. Further down the page was a 'Track on Map' icon. She clicked on it.

And there it was.

Sevastopol. A yellow arrow designated its location. She stretched the image. It was quayside, in its berth. But Debbie knew *Cressida* wasn't in Sevastopol. The berth was empty. The images told her that.

Something wasn't right.

She did five minutes' research on how the tracking system worked. In essence, each ship sent out an Automatic Identification System (AIS) signal, which was used to triangulate where they were. It had been around for ages and seemed pretty bomb-proof.

The AIS from *Cressida* must be broken?

'Rich?' Debbie called out across the office.

'Yup?'

'Can you pop over here, please?'

Rich was on his feet and across at Debbie's side in no time.

He looked miserable; reflective. He struggled to find a smile.

I know how you feel.

She explained what she had found with *Cressida's* AIS.

He pulled up a chair.

'I spent some time working alongside the Coastguard when I was a copper. They use the AIS system all the time. If there's a satellite system fitted, then the ship can be tracked anywhere in the world. If it's VHF, radio signals, it's only trackable to within about 60 kilometres of any landmass. So, some boats can get hidden at sea.' His mood had picked up. He was working.

Debbie was impressed. Rich leant forward and

gently motioned for her to release the mouse. He took it and clicked on the current display.

'No, *Cressida's* is VHF only. Which is a surprise. I'd have thought Sokolov's yacht would have both fitted. Can you throw up the image of the berth?'

Debbie did so on her second screen – it was the latest monochrome from yesterday afternoon.

'Pan out, as far as you can, please.'

She did. The image showed one square kilometre of marina, quayside and sea.

Rich drummed his fingers.

'*Cressida* is not in this photo. But if you look here...' Rich was back on the original screen and playing with the *vesselfinder*. He clicked on a couple of icons. 'You can see the boat's recent movement, with these sets of new arrows – normally a history of the past seven days. According to this, it's been sat quayside for the last four days. Mmm. Photo says "no"; *vesselfinder* says "yes". But...' He paused, rubbing his chin with his hand.

'Go on, Rich.'

'The VHF signal is not wholly accurate. It depends how close you are to the land; it could be hundreds of metres out.'

'But this is a square kilometre? That would subsume any error? The boat would be here on the screen somewhere?' Debbie still thought they had an anomaly.

'It would seem that way. But I wouldn't be so sure.

These things aren't foolproof.'

Debbie was still unconvinced.

'Sam was onto this – It was the last thing she looked at, before, well, you know.' She was struggling to hold it together. She coughed, to clear the frog from her throat. 'What do we do?'

Rich placed a comforting hand on her forearm.

'Somehow, we get a full overview of the shipyard/marina, call it what you will. If Sokolov's boat is there, somewhere, out of picture, this is a red herring. If not, then somebody is purposefully deceiving the AIS system. They want the world to think the boat is in Sevastopol. When – who knows where it is?'

'Do you think the boat could be carrying the bomb?'

There was a pause.

'No. I think this is a genuine gremlin in the system. Sokolov's boat is in dry dock, off image. Or, some other plausible explanation. Come on, let's face it. Would you carry 30 kilograms of uranium waste on your pristine mega-yacht?'

Debbie shook her head. She wouldn't.

'So, we need to sort this. Let's take it to Jane. The earliest we could get a full set of images of the whole area is in, say, 12 hours?'

Debbie nodded. 'A complete set. Yes. Maybe quicker. Or slower? It is a Saturday.'

He rubbed his chin again.

'What are you doing for the rest of the weekend?'

That made her sit back.

'Do you think we should go down there?'

'I've been before. Flown. We could easily be down in eight hours and back within 24. We've got some simple radio detection equipment in the store. We could find the boat, easily enough.'

'And if it's not there?'

Rich shrugged his shoulders.

'It's somewhere else.'

Jane had sent Rich and Debbie off to Sevastopol. There was little else for them to do, and she needed to get some certainty on *Cressida*. She guessed it would also help to take their minds off where they all found themselves.

The quickest way to verify if *Cressida* was in the dock, would have been to speak to the FSB. They could contact someone at the port, and do what she'd asked of Rich and Debbie.

But.

If this *were* an elaborate scam – a sort of pillow-under-your-blankets deception, then she wouldn't put it past Sokolov to own men at the port who would 'see' the boat in the berth, even though it wasn't actually there.

And she needed to be absolutely sure before she alerted the whole of the Western European security infrastructure to look out for a big white boat.

Especially as it didn't fit. She couldn't rationalise it. You don't carry a hugely radioactive device on a mega-yacht. Not without encasing it in lead – or similar. And then you'd struggle to manhandle what you had. You'd need a big crane and a huge truck at your destination to take it anywhere. No, she'd need confirmation that *Cressida* wasn't in the port before she sent those hares running. And, if Rich were as good as his word, they'd be at the port by early evening. They'd taken some gadget with them which Jane had never seen before, but Rich assured her would track down the VHF beacon.

The hares would have to wait.

So, what to do now? She needed to keep herself occupied. She needed someone to give her something to do, like she had for Rich and Debbie. Sure, she had plenty of work – there were countless reports from London from her other desk-officers that she should be reading. But, the sense of grief she felt for Sam was a burden she couldn't compute. It sat on her shoulders like a heavy, damp coat; pulling her down. Tears were never very far away. Throughout the morning she'd spent more time with her head in her hands, than at her keyboard. It was all too awful to contemplate.

She needed to be occupied – on the dirty-bomb case. Helping finish what Sam had started.

First thing she'd called the chief in London. They'd spoken yesterday, but she'd wanted to revisit the discussion she'd had with the director of the FSB concerning Sokolov. C hadn't changed his mind overnight. He reckoned that Pierrot was intact, and Jane agreed with him. As such, they'd leave well alone.

For now. It was the lesser of two unspeakable evils, but only just. C told her to phone him if the situation changed in any way. Then they would reconsider.

Vauxhall had taken full responsibility for their UK's side of Op Samantha. They had a team of seven multi-agency staff working on it around the clock. The assumption was the device was headed west, and likely out of territorial Russia. All national security agencies were alerted to the threat and borders were being monitored. Radiation experts were stood by, but the target list was so long, nobody could adequately focus their efforts. The German Federal Intelligence Service, the BSV, was particularly concerned about the threat to Berlin. They had upped regular police patrols, and were conducting random stop-and-searches on anything van-sized and above. At most it was a deterrent. There was little hope of actually finding the bomb this way.

They had nothing new from Saudi, nor from any of the other out-stations. If it were al-Qaeda, they were doing a very good job at keeping the lid on it.

And 14 Signal Regiment had a LEWT on six hours' notice-to-move. A Special Forces Chinook helicopter was at the same notice. And a government-owned HS 125, twin-jet aircraft, was stood by – should the target be out of Chinook range.

On the other issue, M2 was on the suicide case and handling it well. She was right about Simon Page's staff. After the initial shock of the news, they had settled back into their routine without too much fuss.

Jane drummed her fingers. What to do? Yesterday

came back into view.

Do something!

Her patience snapped.

She picked up her mobile and phoned Frank.

'Hi Jane. Are you OK?'

'Hi Frank. Yes. No. Not at all. But it will heal eventually.' *I hope.* 'What about you?'

Nothing came back initially.

Then, 'Sorry, Jane. I can't begin to tell you. It's Berlin all over again. I'm not sure I'm going to fully recover this time.'

Jane sighed. It was all rubbish. They'd lost Sam once before in Berlin – for two days. But then, they always hoped. This time, there seemed little point in hoping.

'I know, Frank. I know.' She paused. 'Can we do some work?'

'Yes. Please.'

Good.

'Look, this is a long shot. In fact, so long I'm worried about throwing it into the mix – so don't share with the team. I don't want them distracted.'

'OK.'

'We may have lost Sokolov's mega-yacht, *Cressida*. It should be in Sevastopol, but may not be. I've got a couple of staff heading down there now to check it out. Could you get in touch with the Maritime and Coastguard Agency, and put feelers out to see if they have any method of tracking a 200-foot yacht – that doesn't want to be found?'

'You've looked on *vesselfinder*, for the boat's AIS?'

'Yes. It says it's in port; Sevastopol. But the airphots Sam ordered tell a different story.'

'OK. I can see why you might think that's an issue. But, who delivers a nuclear device on a yacht the size of Southampton?'

'Exactly. And the AIS system isn't bomb-proof.'

'Indeed. OK. I'm on it.'

'Thanks.'

Jane felt a little better at having done something proactive.

Crestline, Northeast of Los Angeles, USA

Todd Mason was having another of his 'good days', even though it was only 9am. He loved his job, especially after the move to California. Out in the fresh air all day, with views of Twin Peaks. When he climbed up the largest of the fracking fluid bowsers – which was over 60 feet high, he caught a rare glimpse of the beautiful Pacific Ocean. And nestling on its shore, the metropolis that was Los Angeles.

The drilling looked good. The well had been cased at the end of last month, and they had started preparatory fracking on Monday. It wasn't his side of the business, but Todd, a drilling engineer pal of his, had given him the thumbs-up the other day. They were three weeks ahead of schedule, but starting slow – just 100 barrels a day. That would quickly ramp up, certainly now the Federal Energy Regulatory Commission (FERC) officer had been round and given them the all-clear. Todd reckoned they would all get a $500 bonus for completing early, especially as they were working weekends – which was great. He was saving up for a bright red 1957 Mustang, which was on the forecourt of a dealership downtown. His $500 would probably buy the four hubcaps.

He checked the pressure reading on the main pipe's gauge, the big one that fed the well. It was reading 8,750 pounds per square inch. He tapped it with his knuckles, a sort of 'good luck' tap. Unsurprisingly, the gauge didn't move. He then checked the level of the fluid bowser that was in use. It read 560 gallons; about three days' supply left. The other two towers were empty – it was pointless spending cash on fracking fluid until the well had been given the green light by FERC. He had the order in. The prepared fluid would arrive on Monday, pulled by three Mac trucks. He had them down arriving at 9.30am, from the usual supplier. He'd be ready for that.

'Hi, Todd.' It was Brad, the site foreman.

'Hi Brad. Lovely day?'

'Sure is. How's it going?'

'Good. All good. Thanks.'

'I see you have the fluid ordered for Monday?'

'That's right, Brad. From *Fluid Companion*, the usual

team.'

Brad grimaced. It could have been the sun, which was just beginning to hit his eye line.

'Sorry, Todd. I've cancelled that. We have a new supplier. I've duplicated your order and the first truck should arrive late on Tuesday. We'll balance any drilling to meet the later availability of fluid.'

'But...' Todd was confused. 'Why change the supplier? Are they cheaper?'

Brad smiled. 'Considerably so.'

'And why is it coming so late? Are they shipping the stuff down from Alaska?'

Brad smarted.

'You don't know how close you are to the truth, Todd.'

Sevastopol Port, Crimea, Russia

It had taken Rich and Debbie six and a half hours to get portside. They had booked onto the 3.45pm from Moscow (SVO) to Sevastopol, but it had been delayed. They then had trouble hiring a car and, without any GPS fitted, it had taken them an hour and a half to find the correct entrance to the port.

Rich, who spoke fluent Russian, was having an animated conversation with a marine-security guard. Debbie stayed in the car to keep warm. It was bitterly cold, with a strong, damp wind blowing in from the Black Sea. She could see Rich bent over, talking to a man in a booth through a slit in the window. There was limited lighting, but she picked out Rich showing the man an ID card. It seemed to do the trick. He jogged back to the car.

'What did you show him?'

'I have an FSB pass. It gives me limited access to a couple of buildings in Moscow. Here – I can go anywhere!'

Debbie grinned (which was against the wishes of her persistent hangover). Rich was fun to be with. And relatively normal – for a spy.

The port was half riverbank, half large, industrial marina – they'd looked at Google Maps before they had left the office. The Chrona River, which Sevastopol straddled, didn't appear to be wide enough to be a natural harbour. But, in reality it was bigger than it looked on the map. Even in the semi-dark she could now see why it made a decent port.

They were on the east-side dock. It was filled with an eclectic mixture of ships and boats – Debbie really didn't know the difference between the two. Surprisingly, the latest satellite image showed that there were plenty of grey Russian navy ships moored alongside the tankers and cruisers. As they drove down the concrete quayside, commercial buildings on their left, the back ends of some huge ships on their right, she spotted a submarine. She remembered Sam describing the TK-202; something along the lines of, 'as big as a skyscraper on its side'. This one wasn't that big, but it was certainly akin to a row of terraced houses.

With a blanket of low cloud, and now accompanying light rain, all the boats looked bleak. The naval ones more rust coloured than grey paint. Intermittent, dull orange street lamps, and a line of run-down and rickety buildings added to the gloom.

Debbie was counting the ships. *Cressida's* berth should be the 17th along next to a small naval boat, and just before a non-military boat – some sort of medium-sized, civilian cruiser.

And there it was. Or wasn't. A gap, about 15 metres wide. Naval ship on the right, and a large, ageing pleasure craft on the left. There was a long, possibly 50 metre, concrete and wooden jetty running perpendicular to the quayside. Every eight metres or so a bulbous piece of metal sprung out of the concrete. Hanging from these were a couple of those big, wardrobe-sized rubber fenders; protection for the side of the ship. At the end of the jetty, which was decorated with plenty of carelessly coiled, heavy ropes, she could just about make out an unlit streetlight.

Rich got out. Debbie followed him. He opened the rear door and, from his holdall, took out the 'gadget'. It looked very Heath Robinson: like a large, plastic pistol. At the dangerous end, there was a horizontal metal rod with a vertical spike at either end. Like a TV aerial that had moulted.

It was interesting, but not interesting enough to keep out the cold. The wind whipped Debbie's hair across her face. She was looking forward to supper – in a warm hotel.

Rich, on the other hand, was very excited.

'It's a VHF/HF direction finder. The two antennae here...' he was pointing unnecessarily at the two aerials at the end of the gun-shaped thing (she'd worked that out), 'pick up the signal that you tune to. Because they're separated by a short distance, a clever bloke in here,' he was now pointing at the main bit of the gun, 'can sense two very slightly different angles from the signal. As you turn it...' he now did a short twist of his hips, 'the machine gives out a bleep. The loudest bleep indicates the direction of the signal. It's all very simple!' He grinned. Ear to ear.

Debbie gave him a patronising smile. She hoped he couldn't tell.

Get on with it then...

He did. As he walked around the jetty pointing the thing, Debbie heard him shout, 'I've already tapped in the correct frequency for *Cressida*.'

She heard some beeping, and then a continuous noise. Rich was now walking down the quay. Thankfully he stayed in a straight line; to deviate would have been a very wet experience.

'It's coming from over there!' His words deadened by the wind.

She jogged to catch up with him. The further down the jetty they walked, the worse the wind got. And it had now started to rain heavily. *Perfect*. She put up her hood.

They were at the end of the jetty. Rich put down the direction finder and looked up at the unlit lamp.

Now she knew why it was unlit. It had a box on the top; not a light. Rich had taken off his jacket and he held it out to her; she took it. And then, to Debbie's surprise, he shimmied up the lamp post. It was about four metres tall. She moved closer to the pole, pointlessly preparing herself to break Rich's fall, should that happen. It wasn't necessary. Expertly, Rich opened a small door in the side of the box, and looked in. He then reached into his pocket, took out his phone, and, all with one hand, snapped a photo; the phone's flash momentarily lighting up the sheeting rain, as well as the inside of the metal box.

Then he was down. Debbie stepped away. In the short time he'd been up the pole, the wind seemed to have increased to gale force. She was hugging her arms to her chest. He, seemingly unaware of the cold, picked up the direction finder and brought his face to within a few centimetres of hers. He was wet; rain streaking down his cheeks, dripping from his chin. And he was smiling.

'Success.' He was almost shouting; the wind so strong it was whisking away his words. '*Cressida* is not here. But someone wants us to think that she is.' He pointed at the box on top of the pole. 'The AIS system is in there. Wired into the mains. Very simple *and* very clever. We need to get this to Jane, and then get dry. And then eat some food. They do good dumplings here!'

Was that sarcasm?

Delta Hotel, Sevastopol, Crimea, Russia

Debbie felt much better having had a shower and eaten something that might be called 'food'. She and Rich were sat at the bar. She was exhausted. She had ordered a coffee, he a beer. She hadn't drunk any alcohol. So as not to appear a prude, she explained to Rich about the hangover which, thankfully, was a shadow of its former self. She really didn't feel up to drinking. Not tonight.

Rich had phoned Jane as they drove to the hotel, putting her on speaker so Debbie could hear. He'd already sent her a copy of the photo of the inside the box. The AIS had a serial number on it, which you could see in the picture. He was confident that you could match the number against *Cressida's* designated system. But, what was obvious: *Cressida* was off doing something she probably shouldn't.

Jane was convinced (and pleased) – but she still thought that they were short of conclusive evidence. She needed something that irrefutably tied the device to the boat. Nonetheless, she was sure that Vauxhall would now send out an 'all ports' call, looking out for *Cressida*. She may be 200 feet plus, but there were hundreds, maybe thousands of berths in the Med where a boat of her size could dock, unload, and then disappear back out to sea. Then there was the remaining issue of 'who in their right mind would carry 30 kilograms of uranium on their pristine show-boat?' It was essential that they tie the device to the yacht. Somehow.

Debbie took a sip of her coffee.

'If the device is on *Cressida*, what do you think the target is?' Rich asked.

Debbie's geography of the Mediterranean was restricted to major ports. Her view was that, if you ruled out anything on the north African mainland, you could probably count suitable targets – those with the biggest impact – on just over one hand: Tel Aviv; Istanbul; Venice, Rome, Nice, Marseilles and Barcelona. She spelt them out to Rich.

'I know I suggested Rome earlier in the week, but it's not a port?'

'No, but there is a port a short distance away that services Rome. You could offload the device, and drive it to the front steps of the Vatican, or the Trevi Fountain. Or any of a hundred other spectaculars.'

'OK, I get that. But with the French very jumpy over the whole Islamic terrorist issue, I'd put Marseilles and Nice a close second. Or, and maybe you discounted it, Monte Carlo?'

Would anyone really mind if Monte Carlo was targeted?

'I don't get Monte Carlo. Who would care if a load of rich folk get irradiated?'

Rich laughed at that.

The longer they talked, the more something bugged her. It was Jane's earlier line about being 'short of conclusive evidence'.

Just as they were about to call it a day, a penny teetered, and then dropped.

'Do you have a firm's Nexus on you?' she asked Rich.

'I do, it's in my room. I'll go and get it.'

He was back a few minutes later.

'Can you log in as me?' Debbie asked.

'No, not quite. But I can log in as me, and access your account. If you give me your password.'

Between them, with the Nexus on the bar, they accessed Debbie's files. She opened the two IR images of the berth – the one showing the very bright hotspot, and the second, a much lighter, almost 'stain' of the first.

'What do you think?' She pointed at the hotspot. 'I hate to sound unscientific, but is nuclear radiation in the red or blue part of the electromagnetic spectrum?'

Rich expanded the image.

'Definitely red.' He was concentrating. 'Hmmm. Could be a couple of pixel irregularities – some burnout. But I'm not sure. And why coincident, two nights running? This is a hotspot – either something very warm, like a fire. Or a rectangular block of radiation. And this,' he swiped the Nexus and pointed at the lesser mark on the second image, 'could be irradiated concrete or tarmac, left over from the previous evening.'

Rich sat back on the bar stool. And breathed out heavily. He then picked up the Nexus and compressed the image back to normal size. The hotspot was now no bigger than four or five pixels. He studied it for a while.

'Can I have a look at any daylight images taken between these? I'm looking for something.'

There were two. Debbie brought them up, and handed the Nexus back to Rich.

He played with them for a few of minutes. Debbie finished her coffee.

He then showed the Nexus's screen to Debbie. It displayed a full-size photo, one square kilometre, of a big chunk of the port and river – the 10am shot, the one following the night-time hotspot.

'What's that?'

Rich was pointing at the very top of the screen, in the middle of the channel. Two small things that weren't water. And easily missable, if you weren't looking for them. One was the tail end of something which was off screen. It appeared to be a very small part of a white boat – probably a slice of its stern. Right behind it was a much smaller vessel which you could see all of. With the fabulous resolution they had, you could pick out ropes connecting it to the stern of the larger boat.

Debbie expanded the image and dragged it so that the two objects were in the centre of the screen. It was clear.

'Damn. How could I miss that?' Debbie was furious with herself.

'Nothing to miss. If you hadn't picked up the radioactive hotspot, I wouldn't have given the image a second thought. Instead we've got what looks like the back end of a *Cressida*-sized boat towing a tender. A tender big enough to be full of explosives and uranium.'

He finished his beer.

'We'd better call Jane.'

DESTRUCTION

Chapter 18

38°09'27.1"N 15°36'12.0"E – Short of the Straits of Messina, Sicily, Italy

Sam had worked out the rough time of day. The big woman had just brought in her latest meal. It was fruit, some bread and a glass of orange juice. Breakfast. About 12 hours ago (she couldn't be sure), she had been served a selection of cold meats, cold potatoes, bread, tomatoes, some sliced cucumber and that fabulous coffee. Plus, and this had sealed the timing thing for Sam, a slice of chocolate cake – pudding. That was supper then.

For both of those meals, and the previous lunch, she had accepted the red and green pills from the woman. Sam had assumed that they were antibiotics – to chase away any infection from the gunshot wound. It seemed churlish not to take them.

Every time the woman had come in, Sam had engaged her with simple, non-threatening questions;

trying to build a relationship that she might exploit sometime in the future.

The question she really wanted answering was: 'why are you keeping me alive?' The UK government would be all over her disappearance like a rash. And she was sure SIS wouldn't stand by if there were half a chance that they could extract her from wherever she was.

Surely, from Sokolov's perspective, she was better off at the bottom of the sea? Or they could have finished her off at the log cabin?

Sam pressed the woman on that issue this morning.

'Why are you keeping me alive?' *Positive, passive* – another lesson from training. 'Why haven't you killed me?' would be considered: negative, aggressive. Stay positive and keep the dialogue calm; that was the key to success negotiations. Sam had also switched to English now; her waitresses' preferred language. She was probably practising; Sam obliged.

The woman, who was about to do the iris thing and leave with the breakfast tray, stopped and turned to Sam.

'The boss wants to see you. That's all. I wouldn't get too comfortable.'

And with that, she left.

OK?

Sam wasn't surprised that her stay was an interregnum. They wanted her for something. And then they'd get rid of her. That's what would happen.

Whatever, it had bought her some space. She had to

see this additional time as an opportunity.

She'd worked every square inch of the pod and found nothing that might help her escape. Everything was tied down. Mealtimes looked hopeless – it was all edible, except the tray, which was a thin plastic affair, and a plastic mug. They were hardly weapons.

But, if 'the boss', who she assumed was Sokolov, wanted to see her, at least then she'd be taken from the pod. She'd seize the first opportunity she had. And then the second. Until she ran out of chances.

In the meantime…

The only good thing about the pod was, it wasn't soundproof. She'd spent two hours last night with her ear up against the door. She thought she'd heard at least three people walk past during the evening. There had been the constant hum of the motor, the slapping of the waves, and, just before she'd called it a day, there was some shouting down the corridor that she couldn't decipher.

Sam decided that this morning she would listen some more. She sat with her good shoulder against the door. Her wound throbbed, and didn't enjoy sudden movement, but it was workable.

She listened.

Nothing.

Maybe an hour passed.

She continued to listen.

And then, her first small success. It was two men. They walked past the door talking. She picked up three or four sentences, the voices rising and falling like a siren on a passing police car.

'How long do you think she's got left?' Russian with an English accent.

'Not long. Then it's over the side for the congressman's daughter.' Russian.

'Where will we be for the next one?'

The reply was too quiet to hear. It sounded like a single, or maybe a double syllable word. Perhaps, Venice? Or Rome?

The congressman's daughter? She had seen the deputy director of the FBI on the TV in the cabin. *Holly Mickelson*. The missing congressman's daughter. One of the young women abducted. She had been taken from Istanbul. There were two other women, one had been washed up ashore on Corfu. Kelly Jameson and Lizzie Jefferson.

Holly Mickelson was on the boat. Abducted by Sokolov. As Sam had been. But why? And her days were also numbered? *'Not long'*. How long was 'not long'?

What is going on?

Sam didn't have time to pursue the question in her head; she heard a new sound. The unmistakable slapping of rotor blades as they cut through the air. She listened: *single set of blades; heavy beat; twin engine; medium-sized helicopter*. It could well be a *Sikorsky* S-76D? One of the most popular executive helicopters in the world. Was this the boss arriving? He wanted to see her. Would it be soon?

She stood up and wandered over to the bed.

Holly Mickelson. She was on board. And Vlad? Somehow, she didn't think so. Sokolov was Russian. A powerful one. They could cover Vlad's shooting with something along the lines of trespass. But, would he risk holding an FSB agent hostage? Maybe? She'd need to find out. She couldn't leave the boat without him.

Could she leave without Holly Mickelson?

Her thoughts were interrupted.

The door opened and in came the big woman. She was carrying a pair of handcuffs.

'Wrists.'

Is this an opportunity?

Too late. Sam had instinctively offered her wrists and was now in chains. She hadn't seen a key.

'Don't try anything. I'm quicker than I look.'

The woman opened the door biometrically and pulled Sam out into the corridor by the cuffs. With her hands tied, she couldn't have tried anything even if she'd wanted to.

She followed the woman down a beautifully appointed corridor. Red, exquisitely patterned carpets. Gentlemen's club, rosewood panelling on the bottom half of the walls. The upper wall was finished in deep cream paint. Between wooden side-doors, someone had hung paintings. Sam was no expert, but they all looked very expensive.

After about ten metres, the corridor opened into a wide and deep hallway, with a wooden, double staircase leading up to a gallery. Above normal ceiling height, and in line with the gallery, all the other three walls were glass; natural light streaming in from an outdoors Sam hadn't seen for at least a day and a half. As she was dragged up the left-hand set of stairs, she glanced at the ceiling: a massive hexagonal window, rising to a point, framed a piercingly blue sky.

This must be the Mediterranean?

As they reached the gallery, she turned and looked behind her. Pride of place, and larger than life-size, was a portrait of Sokolov hanging on the far wall. He was dressed in equestrian gear and was stood beside a black horse. He looked every part a member of a royal family. There were no obvious indications, like a crown, a mace, or a chestful of medals. But the artist had been clever and used light to silhouette his head – almost like a halo. It was a clear statement: 'I am an incredibly important person.'

She closed her mouth, which was hanging slightly ajar.

Then they were in a huge lounge. It must have been 15 metres long and the full width of the boat. There was a central fireplace and flue, with surrounding bumwarmer, finished in red leather. There were sofas and scatter cushions, occasional tables laden with fruit and nuts, a bar in the corner, and the biggest TV Sam had ever seen. The decoration was more Scandinavian chic than the English gentlemen's club of downstairs, but she was equally as impressed. At the end of room were a set of sliding doors that filled the whole wall. Beyond that, Sam saw land on either side of the boat, with a channel in between. The boat was too far away to be sure, but the channel was probably about five kilometres wide. The land on both sides was mainly urban; old sandstone buildings intermingled with new high rises. To the left, she spotted an old-walled port, with a huge pillar at the entrance; it was topped with a gold statue. It wasn't the Bosporus. Istanbul was immediately recognisable – a multitude of minarets was the giveaway. They hadn't travelled far enough to reach Gibraltar; the channel wasn't wide enough, and she'd recognise the rock when she saw it.

Her guess: The Straits of Messina. Mainland Italy to her right. Sicily to her left. She'd not been here before, but knew the geography. Next stop – Rome. Or Naples. Or Marseilles. Or Barcelona. You could now discount Venice and Trieste.

Why Rome – or any of them?

'It pains me to use the cliché, but we meet again, Samantha Green.'

It was Sokolov's voice. He was behind her.

The big woman turned, pulling Sam with her.

There he was. As she remembered him. Big. Imposing. Tanned. Good looking, in a chiselled way. He'd lost the black tie and was now wearing expensive-looking, navy-blue chinos, and an open-necked, pinky-red polo shirt, which didn't sport a label. Inevitably, he wore two-tone, leather yachting shoes: mostly tan coloured, but with a cream top. No socks. He looked every part the playboy. Completely at home on his luxury yacht, having helicoptered in from somewhere equally exotic.

As he approached, Sam again spotted the

unmoving, right-hand side of his face; as if he'd had a stroke – or a skin graft, post a burn. She couldn't draw her eyes away.

'Take a seat.' He motioned to one of the huge sofas in the centre of the room. 'Marya. Fix us some coffee, please. And some pastries.'

Sam glanced at the big woman, now to be known as Marya. She looked confused. Wary.

'Don't worry, Marya. Samantha Green is safe with me.' He was standing beside her now. He touched Sam's hip and winked at her. She shivered.

Touch me again...

He didn't. She sat as ordered, and Sokolov slumped into an armchair that even made him look small. There was a table between them. Fresh tulips, reds and yellows, sprung out of a simple glass vase. There was a copy of *Yachting Monthly* to the side of the vase.

'So. Samantha Green.' Sokolov had his fingers intertwined in front of his chin. His legs were crossed. Sam felt like she'd been called into the headmaster's study for 'one of those chats'.

'What a fun time you've had. First you visit my oilfield in Salekhard. You give my boys the slip – I hope you realise they lost a month's wages because of your actions, and then you alert *Médecins Sans Frontières* to our very efficient fracking process. Putting that right was a lot of hard work, I can tell you. But we sorted it. And then you chase about in Arkhangelsk with your friend Vladimir, and end up where we really didn't want you.'

Sam stiffened at the sound of Vlad's name.

'Where is he?' she barked.

'Who?' Sokolov had now placed his hands on his chest, twiddling his thumbs. His head was tilted to one side. Just like a headmaster. He was enjoying this.

She was about to reply with heavy sarcasm, but stopped herself.

Positive, passive.

'Vlad. My FSB colleague.'

He breathed in and out through his nose. Biding his time.

'I'm sorry, Samantha, but he was caught up in a fire at the cabin. We did what we could.'

His condescension flew like an arrow into her chest. Her mind blanked. Then it spun. Sam was sitting with her cuffed hands on her lap. She had her right thumb in the palm of her left hand. She squeezed it so tight, she thought she might cut off its blood supply.

She tried to focus. She couldn't save Vlad now.

I can't save Vlad now.

Concentrate on the opportunities.

She took a breath. And another.

'Where's the target?'

'Ahh. Back to business. Good girl, Samantha. I thought you'd ask that.'

He turned his head to his right and stared out of the window.

Is he going to tell me?

It was surreal, like reciting the script of a James Bond movie. The bad guy confesses all. And then she gets fed to the sharks?

Well?!

'Ahh, Marya is back.'

The big woman placed the silver tray on the table. She stood back, waiting ominously beside the sofa.

Sam's mind wandered. The cups and saucers were espresso-sized and looked elegant enough to be Meissen. Sam's mum had been a very minor collector of fine pottery – she had one Meissen piece, a small milk jug. It sat pride of place in a glass cabinet. She'd have bitten Sokolov's arm off for this collection.

There was a plate full of Danish pastries and various croissants. Sokolov served coffee without asking if Sam wanted one. And he helped her to a pain-au-chocolat.

He took a swig of coffee, his little finger stuck out as if he were having tea with the Queen. Sam was beginning to really dislike his affectations.

'Well?' Sam asked.

'I'm glad you asked, but, you know, I really don't want to talk about it. I find it sensitive – unnecessary. Sorry.' His grin was childlike. He was playing with her.

She broke protocol. Positive, passive would have to wait.

'But not unnecessary enough for you to sell a uranium-laced bomb to a Saudi terror cell, so that they can target a city – I figure Rome? And then sit back and enjoy the mayhem? I'm guessing the price of oil alone will double within a year?'

Sokolov then did that thing again with his face that he'd done at the Embassy. Where his charm deserts him, and anger takes over. But he didn't flinch.

He replied through gritted teeth.

'You're very well-informed, Samantha Green. Very well-informed. But we're well ahead of the game.' He looked at his watch, but didn't add anything.

'And M, you used him?'

He laughed. His flare up of anger had now dissipated.

'He helped, here and there. For a small sum. I was sad when he blew the back of his head off. That was your fault?'

She'd had enough. It was Sam's turn to lose it, the red mist making an impromptu appearance.

I won't be blamed for Simon Page's suicide!

'My fault!' She leant forward, as if to launch herself. Marya, who was still stood by the sofa, put her hand on Sam's bandaged shoulder, holding her down.

Then she squeezed her fingers together. Powerfully.

Any will to be combative immediately drained from Sam. The pain was overwhelming. She held back a tear.

'Leave her, Marya. Let her have her head.'

Marya let go of Sam's shoulder.

'If you had done what Page had asked, and stayed off my case, he would be alive today. I'm sure of it.'

Sam didn't say anything. She sat back on the sofa, raised her shoulders, and instinctively stuck out her bottom lip. She wouldn't say anything else. *Fuck him.* She would sulk.

'That's better. Now, before we move on. I have to tell you a little secret that I have been keeping for a very long time. You are the only person I have ever been able to tell.' Sokolov's mood had changed. He seemed excited. Like a kid at Christmas. There were now two children in the room. Her *and* him.

'Marya. Leave us please.'

Again, Marya's face adopted one of incredulity.

'I'll be fine. I am much bigger than she is. And, as you just demonstrated, she has a weakness. Go on!' He shooed her away with his hands.

Sokolov really was excited. He leant forward, his hands on his knees. His face beamed. It was like being transported back to the playground. One of the girls had a piece of gossip that was so huge, they'd all wet themselves when she shared it.

Sam was intrigued. She leant forward, slowly; her pout gone.

What's this about?

Sokolov looked over her shoulder to check that Marya had left the room.

He leant forward further. He motioned with his hand for her to come closer. Sam moved in as near as she could without lifting her bum from the seat. Their faces were no more than 30 centimetres apart.

He whispered; his face alive – that is, the bit that could move.

'Do you know why no one from your organisation has tried to stop me?' He grinned, again looking over Sam's shoulder. Checking that no one was listening in on his secret.

Was it a rhetorical question?

Yes, she was curious as to why she had persistently been told to leave Sokolov alone. With M's admission just before he killed himself, she understood why he had pressed her. He was on Sokolov's payroll and he was just middleman.

But Jane? She had been very sensitive about Sam's chasing down of Sokolov. Ordering her off his case – twice. And then there was the orange marker on his file. *Special Care – Authorisation Required.*

Sam motioned a 'no' with her head. Her facial expression now shouting, 'Go on – tell me!'

'I'm on your side!' He was nodding quickly, his mouth slightly open, accompanying a smile a mile wide. 'I am an agent for Her Majesty's Secret Intelligence Service – codenamed Pierrot, like the French clown!' A childish giggle followed.

To say that the admission blew Sam away was a fraction of what she felt. *Wow!* Within a second, though, it all made sense.

It all makes sense!

Sokolov and the Russian premier could not be closer; they were old KGB pals. Sokolov knew everything that was going on at the centre of the Russian government. If the Kremlin decided to invade the Baltic States, the UK would know before anyone else did. He was the perfect agent. An informant at the highest possible level.

So, if Sokolov goes down – the British lose their joker.

Sam could picture the finely balanced scales. On one hand – an agent so well placed you might as well be in the mind of the premier. On the other, a dirty bomb which, if detonated, would kill and maim hundreds, and could spell disaster for Europe for years to come.

But. *But.*

It was much more than that for SIS.

Of course! Sam had it all now. Owning Sokolov was a seat at the top table. It was a hugely impressive hand of cards: four aces. Whatever SIS wanted from the CIA, they could get. Lose Sokolov, and you lose access to all manner of American intelligence assets and avenues. They would be set back years.

Sokolov was key. He was SIS's joker.

Sam looked at him, eye to eye. So close she could see a blackhead on his nose. It intrigued her. She had to stop herself staring at it.

Sokolov was still grinning at her, nodding. *The child.*

Sam could visualise the scales and she quickly made her choice: Sokolov was dispensable. The European project, and the hundreds of innocents in harm's way, weren't. She knew what she had to do.

In an instant, Sam thrust her cuffed hands upwards, towards Sokolov's throat, both fists clenched. She put everything she had into the punch. If she found the target, if she connected, she might knock him over – if nothing else, wind him; startle him. One of the huge patio-style doors was open. She would be out onto the deck in a few seconds, find a way to the side of the boat, and dive overboard. She was a half-competent swimmer, even in cuffs. She could make it?

But her fists didn't make a connection. Sokolov was too quick. His head moved out of the way, and her forearms flew past his ear. Her chin ended up on his shoulder and he grabbed her round her back, holding her tight. A bear hug. He was far too strong for her. The pressure on her shoulder sent spasms of pain down her side. She gasped.

His mouth was right next to her ear.

He whispered.

'Ahh, this is nice! A hug.' He chuckled. 'You know, I like you, Samantha Green. Very much. I do. But, now that I've told you my secret, I'm afraid I'm going to have to kill you.'

Aeroflot 737, Sevastopol to Moscow (SVO) Airport, Russia

Yesterday had been the worst day of Debbie's life.

She'd not yet lost a close relative, but she presumed that losing Sam was akin to that? Probably.

Today she felt lighter; as if a small piece of that load had been lifted. The whole world was now looking for *Cressida*. And Debbie had been instrumental in finding the intelligence that made that happen. If they found the yacht, and stopped the bomb, that would make her very proud. And it would go some way to help with the healing.

Both she and Rich had taken a complimentary small bottle of red wine with their lunchtime, in-flight meal. As she stared at the headrest in front of her, she raised her glass and, in her head, she saluted Sam Green.

To you, Sam.

Rich was dozing. He'd finished all his food, his wine and the coffee. He'd woken this morning with a streaming cold, which hadn't surprised Debbie. She'd fished out some paracetamol from her bag and handed them over.

What now? Back to her day job? She was assigned to another case-officer who was working a couple of informants in the Russian army. They provided a link to unit manoeuvres on the border with Finland. Her job was to study satellite photography in order to add veracity to the claims made by the informants. They also had transcripts from mobile telephone comms of senior army staff. Once translated, her job was to sort the wheat from the chaff. It was interesting stuff, but not on the same scale as Op Samantha.

She also had the *ExtraOil* and *CleanDrilling* mini-op that Sam had been running with. Debbie felt really close to the op because only she and Sam had been involved with taking it forward. This morning she'd woken with the lark. She'd spent an hour on the net seeing if there was anything from *MSF* that might indicate that they were even close to whistleblowing on Sokolov's oil exploration shenanigans in Alaska and California. But there was nothing.

However, what had alarmed her was a report she found almost by accident. She'd accessed the US's Federal Energy Regulatory Commission (FERC) website and lifted several layers until she found a page detailing reports and news on oil exploration. There, among several notifications, was a single line:

Authority awarded: the FERC's east coast regulator clears CleanDrilling site at Crestline, CA; oil production can commence immediately.

The notification was dated the middle of last week.

Drilling can commence immediately – bother.

What should she do?

She should take this to Jane as soon as she got back, that's what she would do.

Should she?

M, for some reason, had wanted Sam to stop – he had taken her off the case. Told her to leave well alone. But it didn't stop there. Jane had asked Sam to pass the details to Frank (she'd been copied into Sam's report), so he could take it forward.

But, as far as she could see, nothing was happening. As with all other members of the Moscow staff, she received the daily sitreps from London. Over the past four days none of them mentioned anything about the *ExtraOil* case.

Was Frank sitting on it? Had he also been told to lay off by Jane?

Debbie could imagine the possible fallout of *CleanDrilling's* work in California. Sam had described the conditions in that little village in the Urals. The devastation that a double dose of radioactive water had brought. Sam was almost in tears when she recounted her meeting with the *MSF* doctor. Imagine the effect it would have on those who were supplied via the Los Angeles' watercourse. She was in no doubt that US lives were no more or no less important than Russian ones. But, there were considerably more people at risk here.

What would Sam do? She had spoken about a pal of hers in the CIA – someone she trained with? She'd not mentioned a name, but when (on Jane's instructions), Debbie had looked through Sam's files and emails, she'd come across a Jodie Mountjoy, with a Langley telephone number next to it. That might be the agent she was talking about.

Rich interrupted her train of thought by breaking into, and then out of, a man-snore. With his eyes closed, he grumbled a few words as though it was someone else's fault, and then promptly went back to sleep.

Debbie smiled to herself, but got straight back to her dilemma. To help, she stared at the weave of the remarkably ugly, polyester pattern of the seatback in front of her.

What would Sam do?

She'd phone her pal. Now. She wouldn't wait or ask for instructions. She was a woman of action; action inspired by the desire to do the right thing, and to do it on time. If Debbie went to Jane, she'd demand a report – and, knowing Debbie, that would take a day to get right. And then there might be more questions – more work. And, who knows what the outcome might be? M had asked Sam to leave it alone. And she hadn't. Jane had done the same. If she went to Jane, she might also be stopped in her tracks.

That wouldn't do.

She may only be an analyst, but she had been mentored by the best.

Debbie would go straight into work from the airport. She would find the American woman's number and, regardless of the time and the fact it was a Sunday, she would phone her. She could then do what she wanted with the information.

41°05'06.3"N 13°48'04.3"E – Southwest Coast of Italy

Sam had no idea what was coming next. Not that she cared. At all. She was struggling to find any emotion other than aching self-pity. She knew that sometime soon she was going to die. Sokolov had made that abundantly clear. His parting words to Marya were, 'Turn her blonde. Give her to my brother to have his fun. And then deal with her.' He waved a single hand, dismissing them both as though he was now utterly bored.

She was sat back in her pod, her hair covered in sickly peroxide – which stank to high heaven, the smell of bleach burning at her nostrils. She was definitely going to end up blonde, there was little doubting that. But she really couldn't find the energy to be bothered.

Give her to his brother?

Her mind ran a gentle riot, not that there was a great deal going on upstairs. She was shattered. Broken. Her shoulder ached like it had had a bullet through it *and* then been dislocated. It ached like that, because that was what had happened.

Marya had brought her back to her cell (let's call it what it is), and literally threw her in. She'd left, returning 15 minutes later with a couple of bottles of peroxide. Sam had put two and two together, thinking that she understood what 'turning her blonde' had meant. But couldn't get the context. Was this some form of bizarre ritual?

She then kicked herself. *Of course.* What had the deputy director of the FBI said? They're all blondes. That was the connection. Blonde. And young. And abducted. She could picture a couple of possible outcomes to where this was heading. Neither caught her imagination.

Marya had dragged her into the en suite and removed her cuffs. Sam, who immediately sensed an opportunity, took an almighty swipe at Marya with her left hand. It was pathetic. And such a waste. She knew as soon as her arm wound up for the punch, that it was futile. She wasn't ambidextrous; her left arm was much less of a weapon than her incapacitated right. Marya ducked, but Sam's fist satisfyingly caught her on the ear – but with little effect. Marya pushed her bulk forward at an alarming pace and suddenly Sam felt she was in the wrestling ring with Big Daddy – one of her dad's old favourites. The woman's expansive stomach hit Sam like a small car, and it knocked her backwards into the shower. Sam hit the metal sidewall with her right shoulder and screeched in pain, collapsing in a pile.

Sam looked up. Marya was holding her ear. It obviously hurt. *Good.* She walked to the edge of the shower, towering over Sam who was now curled in the corner expecting some form of retribution.

Marya turned on the shower. Cold at first. And then hot. The woman turned the temperature knob to its highest setting. It got hotter. And hotter. The cubicle filled with steam. Sam, who thankfully had not yet removed her coveralls, curled tighter and tighter, trying desperately to hide any exposed flesh from the steaming water.

Her hair was on fire. The cotton of the coveralls got so hot, Sam felt that they would spontaneously combust at any moment. She remembered from somewhere that showers should be set at no more than 60 degrees centigrade; this must be hotter?

Sam knew that she wasn't being scalded. It just wasn't quite hot enough – especially when everything maxed and she sort of got accustomed to being fried in water. But it stung, her exposed flesh red and begging for it to stop. Her reflex action to try and escape was overpowering and it took every ounce of her inbuilt stubbornness not to push through Marya's tree trunk legs. She wouldn't – *wouldn't* – give the woman the satisfaction of seeing her try to flee.

Fuck her.

Marya turned off the shower.

Sam remained where she was. She felt like an overcooked, drowned rat. Or a boiled carrot. She stared up at Marya and tried her best 'contempt' look.

Marya sneered a smile; because Marya knew what Sam didn't. She wasn't finished yet.

She offered Sam her hand.

Evens?

Sam took it. She wished she hadn't.

In one swift movement, Marya pulled Sam out of the shower, grabbed her by her hair and pushed her head in the sink. *Bugger, that hurt.* She then took hold of her right upper arm, and with strength that Sam thought only possible from male shot putters, pulled it out of its socket. She held it momentarily, gave it a twist, and then let it ping back into place.

Sam only felt the initial surge of pain, which hurt so much more than she remembered from when the bullet had ripped into her at the cabin. After that her mind refused to accept what the receptors in her shoulder were shouting at her. And then she passed out.

She woke (she didn't know how long she'd been out for) to find herself naked, lying on her mattress and stinking of bleach.

And her shoulder! Shit, did it hurt. The pain started in the joint, coalesced with the that from her wound and then went to every corner of her body. She was completely out of it. Like a teddy bear that had been pulled apart by a viscous child, and then poorly stitched back together by a careless mother. She was an idiot. She had wasted her second chance to escape. If another one came, she didn't think she would be able to find the energy to do anything about it.

I am an idiot. A pathetic idiot.

The door opened.

Marya came in. She motioned for Sam to go into the en suite. Sam did as she was told. Meekly. She couldn't have cared less that she was naked. It didn't matter. Nothing mattered; not now. She dragged her sluggish legs, zombie-like, to the en suite. Marya pointed to the shower. She got in. Marya, having turned the temperature knob down to something sensible, pulled up on the lever. Water came. And then from her pocket, Marya removed a small bottle of shampoo. She took hold of Sam's head and gently pulled it toward her. She opened the bottle and tipped it onto Sam's head. And then, as if Sam were her daughter, she washed Sam's hair. It was, for Sam, an extraordinary act. Last time she was with Marya, she had been subjected to an assault at a level of ferocity that you'd only associate with a serial killer. Semi-scalding water and a dislocated shoulder. And now she was being treated as if she were being prepared for her wedding, with overwhelming gentleness.

Sam couldn't take it. The juxtaposition of the two acts, combined with more pain than her body could manage, was too much.

She wept. Her shoulders, one of which was crying out for mercy, joined the pathetic display by shaking up and down. It was pitiful.

She'd been in more pain before. And she'd seen things that had shocked her more. And, at least once, in a warehouse in Berlin, she had willed death to come.

But now, she was more devastated than she had ever been in her life. She'd lost Vlad. She'd been beaten and abused. And she could see no way out. Some ritual was next – and then death. She was destroyed. Smashed to pieces like a thrown dinner plate in a marital argument. If death was next, then that would suit her just fine. She only hoped, beyond hope, that any accompanying pain would be short-lived.

Chapter 19

4th Floor, British Embassy, Moscow, Russia

Jane had eventually settled down to a half-decent day's work. She'd cleared most of the reports she had from London and was thinking about closing down for the day. Debbie and Rich had been due to land half an hour ago. It was past 7pm, and dark and wet outside; she assumed that they were heading straight home.

There'd been nothing yet on *Cressida*. It was a tough one. You would have thought that tracking down a 200-foot yacht would have been simple enough. But the Mediterranean was a very big and very busy sea. Even if they had authorisation to stick up a squadron of NATO Airborne Warning and Control System (AWACS) aircraft, with huge radar domes on their roofs that could pick out ships within a 400-mile radius, they'd still struggle to find an aircraft carrier in a week. *Cressida* was quite capable of hiding away for as long as it took to deliver her cargo.

London had produced a map with concentric rings

on it, centred on Sevastopol. It showed *Cressida's* likely maximum arc, having left Sevastopol on Thursday at 10am. The bottom line was that she could get anywhere from Beirut to the Gibraltar by Monday lunchtime – the whole of the Mediterranean was fair game. The map, which was updated hourly and based on *Cressida's* maximum speed, also gave them an indication of where the boat couldn't yet have reached; as at half an hour ago, the ring stopped on a curve from Tunis, through Sardinia and Corsica, and onto Marseilles. That was about one-quarter of the Med that was not yet within her range.

In short – they needed a stroke of luck. And they needed it soon.

There was some noise in the office – it had been deathly quiet up until then, every sensible member of the organisation was at home sleeping off their Sunday lunch.

Her door opened without ceremony. Rich and Debbie burst in, almost falling over themselves. They were excited. Debbie was giggling.

'Have you two been abusing the Aeroflot complementary drinks? If not, why not?'

'No, no.' Almost in unison. 'We have some fabulous news.' That was Debbie.

Jane was about to reel off a list of possible fabulous news's, when Debbie, who clearly couldn't contain herself, blurted out, 'Sam wasn't in the cabin. It wasn't her body!'

What?!

'What?!'

'The FSB left a message on Rich's phone.' Rich was clearly not going to get a word in edgeways as Debbie continued at a blabber. 'The body in the cabin was a man's. They have no idea whose, but the pelvis is the wrong shape for a woman. It's definitely not Sam.'

Jane was hit by a tsunami of emotions. Sheer joy. Elation. Then, confusion. Followed quickly by fear.

'That's... that's great! But where is she?' The last question was clearly rhetorical.

Rich filled the gap. 'I think we need to look again at the woods. I don't mean to use a dreadful pun, but she's not out of them yet. And we have two other main options: one of Sokolov's residences. Or *Cressida*.'

Jane wrapped her fingers on her desk, and then stood, her hand moving to her forehead.

'Rich, how much clearance around the area of the cabin did the FSB manage to complete?' Jane asked.

'I don't know, but I'll get onto them, pronto. If it's not been thorough enough, I'll see if we can get a joint team down there now. I know it's late, but we have to do what we have to do.'

'Good.' Rich was about to leave the office, when Jane added, 'I hate to say it, but check the lake.' Rich stuck his thumb up, and left.

'And Debbie...' Jane was still thinking on her feet.

'Yes.'

'Get a Priority 1 into Langley for IR shots of a ten-kilometre radius of the cabin. If they've got images from last night, then great. If not, get them onto it now. If Sam is down and in the area somewhere, then she should be a hotspot. Certainly, last night. I know it will be difficult to sort a human from, let's say, a deer, but we have to give it a go.'

Jane had run out of instructions. Instead of leaving Debbie looked like she didn't want to move – just yet. 'Anything else?'

She looked uncomfortable. As though she had something to tell her. Jane raised her shoulders and lifted her hands in an 'And?' sort of way.

'No. Nothing. Thanks, Jane.' And then she was gone.

Jane was just about to think through how they should play the fact that Sam Green, an SIS case-officer, had likely been abducted by a Russian oligarch, when her phone rang. It was Frank.

'Frank, I was just about to phone you.'

'Go on, Jane.'

'The body in the cabin is a man's. It's not Sam.'

Jane could sense the relief gushing down the telephone from over 1,500 miles away. Frank wasn't the emotional type, but she knew he had a very soft spot for Sam; she had that effect on people.

'That's the best news I think I've ever heard.' He cleared his throat. 'Any idea where she is?'

'No. We're about to search the woods near the cabin. And I'm left with the sticky problem of the notion that she's being held captive by Nikolay Sokolov.'

'Mmm. Good luck with that, Jane.' He paused for a second, then added, 'Do you want my news?'

'Yes please.'

'*Cressida* was spotted passing through the Strait of Messina about four hours ago: 14.30 local. GCHQ have just picked it up on Instagram. There were two tourist posts with *Cressida* in the text. When they looked at the post locations, one was from Messina, and the other at Villa San Giovanni, on the mainland side of the channel. The tourists were obviously very excited by seeing such a big yacht close to. Both photos had the yacht's name on its hull. And, have a guess what?'

'What?'

'It was pulling a tender – that's a result.' Frank sounded pleased.

'And now the obvious "so what?" question.'

'London is restricting the target to a choice of two: Rome and Marseilles. They, that is we, have discounted Nice, Naples, Monte Carlo and Barcelona. The view from the Joint Intelligence Committee is that Marseille is the more likely. Drive up, unload, drive away and detonate on the quay. No need for messy additional transportation. The French's recent history with regard to Islamic terror cells also adds weight to that argument. It's a country on the edge.' Frank let it hang.

Jane had yet to sit down; she still had her head in her hand.

'They'd see it coming. It's a 200-foot yacht.'

'But, as your team spotted, the enemy has a tender. The Marines have done some calculations for us. They reckon that *Cressida* could sit up to 100 miles off shore, and with some extra fuel, the tender could make it in "under the radar" so to speak. Especially at night – like now.'

'And, according to your map, she could be there now? And could moor at any number of places, and then get the device to Marseilles by van? Or pick any other French port on their Mediterranean coast, detonate the device, and still cause chaos.'

'Yes – we spent an age on that just now. The French are already soaking the area with troops and police – focusing on Marseilles. And their navy are now about to deploy. The collective view is that the device will be offloaded tonight. *Cressida* will disappear and be back in the Black Sea within three days. At that point she will be impossible to intercept.'

'What are London doing about the 14 Signal Regiment Electronic Warfare team, the LEWT?' Jane asked.

'The French have that covered; their equipment is as competent as ours. They are prepositioning a team to cover Marseilles docks. They've not disclosed anything about timings – they're keeping the whole thing as hush-hush as possible. Any leak and there'll be a stampede out of the city. But we've assumed that you won't be able to play *Pokémon Go!* near the harbour for a while. The problem is, they can't keep that level of blanket cover up for long. The terrorists could hold the bomb, and release it later.'

'Indeed. Although, they'd need some very committed people to stay that close to the device for that long.'

What was she thinking? If they could recruit suicide bombers to blow themselves to heaven, asking some lesser folk to guard a radioactive bomb for a bit wouldn't be a problem. France had a huge Algerian and Tunisian population. Finding martyrs and their assistants shouldn't be that tricky.

'What's the view on Rome?' she asked.

'C's been in touch with the director of their Intelligence Service, the SISMI. As we know, they're slightly less organised than us – and the French. They've got a maritime patrol boat entering the coastal area about now. And the local carabinieri are looking to set up some form of shield around the city, checking major routes in. They hope to have that up and running in the next 8 to 12 hours.'

'By which time…' Jane didn't need to finish that sentence.

The elephant in the room always with the Italians, was corruption – which was endemic. If you couldn't buy an official, then you could pay the Mafia to do it for you. That's why Rome had always been her first choice.

What should I do?

'Do the Italians have a mobile jamming capability?'

'Ehh, not as efficient as ours, I'm afraid.'

That's what I thought.

And that's what they need more than anything else.

'OK. This is what we're going to do. Our office in Rome is scantily manned?' Jane didn't know why she asked Frank that question. She knew the answer, and he, almost certainly, didn't. 'Sorry. Two older men and a worn-out dog. I knew that.' She took a breath. 'I'm going to book a flight to Rome – now. I'll phone C for confirmation on the way, but can you get clearance to get the 14 Signal Regiment LEWT deployed to Rome asap? I'll meet them there. In the meantime, have the section's chief in Rome phone me. I'll expect one of his team to meet me at the airport. Between now and then he can liaise with the SISMI and tell them they should have a LEWT on the ground in, say, 8 hours. OK, Frank?'

'Sounds like a plan, Jane. Good luck!'

The phone went dead.

Jane reduced a couple of tabs on M's desktop and Googled flights from Moscow to Rome. There was a final flight at 21.25. If she got her skates on, she'd just about make it.

41°13'07.4"N 13°42'45.5"E, Mediterranean Sea, South of Rome

The door of the pod opened; Mayra came in. She looked at Sam with her head titled slightly to one side, dangling a pair of cuffs in front of her. Sam offered her wrists. Mayra accepted and attached the cuffs. Sam didn't even ask herself where the key might have ended up.

She was clothed in a new set of blue coveralls. Mayra had washed the bleach out of Sam's hair, running her fingers through it by way of a comb. She redressed her gunshot wound, then carefully helped Sam get dressed, leaving her sitting on the bed. Sam hadn't thought through how long she had been waiting for Mayra to return. It was probably about an hour.

Now she was being taken somewhere. She wasn't sure where. She really didn't care. Her shoulder ached like someone had stuck a screwdriver in it, and was tightening up her recently dislocated joint. Carelessly. The pain was crazy. The whole of her right-hand side was hopeless. She dragged her leg. Wherever she was going, she hoped she'd get there soon. And whatever bizarre ritual she had been prepared for, that too.

And then she'd be happy to jump off the side of the boat and into the drink herself. *Glug glug*.

It was about context. Her life, against her death.

She had no friends, no relatives, and a shitty job that took all her time and gave little back in return. Christ, she'd not even got to the end of the *ExtraOil* case. She was a poor case-officer. Chasing shadows where there was no sun. Impetuous; maverick; irresponsible; irrelevant. She had brought Simon Page down – she knew that now. And she had cost Vlad his life. *Poor Vlad*. Vlad – the only one of them she could really trust? Even her quasi-best friend, Jane (quasi, because your boss can't really be your friend), had let her down. Jane should have told her about Sokolov.

She might not have agreed with the party line, but Sam would have towed it. She could have stayed away. Not chased after Sokolov – as both M and Jane had ordered. Saved Simon Page.

And prevented Vlad's death...

...If I had known, would I really have done as I had been told?

Maybe.

Hah! Even now, after all this, she was questioning the defined authority.

Who the hell did she think she was?

Who?

So, it was about context. Her life, which was rubbish; worthless.

Against oblivion.

Oblivion won. Hands down.

Mayra had reached a door. It wasn't a door like hers to the pod, squeezed between two others. This one was on its own. It had a grandness to it. Maybe a single sheet of oak, planed to an inch of perfection. Polished with the finest of waxes. The door handle looked gold. Proper gold. The doorframe, equally as sturdy, was beautifully crafted.

There was a key in the door, and an iris reader in its usual place.

Mayra did the business with her eye, opened the door, and led her into...

...If you had to choose a single word: a hareem.

What Sam saw hit her like baseball bat. Her current state of emotional stupor vanished. In an instance. Her previous trance-like state received a jolt as if she'd been plugged into three-phase power, and someone had thrown the switch.

Her mind cleared.

All thoughts of self-pity and pending death evaporated. It wasn't that they weren't there. Or that she didn't deserve to be feeling so wretched. It was that one huge emotion, *fury* – red mist on steroids, smashed aside all others; like a prize-winning, full-sized bull, flinging a teenage matador from the ring.

With it, and this surprised her, came a calmness that so complemented the rage she felt that she could conquer the world. Even the oversized and overweight Mayra was a takeable target. *The bitch*.

She took it all in.

White and gold room. The size of country kitchen. Opulence – painted wood, and gold-leaf. Mirrors (*check* – a weapon) on the dressing table, and on the ceiling above the bed. Ornaments, pristine pottery and glass vases (*check* – more weapons). A gold, wooden chair, with a seat covered in green satin (a weapon). Three portholes (*check* – no latches/locked). A pile of men's clothes on the floor.

A king-sized bed – she could only glance at it, her mind choking at what she saw. She quickly refocused. Naked, over-sized man on top of slim, equally naked, blonde woman. The woman had her eyes closed. She was in pain. No, that wasn't any way close to being a strong enough description. Her mind didn't have time to register a more apposite one. The over-sized man turned his head and glanced at Sam – again, her mind stammered. He was ugly. Not quite deformed, but not a picture. Like a more handsome version of the big guy they kept in a shed by the cave in *Goonies*. A child in a man's body?

Pumping away.

Slap. Slap. Slap. Slap.

He showed no emotion. No hint of a smile or a frown. He was doing a job. Something that needed to be done. He turned his head back to his victim. And kept pumping.

Slap. Slap. Slap. Slap.

Her rage was looking for an outlet. Pressing against the wall of her chest. Making her fingers throb. Her head bulge. But it was all under wraps. In control. She had it where she wanted it. On tap.

For now.

Myra opened a door in the far-right corner of the room (key on outside – *check*), and led Sam in. She closed the door. She undid Sam's handcuffs and placed them, with the key still in the lock, in a pocket. *Check*.

'Undress.'

Sam did as she was asked – her shoulder screaming at her. But she was no longer paying any attention to its protestations. She was taking in the new room. It wasn't metal and rivets, like the pod. This was a porcelain, tile and mirror bathroom. Sam could sense opportunities everywhere she looked.

Just for a second, her strength almost collapsed. Having tuned it out, from next door she heard the rhythm of the *slap, slap, slap, slap*. Its beat had increased slightly – the tempo picking up. She bit into her tongue and scrunched her fists. And got a grip – blocking out the hateful noise. She didn't need any distractions.

'You be good. It will be over soon. All of it.' It was an instruction from Mayra. Kindly, but firm.

Sam nodded and smiled sheepishly. An Oscar winning performance.

Mayra left, and locked the door behind her.

Sam, naked as the day she was born, picked up a beautiful white bath towel from the rail. She folded it in four so it was slightly wider than the mirror above the sink. She placed the towel against the mirror and waited.

Slap, grunt. Slap, grunt. Slap, grunt. Slap, grunt.

Could the soundtrack be any worse?

As the tempo quickened, the grunts became louder. Sam knew where this was heading. She had to get the timing right.

Slap, grunt. Slap, grunt. Slap, grunt. Slap, GRUNT!

On the last stroke of the man's evil ecstasy, Sam smashed her left elbow into the bathroom mirror. It broke into a myriad of pieces. She watched them fall into the sink and onto the floor.

Clatter.

She checked that the mirror had all come off the

wall. One piece was caught behind a screw. She removed it. She didn't want anything left on the wall that might catch someone's attention.

Then she paused. And listened.

Sloppy noises next door – some mopping up.

She had some time.

Sam looked down among the shards of glass. She picked up a piece that seemed the most knife-like – it was shaped like an elongated triangle. She wrapped the larger end in a wet flannel. She held it in her unfavoured left hand – she might have conquered the pain, but her right arm was next to useless; if she exerted it in any way, it could easily pop out of its socket. And she couldn't have that.

Hastily, but efficiently, she pushed the remnants of mirror that were on the floor, under the sink. She couldn't hide it, she didn't think she had the time. But a casual glance might miss the mess.

She then turned and faced the door. The weapon behind her back, in her left hand. Her right hanging loosely by her side. Still naked, other than a dressing and a bandage.

And a weapon.

She didn't feel naked, or vulnerable. She felt pure. And powerful.

Let it begin.

The lock in the door made a noise. It opened abruptly and there was Holly Mickelson. She must have been a staggeringly beautiful young woman before the ordeal. Before the abuse. Now she looked like a shell. A fragile being, scrunched up like waste paper and thrown away on the floor.

But Sam had missed something – just for that instant. Something hidden deep in the recesses of Holly Mickelson's soul. She and Holly's eyes met. Sam knew hers would betray no emotion. They would be glass replicas, devoid of feeling.

Holly's weren't. Underneath an opaque sheen, formed from the worst degradation known to woman, there was fire. An unquenchable fire. Sam knew this girl had guts and courage. And there was plenty left; it was just not ready to be unleashed. Yet.

The over-sized man pushed Holly into the bathroom, revealing his own naked body. Sam blanked it – her brain refusing to accept the images that her eyes had seen. He gave Sam a once over, grabbed her by the scruff of the neck and launched her into the bedroom. Sam almost fell, but took a couple of quick steps and managed to stay on her feet. She immediately turned, the weapon still hidden.

The over-sized man was closing the bathroom door, his back partially toward her. He started to bend at the waist to reach for the key that was in the lock. It was obviously fiddly – if you had hands the size of dinner plates.

It was then that Sam's brain accepted what her eyes were relaying.

He must be six feet two inches tall. Very broad, but flabby round the waist. Thick thighs, some fat, that met above the knees. He was lightly covered in hair –

except around his backside and his, now exposed, testicles. The hair in that area was plentiful. Sprouting out of the crack between his cheeks. And hanging down between his legs.

Sam had enough information. It was all she needed.

She struck.

The tip of the broken piece of mirror hit the oversized man in the soft flesh between his anus and his testicles. Sam had forgotten most of her human biology GCSE, but she reckoned that that area was probably boneless and the best target.

It punctured his skin. Sam forced it in with all her might behind a straight left arm, the blade didn't stop until her hand reached his flesh. Instinctively, she turned the blade, but to her surprise the mirror shattered and all she was left holding was a flannel and a smattering of silvered glass. She couldn't tell, but she didn't think much of it had landed on the floor. Most of it was inside the underparts of the over-sized man.

Who roared...

...And arched his back, bringing his buttocks together, which could only have compounded the pain.

Sam, who had started to pull back, was surprised by how much blood there was already. She had dropped the flannel and, after a period of such clarity of thought, her mind was now scrabbling around, trying to work out what to do next.

The over-sized man made that decision for her.

He turned and span, striking out, his arms whipping

around like a windmill that was toppling in a storm. One of his hands caught Sam on the face, the force of which sent her flying backwards onto the bed.

And then he was on top of her.

How could he be? Why wasn't he writhing in excruciating pain on the floor? Bleeding to death.

She was immediately winded. And with his weight on her, she was struggling to breathe. He was raising himself up, his fist now high above his head, which, when released, would be on a trajectory for Sam's head. There was noise, and grunts, and spittle, and pain – her shoulder now very much back in the business of letting her know how it felt.

She looked into his eyes.

What is that?

Pain – certainly. Confusion – yes? Terror, like a child who has just lost a parent – absolutely. And a clear determination to kill or maim the woman who had just stuck a knife between his legs.

His fist began its short journey toward her face.

Sam closed her eyes and turned her head away from the punch.

I might not survive this.

But there was no contact. *What?!* His fist lost momentum and slammed into the mattress beside her. He yelped and gurgled. And then the whole weight of his over-sized body collapsed on top of her. *Lifeless?*

She almost panicked. Enclosed spaces. Not for her. She tried to move him, but her shoulder popped –

pain beyond all pain followed, and dizziness swept over her. She wouldn't try that again.

The man moved. A touch.

He was dead?

A female 'grunt'.

The man moved some more.

And then it became clear.

Holly Mickelson was pulling the man from her, dragging him by an arm. It took her two more attempts. And then Sam was free.

Holding her shoulder and breathing far more rapidly than was good for her, Sam swung her legs round, off the bed and onto the floor. She stood. Holly was next to her. Her eyes glazed, her lips slightly apart – rasping coming from her mouth. She was in shock.

Sam looked at the bed. There was blood everywhere. Not all of it was from the wound she had created between the over-sized man's legs. In the middle of his back was the fat end of a shard of mirror. Blood bubbled from the wound. Blood that was being soaked up by a hand towel.

Holly Mickelson had followed Sam's lead. She had made a knife. And she had killed the man who had raped her.

Sam nodded. Her breathing returning to normal; her shoulder no longer the only thing that was controlling her life.

'Holly. I'm Sam. We need to get out of here. Can

you swim?'

She nodded quickly. No words.

'In the bathroom is a pair of coveralls. Put them on now.' Quick, clear instructions. Holly disappeared. Sam jogged over to the pile of men's clothes. She picked out a shirt and put it on. She struggled with the buttons, but Holly was with her a few seconds later. She helped her finish them off.

They now had to get out of the room.

We can't lift the man. Can we? No.

Plan B.

'Holly, I want you look away.'

Holly was in automaton mode. She did as she was instructed.

Sam went across the over-sized man. The right side of his face was pointing to the ceiling.

I hope this works.

With her left hand, Sam formed her index finger and thumb into a claw. She placed them around the edge of the man's eye socket and, with her teeth and stomach muscles clenched (she really didn't want to throw up), she forced them around the eye.

Gross.

The first time she tried, she couldn't get leverage – her thumb slipping out of the socket.

The second time she had it. She tugged.

The eye popped out like pickled egg from a tight jar, and then fell from her hands as the optic nerve and associated muscles refused to let go of its owner.

'Here.'

It was Holly. She wasn't looking away. She was handing Sam a slither of mirror from the bathroom floor.

'Thanks.'

Sam cut and cut. More blood.

Then the eye was free.

Now we need to get off this boat.

As Holly chased after the woman who had come to rescue her (in the heat of the moment, she had forgotten her rescuer's name), she couldn't begin to rationalise what was going on. She had just murdered the oaf who had systematically raped her evening after evening for, how long was it, a week? Was it more? Rape and murder. Two despicable things that should make her want to curl up in a ball and hope they went away.

And yet…?

…They were rushing down a corridor. They turned a corner and were met by a set of metal stairs, rising upward to a hole, and into the night.

'Stay here. I'll be back.' The curly haired woman, wearing nothing more than the oaf's shirt, spoke quietly. And authoritatively.

…And yet, her overriding emotion was one of elation. Success. Victory! She was high. As a kite. Soaring on the wind.

Copying the woman, by making a knife from a piece of mirror and creating a handle out of a towel, was genius. Stabbing the oaf with it was such a release. All those evenings being subjected to the abuse had filled a deep well of anger to overflowing. When the opportunity presented itself, she couldn't control herself. It was spontaneous. She smiled as she thought about it. She had no regrets; felt nothing for the oaf. At least now he couldn't do the same thing to some other poor girl.

'Holly!' A whispering shout from up the stairs.

She stuck her head forward so that she could connect with the woman – who was beckoning her upward.

Holly climbed up, and out into the night. As soon as she emerged onto the deck, the woman pushed her down, so that they were both crouching. There was a wind and, with the reflecting moonlight, she picked out white horses on the tops of the waves. Land was about half a mile away. No distance for her. She saw what looked like a small fishing village and a harbour; the end of the breakwater signalled by an illuminated statue of, almost certainly, the Virgin Mary.

Off to their right was the stern of the boat. It was a hive of activity, which made her crouch lower. A couple of men were stood by the rear rails, shouting to a further two men who were on a much smaller craft. She couldn't make out any of them. But the language sounded Russian. One of them on their boat released a couple of ropes and threw them across to the smaller one. Its engines throttled up, the bow turned and it headed off toward the village.

Throughout this, her rescuer was knelt beside her, looking on with great intensity. As soon as the smaller boat started to move, she took hold of Holly's hand, and, still crouching, she pulled her off to the left. After about ten paces they were out of sight of the stern of the boat. The woman turned to her, their faces no more than a few inches apart.

'See the harbour?' She was pointing vaguely landward. 'Left of the statue? It looks like the beach there is sheltered and in shadow.'

Holly nodded.

'We'll swim to there. Stay together. Just in case. OK?'

Holly hadn't stopped nodding.

'Let's go.'

The next thing she knew, she was in the water. Their entry splashes were lost in the noise of the choppy sea.

It was cold. Cold enough to take her breath away. She didn't know what to expect, having never swam in the Mediterranean before, but she didn't expect this. She was used to the water off the coast in Florida. In comparison to what she was currently experiencing, that was like getting into a bath.

She took in some water – the cold penetrating her broken tooth. *Ouch!*

But as the coldness washed over her it heightened her sense of achievement. She was alive – and free!

She swam. Expertly; even though her other injury,

the bent finger, hurt like hell. She was a high school 800-metre freestyle champion. It may have been a few years ago now, but as her coach used to say, 'swimming is 50% strength and 50% technique'. She'd not forgotten the latter.

Holly covered the distance effortlessly. She kept an eye on her rescuer, who looked to be an adequate swimmer, but was obviously hampered by her bandaged shoulder; she was patiently using just her good arm. Even so, they covered over half the distance in around 15 minutes. As the harbour wall got closer and the beach beyond it came into focus, Holly couldn't stop herself. It was like being back in the pool. All that mattered was hitting the end wall first. She took off.

Stroke – stroke – stroke – breath right, stroke – stroke – stroke – breath left. Legs kicking with a freedom that felt so good, even though they were slowed by the weight of her clothes. Pain was burning in her muscles, lactic acid flooding them. As the waves lifted and fell, she took in water (her tooth shouted at her), but she spat it out on the next breath.

God, this feels good!

Her knee hit a rock. She stopped swimming, looked up and saw that she was nearly at the beach.

She stood, slipping on a seaweed covered rock; she put a hand down to find her balance. Then she stood tall. Upright.

Freedom!

She turned, looking for her rescuer. In the distance she saw the lights of the yacht. It looked majestic and becalmed. But, she guessed, all hell would break out when they found the dead oaf. Would they come ashore looking for them? She would.

They needed to get a move on.

Where was the woman?

She looked. A minute passed; it may have been longer.

Holly was worried now. She scurried to her left and clambered up a couple of rocks which helped make up the harbour wall. She looked again.

Shit!

There she was, maybe 100 metres out. But she wasn't swimming. She was floundering. Her head was bobbing about, and her arm was up in the air. Holly lost her in a wave, and there she was again, no further forward.

And then she went under.

Holly didn't think. Everything she did from that point was completely instinctive.

She whipped off her coveralls, pushed off from the side of the harbour wall and swam the race of her life. She lifted her head after about 50 metres on the crest of a wave, caught a glimpse of a hand in the air, adjusted her route and ploughed powerfully toward the arm.

When she thought she was at the right spot, she stopped, treading water. She looked. Nothing. She turned herself in the water. Still nothing.

'Hey!' she shouted.

Nothing.

And then a hand broke the surface off to her right, about ten metres away, and then it was gone.

Holly had to dive under the water to find the woman. It was dark, but the water was clear. The woman was floating about a metre below the surface, her eyes wide open and her cheeks pushed out. Her last gasp of air. Holly grabbed her under her arms and pulled her upward until their heads were free of the water. It was not without effort.

Having attended life-saving sessions in the pool, she knew that at this point the woman would either take a huge gulp of air and recover, or she was already drowning and nothing would happen. If it was the latter, Holly would have to attempt mouth-to-mouth. Here – in the choppy sea. She'd practiced that once; in the calm of the pool. It was impossible.

Holly treaded water with all the strength she could find, keeping the woman's shoulders high. Her head flopped back, which wasn't a great sign, and Holly started to rehearse what she needed to do next.

But it wasn't necessary. *Thank God.*

The woman coughed and spluttered, and took in huge gulps of air. Her arms and shoulder rising and falling with the effort she needed to find her breath.

Holly knew that it wasn't over yet. Now she'd be faced with one of two scenarios. Either the woman would panic, hold onto her for dear life, and, if Holly couldn't get her to calm down, they would both drown. Or, the woman would accept her rescue, lie back and allow herself to be slowly towed into shore –

backwards; Holly's body under hers, her hand on the woman's neck and a kick stroke to propel them.

'Lie still! Lie still!' Holly shouted.

The woman immediately did as she was told. She was the perfect rescuee.

Too perfect?

As they approached the shore the village provided some ambient light. Holly's chin was resting on the woman's right shoulder, her legs screw kicking. She'd tried talking to her as they'd come in; to reassure her. But had got nothing back. The woman's body was limp; flaccid.

She looked back toward the yacht. Two things disturbed her. First, there was another small boat heading inshore from the yacht. It looked like a rib. On its bow was a light. It was swinging left and right.

Searching.

For them.

And second, she remembered that her rescuer had a dressing on her right shoulder. That was definitely gone. Holly lifted her head further to the vertical, and looked at the woman's chest. She wore a cream and light blue, thick-striped shirt. It's what the oaf wore every time he had 'visited'; Holly hated the sight of it. Worryingly, where the woman had been wearing a dressing, the shirt had a stain that was darker than the surrounding material.

Blood?

She had to get her to shore. And then to a hospital.

Without the boat with the light spotting them.

Holly kicked the last couple of strokes, found her feet, and then, with strength she didn't know she had, pulled the woman quickly onto the beach. She looked for some shade from the ambient light of the village, and saw some a few metres away beside a large rock. She dragged the woman to the shadow and lay her down.

She checked for a pulse. And for breathing. The woman had both, but the pulse was very light.

What now?

Recovery position. Then find help.

Holly put the woman on her side with her bottom leg straight and her top leg bent to stop her from tipping onto her front. She checked her airway and, although not part of her life-saving training, she looked inside the woman's shirt at her wound.

What she saw looked like someone had ripped a small hole in her shoulder. It had been stitched, but in one corner the stitches were hanging loose. Blood oozed slowly from the wound.

To add to her worries, the woman had started shivering uncontrollably.

I have to get help.

But first, I must get dressed.

Holly threw on her coveralls, raced up the beach and found a path. Within a minute she was in among the dark alleys of a beautiful seaside fishing village.

What am I looking for?

She didn't know, but a light drew her to the end of a narrow street – in the direction of the harbour. As she got closer, she slowed. And then stopped. The harbour was right in front of her. It was small, maybe 50 metres across; on the far side were more fisherman type cottages. The harbour was full of all manner of boats. Some looked like small fishing craft, and others were sailing yachts. Looking left, she picked out the two boats that had come from their yacht. One, the craft they had seen tied at the stern, was dockside. It had one man on it, and two more on the shore. One of the men was operating a small tractor-type vehicle fitted with a crane. He was in the process of lifting a big metal box from the boat.

The rib with the light was in the harbour. A man on its front was shouting at the men on the shore. He definitely sounded Russian.

Once the exchange finished, the rib turned, revved its engines and drove slowly out to sea, its light flicking left and right.

Holly was just about to go back down the alley and maybe, *Knock on any old door and ask for help?* when she recognised one of the men on the shore. He was one of the thugs who had abducted her from Istanbul. He was talking to a new, fourth man, who she didn't recognise. He looked different to the others. Even in this light, she could see that he was darker skinned. He was also very tall and slim. North African?

Both men walked a few yards to their right, to a van which she hadn't noticed before; it had its sliding door open. Under the light-orange street lights, it appeared creamed coloured. The van was different from a standard goods van. It had a window in its side door, and what looked like an awning running along the top of its roof. A vehicle you might own if you were a market trader?

Were they running drugs?

Holly had seen enough. She had to get help for her rescuer.

She was about to turn, when something touched her shoulder. She immediately flinched; somehow, suppressing a scream.

She couldn't run forward into the light of the harbour area. And she really didn't want to turn and face, what she thought would be an inevitability: chloroform followed by abduction.

But nothing horrible happened.

Still cowering, she slowly turned round.

Relief flooded her senses.

She was met by the sight of a short, elderly woman with a walking stick. The woman had a wrinkled face, a kind smile and very few teeth.

'Posso aiutarla a tutti?'

Chapter 20

Scauri, Italy

Sam had a recurring dream that she had to get somewhere very quickly, but, no matter how hard she tried, her limbs wouldn't propel her forward as fast as she needed to go. Thus, she was going to be late. And she hated being late. In some dreams she'd be inappropriately dressed, or not wearing anything at all; she would scour her dream world, but would be unable to find the correct clothes. Or, sometimes, any clothes. Neither dreamscapes, nor sometimes both concurrently, made for a restful night's sleep.

Worst of all for Sam, was one of those sleeps where she'd try to wake, but couldn't. Or she thought she had, but hadn't. And then she'd get fretful – and try harder. But, no matter how hard she pushed the boundary between asleep and awake, it wouldn't budge. Or it did, but only to accommodate and fool her. She'd eventually think that she was awake – but she wasn't. She hated those.

At the moment, Sam was sleeping through all those scenarios – combined. It was a nightmare; both as a noun, and as an adjective. Except it was worse. She also was carrying an old war wound that hurt like hell.

It was the mother of all nightmares. She was going to be late for something important, she'd likely turn up naked, she was in pain, and whilst she knew she was dreaming, she couldn't shake herself from the dream – no matter how hard she tried.

Aagghh!

She was being shaken.

Leave me alone! I need to get out of here!

Shaken some more.

Her dream was disturbed – she woke. But was she awake? She wasn't sure. Not yet.

She kept her eyes shut. She had to cough. She did. The pain in her right shoulder burnt like a hot poker.

Fuck!

She instinctively opened her eyes. She was in a small, dark room, lying on a bed. *Come on, eyes – adjust!* Sitting next to her was an elderly man. He had a stethoscope around his neck and was gently rocking her, by the hip. *It was he who was waking her. Who was he?*

There was a window opposite. The curtains were closed, but through the small gaps she couldn't any see light. *Night-time. Come on, think...*

'*Signorina, signorina.*' It was a melodic, soothing call from the old man.

What?

What is happening? Who is this man? Where was she?

She tried to sit up, but the pain was debilitating. She closed her eyes, a tear formed, squeezing out from the corner of her left eye and dripping down onto the sheet. She opened her eyes again. The man must have been in his 80s. He had a warm, tanned face with more wrinkles than a shar-pei. And he wore a tender, old gentleman's smile.

Sam smiled at him by way of a defence mechanism. Buying some time as her brain started to boot up and race through all of the permutations of what was happening – and where she might be.

She glanced behind the man. *Ahh*. There was someone she recognised. *Holly Mickelson*. Things started to coalesce.

Ask her, she'll know.

'Hello, Holly.' It was a rasp. She suppressed a cough. The pain was ebbing. She really didn't want it flowing again.

Holly smiled. It was a glorious beam of a smile from a young woman who looked like she had just won the state lottery. Or had fallen head over heels with the nicest, most handsome man on earth. Or woman. Sam didn't care.

'I'm so sorry, but in the excitement, I've forgotten your name. Are you OK?'

The man was still looking at Sam in a quizzical way. Sam guessed he was a doctor. Or someone who had bought a stethoscope from a market, and was pretending to be one. Whatever, she thought that she was one helluva patient. A gunshot wound. A semi-dislocated shoulder. *And, a set of lungs full of seawater!*

Latent terror washed over her. She flinched inwardly. It was all pouring back in a tsunami of feelings, all of which hurt. The bit about the swimming, the going under, the fear of being in a place she couldn't get out of, the drowning – it all spat at her with disdain.

Sam's stomach couldn't take the emotion and tried to retch. Her oesophagus closed just in time, but that didn't prevent the old man from moving his legs so that any vomit would have missed his worn-at-the-knees green cords.

She forced aside the memories and tried to focus on the present. Her mind span like a roulette wheel, loaded with multiple balls. As one stopped, a thought came to her; then another.

And she still hadn't answered Holly's question.

What day is it? What's the time? Where am I? How close is Rome? Does anyone have a telephone?

Sam stopped her cacophony of thoughts in their tracks, and focused on two: *what time is it; I need a telephone*.

'My name is Sam. What time is it?'

The old man, who didn't seem to understand a word, looked from Sam to Holly.

'It's about 5.30. In the morning.' He looked back at Sam again. Centre court at Wimbledon.

'How long have I been out?' The man continued to follow the conversation.

'About two and a half hours?'

Sam looked at what she was wearing. A pair of joggers and an, oversized for her, woollen jumper. *Bless them*.

'I need a telephone. Do these people have one?' Sam nodded at the old man/doctor, who smiled at her. She smiled back.

'Yes. A landline.'

'Take me to it.'

'But. You're badly injured. The doctor here has patched you up. He's put a drip in to rehydrate you…' Holly pointed at the plastic bag that hung from the wardrobe, and a tube that ran from it to Sam's right forearm.

How did I miss that? Sam pushed herself up (*Ouch!*), and swung her feet off the bed. The doctor stood to give Sam some room, and reached for the drip which was in danger of being pulled from the wardrobe door.

As Sam positioned herself to get off the bed, she looked down at her right arm; she used her free hand to remove the medical tape that was holding the cannula in place and detached the drip. The doctor sighed, collected the line and turned off the butterfly switch to stop it from leaking.

'Have you phoned the police?' *I should have asked that first*.

'No.' Holly looked agitatedly at Sam. She had her

hands out, preparing to accept Sam as she stood. 'The doctor and his wife wouldn't let me. I speak a little Italian, and they can't speak any English. But it was clear to me that they don't trust the police round here. At all.'

Bloody Mafia.

Sam was on her feet. And then she sat back down again. *That was tougher than I expected.*

Then she was up. This time using Holly's arm for support.

'I have phoned my daddy, though.' Holly stopped there. Sam looked at her. She guessed Holly was waiting to see if she approved.

'Congressman Mickelson? Good. What did he say?' Sam was waddling now. Out through the bedroom door, half following, half leading Holly. She was looking down to see where she was placing her feet. But she could sense another one of those broad, beautiful smiles on Holly's face.

'He was over the moon. He was crying. I've never heard him cry before. Anyhow, I told him where I was, which is a fishing village called Scauri, and that I was being really well looked after by an elderly Italian family…'

Sam put up her good hand to stop them both. They were at the end of a short dark corridor. It looked like the lounge ahead. She needed a quick breather. This walking malarkey was tougher than she remembered.

Holly stopped and turned to her.

'Are you OK?'

'I'm fine. How far from Rome are we?' Sam asked.

'I don't know. All I know is that Daddy said to stay where I was, and that they would get someone from the Embassy in Rome to the village as soon as possible.'

They were walking again now. Sam spotted an old, red plastic telephone on a wooden sideboard a few metres away.

'Did you mention me?' She picked up the phone.

'I was going to. But Daddy cut me off. He said he had to get hold of the Embassy as soon as possible.'

Sam was dialling now.

'How long ago did you have this conversation?'

'About an hour ago. I was just about to phone Daddy again to check how things were, when you started making noises in your sleep...'

Sam put up her hand. The phone rang twice and then it was picked up.

'Jane Baker? Who is this?'

Sam knew that Jane would be looking at the Italian number and trying to compute.

She took a deep breath.

'It's Sam, Jane.'

Nothing.

'No. No!! Sam, where are you? Oh my god! Are you OK?' The emotion poured down the line.

And to think, last night I was wishing myself dead – when I have people who care about me as much as Jane.

'Apparently, in a little fishing village called Scauri: S-C-A-U-R-I. I'm guessing close to Rome, but without Google Maps I have no idea. Listen. The bomb has been unloaded. Probably between midnight and two this morning. I'm pretty confident that it was on a tender which was being pulled by *Cressida* – it looked like a small fishing boat; wooden, just about seaworthy. I reckon they have a two-hour head-start on us.'

There was a pause. Holly was hopping from one foot to another, obviously excited about something. Sam looked crossly at her, and turned away.

'So, that's where you've been. We should have guessed. God, Sam, it's so good to hear your voice. Look, it's a long story, but I'm in Rome – at the Embassy. Everyone assumed the target was Marseilles. I guess I don't need to explain why, but in short, it's the French connection. Anyway, I was surplus to requirements, so came here.'

Holly had walked round Sam and was facing her. She had her hand up like a young kid in class, impatient to go to the loo.

Exasperated, Sam asked Jane to wait, and put her hand on the telephone's mouthpiece.

'What?' *We've got a terrorist bomb plot to prevent.*

'I saw the bomb, or whatever it is. It was being offloaded onto the dockside. I think it was being transferred to the back of a van.'

Sam dropped her hand from the mouthpiece and held the receiver out so that Holly would be speaking to both she and Jane.

'So sorry, Holly.' *She really was.* 'Tell both of us. Jane,' Sam bent her head to the phone, 'this is Holly Mickelson. It's another long story.'

Sam didn't allow Jane to ask any questions. She mouthed at Holly, 'Go on.'

Holly bent her head forward.

'Hi. When we got ashore, I ended up at the harbour. There was a boat and a crane. And three men, I think. And a van.'

Sam interrupted.

'Tell us about the van, Holly. We don't have much time. This is really important.'

Sam could see Holly trying hard to piece together what she had seen.

'Sorry, I'm not very good at this. It was small.' She dithered. 'Like a van you might see at a market stall. That's all.'

'Colour?' The screech came from down the telephone line.

'Light. Maybe, orange.'

'Were there any street lights lit at the harbour?' It was Sam's turn.

Holly closed her eyes in thought.

'Yes. The orangey type, overhead ones. Pink tinge possibly.'

'The van is white, Jane,' Sam corrected. 'Not much help.'

'How big?' Sam pressed.

'Not much bigger than a car.'

'And the men?'

As best she could, Holly described the two white men who were on the dock and the man in the boat. She was able to give a much more accurate description of her abductor. But for the others, it was very outline stuff.

'There was a fourth man. On the dock. He seemed to come from the van. He was taller than the others. Dark skinned and slim. I thought maybe he was Asian?'

'Or North African?' Sam added.

'Exactly. Yes, I thought that as well.'

'What was he wearing?'

'Sorry Sam. Clothes is the best I can do. Although, possibly a leather jacket?'

'He must be the driver,' Sam added for Jane's benefit; it was an obvious conclusion.

'Anything else, Holly?' Another screech from the telephone from Jane.

Holly scrunched her face up.

'The van, Holly. Think. The van. It's very important,' Sam added.

Holly looked beyond Sam, who glanced over her shoulder (*God, that hurt.*) to follow her gaze. Holly was looking at a small oil painting of the Virgin Mary – it was above the fireplace. The room's centrepiece.

A light seemed to go on in Holly's head.

'It had an awning. Like you'd need for a market stall. And a window in the sliding door.'

She thought some more. 'That's it. Sorry.'

'No, that's really good and very helpful, Holly,' Sam said, bringing the receiver back to her ear.

Jane interrupted them.

'One of the guys here has come back with a distance between you and Rome. Let's round it up to 180 kilometres. They could be in Rome already, or close. Although, Roman traffic is notorious, even at this time of day. Whatever, we don't have much time.'

Sam checked the clock on the mantelshelf. It was 5.50am. Jane was right. The market van could be in Rome already.

'Sam. I need to get this to the SISMI liaison officer, who's having a nap in the corner of the ops room. We have the LEWT on standby at St Peter's – any mobile within a click's radius would be disabled the moment the team switch their machine on. I think the Vatican is the most likely target.' Sam wasn't sure if Jane wanted her to comment – she certainly agreed with the choice. 'As soon as I kick him, we'll have it up and running. And, when they get this message, I'm sure the carabinieri will stop and search every white market or delivery van in Christendom. I'd better go.'

'Do you have this number?'

There was silence. Sam assumed that Jane was checking the screen on her phone.

'Yes. Got it. Great to hear you, Sam. Speak soon.'

The phone went dead.

Sam looked at the receiver. And then put it down in its cradle.

That was it. She had done everything she could. There was nothing else to do, other than wait.

Could she wait?

She wasn't sure. Especially as there was something at the back of her mind that was bothering her. Some snippet of intelligence that she'd picked up on the way and discarded. Something that she now thought might be important, but couldn't find it in her memory banks. She'd keep trying.

They were joined in the room by the doctor and an elderly woman (*wife?*), who was even shorter than her husband. In one hand, she was carrying a plateful of pizza slices. In the other, a hexagonal silver pot – that looked like it might be holding coffee.

'*Pizza al trancio? Caffè?*'

Sam smiled and nodded.

The smile was for effect. She wasn't happy.

She was restless.

They didn't have enough intelligence.

She hadn't seen the van. No one, other than Holly, had seen the van.

How many white vans would there be in metropolitan Rome?

Thousands. Maybe tens of thousands.

And, if she were a terrorist, she would pick an obscure route; avoiding nosey policemen. They'd already dropped the device off some distance from Rome, at an unlikely harbour. 'Tick' against them for that. These people were working hard to get this right.

Worse still, if the van got stuck or compromised outside of the LEWT's jamming zone, the terrorists could detonate it anyway. They may not get to the Vatican, but they could pick anywhere in central Rome and still have a devastating effect.

A white van, somewhere in the centre of Rome.

A white van…

…That only Holly has seen.

'Holly!'

She had a mouthful of pizza.

'Whacfts?' Holly swallowed quickly. 'What?'

Holly put the half-eaten slice of pizza back on the plate that the old-lady was holding. Sam sensed that Holly knew where this was going.

'Would you recognise the van if you saw it again?'

'I don't know, but I could give it a try.'

'How's your Italian?'

'Adequate, why?'

'We need a car. And a mobile. Now!'

The expression on Holly's face went from 'confused' to 'excited' in less than a second.

'You and me? Looking for the van?'

'Yes. You're the only person on our side who will recognise it. And I know some people who can help.'

Sam pointed at the phone. 'Between us, I think we make a good team.'

'How big is the bomb?'

Sam didn't see fear in Holly's face – she saw determination.

'It's not its size you need to worry about.'

It took the pair of them about ten minutes to persuade the good doctor and his wife to lend them their only mobile phone (an old Nokia 3310, with a battery life of about a month – Holly had never seen one before), a map book (no GPS), and a car.

Holly was doing her best to translate the elderly couples' concern about the car.

'I think they're saying it's their grandson's. He's away at school. No, university. It's very special. Please bring it back in one piece.'

Sam put on her most responsible face.

'*Si, si.*'

If you added '*Per favore*' and '*Grazie*', Sam was at her limit of Italian.

'*Grazie. Grazie.*' She was almost done.

It was just about getting light as the doctor walked Sam and Holly to a small garage behind the house. Without ceremony, he unlocked the double doors and opened them.

And there it was.

Sam was impressed.

A flame-red, Lancia Montecarlo. Probably 1980 vintage. A two-litre, two-seater, mid-engined, Pininfarina-designed rust bucket. The latter certainly applying to any of the cars imported to the UK. A mirror image of the fabled DeLorean.

And her dad's favourite Italian after Sophie Loren.

Thank you, God.

The doctor sheepishly handed over the keys. Sam, who, ten minutes ago, had taken all the four Valium that the doctor had given to her – was up for any challenge. Her shoulder ached, but she was very relaxed about it…

'Get in the passenger side. I'm driving. You're looking for the van; "spotting". And map reading.'

Holly got in. Sam turned the car over. It failed to start. She turned it over again. Still nothing.

Come on!

Third time lucky. She threw it into gear and they were off, a peppering of gravel the outcome of some serious wheel spin.

Sam glanced in her rear-view mirror. The doctor had his hands raised to shoulder height. He mouthed something. It might have been, *'Mamma mia!'*

In the excitement of starting the chase, Sam had forgotten to ask Holly about her dad and the CIA. Wouldn't he be worried if she weren't at the house? Above the noise of the engine, which was behind her right ear, Sam almost had to shout.

'What about your dad and the CIA?'

Holly, who had her finger placed on the map and was following their route intently, replied, 'They'll be fine. I'm sure Daddy will understand when I tell him. He does worry. But, this is the sort of thing I want to do.'

'What, join the CIA or FBI?'

Sam changed down to pass a slower car. *That hurt.* She'd forgotten that the car might be left-hand drive. Changing gear was giving her shoulder so much gip.

'Actually, I want to become a war correspondent – Syria, Afghanistan, hot spots, you know.'

Sam nodded – *If she can write, she'd be good at that.* She looked down at the speedo. They were now on the main dual carriageway, the SR 148, heading northwest. And squeezing out 140 kilometres per hour.

'Where in Rome should we be looking?' Holly asked.

'The Vatican. I think it's the target. I visited their once. It's on the left bank of the Tiber which flows north to south, bending its way through the city. Look close to the centre and you should find it. We need to try and come at it driving down an obscure road – not one of the main ones. The police may have roadblocks on the motorways and we don't want to get caught. Can you do that?'

Holly looked across at Sam and grinned.

'I have no idea! All our cars have GPS. Paper maps are news to me. But I'm keeping up so far.'

Sam reckoned they were halfway there. She checked the gauges; all was well with the Lancia. No panels had fallen off so far. Her dad would be pleased.

She reached into the pocket of her joggers and took out the Nokia.

'Phone the following number.' She gave Holly Jane's mobile number.

It rang twice and Jane answered.

'Hold it against my ear.'

Holly did as she was told. One finger on the map. One hand against Sam's head. Eyes everywhere.

'Jane, this is Sam. Have you got this number?'

A pause.

'Yes. Got it.'

'I'm with Holly. We're about 50 klicks short of Rome centre. We're coming in, driving a Red Lancia Montecarlo; early 80s. Let the carabinieri know to let us through. We're not taking the main roads, trying to avoid any road blocks. I reckon we could be at the Vatican in 25, maybe 30 minutes. Any news?'

'No. Nothing And why are you bringing an unqualified civilian into a city where it's likely there's going to be a major terrorist blast?'

'Because she's the only one who has seen the van.'

There was silence, apart from a strange knocking sound that was now coming from the engine compartment. Sam didn't think it was good news.

'You... look, I'm sorry Sam, but I can't sanction this. You really ought to turn back. Or at least drop this Holly woman off on the side of the road.'

'No, sorry Jane. We need her.'

More silence.

'I'm prepared to order you to do it, Sam.'

Sam grimaced as she changed gear again.

'Like you ordered me to stay off the Sokolov case?' She was now gritting her teeth. 'He told me, you know.'

The pause that followed allowed Sam to overtake two more cars and push the Lancia up to 150 kilometres per hour as the road gently dropped into a dip.

'Told you what?'

'Everything. Just before he tried to get his brother to rape me. And then throw me overboard. You could have told me, Jane. I would have got it.' Actually, Sam wasn't sure she would have got it. Maybe that's why Jane hadn't shared her secret?

'There are only four government positions who have access to Sokolov's full file. Me, the chief, the permanent secretary and the prime minister. It was never within my gift to tell you Sam. And, I wouldn't change that position even now. Sorry.'

Sam blew out, her cheeks extending like a trombone player's.

'OK, Jane, I get it. I think.' She didn't. It was a matter of trust. But maybe that was a naive, innocent way of looking at it. 'But I'm not letting Holly go. We're going to do our best to find the van.'

'OK, Sam. Have it your way. We'll chat when this is

all over.'

And that was that.

Angry with herself and Jane, Sam pressed the car even harder. As she did the knocking got louder and louder. She caught a road sign that displayed 'Rome, 35km'. She hoped the old girl held out for that long.

Tiredness gripped her, and her shoulder was knocking as loudly as the noise in the engine compartment. The Lancia had an awful ride. It was harsh – good for cornering, but not good for her joints. Changing gear was becoming more and more of an effort, every movement was accompanied by a scream of pain that sapped what little energy she had left.

'Change gear for me, Holly. Can you do that?'

'What?'

'My shoulder is not happy and needs a break. I'll shout "up" or "down" and you change gear accordingly.'

Holly looked at Sam nervously.

'Let's give it a go,' she said reticently.

'Down!'

The gearbox crashed as Holly moved the stick from 5th into 2nd.

'Sorry.'

They had a couple more goes and then she had it.

'After a while I won't need to shout. It'll come naturally.'

Holly didn't look overly convinced of that.

However, after a while she was seamlessly changing gear and barking instructions that Sam then followed religiously. It was properly light now, and, as the SR 148 turned north toward the centre of Rome, Holly started preparing Sam for some new directions.

'We need to come off before the ring road, the E80. Look for a slip road to "Spinaceto". S-P-I-N-A-C-E-T-O. And then we need to follow signs for "Mostacciano"'

'No need to spell it. I've got it.'

The traffic was building up and their speed reduced. Sam spotted the first roadblock ahead and took some lefts and rights that Holly hadn't prescribed. They worked their way past the constriction and somehow kept heading in the right sort of direction. Sam had a sixth sense with navigation – it followed the same pattern as her photographic memory and her visual perception. It was all perfectly natural to her. She'd also visited the Vatican seven years ago and could picture it, set back on a sweeping bend in the Tiber. When they got close, she'd know where it was.

'Keep an eye out for the van.'

'I am. I am.'

She's good, this girl. Navigating, changing gear, and spotting, all at the same time. A neat trick.

To their left, between two large buildings, Sam spotted the Tiber flash past.

'We need to be on the other side of the river. It's just there.' Sam threw her head to her left, indicating where she'd seen the river. 'I don't need any further instructions. I'm going to cross the river at the first bridge... hang on!'

Sam slammed on the brakes as the traffic lights turned red ahead of them. The Lancia stopped a couple of inches short of the car in front. A pair of businessmen waltzed across the zebra crossing.

'No vans?' Sam had craned her head forward to look out of the sports car's low-raked front windscreen. They'd probably seen no more than 20 vans in the past ten minutes. Only one was white and Holly had said, 'No, that's not it.'

They took off again, the knocking in the engine, now reverberating violently around the cab. The car was on its last legs. It didn't seem to help that they were stopping and starting. She noticed that the temperature gauge was climbing dangerously high.

Sam spotted a bridge ahead, the 'Porta Portsee'. She turned the car left, got halfway across the bridge, and then it died.

She turned it over. Nothing.

Everything smelt hot.

She tried again.

Nothing.

Again.

'Sam! Sam!'

'What?'

'That's it!'

'Where?'

'There!' Holly was pointing at a white blob that was in traffic on the far side of the river, moving along the Tiber heading north. *Toward the Vatican.*

Except it wasn't a white delivery van; or a market trader.

It was a white campervan. A Ford Transit – third generation, short-wheelbase, high-top. Probably self-converted, but competently so. And it had an awning on the side – the connection she'd missed from Holly's description.

Of course! An awning. Campervan! How could she have been so stupid?

The carabinieri weren't looking for holiday makers – they were looking for workmen. Delivery drivers. A campervan was the perfect disguise. *Genius!* And it was getting away from them. The river bent left just ahead; and the camper would soon be out of sight.

Sam turned the car over again. Nothing.

The traffic behind them was tooting away. Sam ignored them.

Shit! She smashed her good hand against the steering wheel.

'Give me the phone.'

Holly obliged.

Sam got out of the car, her shoulder reminding her that she was making a big mistake by treating it so poorly.

'Stay here! Please. You've done everything you can.

The bomb is radioactive. If it goes off, you really don't need to be in the thick of it.'

Holly nodded. Reluctance spread across her face. Sam thought, this time, she'd do as she was instructed.

Sam was out, on her feet. There was probably a quicker way to get to the Vatican than follow a river that was never straight, but she really couldn't afford to get lost. And she needed to get visual on the camper.

She ran. Not a sprint, but a fast jog. She had no idea how far it was to the Vatican and needed to pace herself. And, in any case, her body was a reluctant competitor in this race. Every step was an effort, and every placement of her feet sent a jolt to her shoulder.

The pavement was littered with pedestrians. Men in suits. Men and women in smart, designer clothes (*Why do they always look so much better than we do?*). Young kids on the way to school, many of them smoking – *How typically Italian*. And, even at this hour, as many tourists as there were commuters. Sam weaved in and out. She hadn't the energy to say 'sorry' or 'thank you', as people got out of her way.

As she jogged, the thumb of her good hand, pressed buttons on the Nokia. She scrolled to their latest call, Jane's number, and pressed the green button.

She had to tell her about the camper.

It had only been a few minutes and she was already breathing hard. Having a conversation was going to be difficult.

It rang twice.

'Sam?'

'Hi, Jane…'

It disconnected.

Shit.

She looked down at the screen. The phone had no signal. She jogged past a Far Eastern tourist who was taking a photo of an island in the middle of the Tiber with her iPad. Sam shimmied left, then avoided a tree that was growing up from a prepared hole in the pavement, before getting back on track.

She checked the phone again.

No signal.

She kept jogging.

And looked down.

No signal!

Was the LEWT doing its stuff?

She slowed her jog – slightly, taking in the myriad of pedestrians. A man across the road was looking frustratingly at his phone. She picked out another – a young woman, who held hers in front of her face and was screaming at it. Then another… it was the same story.

14 Signal Regiment were earning their pay.

Great. There was no way the bomb could be detonated by mobile phone.

But why didn't she feel the sense of relief?

Why? What was it that was nagging at her?

Come on!

She jogged some more. The traffic had slowed. She spotted the camper. It was 300 metres ahead. Beyond it, the river bore right.

Tourist taking photo of an island on right – a minute ago. Right bend in the river at 300 metres.

She tried to piece together what she remembered from her trip. She had done the whole of Rome in two days. It was only seven years ago. She never forgot.

But... that was when everything was working. Things weren't operating as they should in Sam Green's world. Not now. Her shoulder yelling at her. Telling her to stop. It had had enough, thank you very much. Doing stuff to her head. Her breathing was laboured. And she was so tired. She needed to call it a day.

Extreme pain does something to a body. The brain can shut the pain out; pretend the trauma isn't happening. And that works. Or, and there's no guessing which one will come first, the body shuts down organs that aren't helpful to recovery. And, sometimes that's the consciousness bit of the mind. It sends you to sleep, so the vital stuff, like the lungs and the heart can get on with the job of keeping you alive.

Sam knew that's what was happening to her.

Her brain was shutting down. Bit by bit.

She gritted her teeth and soldiered on.

And then a light came on.

Got it!

The Vatican is set back from the corner of the river. Opposite the *Ponte Principe Amadeo Savoia Aosta*. An unremarkable bridge, but she remembered crossing it from the city centre. You can see the dome of St Mark's behind some buildings. Which is up ahead. Where…

She looked up, her eyes losing focus… Where the van was now turning left.

Keep going.

She jogged and weaved.

Get out of my way!

The number of pedestrians were increasing; her passageway was becoming more and more constricted.

'*Idiota!*' The retort from a man who she hit, thankfully, with her good shoulder. His corrugated cup of Starbucks coffee spilt on the floor.

Sorry.

Dizziness now. Pain and fuzziness.

One hundred metres. The bridge was ahead. There flashing lights of police cars on the junction.

But the camper has already turned left? It's ahead of them.

Apart from the pain, and the wooziness, what was at the back of her mind? Something key. Something important – pushing her on.

She jogged some more. Another hapless businessman was looking at their mobile with complete disdain.

How did they used to cope?

Sam could see the end of the bridge. When she got there, if she got there, she'd need to follow the van left, then jink right after about ten metres, followed by an 80 metre stretch, and then left again – and the Vatican would be dead ahead? She hoped.

Smack!

She hit a man – actually she couldn't determine the sex. It was a big person, more likely to be a man than a woman. She went down with a *thud*, right shoulder first.

The shock of her arm popping out of its socket and then back in again jolted her into consciousness, when passing out would have been a much more preferable outcome. It was if the whole of her body were having one big joke at her expense. 'Look at her! Let's make Sam's life as miserable as we can!'

Searing pain. Tears. Short breaths. Dizziness.

Her face pressed against the cold, stone pavement. People were already starting to mill around. Forming a circle, a mass of concerned and just a little bit voyeuristic, people.

Give up, girl. Like Holly. You've done your bit. Why do you have to find the van?

Because.

Because of something that was nagging her.

Because…

Then she had clarity. It all came into focus.

Log cabin. Her and Vlad. Looking over the jumble

of stuff in the room. Radioactive jars. Countless waxy wrappers from sticks of PE4. The empty sacks of sand and gravel. Vlad finding the discarded containers for the mobile phones and laptop batteries.

And the small piece of packaging that she found at the end. She'd almost missed it.

The box for the escalator 'Stop' button. A big, red button. You can't miss them. Press to activate. Thump it in panic. Everything stops. If all else fails…

Press to activate. Everything stops. *Or everything goes.*

The terrorist had been clever thus far. They had covered every eventuality. What if the mobiles didn't work? One of them ran out of batteries? Or the network was down?

Press to activate.

The tall North-African looking man who Holly had described – he was due martyrdom. He knew he was going to die. He longed for it? But the terrorists wanted to be completely sure. Could they really trust him with something so crucial? Yes? Maybe? There was always enough doubt. So, they'd detonate it remotely. Take the man out of the loop. That's what she would do. Plan A.

But if Plan A failed. They'd need a Plan B. Back to the man in the van.

Pan B. A big red button. *Press to activate.* And fingers crossed that he was still up for martyrdom.

Lying with her face pressed flat against the cold stone, her body racked with pain, surrounded by voices asking her if she was OK in languages she didn't begin to understand, Sam now knew why she had to keep going. The man in the van was going to press the big red button. He had been told that if, after a certain time the bomb didn't go off, he was to self-detonate. His guaranteed ticket to heaven.

Press the big red button.

Her mind was back in the game. Her shoulder was relegated to a nuisance. Nothing was going to stop her from finding that van.

As she got up, a man helped her.

'*Stai bene?*'

Sam turned to him. She thought she understood.

'*Si. Per favore.*'

She had to be OK. She had no choice.

As she staggered forward, people moved out of her way. It was almost Biblical. Like the parting of the Red Sea. Soon she was out of the crowd. And back in the game.

She reached the bridge and held onto a lamp post for support.

Cross the road here. Then turn immediately right. 80 metres. Then left...

She crossed, trying desperately to keep up a jog. She knew she wasn't travelling in a straight line and several pedestrians avoided her as though she had some infectious disease.

She turned right.

About 80 metres, then left...

A group of tourist were gathered on the pavement in front of her. In the middle was the tour leader, a bright blue umbrella stuck up in the air, shouting, 'Follow me.'

By now she was dragging her right leg – and she thought she was probably dribbling. But couldn't be sure.

'Get out of my way!' She screamed when she was a couple of metres out.

A few of the group (they looked German – the men had beer bellies, the women efficiently dressed in tweed and wool), spotted the crazed woman and parted to allow her through. One man, wearing a green jacket and a trilby hat with a feather in it, didn't see Sam until it was too late. He was pushed aside, and had to grab a fellow tourist to stop himself from falling over.

'*Entschuldigen sie.*' Sam's German (she hoped she had chosen the right country – they could have been Americans?) was adequate. 'Sorry' was the best she could manage at the moment.

And then she was at the corner. 80 metres – tick! Turn left. Then the Vatican. She staggered out into the road; her first attempt to cross. She stopped and put her hand on the bonnet of a stationary Ford Focus to catch her breath; the driver looked at her with amazement. But stopping would almost certainly mean that she would pass out.

She couldn't have that.

She crossed the road. Now restricted to a walk, she dragged her right leg up a slight incline toward the

Vatican. Fifty metres in front of her, she could see the beautiful, curved, covered walkway that surrounds St Peter's Square. Tall, multiple Romanesque pillars, holding up a red, lightly-angled tiled roof. The low morning sun catching the tops of the pillars. On any other day it would have been breathtaking.

Now, it meant she was almost there.

But where was the van?

Sam half jogged, half walked, half dragged herself on. She hadn't thought this through. The camper could be anywhere. The Vatican was huge. And its surrounding environs, doubly so. It was hopeless.

Hopeless! Getting here without a plan.

She had to think. Where would they park the campervan?

She reached the corner of the street, just shy of the Vatican. The number of people had increased. One or two pushed past her.

She felt her legs wobble. She was going to collapse. Any fight she had left was gone. It was over. If what she thought might happen, happened, any moment now the man in the campervan would press the big red button. There would be a huge explosion. Many would die. Hundreds would be injured. And the Vatican would out of use for a decade. The impact on the world would be unthinkable.

And she hadn't been able to stop it.

She teetered, looking for something to hold onto. She didn't want to fall to the ground again.

She reached left, stretching for a railing she'd spotted a few seconds ago.

And there it was.

The campervan.

Down the side street from the junction. Six vehicles down. With its back end to her.

The man in the campervan. With the big red button.

Six car lengths away.

She didn't fall. She didn't even take hold of the railing. She steadied herself on her own legs. She forced her body to pivot left. And then she moved. She didn't run. She didn't want to alert the man. She walked. It was all she could manage.

Walk. Like a normal person. Don't draw attention to yourself.

Casually.

She walked. Step by step. The man with the campervan had a schedule. Would she be too late?

She wasn't scared. Death had never been a concern of hers – at times she would have welcomed it. If the bomb went up, she'd be blown into a thousand pieces.

So be it.

She walked.

Five cars.

Four cars.

Three.

The second.

And then the campervan.

She knew the driver would be just to her right. Percentages had it as a left-hand drive vehicle. The van was parked on the left-hand side of the road, facing away from her. The north African looking man would be in the driver's seat.

Just...

...*Here.*

Her right hand still hopeless, Sam reached her left hand round the front of her body and yanked at the door handle. It flew open. The man was facing away from her, bent down, looking at something between the seats.

The movement of the door startled him and he jerked upright. She couldn't see his face. She was concentrating on her next action.

Was he wearing a seatbelt?

No.

In one seamless motion, she put one foot on the driver's entrance step and, again with her left hand, grabbed the far lapel of his leather jacket. As tightly as she could...

...And pulled with all the strength she could muster, purposefully falling out of the van as she did. It was about momentum. She was small. He was much bigger than her. She had to get him moving. Out of the campervan. Away from the big red button.

Her momentum. Against his inertia.

It worked.

She and the man fell out of the van onto the pavement. As they fell Sam caught sight of his face. Sweat was pouring from his forehead, his eyes were wide and full of fear. They both reached the ground together, but he fared considerably better, bouncing as he hit the pavement. Sam slumped like a sack of potatoes. She prepared herself for a fight; for another launch. But immediately she knew that it was over.

She was out of it. There was nothing left. She had lost. He could do what he wanted.

The man, shocked but obviously unhurt, scrambled onto all fours. He looked at Sam, the fear still present – she could smell it. His breathing erratic. His pupils dilated. His head twitching from side to side.

Still on all fours, he glanced at the open van door. And then in the direction from where Sam had come. Toward the Vatican. The home of the Pope. The very heart of Catholicism.

'Don't do it,' she whispered in English.

She repeated the same in Russian.

'Please.' In both languages.

Sam could sense the man was torn. Between the promise of martyrdom and the reality of death. His glanced again at the van, and then back to the Vatican.

In flash of movement he stood, turned on his heel and sprinted down the pavement away from his intended target. Sam craned her neck to see more – he was gone.

It may have been a minute. Or two. She noticed a pedestrian coming toward her. It was a man in a grey suit. He stopped short, turned into the road and crossed the street. *A bad Samaritan?*

Sam found the strength to sit up. And somehow reach for the door of the van, pulling herself to the upright. She crawled, face down, onto the driver's seat and, with even greater effort, put one foot on the entrance step. With that she was able to force her torso further into the van.

And there it was. Between the front seats.

A small yellow box. And a big red button. Wires ran out of the box into the rear of the van.

The sound of police sirens joined her consciousness. But not for long. A few seconds later she was out cold.

Epilogue

One Restaurant, Porto Montenegro, Tivat, Montenegro

Four months later

Sam had ordered a double espresso – decaffeinated. It was her second of the morning. The small white cup and saucer sat on the table in front of her, next to a pair of very competent, stabilised binos she had signed out from Q's stores in Vauxhall. Beside the binos was a small flower arrangement: oranges, reds and greens in an ornate glass vase that glinted in the low, mid-morning sun. Even though it was very early spring, the sky was cloudless, the sun shining and temperatures were in the high-teens. It was a beautiful day to be sat outside.

She'd left her hotel, the Hotel Palma (which was right on the seafront in the main town – *unextravagant, but lovely*), straight after her continental breakfast. It had taken her ten minutes to walk to the port and she almost tripped over her tongue when she got there. *'Move over Monte Carlo, Porto Montenegro is the new hotspot for the rich and famous,'* was the cry from anyone with a superyacht who needed somewhere to park it. She could see why. Nestling in Kotor Bay, the deepest natural harbour in Southern Europe, and with a backdrop of spiky, Adriatic hills, it was glorious. The port was originally the main base for the Austro-Hungarian navy and, until recently, resembled a bombsite; it had now been transformed into a new playground for the super-rich.

There were boats everywhere. All of them fabulous. Most were bigger than a couple of houses, and five or six of them were 200-footers. They were all very shiny, and very expensive. And, in her mind, they all smelt of money made on the back of someone else's misfortunes. She couldn't help but admire the glamour; but despised its source.

Sam would never have chosen Tivat as a holiday destination. She'd been to Dubrovnik, Croatia, 30 miles northwest of where she was. But that was a country *and* a completely different culture away. Head south a couple of hundred miles and you hit Corfu, Greece. Again, she'd been there – that, again, was an altogether different experience.

So, it was her first time in Montenegro – and it was lovely. Although, in general infrastructure terms, it was light years behind Croatia and Greece – and that was saying some. But, that all added to its charm. The clientele was less charming though, especially here in the port area – they were very 'in your face'. More Lamborghini Diablo than Jaguar F-Type. There were a couple of the former in the quayside carpark.

Sam hadn't chosen Tivat. It had chosen her. More

accurately, *Cressida* had berthed at Porto Montenegro – somewhere new to rest her weary propellers. And Sam had followed her there. That was the beauty of *vesselfinder.com* (now that Nikolay Sokolov's boat had had its AIS refitted). You really could follow any ship, pretty much, anywhere.

So far, three months into a sabbatical from SIS of 'unspecified length', she had chased *Cressida* around most of the Mediterranean: Monte Carlo, Naples, Palermo, Venice (*that was particularly nice*) and now Porto Montenegro.

It was stalking on steroids. And in her present mind set, that suited her.

After the Rome incident, she had been whisked straight home to London and given a private room in St Thomas's. It had taken her a couple of weeks to get close to having normal energy levels, and a further month of intensive physiotherapy to get her shoulder working properly again. The consultant reckoned that her shoulder would be susceptible to 'popping out' if it were put under any lateral pressure. She should avoid gymnastics and rock climbing.

OK then.

Insofar as work, it was not until Jane's third trip to the hospital that they eventually got round to talking about the future. Sam had already been subject to a severe debrief by her own kind, initially at the airport in Rome, and then again in Tommies – as soon as she was back in London. That, in itself, had been an exhausting experience. She also had a whole day with the CIA at her bedside, eating all her soft fruit and chocolate that her few friends had brought in for her. They were more fun though, and much easier to take the mickey out of.

On the plus side, was a welcome visit by Holly and her father. As well as thanking her (continuously), her 'daddy' came to tell Sam that the US Congress had agreed to present her with a Congressional Gold Medal, the highest accolade bestowed on non-military personnel in the US. Sam said 'thanks' several times, and wondered what 'Daddy' must really think about her dragging his cherished daughter into a city centre just before a dirty bomb exploded, irradiating the Pope and all his cardinals. She hadn't asked.

The second real piece of excitement had been a phone call from Debbie. They spent ages talking about all manner of stuff. But the call brought with it two bits of fabulous news. First, Vlad had survived the fire. He was well and back at work, although in a wheelchair. The doctors had had to amputate both his legs below the knee, due to the fire damage caused by the falling lintel. After Debbie's call, Sam had spent many evenings reflecting on her involvement in Op Samantha and the pain that had caused her friend and colleague, Vlad. She had come close to phoning him a couple of times, but never summoned the confidence. It was just great news to hear that he hadn't been consumed by the fire – but she was so sad that he had been left permanently disabled. She would get round to calling him at some point. Once she could face it.

The second snippet of good news was that Debbie had spotted a report from the US's Federal Energy Regulatory Commission (FERC), that *CleanDrilling's* fracking operation in California had been closed down – and that the company were being investigated by the FBI for illegal drilling procedures; both in California and Alaska.

'That's brilliant, Debbie. Just brilliant. *MSF* must have used their US offices to press some buttons?'

'Or, I spoke to your CIA contact, Jodie – who then made it her personal crusade?'

'You did that!'

'Yes. I did!' Debbie was very excited. 'When I thought you hadn't made it out of the fire. I couldn't let it rest. Not after what you had been through.'

'Well done you, Debbie. Does Jane know?'

'Nope – it can be our secret.'

'Again, well done you!'

The news from Debbie had scratched an itch that had been bothering Sam. She was delighted that *CleanDrilling* and Sokolov had got their comeuppance.

Really well done her.

But, it was Jane's third visit that had brought the issue of a sabbatical onto the table.

It was clear to both of them that Sam couldn't go back to Moscow. It was too risky. Both from the organisation's perspective, and for Sam's own safety. Sokolov was at large, operating pretty much as he had before the incident. According to Jane, the CIA were still ruminating over whether to go public with his involvement in the abduction of the three women – and the murder of two of them. And, on the back of that, demand that Sokolov be extradited to the US; not that the Russians would have allowed that to happen. With Holly's and Sam's testimonies, the UK and the US were certain that the abuser was dead – indeed, Sokolov had held a very public funeral for his brother in Moscow, just a week after the bomb incident.

So, the CIA was still ruminating; but not taking action.

Sam guessed that, between the CIA and SIS, the considered view was to leave Sokolov where he was. Where he could be of best use.

And she and Jane had discussed that too.

As Sam was now 'in the loop', C had authorised Jane to include her as one of the, now, 'gang of 5' – although she wasn't allowed access to the complete Pierrot file. It was a brief discussion, mostly because Sam was bored by it. The outstanding question remained: 'when is an asset so precious that you're prepared to sacrifice scores of lives in order to keep the asset operational?' Sam remained unconvinced by the UK government's position.

'Why did you choose the codename "Pierrot"?' Sam had asked.

'Did he tell you that as well?'

Sam nodded.

'He was recruited whilst he was at Cambridge. He got involved in a fight in a pub. He took a glass to the right side of his face; the other guy didn't fare so well, and was carried off in a body bag. Sokolov is the son of, who was then, a big cheese in the communist party.

We were within our rights to prosecute him and stick him in jail – for a long time. Or, they'd accept a prisoner exchange. It was 1983 and there was a lot of that going on at that time. As MI6, as we were then, were preparing him for exchange, some bright spark decided to see if he could be recruited. He could. All it took was money. And that's all it's taken for the last 20 years. We had no idea at the time that he would end up as one of the premier's right hand men. As is often the case with sleepers, these things are mostly down to luck.'

'You haven't answered the question. Why Pierrot?'

'His facial scar. Like the French clown.' Jane used her hand to demonstrate a vertical mark to her face.

Sam understood.

'The scar's been covered by plastic surgery?'

'Yes. Correct. He looks like he's had a stroke.'

Sam nodded in agreement.

'But he has more money than he needs – surely he could stop whenever he wanted?' Sam asked.

'Except that we would then expose him as a British spy, and he'd end up with a bullet in his head – or similar. My view is that he also quite likes all the clandestine stuff. Very *James Bond*. And he was very good at it. If you were able to look through the file, you'd be amazed at how much valuable intelligence he has fed to us.'

Sam still wasn't convinced. And didn't think she ever would be.

There was an uncomfortable silence.

'Why don't you take some time off?' Jane asked.

'What, don't you want me back at work?'

Was she right to feel affronted?

'No, no. It's not that. It just that... well, I can see that you're struggling with all this, Sokolov and everything. And it's been a tough time over the past month or so. Maybe you need some time to reflect?'

Sam didn't know what Jane was saying.

You don't want me back at work? Am I too much of a risk?

She was about to ask, but a bout of tiredness crept over her and she thought better of it.

Sod them.

And that was that.

Sam took the sabbatical on half pay. The agreement was for up to a year; anything beyond that and SIS would consider her position. They didn't discuss what she might do if she did come back, but Sam really didn't have the energy to get excited about it.

She'd bummed around for the first couple of weeks, and then, with nothing else to do other than watch the complete series of *The West Wing* for the sixth time, she opened the *vesselfinder.com* web-page, and there she was: *Cressida*. Berthed in Monte Carlo.

She'd never been to Monte Carlo before and there was nothing stopping her from getting on a cheap flight to Nice and then bussing it to the rich man's playground. So, she did – the next day. And she hadn't been back to the UK since.

And now here she was. With her new best friend. A 230-foot super yacht.

She didn't spend every day staring at the back of the boat, catching the occasional glimpse of her nemesis: Nikolay Sokolov. Watching him with his arm round a bikini-clad gorgeous thing, who certainly wasn't his wife. Keeping an eye out for Mayra – she was often there, laden with a silver tray of pastries and fabulous coffee. And making sure that his brother didn't make an appearance; that he truly was six-feet under in a Moscow graveyard.

She also did some touristy type things. And she ran; and trekked.

But Sam did keep a watchful eye on the boat. She considered it to be part of her rehabilitation. Seeing Sokolov from a distance. Getting used to the fact that he was alive, even though he really should be in a grave next to his brother. Preferably still conscious. At some point, she was sure that the fascination would wear off. It would.

And what would she do then?

Third Floor Room, Above the Moritz Eis Cafe, Porto Montenegro, Tivat, Montenegro

Iosif Ergorov was a thorough man. He had exacting standards. Nothing was left to chance. Where he could, he rehearsed every hit, even if the target wasn't in the frame at any point during the rehearsal. For this one, he'd practiced on the first day, and again yesterday morning. The target had been in sight on the second day. But he would bide his time. Follow his meticulous plan.

He'd rented the second-floor room as a six-month let, but he only needed it for three days. He preferred not to work from hotel rooms – you were never sure when the cleaner might barge in.

He'd arrived the day before yesterday and had travelled by car – he *always* travelled by car. It was safer that way. It did mean that his area of operation was restricted to Europe and central Asia. But, you'd be surprised at how much his services were in demand, even if he refused to fly.

His car was in the carpark behind the apartment block, packed and ready to go. He would be out of here in 15 minutes after the hit, and across the border into Bosnia-Herzegovina within the hour. Yesterday, he'd recced the escape route, and an alternative, should the former be closed. Both would work well.

Ergorov had the right-hand apartment window ajar. About 40 centimetres. Using his own lightweight, metal and wooden frame, he had erected a sniper's platform in the room; it was set back from the window and almost impossible to see from the outside. You'd need a pair of decent binos, and know exactly what you were looking for, to have even the slightest chance of guessing what might be going on behind the gap in the window.

He had zeroed his rifle, an *Accuracy International* AS50 (the British Army's latest long-range harbinger of death), three days ago in one of the many Montenegrin forests en route. He'd set up a head-sized target at 1,000 metres and hit it first time. That was the beauty of the AS50 – you had to run over it with a tank before it lost its zero. But he always checked, just in case.

Today's target was 340 metres away. It was going to be simple.

He was lying on the platform, which was at a height of 1.5 metres above the floor. The gap in the window afforded a very clear view of the target area, and allowed him to switch left and right and acquire others. That always made him feel like God. Anyone in his sights was never more than a split-second away from death.

But he never killed anyone without good cause; and without being paid. And he expected his employer to meet both requirements before he accepted a task.

He snuggled the butt of the sniper-rifle against his cheek and placed his right eye against the Nightforce NXS sight. He kept his left open. He could do that. Pick out a target at up to 1,500 metres through the scope with his right, whilst looking out for peripheral trouble with his left. Not many could do that. And that's why he'd survived this long.

He gently placed his right hand on the trigger guard and slipped his index finger in front of the trigger.

Looking through the scope, he made very minor adjustments to the direction of the weapon – which pivoted on the forward bipod.

He controlled his breathing. In. Out. In. Out. He would shoot when his lungs were empty. And just after a heartbeat. When any body movement was minimal – and success guaranteed.

He never missed. Well, that's not exactly true. He'd missed once, when the target tripped over something just as he had pulled the trigger. Ergorov had got him with a second shot, when the target had stood up, and was brushing himself down. He didn't really consider it a miss.

Today's was a key job – there was little questioning that. He didn't get many taskings directly from the Russian government. He had no idea exactly which department, but the tell-tale signs were clear – he had his methods. The detail came from, he guessed a man, who addressed himself as 'V'. They'd not met, which was not unusual, but he had agreed to one of Ergorov's key prerequisites: that he should know why the tasker wanted the person dead. A single line would do. Like, 'the target is having an affair with my wife'; or 'the man has embezzled over $1 million from the company'. Ergorov needed his conscience clear. And either of those, or something similar, would do.

The line he'd got from his contact couldn't have been more unequivocal.

A threat to national security.

That was a good enough answer.

And the money was acceptable.

So here he was. Regulating his breathing.

In. Out. In. Out.

He twisted the near focus on the scope a fraction of a millimetre.

There she was. The woman. In the centre of the lens. The one with the coffee, the vase and the binos, sat outside the restaurant. She had been looking at the boat for an hour. And she'd been there yesterday, doing the same thing. She was in perfect focus. The beautifully constructed crosshairs were poised, hovering over her left ear.

He carefully closed his trigger finger, taking up the tiny bit of play there was in the mechanism.

She moved. She was picking up the binos.

Now she was back in focus. He adjusted himself.

In. Out. In. Out.

His left eye picked up some movement on the stern of the boat, a deck up. Two people had come out through the sliding glass doors. A large woman, carrying a tray of drinks, and a man. He recognised him immediately.

Perfect.

It took Ergorov three seconds to switch the barrel of the rifle so that the crosshairs were on the man's forehead.

Nikolay Sokolov. He knew him. Everyone in Russia knew him. He was all over the news. The oligarch of oligarchs. And, surprising for Ergorov, a former client of his. The cafe bomb in Moscow last year.

How things come around.

In. Out.

His trigger finger took up the slack.

In. Out.

Heartbeat...

Bang!

The noise was muted by the silencer, a car backfiring to the outside world. But it was still deafening at the shooter's end.

A quick move of the scope downward showed that the target was down. When a 0.5 inch round travelling way beyond the speed of sound hits your head, there's rarely anything left of it.

There wasn't.

Just a flaccid body with no face to speak of. Lots of blood.

He remained still, gauging the reaction on the ground. Checking if anything had happened that would upset his planned escape. As he looked, focusing on the target area, he reached for his mobile which he'd left beside him on the platform. He had already prepared an SMS to send to 'V'.

It simply read:

Magpie is down.

A threat to national security.

Not any more.

He pressed 'Send'.

As he lifted his chest from the platform, he looked down to the restaurant.

The woman was gone. All that was left to remind anyone that she had been sat there was an empty coffee cup and a €10 note, tucked under the vase to make sure that it didn't blow away.

Sam Green books by Roland Ladley:

Unsuspecting Hero

Sam Green's life is in danger of imploding. Suffering from post-traumatic stress disorder after horrific injuries and personal tragedy in Afghanistan, she escapes to the Isle of Mull hoping to convalesce. A chance find on the island's shores interrupts her rehabilitation and launches her on a journey to West Africa and on a collision course with forces and adversaries she cannot begin to comprehend.

Meanwhile in London, MI6 is facing down a biological threat that could kill thousands and inflame an already smouldering religious war. Time is not on anyone's side and Sam's determination to face her past and control her future, regardless of the risks, looks likely to end in disaster. Fate conspires to bring Sam into the centre of an international conspiracy where she alone has the power to influence world-changing events. Blind to her new-found role, is her military training and complete disregard for her own safety enough to prevent the imminent devastation?

Fuelling the Fire

Why are so many passenger planes falling from the sky? Why are two ex-CIA agents training terrorists in the Yemeni desert? Why is a religious cult transferring millions of dollars to unattributable bank accounts around the world? Are these events connected? If they are, is this the mother of all conspiracies?

MI6 analyst Sam Green desperately wants to establish why her only surviving relative died in the latest plane crash. But can she put aside her grief and make sense of it all? Or is the clock ticking just too quickly, even for her?

Printed in Poland
by Amazon Fulfillment
Poland Sp. z o.o., Wrocław